Words of Praise for Cholama Moon

My non-traditional historical Western novel pick of the year.
　　　　　　　—Stu Rosebrook, *True West Magazine*

"A gritty, beautiful picture of life on the Western frontier. The characters are realistic and compelling. This is a rare gem in historical fiction." —Amazon Reviewer

"The characters are very fleshed out, and come alive with deft use of colloquial speech. You find yourself drawn into their lives. Even the antagonists of the novel are richly developed and sympathetic. From the father too consumed with grief to care for his child, to the banker that proves abusive in his moments of weakness. The stories will keep you reading every word." —Amazon Reviewer

"An exciting Western saga. Well researched and finely written historical novel. Schroeder has a knack for placing her readers directly in the path of stampeding horses so that we smell their animal sweat, taste the grit of the dust, and envision the beauty of the land that surrounds us."
　　　　　　　—Velda Brotherton, Author of *Rowena's Hellion*

If you enjoyed this book, please leave a review at Amazon, Goodreads or Bookbub. The author and other readers will appreciate your kindness.

Cholama Moon

Printed in the United States of America.

First edition, April 2014
Second edition, October 2018

ISBN: 978-1-7256-0691-3

All rights are reassigned to author with written permission of Oak Tree Press.

Discover other books by Anne Schroeder or contact the author at
http://anneschroederauthor.com

CHOLAMA MOON

By

Anne Schroeder

Acknowledgements

To my husband Steve, for his unfailing enthusiasm of the next bend in the road.

To Donalee Thomason, for her detailed book, *Cholama, The Beautiful One*.

To Marlene Thomason, for Cholame Valley history and for a white-knuckle tour of the hills in her farm truck. Thanks also to her husband Doug, a classmate of mine at Shandon High School.

To Robert Natiuk, for his help in building this into a fuller, richer story.

To Nancy Mickelberry, for the tour of her two-story adobe home, Casa Cholama.

To Cindy Van Horn, for a horseback tour through Cholame Valley.

To Sam Kaffine; Susan Hohenstein; Doris Shaffer; Ellen Schroeder; Hank Hohenstein; Martha Natiuk; Pamela Barrett; Joan Kelley; Monica and John Rosecrans.

To my editor, Leslie Kallas Payne, for substantive suggestions.

To the docents at San Luis Obispo Mission, San Miguel Mission, Santa Cruz Mission, the Rios Caledonia Adobe, and the King City Historical Museum.

To the many regional authors whose family histories create textured local history.

To the Cholame Valley residents who shared stories at the Jack Ranch Café and Parkfield Café.

And thank you to my valued readers.

Thank you for reading this story. If you enjoyed it, please leave a short review on Amazon, Goodreads and/or Bookbub.

Chapter One

Ginny

Cholama Valley, Central California
April 1878

"She'll be coming 'round the mountain when she comes. . ."

Sunrise shining through a crack in the wall caught Ginny full in the face and her voice dropped to a warble. She tried to resume the melody, but the song had lost its appeal. Most days singing made her feel closer to her mama, but today the words caught on her tongue like dust on old leather.

Time to meet the day, her mother used to say. Her mother had been a lady and she planned to be one, too, some day.

The sun crested the ridge and she found another distraction. By squinting just right, she managed to tangle the sun's rays in her eyelashes, weaving a spider's web across her vision until a shout from the yard broke her concentration. She blinked and the web disappeared. With a sigh, Ginny climbed from the bed.

The sun was lighting a path across the low adobe bunkhouse, spreading to the round corral north of the tack room where Sancho kept his gelding and a few mares waiting to be broke to saddle. The barn stood taller than the house, with rough-hewn boards tacked to its sides. The heart of the rancho, Sancho called it. The vaqueros had built it before she was born, along with the adobe bunkhouse where they slept. Sancho said the ranch was fair-to-passable; it was only her mama's house that waited finishing, and that would never happen now.

A narrow wagon path led from the corrals, past a big cottonwood shading the yard, west to Slacks Canyon, and from there to the outside world. One day she'd take the mail stage north to Hollister and see the town for herself. She used her finger to trace an imaginary road in the dirty glass window, a road leading to Soledad and San Francisco. The imaginary trail wasn't wide enough to accommodate the sprung buggy she'd have one day; she made a wider streak and peered through, catching the movement of a herd of pigs in search of acorns. They were heading to the huge valley oak at the end of the lane, her dreaming tree, Sancho called it.

She pulled her hand away and noticed the grime on her fingertips. Maybe it was time to take a bath. Her mother had taken one every week, with hot water the vaqueros hauled into the cook house, afterwards sitting in the tin tub with a view of the golden grass growing up to where Table Mountain touched the sky.

Ginny liked to think about a buggy coming around that mountain carrying her mama and her little brother. When she closed her eyes she saw them racing along in a frightful hurry to get home. But that wasn't likely— not with both of them dead and buried in the family cemetery up top of the hill. Dead because of her.

Daylight was burning leather. She tugged on her soiled britches and reached for her second-best shirt hanging from a hook with her only dress, both so mended they were more thread than cloth. Above her straw mattress a spider stitched its web while she buttoned her shirt. Miguelito and the other vaqueros were dawdling at the sawbuck table under the cottonwood tree where they took their summer meals. Judging from the nervous jingle of their spurs, Patrón was nearby. He was probably in a sour mood again this morning. No big surprise; he'd been that way every day since her mama passed.

Sure enough. Patrón was yammering at anybody with half an ear to listen. "That damned Mustang Saddle is hiding strays. Comb those hills and find them, dang it! Before the bandidos do!" He was on a roll today. His anger carried to the second floor.

Miguelito turned and wiggled his fingers. She tried to duck away from the window, but it was too late—Patrón had already seen her.

"Kid, get down here and stop acting like you're loony."

She remained at the dirty window while Patrón flung his leftover coffee onto the ground. Quicker than he could sail his tin cup onto the dirty table, the sand swallowed the dark liquid. The vaqueros jumped to their feet and fell in behind him.

At the sound of benches scraping, she shimmied down the ladder into the hallway where a staircase would be built if they ever got around to finishing the house. She made her way down the hall, past Patrón's room and the parlor in time to watch the men sauntering out to the corrals, her father in the lead.

Miguelito followed, his silver spurs clinking like the tiny bells he hung on his bridle when one of his friends got married. His yellow scarf caught the breeze and made him look dashing and slightly dangerous. Antonio, the newest hire, tried to look fierce with the handle of his knife peeking out of his right boot. He bragged that he would cut off the tongue of any gringo who dared to look at him, but it was unlikely any gringo would bother with a skinny boy like him. Jose Luis, the hungry one, picked food from his teeth with a piece of straw. Perez followed, his hard eyes glowering beneath the brim of his flat vaquero hat. One by one, they disappeared around the corner, taking with them the smell of sweat and raunchy leather. A minute later she heard them mount and ride off.

Sancho sat alone at the end of the table, sipping from a battered tin cup. He squinted and started to turn, but she ducked back and pressed her ear against the plank door, wincing when the rough, unfinished wood bit her cheek. She closed her eyes and imagined the smell of her mother, but the house had forgotten. It reeked of Maria Inés's fried lard, burned beans and kerosene. Only the parlor remembered, and that was because none of the men were allowed inside to traipse across the floor in their filthy boots.

Outside, Sancho clapped his mug onto the table. She inched the door open with her bare toe and waited for him to stomp off as he did every day, venting his broody mood for everyone to see. It was only sunup, but it was unlikely that his disposition would improve. He sat with his head cupped in his hands like he was pained—but he didn't get headaches, only Patrón. Finally, he pushed his plate back, picked himself up from the scarred table and limped off toward the orchard.

"Mawning, Miss Virginia!" he called over his shoulder.

"Morning." She watched as he cleared the yard, his worn-out boots dragging from what he called the hitch in his get-along.

On her way to the outhouse, she detoured past the huge rock fireplace in her father's library to grab a scrap of newsprint from his desk. The paper was old and yellowed; who knew how much time had passed since the mail stage had brought it—could be a year or two—but it was still readable. A letter sat nearby. She picked it up and started to sound out the words, but the effort of reading caused her to skip to the end.

 . . . expect me by late summer. Sincerely, Jeremy Lawsen.

She set the letter back with a sigh of satisfaction. In another month a stranger would drop by and maybe change her life for good.

The yard was empty except for the goat. Ginny's stomach rumbled at the smell of bean juice and ham fat, but the vaqueros had scraped the skillets clean. The other men teased Miguelito because Maria Inés always served him the biggest portion, but he was the top vaquero so he grinned and ate every bite.

Cholama Moon

Underneath Sancho's overturned bowl, Ginny found a slice of salt pork beside a cold tortilla. Sancho had started leaving scraps as a joke, in case she had a falling out with the cook, he said, and on most days he had a point; it was easier to grab leftovers than to get stuck with a dozen chores and no thanks when the work was done. She tried to roll the tortilla around the meat. When it broke in half, she swiped the dribs of bean juice and popped the tortilla into her mouth. She filled a tin cup with coffee while a squirrel waited at the edge of the table. When she finished, she threw her crumbs at it and carried a load of dirty plates to the wash basin.

The summer house was the place where meals were prepared to keep the heat away from the main house, but it was hotter than hellfire in there. Maria Inés was inside, banging pots, probably stewing over Patrón's broken promise to fetch a hired girl. But Patrón only cared about his horses and his headache potion. He didn't see the sour, stinking pots or the goat that needed milking twice a day. He didn't care about the fresh steer carcass hanging in the yard or the effort it took to cut the meat into strips for drying before flies got it.

Patrón was gone. She wiped her hands on her jeans and decided it was a good day to hunt for Mama's left-behinds. Maybe Patrón had left the wardrobe unlocked, like the time she found it open with her mother's camisole inside. When she buried her nose in the folds of lace, she smelled the lilac talc her mother had worn for special occasions. The camisole was hers now, hidden under her straw mattress where Patrón wouldn't find it.

The key to the wardrobe was stowed safe in Patrón vest pocket. He was big on hiding things. He had locked her mother's tintype in his desk, but she'd found it and set it on the top shelf of the wardrobe. Caroline Foster Nugent's image, made before she was born.

Ginny turned to pull a dirty shirt from her father's floor when she saw the frame lying upside down with a jagged crack in one side. *Not Mama's frame!* He must have broken it in one of his rages. The frame was damaged, but the daguerreotype was intact. No point in crying over spilt milk—it wouldn't be the last thing he broke.

The cook's voice came from the other side of the yard, her voice warbling low and high again, like she was scouring the yard for a missing kid and not sure where to look. "Señorita Geena, es time you scrub up the dishes. The water es boil!" Ginny clamped her hands over her ears when the cook called again, this time in the exasperated tone that meant the day was going to be hard. "Señorita—you old enough. You work. Or no food 'til the sun go down!"

5

Ginny set the frame upright and ran her hand over the carved oak mirror that stood in the corner, oval, with its legs sitting flat on the floor and the top nearly touching the ceiling. She struck a pose, practicing for the day that she reached her majority. "I'm no beauty, but Sancho says my chin is strong, whatever that means," she whispered. "It's a crying shame my hair's the color of summer straw. Rather it be the color of an Appaloosa. Nobody'd ignore me then. "

She might not have her mother's looks, but at least she had her blood. None of the vaqueros, or the cook—not even Sancho—could claim that. Not even Patrón. She wanted to hear about her mother, but Patrón was wrathy on the topic, and he wasn't the only one. All the others kept their secrets to themselves: their memories of her mama, what she looked like and smelled like, what her laughter sounded like. The tricks she played on them was pay-back for holding secrets from her.

Maria Inés was crouched in the cookhouse with her head inside a tule basket. She straightened at the creak of the door. "Señorita Geena Nugent! You stay put. God, He will punish you."

When she saw her glare was having no effect, she turned back to scoop a sifter of cornmeal from the basket. Ginny grabbed a warm tortilla off the griddle. She ducked under the ropes of dried chilies hanging from the rafter and slipped through the door. With the tortilla flapping, she spread her arms and ran past the water bucket that needed filling, not stopping until she reached the thick branches of the apple orchard.

Maria Inés carried her bowl to the outside table and began working *masa* between her palms, forming tortillas for the noontime meal. Sancho said Indians like her were tough, and he was right. Bent over her work, she looked hard-bitten and brooding. The late spring sun had just risen over the foothills and already the cook's brown cheeks were shiny with sweat. By afternoon her graying hair would be plastered to her face from the *ilne'*, as she called the hot, dry summer days that were not her friends. She nodded and smiled when she shared her chores with other Indian women, but it was unlikely that anyone would stop by for a few weeks, not until the fall roundup.

Until then the cook had only her, *Señorita Virginia Foster Nugent.*

Chapter Two

Jeremy

Charlottesville, Virginia

"Coffee's brewed, Son. Best take a cup before you commence your errands this morning. That Yankee banker can just wait."

Jeremy Lawsen winced at the mention of food, his breakfast forgotten in the details pressing his mind. He accepted the bone china cup and saucer from his mother and took a sip, not surprised to taste real coffee beans. It might be his responsibility to provide for her, but his brother-in-law Jeb excelled at black market endeavors—anything that thwarted the Yankee retrobates. The coffee was brewed to half-strength and the cup was chipped, but it was a welcome change from the meager meals they'd endured of late.

"That damned carpetbagger banker has rubbed my face in defeat one too many times. I swear, Mother, duty has a hard edge."

His mother's deep azure eyes faded to steel gray, as they were wont to do whenever she fretted. "I watch you, Son, and I understand. There's more than one way to die."

He studied his mother's mouth, pinched with worry and regretted his rant. Her gentle tone was already filling him with guilt. "War didn't take me, Mother; damned carpetbagger politics won't, either. Pardon my language."

He hated when his mother took him to task for his tongue, but her lengthening silence felt worse. His glance swept across the shabby parlor to where a strip of lilac wall paper hung loose on the wall it had graced for five generations. A side-table with its glass top shattered by a bullet held what was left of the company silver, a tarnished spoon and sugar bowl his mother had dug from the garden after the Yankees left.

He glanced back to see tears in his mother's eyes. Rising, he leaned close and kissed her, feeling her fingers pressed into the worn shawl she had received as a gift from her husband before the Rebellion. When her tension eased, Jeremy escaped through the French doors to the crumpling veranda.

From his vantage, a sharecropper family seeded tobacco starts in a creekside field, digging furrows with a lame mule. A partially-destroyed fence held the remains of a herd of sheep being tended by a boy with a shaggy dog—scenes both familiar and heartbreaking. To him, it seemed as though life was standing still because it didn't know how to move forward.

A plume of steam rose above the foothills a dozen miles distant. He heard the locomotive's mournful whistle and for a moment he imagined he was on it, headed anywhere. West, where people were building new lives, where strangers didn't inquire about a man's politics, or often, even his last name. Where the son of a former slave owner could make a living with his own two hands and whatever luck he could muster.

He returned to the breakfast table.

"Mama, I've given thought to Missus Foster's request. She wants to get word to her granddaughter. I intend to deliver the message." When he saw his mother's nod and the satisfaction coloring her cheeks, he released his pent-up breath. He had anticipated this moment for weeks; in his mind it had been more difficult. "You knew?"

"I had hoped, Son. For your sake, I had hoped." She cleared her throat with a lace handkerchief pulled from her sleeve and continued. "Charlotte has suggested she and Jeb move in here with me. I've held off saying *yes* for a spell now. Until you came to a decision."

Jeremy looked up to see her eyes brimming again, happier tears than the ones she'd spilled for her older son the week Richmond fell. More like the tears she spilled on the day he stumbled back up the river road, carrying his musket and a flesh wound in his thigh that troubled him now and again.

"You have my sisters. And the grandbabies," he continued as though she needed convincing.

She nodded and he noticed strands of gray hair for the first time. "I'll always have a home with them. Unlike you, they feel a kinship to this place."

He lowered his face into his hands when his head suddenly seemed heavy. "I would stay if I were needed. You know that."

She smiled. "Fiddlesticks. If your brother had lived, it would have been he who took over here. I would have set you packing for distant shores. Mark my words."

Jeremy felt no joy in the mention of his brother. Unlike his thigh, the wound was still too fresh. "Missus Foster has a package she wants me to take to her granddaughter, Virginia. She insists on setting up a trust fund, on the chance I find the child."

"It's all she has left, the hope."

Jeremy smiled, and this time it felt genuine. In the distance, the train picked up speed and made its way toward the sea.

***

The Union Pacific rumbled through another day of flat prairie devoid of buffalo or Indians, the tribes sequestered on distant reservations with Yankee efficiency as though the Indian Wars had never occurred. The vastness was scored with wagon tracks and wheel ruts, the grassland studded with wooden crosses and discarded supplies from the great exodus across the plains. The government's bold declaration of *Manifest Destiny* in action. Occasionally, Jeremy saw a clump of stragglers on their way to California and Oregon—a few families traveling in caravans with surreys and porters, followed by wagons loaded with farm implements and goods; a new batch of emigrants to replace the penniless Argonauts that had abandoned the gold fields to return to their families in the East.

The hours dragged with the slow, steady undulation of a rocking passenger coach, the drumming heat, the clicking of crickets, the insistent drift of ash from the smokestack, paired with a slow-building stench of body odors and the drone of flies against the windows. The narrow wooded benches were scarcely adequate, but even less so for women whose bustles and petticoats crushed against the seatbacks and spilled into the aisle. Still, the ladies' garments provided enviable posterior cushioning. Jeremy drifted in and out of a heat-induced stupor. He carried a book, but his eyes blurred from reading. Occasionally, the conversation of free-thinking people proved to be superior entertainment.

Rattling through Kansas on the third day, he shared a table in the dining car with a fellow traveler, Rufus McNeely, and two other men.

McNeely was a talker, the first to offer an introduction. "I'm on my way home to San Francisco. Attended a county fair in Illinois that has me thinking."

One of the other men nodded. "County fairs are where you find new inventions."

McNeely continued as though he didn't notice the interruption. "One of the exhibits was fairly simple. Nothing more than a bunch of twisted spikes on a wooden strip of wood. Fencing, it was purported to be."

"Fencing?"

"It's the latest thing. Apparently, three competitors, used to be friends, are each working like the devil to create something they call 'barb wire.'"

"Barb wire," one of the others said, "well, I'll be damned!" He looked around in haste to see if he had offended any ladies present.

"One of them has formed a tiny company in De Kalb. He's manufacturing a twisted barb made of wire. I saw his prototype. He uses barbs held in place by wooden bits."

Jeremy laughed. "Take a month of Sundays to build enough to keep hogs out of a woman's garden, sir."

McNeely turned and smiled. "That's what his competitors say. They've filed patents for other designs. The three are having quite a battle over rights."

One of the other men smirked. "Poppycock! Hedgerows and rock fences are nature's answer for restraining livestock."

Jeremy hooked his thumb toward the flat, treeless land outside the train window. "Providing you possess the materials."

The man from New England laughed. "In my area, a farmer buys two acres, one to farm and the other to hold the rocks he picks off his productive acre."

Even McNeely laughed at that.

Jeremy spent the rest of the day watching the unbroken prairie: thousands of miles with no trees, no sources of wood or rocks, even for shelter, let alone for the protection of cropland. But—a wired fence? The idea would spread like wildfire. As soon as the homesteaders got wind, they would stretch it from one end of the prairie to the other.

Hours sped by while possibilities filled his mind. By the time the train pulled into San Francisco, he had formed a plan.

Chapter Three

Four months passed while Ginny waited for the stranger to arrive at the Bar N. Summer blasted into her loft through the cracks that still waited fixing. From her cot she watched clouds gathering above Coalinga Mountain, five miles distant, to drop rain on the tall, skinny pines that Sancho called widow-makers, because the huge pinecones could kill a man. *Coulter Pines*, he called them.

Bluebonnet clouds wisped the sky this morning. At breakfast Miguelito sounded hopeful for rain. The past year had been hard on the cattle, but maybe they would see a late summer rain to feed the struggling grass. She hoped for a thunderstorm; she could climb into her loft and listen to the music of the wind blowing through the digger pines.

Behind the orchard, the dry Joaquin Creek waited for the few weeks each year when water tore downstream to meet up with the other creeks, each pretty paltry by itself, but where they joined, water cut the banks like a knife slicing butter. Farther south the Little Cholame flowed on the surface for most of the year, and the groundwater created a shady park. Nettie Imus lived there. Her mother said their property would make a fine town setting one day.

Nettie had sent word that she and her mother were due to visit her Uncle Edwin at his cabin today. It was on the stage road through Slack's Canyon, close enough to walk. She'd need to slick herself up if she planned to go visiting; a lady shouldn't smell sour, even if she came from the Bar N. Ginny looked down at her threadbare clothes and wished for the hundredth time that she had something finer to wear. Missus Imus had quit sending over Nettie's cast-offs after she hit a growing spurt.

She gathered her bar of lye soap and a rag scrap, and headed for the spring where she was guaranteed some privacy. The men were all out riding, and no one would think of looking for her there.

Sancho claimed a person could get the chilblains from bathing too often. She didn't believe him—it was tight spaces that killed a person. She'd had a dream just the night before, she was buried inside her mother's casket and the lid nailed shut. The dream was still fresh. She needed to be outside today.

Ginny pulled off her britches and added her sour shirt to the pile. She caught her reflection in the pool of water, and for a moment the ripples made her plain straw hair and sprinkling of freckles seem pretty, almost like her mother's tintype. Stripped naked, she wondered if her mother had ever looked like her, all legs and arms. Her body was changing in slight ways, and only this week Maria Inés had said 'she was old enough now,' whatever that meant. She wondered if Patrón knew how old she was. Sancho said she'd been born after the War.

The scanty late-summer water was algae green with little mosquitoes floating on it. She brushed aside the plants and scooped water with an old gourd someone had left there. The soap was contemptible; she'd scrape her skin raw by the time she rinsed. The sun dried her as she unrolled her dress and shook out the wrinkles. Draped over her thin frame, the hem was high-water, four inches shorter than when Missus Imus made it for her, even though she had picked the stitches from the hem and added a ruffle when her growing spurt came on. Now her budding breasts strained against the bodice and caused her chest to itch. She wasn't sure if this incessant itching was normal, but she didn't know who she could ask. Maybe Maria Inés would know. Some days it drove her crazy.

She finished dressing and rinsed her britches in the murky water, twisted them dry and rolled them in a ball. An apple tree on her way to the house made a great clothesline. She flung them on a low branch, making sure to stay hidden from the house. From behind the tree she watched the cook limping to the spring for a bucket of water, favoring her feet as though every step was agony. Ginny turned in the opposite direction and started walking.

The Imus place was a stout cabin with prime grazing land shaded by full-grown oaks, some with moss on them. A pile of pine and trash wood kindling was stacked near the porch, alongside a dwindling pile of last winter's pumpkins and squash destined for the pigs. The orchard behind the cabin was in full-ripening; a couple of wooly ewes stood on hind legs, feeding on low-hanging apples and pears.

Nettie and her brother were playing in the orchard while their mother sat on the porch with Nettie's uncles. The two men were tall and fierce looking, with sharp eyes and long beards. Ginny hid behind an oak tree, not sure whether she should intrude. Everyone was having a fine day without her, and as soon as she showed up, everything would change. Missus Imus would feel obligated to get up and offer her something to eat. Nettie would stop playing with John, and he would go off and sulk or play tricks on them to get their attention. She swallowed the lump in her throat and considered whether to turn around and go home.

Just then Nettie spied her. "Ginny, finally! We've been waiting the watermelon on you."

John grinned at her like she was the one bringing the melon, when it was one of his uncle's cash-crop melons they planned to serve, probably cooling in the springhouse. She moved from the shadow of the oak and smoothed her dress so that Missus Imus wouldn't feel obliged to stitch her up a ruffle to add some length.

Her hair was still damp from the vigorous scrubbing she'd given it.

Missus Imus noticed right off. "Come sit, dear. I'll braid your hair. It's so shiny and long."

John snorted. "Yeah. Like a horse."

"Hush," his mother warned him with a swat. "Our Ginny's hair is lovely."

Ginny closed her eyes and imagined it was her own mother doing the plaiting, while feathers of feeling ran along her skin until she wanted to cry.

"Your mother would have relished this, Ginny,"

Missus Imus's kindness didn't help matters. Suddenly the pull of the braids seemed to be taking Ginny's scalp right off. She bit her tongue and endured the pain, half-glad of it.

Missus Imus served the watermelon and waited for the children to finish before she pulled out a picture book with a story about a rabbit and a farmer's garden. Ginny sounded out one of the words and felt her face warm with pleasure at the pleased nod Missus Imus gave her.

When the watermelon rinds were cleared away and preparations made for Nettie's family to leave, Ginny tried to hide her pleasure when Missus Imus insisted she ride with them—and even better, suggested she keep the book on loan to practice her reading.

After waving Nettie and her mother off, Ginny watched the wagon round the bend and disappear. She'd overheard Nettie's uncles arguing, and something they said stuck her as worth remembering. She'd have to ask Sancho. Nettie's father was for riding the stage to San Francisco, registering their claims with the land office and paying their back taxes, but the two uncles said it was a fool's errand. They were for saving their money and buying more stock. "Land is free for the grazing and that won't change," one of them claimed. His voice had drifted into the meadow where she and Nettie were playing hide-and-go-seek with John. It seemed right, the land-aplenty-for-cattle-and-horses part. Sancho would know what happened to people who didn't pay their taxes. Of any ranch in the valley, Patrón's would be the most likely to scrimp on obligations.

Chapter Four

Ginny climbed into a huge oak shading the entrance to her father's ranch. She shinnied up the lowest branch and settled onto a convenient crotch with her new book, but when the afternoon glare made reading impossible, she turned her attention to the summer house where smoke was rising from the chimney.

Sancho claimed Maria Inés's man had spent a summer packing adobe mud into rough-sawn wooden forms that still bore his finger marks. He had died before she was born. She didn't remember what he looked like, but Maria Inés often gazed off into the sunset as if she were watching for him. Jose Ignacio had left his mark on more than just the bricks. Sancho said Maria Inés missed the rhythm of his hands. He was the one who made the soap, and cut and sewed their sandals. He made the candles, burned the lime, pressed the olive oil, rolled Patrón's cigars, cut the vaqueros' hair and doctored them when a longhorn cow split their skin open. Before he died from hard work and a poor life, he saw to it that his wife had a sturdy room to work in. Afterwards, Maria Inés had to do his work, too. It was little wonder that she was silent and worn-out most of the time—she hardly had time to sleep.

Today was the day for hanging branches of pears from the beams of the summer house so they could dry. If Ginny didn't help, the cook would have to do the work of two women. When the noontime meal was put away and the dishes washed, Maria Inés would start on the fruit. She would work until time to serve the next meal, with wadded dish rags stuffed under her armpits to catch the sweat.

Ginny saw the large red clay ollas that stored water for the house. Behind them, the window of her mother's parlor showed a pair of lace curtains hung to block out light. Patrón kept the room locked. Sometimes at night she sat with him in the corner of his library, drawing the squirrels and the jackrabbits she'd seen that day. When he was in a good mood, with his whiskey and his rolled smokes, he let her describe her drawings, but most nights he stared himself into silence and ignored her. On days like today, she wondered what her mother would think of their house. Patrón had stopped working on it the week she died. Lucky for them, the summer cook house had been finished beforehand, because Maria Inés slept there on a coarse mat she'd woven from cattail tules.

When I'm grown, Mama, I aim to live in a garden.

***

Ginny found Sancho in the stone-fruit orchard, hobbling on his bowed legs. Once, when she had asked him why his legs were crooked, he claimed he couldn't remember them being any other way. He allowed as how he'd started riding so young, his legs just naturally grew in the shape of a horse's belly.

"Hi ya, Sancho. Need company?" She called out her approach before she got too close so he wouldn't startle on his bad-ear side. He liked that. They held to arrangements that suited them both. He let her call him *Sancho*, when he was no more Mexican than she was. She'd given him the nickname because she couldn't pronounce his real name, and the ranch had followed suit until his real name had been forgotten. Sometime she'd ask him, but judging from his mood, today was not the day.

"About time you showed up. Thought maybe the buzzards got you," Sancho growled.

"Been over to Nettie's. Her mama loaned me a book. She's hell bent on making a lady out of me." Ginny kept her head down, hoping he'd overlook the rule-bending. No chance.

He looked up, frowning. "Mighta let me know you'd skedaddled over there. We got a rule 'bout that, Missy!"

She studied his salt and pepper hair beneath the battered Stetson he'd bought off an old miner for five dollars in the old days, back when gold was plenty and hats were scarce. He referred to it as his "John B." Claimed he'd bought it nearly new, dipped it in the horse tank and shaped it on a tree stump. The hat came with its own history; the fellow who sold it to him bragged that John Stetson had sold it to him right off his own head. Whether or not that was true, the hat had seen a lot of use. They were the same, Sancho and his hat, plenty good on the inside even if they didn't look like it at first glance. He was losing his teeth, at least the ones in back. That made it hard for him to chew, no matter that the cook boiled his beef instead of frying it. In the late afternoon sun, his eyes were a faded robin's-egg blue. Just now, he squinted and the lines in his face deepened.

"Patrón says a man can do whatever he wants, once he's grown," she said.

"That so?" He set aside the branch he was stripping, his attention on something in the distance. Maybe he was in pain. He was close-mouthed with his aches and pains. Sometimes the vaqueros hid their injuries until it was too late for Maria Inés to tend them. The unlucky ones were buried in a draw below the creek, those souls hadn't died in God's grace.

"Ever tell a lie, Sancho?"

The scowl on his face deepened. "If I did, it was for good cause."

"Patrón says you keep your own counsel."

"Expect he'd know." His branch hit the tree with a thwack.

"Who's smarter, you or Patrón?"

"Give me a hand, will you, Missy? Careful you don't ketch yourself on that limb over yon."

She considered as she bent to pick up the fruit he had dropped. Sancho was a mystery; that much was certain. Even in the orchard he wore his range outfit, the sturdy trousers that Levi Strauss had brought to the high country when Sancho was hunting gold. He concentrated on a fresh branch, seeming to forget about her morning adventure.

She diverted his attention, just in case. "You wear those Levis day and night. Might be they need a good airing."

"My britches get washed every spring." He filled one basket and started on the next.

"You ought to take a bath once a week or so. That's what my mama did."

"Do tell. I don't recall asking for your opine about my personal hygiene." He turned and his battered cowhide gloves dangled from his hind pocket. He'd bought them for ranching, but nowadays they saw more use pruning roses than handling a reata. He had a way with the yard. Once, he'd pounded an old bear trap into a pruning shears as a surprise for her mother. Even now he kept her sweet Castilian roses and hollyhocks blooming. He even carried mountain lion droppings from the hills and laid them around the roots to keep the deer away.

Each day he wore the same faded-green shirt, its buckthorn snags mended by his own hand. Days like today, he left off the leather vest with its pockets for his Barlow knife, chewing tobacco, matches and liver pills. Around the yard he didn't need the leather vest and chaps, but his kerchief was another matter. It was always around his neck, partially to block the sun and wind, and partly out of habit.

Gawking was no way for a lady to act, not even a tomboy. She began chattering to cover her embarrassment. "You ain't that much older than

Patrón. You just limp, that's all. Maria Inés says you shouldn't brood over things you can't change. Can I borrow your kerchief?" She held out her hand without waiting for an answer. That was the thing about Sancho; he was not above helping her out. He fished his scarf off his neck and tossed it to her.

"When yer're done, fetch them things up." He pointed toward a pair of woven baskets. "We'll give Maria Inés some makings for a pie. Got me a hankering for a pear cobbler with sweet cream floating atop like clouds."

Ginny laughed. "We ain't got a cow. Or any clouds for that matter. Better you wish for a watermelon. I know where we could get one of those."

It didn't matter. Somehow the cook would furnish Sancho his hankering. No matter how much work of her own she had, Maria Inés tried to make it appear that Sancho did the work of two men. She'd seen Patrón give some of the vaqueros their pay when they got sick, and tell them to ride on; she was not about to see that happen with Sancho.

Ginny finished with the kerchief and handed it back. "Sancho, why don't Patrón talk nicer to you?"

He swatted a gnat away from his face and growled, "Why the tarnation you call him thet Mex name, anyhow?"

She chewed her bottom lip and considered. "Nettie Imus calls her father 'Pa.'"

"'Pa's' a dang-sight better than the one yer're using." He turned back to work and she wandered into the shade.

The apples, peaches, pears, plums, quince, and black walnuts were in bad need of water. The pomegranate was her favorite, even if it was twisted and humped. It bore colorful red fruit each fall, and she helped the cook press the seeds into juice. Sancho had brought it back for her mother from a cattle drive to Monterey. That was why the trunk had grown so twisted—from being wrapped in a damp burlap sack and tossed into a horse pack for the long trip home. By December the persimmons would be the size of crabapples. Every year when they turned the color of a western sunset she knew Christmas was just around the corner. She loved winter, when the ponds froze over and the persimmons hung alone, the last fruit in the orchard, with their leaves all brown and lying on the ground.

Today the pears were ripe. She pulled up her basket and reached for one. Sancho opened his pocket knife, pared a slice and handed it to her on the edge of his blade. She chewed slowly, enjoying the sweet-tart taste on her tongue. When she finished, she held out her hand or another. "Why are you and Maria Inés friends?"

He chewed on a wedge and considered. "Reckon yer're old enough to understand a friendship twixt man and woman."

"But Maria Inés's a squaw."

She watched Sancho's face turn red. His pear dropped when he raised his hand to shake a finger at her. "You say thet again, I swear I'll take a switch to yer backside."

Ginny nodded while the heat of Sancho's glare threatened to bring up shame tears.

"Where'd you hear those words?" he demanded. "Somebody puttin' ideas in yer head?"

She nodded again, and this time she couldn't hold back the tears. "One of the homesteaders' boys says I'm being reared by a squaw."

Sancho reached to retrieve his fallen fruit, but it was a while before the storm left his face. She began picking pears while she waited for him to say something. Maria Inés shared her tobacco with Sancho, and sometimes laughed at the things he said, and when she was in the mood, she told stories about life at San Miguel when it was a Spanish mission. Maybe Maria Inés felt kindly towards Sancho because he'd been the one to help when her husband died one night, with no priest to pray over him.

Finally, Ginny broke the silence. "You told me how she washed her husband's body and wrapped him in a blanket. You carried him to the Mission on the back of a mule." She looked to see if he was listening. "You said it didn't matter if the padres were gone and the church locked up. You buried him with the rest of the holy dead Indians."

"That's a fact." His tone was calm, but his face remained stony.

Ginny felt her face heat. "I don't think she's a squaw. I don't even know why I said that."

Sancho's gaze met hers. "Don't let folks cripple yer thinkin' with their gum. You keep going straight across lots. Don't shift your path for no one. Yer ma wouldn't want that."

She nodded. He didn't mention Patrón. Sancho had reason to hate her father. He was the only person on the ranch who didn't call him 'Patrón.' She did because Maria Inés said it sort of meant 'Papa' in Spanish. Papa. Sometimes she whispered the words to herself so she wouldn't forget their sounds. *Mama and Papa.*

Judging from his stony continence, it was going to take time for Sancho to forgive her. She turned and gave him her sweetest smile. "Sancho, tell me again about the day you and Patrón found this valley."

Sancho hesitated with a hand on the smoke he was trying to roll. "Reckon so. Haven't forgot much about that day." He gazed into the distance. "It was back in spring of '65—"

Ginny gave an impatient swipe. "Not like that. Like Mama would tell it."

"She wasn't around back then. You know that."

"I don't care. Like she would, with all the pretty words."

Sancho's ears reddened. "You want the fancy words, you tell it."

Ginny beamed. "Okay, I will." She began reciting the story she had created from the one the vaqueros told at the campfire. In her mind, the story sounded like she had been there.

"'Hold them back, Sancho!' Patrón was yelling like he always does. '*Arrimate!*' You yelled back just as loud, never even looking up. Miguelito and the vaqueros were working the herd, laughing and joking like they were part horse themselves." Ginny grinned. "That's 'cause they are. Especially Miguelito."

Sancho glared. "You telling the story or just jabbering?"

"Telling." She shifted.

He reconsidered. "Say, missie, yer're doing fine. Haven't left out a thing."

"Heck no. Mama wouldn't want me to." She thought a moment and continued.

Chapter Five

Sancho

Thirteen years earlier

The herd stallion stood like a statue, sensing something in the air. Nearby, the mares milled nervously, their ears jutting forward. Suddenly a piebald mare let out a scream and bolted when a dust plume escaped from a crack in the adobe. In quick order the earth bucked and folded into ribbon candy, rippling the land while thunder poured from deep below. A pine tree toppled, crowding the horses together. A hawk screamed and took flight, the movement driving fear into the already panicked herd. Sancho strained to see through the dust, worse than he'd seen on a dozen Texas cattle drives. In the charged stillness he swabbed the grit of his mustache. The kerchief helped, but his throat felt like the jerked beef he'd carried in his pocket all the way from Sacramento. He coughed and spit out a wad of adobe mud caught in his lung.

Young vaqueros circled the herd, calling out in soft voices that held no fear of the earth rolling beneath their horses. They were good hands—native Californians more used to the earth's quaking than the gringos. A shout from one of them warned him when a whiskey-colored mare took off up the rise. The herd stallion screamed and charged after her, biting hard enough that she squealed.

As suddenly as it began, the earth settled. Through his good ear, Sancho heard the Boss say, "Pull up! Pull them up!" Suddenly the lead mare crashed into a sandy wash and the others followed.

"Yeeeeeeyeiiii!" Miguelito thundered past. A second later he slipped down the side of his horse, held up only by a boot wedged against his left *tapedero*, his fancy covered stirrup, and by the pressure of his knees. His right hand grasped the horse's mane while his left dangled inches from the ground. By the time Sancho cleared his eyes, the boy was astride again, drinking from his cupped palm, his yellow scarf fluttering in the breeze like a yellow-billed magpie.

The devil-may-care vaquero glanced around with a grin for anybody watching. Sancho opened his mouth to growl a warning, but thought better of it. A fool stunt, but what did he expect? The Boss had taken on four strutting bantams not old enough to shave. This one wore his worldly fortune in his silver tack, tooled leather britches and buckskin jackets. He sported a jacket edged with silver *conchos* that the others eyed with envy, but wealthy or not, none of them ever lost an opportunity to show off—for their gringo bosses or each other.

A warning was unlikely to be heeded. Today was a day for celebration.

He rejoined the riders circling the nineteen Spanish mustangs—bought off a band of Indian mustang hunters for Yankee gold and a pair of weathered Winchester rifles. The trade had been a good one. On his way from the gold fields, the Boss had found a starving Yokut Indian tied to an oak tree while his cruel master slept off his whiskey. The Boss gave the Indian his freedom and a leather sack of jerky. To repay him, the man had led them to the Cholama Valley before he slipped away into the night. The lean mares and the clear-eyed stallion were remnants of a herd living in the Tulare Plains since the time of the Spanish *soldados*. Now the herd had spread out across a narrow valley where sycamores hugged the creek and oaks and pines filled the skyline.

From the corner of his good eye, Sancho watched a line of mules pick their way up the rise, guarded by a vaquero to protect their supplies from bandidos—men of every nationality who raided for a living. But the Boss had hired his vaqueros for their bravery; he had no intentions of losing his possessions to earthquakes—or outlaws.

When the stream cleared, Sancho slipped from his saddle to refill his canteen. He drank his fill while he scanned the ground for telltale signs. Finally he straightened. The old Yokut Indian trail behind them was pocked with the hoof prints of their horses, but ahead the mud had dried. Judging from the grass in the faint track, no one had passed since the last rain.

"Boss, we're biting on fresh trail here. Good Lord's leading us to the promised land."

Overhead, sunshine filtered through an oak tree. Blooming buck brush grew in the low basin and below the hills, filling the air with sweet scent in a rolling carpet of new grass. Purple lupine colored the countryside. Bees buzzed overhead, eager to fill their sacs after a long winter. The land of milk and honey, like God had promised Moses. Milk in the low hills where sheep and goats could range, honey in the flat lands where orchards could thrive.

Sancho stood and waved his Stetson. "This is it, Boss. We've made it to the Cholama."

The Boss nodded and gestured toward a line of mules struggling up the rise, led by an Indian woman leading a young goat. "Hurry them up. We need to make camp before nightfall."

Sancho listened, but he didn't hurry. He had found the Salinan woman, Maria Inés, and her husband Jose Ignacio north of San Miguel while the Boss was asking around for a white man to do the cooking. The woman was dressed in a tule-reed skirt. Both of them had tattered, coarse-woven shirts hanging off their backs, and the hard, gaunt look of people used to living off the land. The couple hadn't said much, but their eyes lingered on the cattle long enough that he knew they hadn't tasted beef in a while. They didn't speak English, but his Spanish was passable. The husband knew the making of adobe bricks, and Sancho saw in the man's eyes that he would work hard for his wages. The woman would work for free.

Sancho loosened his scabbard and followed his boss up the trail. Maybe it was a day for celebration. If Charlie Nugent turned out to be an honorable man, he'd plant his boots and stay a spell.

He studied the arid north side of the Cholama Valley from astride his horse; rugged hillsides scattered with oak, buckeye and small bushy pine, a land carved into arroyos dotted with green areas and hidden springs irrigating patches of fresh grass. Chamise, buck brush, holly berry and a half-dozen varieties of trees scattered the hillsides, hiding bobcats, cougars and even grizzly. The land was prime grazing land. The Boss agreed. When the Mexican longhorns arrived from Los Angeles, after the vaqueros burned the Bar N brand on them, Nugent's cattle would have their run of the valley.

By evening, Sancho had his report. "Those vaqueros will earn their keep," he told the Boss. "They'll sleep on their horses. Stay out there all night long." He squatted alongside the oak stump someone had rolled alongside the fire for a seat, and checked the coffee pot. "Grub ready yet?"

The Indian woman kept her eyes to the ground as she shook her head and gestured toward the pot of beans simmering on the stove. No coffee yet, either. He didn't want to complicate her first night by hanging around camp. On his way out again, he reached over, plucked a blade of new grass and rolled it lengthwise like a cigarette. He bit off the end. "I like this place. Heavy feed. Keep the cattle on their feet."

The cook looked up and nodded, confused. "*Sí*," she replied. She had no idea what he'd just said, but she was agreeable.

On his way to check his horse, Sancho dipped his hat in the Joaquin

Creek. He pulled up a brimful of sweet water and drank deep. The moon was rising in a thin crescent over the valley's eastern ridge. "This'll do just fine," he repeated to himself.

On his return to the camp, Maria Inés shy offer of coffee really hit the spot. She waited for him to take a sip and nod his approval before she turned away. She wasn't a talker. Her husband either—both like ghosts, everywhere at once, but nowhere to be seen.

By the time Maria Inés had the beans and tortillas ready, her man had one of the Boss's stiff new *reatas* strung up over a branch and a skinned possum hanging from the rope. When supper was over, the woman scrubbed the dishes with river sand in the light of a sliver of silver moon cresting the hill. Night birds were calling from cover as the Indian couple moved to a nearby copse of oaks toting one of the woman's woven baskets.

Sancho was fighting the pull of sleep at the fireside when he heard the woman grinding acorns in a set of mortar holes pounded into the rocks by Yokut Indians who had camped alongside the creek.

The Boss settled himself with another cup of coffee, his mood in harmony with the night. "I expect the cattle in a week or two. Paying on delivery. By then we'll be ready."

The two of them were the only ones left at the fire. "Vaqueros started gentling the horses," Sancho said.

The Boss nodded. "I'll put the Indian to channeling the spring. Spare time, we'll start on the bunkhouse." He swept his arm in a broad sweep that included the creek. "It appears the water around here falls as quickly as it rises."

"In'jun woman brought some seeds. Says she's some good with a garden."

Before they left San Miguel, Sancho had watched her dig up a couple dozen starts from a plot alongside the Salinas River where she and her husband had been scratching out a living in a patch of willows alongside a hungry-looking bunch of Mission Indians. It was no wonder they called the times they were living in, the *Time of the Trouble*. Most of what their ancestors ha d known was long forgotten. The Spanish priests had set them adrift from their old ways. After the Mexican government set them loose to fend for themselves, most of what they owned had been stolen or burned off by Yankees bent on driving them off the land. Most of the survivors had died of sickness or starvation.

The Indian woman wore a wooden crucifix around her neck. Maybe it was peace Sancho saw in her eyes. A woman on a ranch was a stabilizing influence, a married woman even more so, Indian or no.

He shook off his thoughts and gestured toward the coffee pot. "Drink up, Boss. Cook left some for you."

The two sat in silence while a night bird twittered in a nearby meadow. The Boss listened intently. "This time next month, I'll know that bird. I'll know every coyote howl."

"Whippoorwill. Place'll likely get under your skin," Sancho said.

"Home finds you, not the other way around."

"Yep." When the whippoorwill quieted, Sancho added, "Right nice place to start a family."

The Boss watched the flames. "Haven't had much luck with family," he mused.

"No kin?"

He shifted, trying to find comfort on the hard ground. Finally he spoke. "None to speak of. None alive, anyway. I had four brothers, but they all died before I was born. My father got killed by Indians. Mother died bearing me." He jabbed a shaft of wild oats into the fire and watched it burn down. When soot tinged the tips of his finger, he tossed it into the flames without flinching. "You got kin?"

Sancho found himself staring into the same flames. "Ma had a passel," he said. "Don't know anyone ever counted how many. Sisters got themselves a brood, too. Kentuck women, they birth easy."

The Boss slumped forward, his body still. "Feast or famine with women. Strange the way nature works."

In the darkness, Sancho nodded. "'Spect by 'nature,' you mean the Almighty."

The Boss's grunt was clear enough he didn't need to use the words, but he growled them anyway. "Didn't feel like the Almighty when I was growing up orphaned, traded off between families thought I was their slave. Felt piss-mean and hungry."

"Some fellows know that feeling, even with kin," Sancho muttered, half to himself.

The Boss shrugged. "I had to call them 'pa' and 'ma,' but they were no kin."

"Oughtta get yourself a Kentuck woman," Sancho said. "Ain't a man ornery enough he don't dream of having a Southern lass in a white dress serving him mornin' vittles."

"Maybe I will—on your recommend. Soon as that cussed war is over. Never thought the South could hold out so long."

"Glad you didn't bet your boots on it," Sancho said.

"Sorry, I forget you're a sympathizer." The Boss shifted and turned to watch the moon. "For now, those horses are my kin. I sure have a fine start."

Sancho let out a snort. "They ain't the prettiest things I ever laid eyes on."

A moment passed before the Boss answered. "I have to agree. They need some fresh blood. I met a fellow over in San Francisco said he'd contracted to buy some purebred stock off a widow in Virginia, somehow managed to hang on to hers with both armies shooting mounts on either side. Says the army has a fort at the Presidio in San Francisco needs a steady supply of horses. Wants me to negotiate the deal, arrange for shipment before the army confiscates them all. He isn't up to the trip."

Sancho considered. "You figure to ride back there?"

"Yes I do. Virginia." His voice grew quiet as he watched the fire.

"Well, close enough to Kentuck, I reckon." Sancho slapped at a mosquito on his cheek. "Dangnabbit, Boss, maybe you'll find yourself a wife."

In the darkness, Charlie Nugent sounded wistful. "If I do, she'll have to be something special."

***

Sancho joined Ginny in her silence when the story was ended. After a few minutes he stirred and relit the cigarette that had gone cold in his hand. "Dang, Missy, you got every single word in, just like she woulda told it."

"I don't have her fancy language. Hers would have sounded better, she been here to tell it."

Sancho held his smoke with a hand that shook. "Who told you that story? Your pa?"

She ignored his close inspection. She wasn't up to pity. It was nobody's business if Patrón told himself the story at night when he got sick from the bottle. Maybe he was afraid he'd forget what it felt like back, when he was hopeful.

She stood and started toward the summer house. "Guess I'll go help Maria Inés with the fruit."

Chapter Six

Sancho watched Ginny walk away, her spine so straight and determined that he was hard-put to swallow. Seeing her half-ways to grown brought a dizzying rush of guilt. With the grit of recall rubbing his insides, he picked up his kerchief and wiped his hands. One of these days the little gal was going to press him to tell the story of her mother; maybe it was time he got his facts in order. Some parts he was responsible for. Other parts he'd witnessed, standing in the shadows of the half-built house, his heart halfway to breaking. He gripped his kerchief and let his mind recall the events.

***

Nine years had passed since the day Caroline Foster Nugent pulled a lace hankie from her sleeve and dabbed at the beads of sweat running down her temples. The Indian summer heat had sapped her strength. She rested in the shade of a cottonwood tree shading the table where she trimmed the last of the roses. She paused to glance out at the hillsides of the Cholama Valley, a golden paradise and suddenly grabbed her belly. Without speaking, she gathered the roses, struggled to her feet and started toward the unfinished portico of the adobe.

Ginny, an energetic image of her mama, skipped up with another rose.

Her mother pressed her swollen belly and forced a smile. "Ginny, darlin'! What a helper you are with Mama's roses." The little gal glowed with pride as her mother added, "Won't Papa be surprised when he comes home and sees our pretty lil' table! Can you hold the door? Mama's just all butterfingers today. She has a tummy ache."

The little gal ran ahead, careful her pinafore and her waist-length hair didn't get caught in the door. The new door was rough and scratchy. She waited for her mama and carefully closed it door behind them. "Where's Papa?"

"Papa's gone far away out where the railroad ends. To a town called Hollister. He's going to sell our cattle and horses." Missus Nugent ran water into a glass and took a long drink. She poured a glass of milk and set it in front of Ginny.

Sancho heard the scrape of a chair as Ginny helped herself to a cookie.

When she finished, she touched the spot her mama was rubbing. "Does Papa know about your tummy ache?"

"Oh, no, Peaches, he would only fret. He will bring us back some gold coins so we can finish our house. Won't it be perfectly ma'velous when the parlor is finished? Papa will buy us a piano and I will teach you to play. You'll be a proper belle. A California belle."

"When?"

"Soon. Papa will ride over to Santa Cruz and see it unloaded from the steamer ship. It will come all the way from Boston."

"When?"

"We have to wait for your brother to join us."

"When?"

"Soon. In three more months."

Ginny proudly held up her fingers. "I'm three months."

"No, darling.' You're three years. Three years is very big. Three months is not long at all. In three months Mama will be well again and we'll have a Christmas tree and dried apple pie. And you will have a special gift."

"A baby doll?"

"Maybe. A fine baby brother or sister, for sure. Won't that be ma'velous? Papa will be so happy to have a son. Now let's ask Sancho to get us some fresh water for our roses. Maybe he wants to help us."

The little gal ran off to find him, but Sancho remained in the shadows.

It was hours later, when the sun was low on the horizon and his stomach rumbling from hunger, that things turned for the worse. He remembered it now, all those years ago as if it were yesterday, the memories: becoming aware that he hadn't seen the little gal for some time and wishing again Maria Inés was there. He threw down the shovel of manure he was moving and strode toward the house. Once there, he halted, unsure whether to knock or enter. Instead, he pulled off his hat and waited in plain view for the Missus to notice him, sooner or later.

His gaze settled on the unfinished walls of the hacienda. The house was well-fixed with windows—he should know, having set every one himself—and he recalled the thought that he needed to finish chinking the spaces between the adobe bricks before he could begin whitewashing. Finished, it would be the pride of the valley. *His* pride, too, since he was doing most of the work.

Minutes passed while he studied the poison oak turning colors around the trunk of a valley oak just across the buggy track. He listened for the little gal's laughter, or the mother's, but for once the house seemed too quiet. His fingers felt twitchy with the need to do something. He opened the front door and stepped into the common room where the hands took their winter meals with the family. From the hallway, Missus Nugent appeared, hollow-eyed like she hadn't slept. His throat tightened when he tried to speak, and when he swallowed his kerchief cut off his windpipe. Her usually neat hair was mussed. Ginny was tagging behind, rubbing sleep from her eyes. In the hallway behind her the Grandfather clock was striking five o'clock.

"Oh, Sancho. You caught me resting." She fussed with the front of her blouse as if she expected her buttons to be askew.

He started to stare, caught himself, and shifted his glance to the floor. "Sure yer're alright, ma'am?" In his recollection, the question came out like a croak.

Her laugh was sunshine in the evening gloom. "Fiddle-fits! I'm just weary." She indicated the lamp. "Maybe you could prepare some lamplight while I start the kettle. We'll have a tea party." On her way to the kitchen, she chattered like a jaybird. "My stars but I do wish Maria Inés would hurry back. This loneliness has me feeling irritable." She smoothed her hair.

He scooped Ginny up, swung her over to the basin and scrubbed her little hands.

"I believe a light supper will make me feel better. Don't you agree, Sancho?"

"Yes, ma'am."

The vittles she sat out for him, fried bread and white gravy, stuck in his craw while she kept him at the table with questions that didn't need answering. He ate enough to keep from hurting her feelings, but she didn't act like she noticed. It was late when he made his excuses and escaped to the bunkhouse where he could fret in private. Something was wrong; he wasn't so blind he didn't see the signs. He was some worried about the birthing, afraid something would happen to hurry nature's purpose.

"That blamed cook chose a fine time to go off visiting. Thet Indian clan of hers ain't going nowhere—they been living alongside the river for a thousand years. Coulda waited for another woman to come along, just in case this baby causes any fuss. Not much use, a washed-up old cowpoke like me." He was glad that no one heard him.

The path to the corral was lit up by the full moon creeping over the Diablo Range. The vaqueros called it *la luna Cholama*. Every month it was a sight for sore eyes, but this night the harvest moon skimmed the mountains on the other side of the Rancho Cholame like a big orange ball. It was too bad his eyes were failing. Still, he squinted upwards and caught the fuzzy aura. Maybe the old women were right when they claimed moonlight caused a baby to stir.

He waited for the moon to clear the hills before he headed back to the house, carrying a pail of water as an excuse. Inside, he stoked the cookstove, rattling pans to announce himself. From the bedroom came a sound like a moan. He edged down the hallway and listened for signs of stirring. "Missus Nugent?" When the Missus failed to answer his tap, he cautiously opened her bedroom door.

His eyes adjusted to the gloom and he saw the Missus and Ginny asleep on the bed. The room was dark enough that he'd scare them if they woke and saw him standing there. His hands were shaking as he lit the lamp. When light filled the room, he said softly, "Missus Nugent?"

Ginny raised her head and rubbed sleep from her eyes. "I waited for Mama, but I got tired so I took a nap, too. Now I'm sleepy for bedtime. It's time for us to go night-night, isn't it, Sancho?"

He nodded, listening to her mother's shallow breathing. "Ginny, why don't you go make a bed in the parlor? I'll be there to tuck you in. Your Ma's pretty tired. Looks like we need to let her rest."

The little gal swung out of bed and padded down the hall. He heard her pull a quilt from its shelf. The door shut behind her before he realized she'd probably need her flannel nightgown and some sort of rag doll to keep her company. And he needed time. "Missus Nugent, wake up."

She stirred, threw her arm over her eyes and twisted as if fighting a bad dream. When she moaned, he reached to feel her brow. It was on fire. Sweat clouded his eyes. He swabbed his face with his shirtsleeve and tried to think. Horses he knew; even cattle and pigs. *But a woman?* He noticed a pitcher of water and poured it into the basin. Hanging from a hook was a piece of cloth. He soaked it and brought it dripping to her mouth.

Ginny returned with the quilt. He led her back down the hall and made a nest on the floor near the fireplace. He found a lantern in the hallway and lit it, gratified to see she was asleep before he was out of the room. By the time he had the firebox built up and a kettle of water heating, the moaning in the bedroom had grown louder. He poured a glass of fresh water and hurried down the hall.

Missus Nugent had tossed her quilts aside. The babe in her womb should be moving; he thought about the calves he'd pulled from first-time mothers and recognized the fact. He knew trouble, and it was lying fevered in front of him. He reached his fingers along her belly. It was burning like the enflamed womb of a mare with a breech colt.

He rushed to the kitchen to soap up his hands and returned, hot water still dripping from his fingers. He slipped his hand low and tried to keep his nerves steady while he probed for the babe. He had seen it move a few days earlier when Missus Nugent sat on the porch, snapping beans. She had laughed when her pan bounced off her lap and spilled onto the floor. Now, nothing bounced, nothing moved.

Sweat ran down his face, blinding him. With a horse he could pull the foal and douche the cavity with carbolic acid to stem the infection. He stood and cursed himself for a fool. He should have been on the trail. He had no business staying behind and playing nursemaid. The Missus needed a midwife, but he couldn't leave her and go for help; couldn't leave the little gal behind, either. He couldn't even take the two of them on a flat-out race to the new clinic at the El Paso de Robles Hot Springs. No way to get across the river. The Imus woman would be willing, but she was laid up with the ague. The Choyboa Family lived to the south. The woman might have some Mexican herbs, but there was no time. Señora Gonzales or one of her women might know what to do, but he couldn't risk the ride in the dark. What if he had an accident or the horse stepped in a squirrel hole? He might not make it back for a day. He couldn't leave the child. There was no way he could take the mother in an open wagon. If she didn't die of the fever, she could die of the ride.

The Missus groaned and the sound filled the room. He watched her eyes flutter open then close again.

"Missus Nugent? Caroline?" He had never used her first name before.

Her eyes cleared and she smiled. "Charlie?"

"No, it's me, Sancho." Missus Nugent, you're in a poor way. You have a fever and the baby . . ." He tried to clear his throat. "How long since you felt the baby move?"

"A . . . a few days. I hoped . . . ."

He needed her say-so. "Missus Nugent, I may have to take the baby. Don't see any other way. Do you hear me?"

"I want it to kick." She sounded too weak. "Want it to move. Charlie needs it."

"Missus Nugent—"

"Carrie. Call me Carrie like my mother did." She was rambling, her mind fevered.

"Carrie. I've got to try. Do you savvy? There's no other chance. You'll only get sicker." His shirt clung to him, soaked with sweat.

"No. I want it to . . . . "

He watched as the fever claimed her and she fell back asleep. "Damnation!"

He swabbed her with wet towels and hoped she'd come to. When she didn't respond, he grabbed the lantern from the hallway and took off across the yard to the tack room where he kept the horse liniment. He held the lantern up so he could study each tin and cursed himself for not knowing the words on the labels. He pulled down the tincture of aconite for reducing fever, and a smelly brown liniment for drawing out boils and skin infections on the horses. He brushed rat droppings from the top. The tin of aconite felt light to the touch. He peeled off the lid. Empty! Used up on that damned ham-strung buckskin mare that never did foal right. He cursed the day Miguelito doctored her. He threw the can to the ground and searched for the tin of smelling salts, anything that might help, but he could find none. Most likely stowed on the chuckwagon halfway to Hollister by now.

He passed from the tack room to the blacksmith shed and then to the corrals, shoving horses out of his way. Back in the summer house, he threw aside the lye and the bluing he found alongside the wash tub. In the Boss's cabinet he found a pint of whiskey. He searched the pantry for anything that might stem a fever, and found a book of remedies on the top shelf. In the dim lantern light he tried to match symbols with something similar on the boxes he found, but the words made no sense. He pulled open half a dozen tins and smelled each of them. Finally, his shaking hands caught on a small bottle of laudanum. He tossed a dozen drops into a mug, added the whisky and enough water so the Missus wouldn't gag on it.

His chest was rasping by the time he limped back to the bedroom. He stood with one ear trained on the sounds of the sleeping child and the other on the moaning mother while he summoned his nerve. Finally, when the Missus gave a wretched, keening moan, he knew it was time. In the kitchen he soaped his hands with hot water and lye soap. When his cracked, gnarled hands and arms were clean to the elbows, he greased them with lard and returned to the bedside.

Slowly, he moved his fingers. For the first time he was grateful for his small build, but even so he winced at every moan she made. His fingers were so numb he could scarcely feel the water inside her when it broke. He took a breath and cursed himself for his lightheadedness. He tried to think, but his brain stalled. With his nerves bound up like knots, and her body cramped and heaving, he pulled.

The baby came out still and lifeless. He swung it upside down and gave its backside a gentle swat after clearing its mouth. Gently lowering his ear to its chest, he listened for breathing. Only silence. The mother moaned and made as if to turn. Hurrying, he tied off the unbiblical cord. Before she could open her eyes, he shrouded the baby in a piece of swaddling flannel and set it low on the end of the bed where she would not see it when she came to.

That done, he prepared to pack her womb with squares of clean flannel he found in her bureau. The afterbirth came and he waited for the bleeding to stop, but it seemed to increase. The pressure he applied slowed it some, but nothing stopped it completely. Frantic, he lifted her head and studied her pinched face for a hint of what she might need.

Her nightdress was wet through and she was shivering. He struggled to unbutton the rows of tiny buttons spanning from her waist to her breast, and by the time he finished, his fingers were stiff. He found a clean nightdress, slipped it over her head and tried not to think on what the Boss would have to say about the matter. Finally, he eased her back under the covers.

There was nothing more he could do. Ginny was stirring. In minutes she would need to be fed and occupied. He dragged himself back into the kitchen to refill the kettle and set it to heat so the Missus would have sarsaparilla tea when she woke. If she woke; the possibility drained his hope. He took a gulp of the Boss's whiskey, then another—two gulps more than he'd drunk since Missus Nugent had arrived four years earlier.

When he emptied his glass, he forced himself back down the hall. Missus Nugent lay too still for his comfort, her breathing shallow. Filled with longing, he collapsed to his knees and prayed to the God he'd ignored since the day he left his mother's house. He'd learned to use the Lord's name in ways that would have shamed her, but this time he bowed his head and sobbed out promises. "Let her live, Lord. She's a fine woman. If you need someone, Lord, take me. I've got no one. Let her get through this night and I promise—things'll be different."

Outside, the first rays of sunlight lit the sky; he caught their pink glow through the windows while his mind wandered. Even in his shattered state, he had the thought to be grateful that the sun rose early and set late in the valley, not like in the Sierra Nevada where a fellow was always cold, and most of the time living in the dark.

He checked on Ginny. Mercifully, she was still asleep.

When morning light was full in Missus Nugent's bedroom, he reached across the mound of quilts to feel her fever. He felt her pulse and had a quick hope when he did not find the rapid fluttering that had plagued her earlier. But when he took a firmer grip, the truth drained his short sense of relief. He held her hand gently and felt his heart hammering in his chest. He placed his fingers on her neck to feel the artery along her throat. There was no beat. She lay as still as porcelain.

Slowly, he lowered his head and tried to absorb the past hours. He was too ashamed to feel anything, but there was no time for reflection. In the parlor, Ginny was rousing. He had scarcely time to close the door behind him before the little gal came into the hall and asked quietly, "Sancho, why are you sad? Does Mama still have the fever?"

***

Sancho felt shame again today. He had failed the mother and here he was, failing the daughter.

Chapter Seven

The intense August heat sucked Ginny's desire to do anything but lay under the cottonwood and dream of San Francisco. Sancho had been there once. According to him, the city had cool breezes that sprang up fresh every morning. On the Bar N, each day passed with a lazy tempo that made her think the sun had nothing better to do than to pester the life out of her. She watched fleas fighting for life in the dirt.

"Leastways the heat's killing off the vermin," she muttered as she kicked up a dusty patch of turkey melon on her way to the outhouse. She hurried her business, all the while holding her breath from the stench. When she finished, she pulled a clump of Spanish moss from a pile and brushed off the spider she saw crawling across it. She slammed the outhouse door with a satisfying *thunk*, wiped her hands on her shirt and looked around for something to occupy her. Sancho had calculated that two of the hens weren't laying anymore. Likely they'd be having chicken and dumplings for supper.

She occupied herself while an hour passed, until boredom again rode her like a green-broke colt with no manners.

"Maria Inés is needing my help again," she mumbled to herself. "But I don't relish plucking feathers off dead hens. I done enough pulling off their heads and watching them squawking around in the dirt."

Sure enough, the cook sat under the cottonwood with a sour look, plucking feathers. Ginny edged closer, watching the way she grabbed a hen, dipped it in boiling water and pulled the feathers out. Ginny gave a sigh and reached for a hen. She plopped it into the steaming water and managed to drown three angry yellow jackets before she started plucking a chicken wing. "I hate these dumb quill feathers."

"Give thanks for the meat, niña," Maria Inés murmured. "It is not to be taken for granted."

Ginny's fingers struggled to keep up. When she finished, her chicken looked too scrawny to offer more than a mouthful for each of the hungry men. Probably all she would get were some dumplings and broth.

"Maria Inés, where do earthquakes come from?"

Maria Inés sounded wary. "The padres say they God's will."

"What do you think?"

The cook slapped the chickens down side-by-side on the table. "My people say we live in this world. But also there is a world above us. And one below." She indicated the ground beneath her feet. "Two serpents have been sent to hold our world up from below. But like me, they grow tired. That is why the earth shakes—because they move their bodies to ease the weariness." She stood and pulled her sticky smock loose from her underarms. "There is more to the story, but I have no time." She pointed to the bucket. "Take the guts to the pigs."

The old wooden gutbucket stood near the table, its heap of putrid entrails covered by a battered lid.

"Then where do the rivers come from?" Ginny stalled. "And how come we ain't got a big one would take us clear to the ocean if we wanted?" With Maria Inés, persistence almost always worked

The cook pointed to the bucket, her voice hardening. "My people say water in the springs and streams of this earth is the piss of the frogs what live there." She started toward the summer house without looking back. "Water here tastes like piss!"

Ginny kicked at the pot and followed the cook to the cook house. A minute later she was sorry she'd bothered. Maria Inés opened the firebox lid and dangled each bird over the snapping flames, and Ginny felt her skin puckering like the hens'.

The cook scooped them into a cast iron pot. "Señorita Geena. Outside, there some snap beans. You pick!" She nodded toward the door.

Ginny started toward the garden. Across the yard the sun created shadows beneath the adobe bunkhouse. She took a dozen steps and halted. Patrón had made it plain she wasn't to go into the men's quarters; he had threatened her with a peach switch if she did. Still, he was seldom on the ranch anymore, what with his trips to town and his headaches. She'd heard some of the vaqueros talking.

Inside the bunkhouse, a row of hooks held spare trousers and winter calfskin coats. Four cots lined up in a neat row, a brown wool blanket over each. A whiskey bottle stood next to a lantern on a table with a couple of stools kicked out of place. The room smelled like sweat, dirty leather and candles. Maybe that was just the smell of men, but Patrón had a sickly sweet smell that he couldn't hide with his cigar smoke. At any rate, there was nothing to see, and she didn't need to spend time indoors on such a fine day.

There was no one around at the corral, only horses standing head to tail, swishing flies and biting gnats. A small roan mare leaned into a tall bay mare. When it nickered, she reached to stroke the roan mare's neck and felt it twitch in pleasure.

***

Sancho came walking up, trailing a rag in his hand in time to watch Ginny make her way over to the corral, her saucy gait looking for all the world like she was queen of the ranch. The little gal looked like she was up to something. He'd seen that look enough to know she was fixing to ask something that he'd rather not hear.

"Sancho, it's time I got myself a horse of my own. It's not fair I'm the only hand on the ranch doesn't have one. Patrón's too occupied to notice that I'm growing up. I need to take care of myself."

Sancho swallowed the lump in his throat. "Maybe so, Missy."

Ginny whirled around, her eyes shining. "I already picked one out. Named her, too."

He snorted. "Horses don't carry names."

"Well, this one does."

As they approached the round corral, he glanced at the sorry-looking pile of stones on the ground, left over from a time when the ranch was part of a Spanish land grant.

"Sancho, how come rocks split out of the earth?"

"This is quakin' country. Back in '68, seen the creek wobble like a drunked-up vaquero. Was riding across when it broke in two. Sin to Moses, it was the dangest thing a man ever saw."

"Was '68 the 'big one'?"

"Big enough for me. Picked up the countryside, laid it down like a lumpy quilt."

Sancho followed Ginny to the corral at a slower pace, burdened by recollections. How old was this little gal? Sometimes she acted like she was twenty, the way she tended her pa when he was down. Other times, like today, it seemed like she was about eight. He counted back to the year her mother passed. Twelve was about right, almost thirteen.

He bent to replace a stone. The corral was falling down, likely built to hold Spanish horses back when everybody was trying to get their hands on California. If it wasn't the Spanish or the Mexicans, it was the Russians up at Fort Ross until the Americans run them off. Looked to stay run off, too. Yankees were born stubborn. Nobody was likely to run the Boss off his land unless it was this cursed drought. The vaqueros had driven most of the steers up to the Sierra Nevada's earlier in the summer. Over at the Rancho Cholame, the fields were empty of sheep—their flocks gone to the mountains as well.

He adjusted his eyes to watch Ginny. The kid had eyes for a roan, a Spanish Bard just over fourteen hands that was nuzzling up to her like they were old friends. He watched as the mare nosed the little gal and found a piece of tortilla hanging from a torn pocket.

Suspicion hit him. "You been sneaking off with that mare?"

Her chin went up. "I'm not allowed to. Patrón said."

He made a vain attempt to hide his smile. "Not what I asked."

"Some . . . ."

"Bareback?"

"Yessir."

"Never cared for mares. Too damned spooky." He spat into the dirt, wiped his hands and avoided her eyes. No point in adding to her misery; her old man did enough of that.

"Caroline's not jumpy."

"Wal, maybe . . ." He hoped his voice held steadier than it felt. "What did you say her name was?"

"Caroline!"

"Your ma's name." He watched her fiddling with a handful of tangled black mane, trying to act like she wasn't quailing inside.

"Yep. This way I can talk to Mama and he won't know." She looked up. Tears glistened in her blue eyes as she leaned into the mare's neck.

He leaned over and caught a piece of straw, swiped the stem clean and stuck it in his mouth. He couldn't keep his fingers from trembling. "That so?" He shifted onto his good leg and lifted his arm to hug her, but he let it drop when his nerve failed him. "Don't be too hard on your old man. He's got his reasons for what he does. He was good to yer mother. *Comprende?*"

She nodded. "You think people in Heaven can see us?"

"Reckon Maria Inés would say so," he mumbled. The kid had some odd questions.

"Your mama teach you about Heaven?" she asked.

"Reckon she did."

He was some younger than this little gal when he hit the trail with a survey team that rode by his ma's place. He'd seen her twice more over the years. First time he rode home to leave off money he had saved up, he'd stayed just long enough to say hello. Last time, his sisters and their brood of youngsters were crowded inside the cabin, their men folk killed off in the

War. He remembered riding into the wind-swept enclosure that surrounded the tiny cabin, proud to be a full grown man. Near as he could figure, he'd been fourteen, filled with pity for the hollow-eyed bunch of kin staring back like he was a stranger. Come to that, reckon he was. The whole brood had been too much for one kid to worry over. He'd done what he could. He remembered placing a wad of money into his ma's worn hands and allowing her to wrap her arms around him one last time before he rode off again.

Squaring his shoulders, he let his arm drop. "Well, Missy, got yerself a dandy horse there, needs a saddle. Let's go have a look."

Ginny started off ahead, wiping her eyes with the tattered tail of her checkered vaquero's shirt. She stuffed it back into her britches and glanced over to see if he had had noticed.

The tack shed smelled of bear grease, leather and mice. He kept the door closed against possums that would chew the sweat off the leather straps. Spare saddles were lined up on a rough-cut pole braced between two saw-horses. Rows of reins hung from square nails he'd pounded out on a forge. He kept his saddle inside, out of the weather, but the vaqueros kept their horses saddled all night. They trusted nothing and no one.

"Yer pa's not going to take kindly to what we're doing, Missy." Her mother's saddle was still in the corner where the Boss had given strict orders it was to stay, still soft and supple from the neat's-foot oil Sancho rubbed on it. Wasn't a man on the ranch would care if they saw the little gal riding. Way the Boss was drinking these days, the whole ranch would belong to her before long. "Go pick yerself out a bridle."

The mother's saddle had been custom made for her, over the Boss's objections. He'd wanted her to ride side-saddle, but the Missus had been right; the hills were too steep for riding that way. The saddle hadn't gotten much use. She'd spent most of her four years in California carrying babies.

He handed the little gal a rat-chewed Navajo saddle blanket, and its sour odor followed them outside. She tossed it on the horse. When it landed squarely on her very first try, she looked to see if he'd noticed. He gave her a nod and lifted the saddle on.

"I'm not as big as my mama," she said.

"You'll do." He shortened the stirrup by two notches and tried to ignore the lump in his throat. "Keep your eyes peeled. It ain't the animals you need look out for."

Ginny scowled. "Yeah, I know. Bandidos. Been hearing 'bout them my whole life."

"Good reason. Countryside's festering with 'em."

"Tiburcio Vasquez wouldn't hurt me. Miguelito says he's gallant to women. You said so yourself. Just like you seen Joaquin Murrieta's head pickled in a bottle."

"True enough. But the Boss lost nine head of cattle just last week."

She hadn't heard that news. "How come men steal?"

He gave the cinch an extra tug. "Expect there's a lot of reasons. Some were high-placed sons of the Spanish dons before the Mexicans took over. Got a grudge to bear, I reckon. Some were born into it—too lazy to earn an honest day's pay. Some are just plain mean—and those are the ones you have to look out for—the ones that'll skin you alive just to hear you holler."

Ginny shifted in the saddle. "You afraid of them?"

"Bet yer sweet goodnight! The way those *cholo* bands carve up a man— 'specially the gringos. They hate the whites." He turned back to his stirrup. "If a man had a nickel in his britches, they'd as soon truss him up and drag him through the buckbrush as look at him."

"Those bandidos ever kill a kid?"

Sancho grabbed her reins and jerked her horse toward the gate. "Just stay in sight. No riding off alone—ever." She was glaring up at him, but her heart was thumping like a wild thing's. He could see it in her eyes. "Here, put these gloves on. Go run yer mare into the round pen, couple of laps. Get the vinegar out." He fought the urge to smile, instead cleared his throat in an exaggerated cough. "You get her warmed up, we'll take out together. That's the rule Comprende?"

"Comprende."

Chapter Eight

Ginny wheeled off toward the shallow ravine where a herd of longhorn cattle were spread out across the white sage. She and Nettie had agreed to meet halfway. By the time she rode up, Nettie was sitting on a boulder while her mare cropped wild oats.

"'Bout time you showed up. I was ready to ride home."

Ginny drew a sweet fresh breath of freedom. "Sancho's up in some draw tending a rattler-bit calf. Couldn't wait any longer so I just left. " *Snuck* was more accurate.

Nellie snickered. "He worries about you more than your pa does."

"He's bent on laying down rules, that's for sure."

"You—rules? Pa says you're the most unruly girl he ever met." Nettie's face blazed and she quickly added, "'Course, Ma makes him hush."

Ginny wasn't sure what "unruly" meant, but it was too nice a day for getting peevish. "He never kept such a tight eye on me 'till now I ain't a kid anymore."

"Pa, too. He'll skin me six ways to Sunday if he catches us."

"Sancho won't dare switch me, leastways he hasn't yet. And Patrón ain't around today." Ginny waited while Nettie used the boulder to reach her stirrup. "Anyway, a couple more rides and he'll see I'm practically a vaquero—I mean *vaquera*." The trail led around the crest of the hill. "If we hurry, we can make it up to Joaquin's Pasture before it gets late."

"Pa says we're not supposed to go there."

"You're just scared." Ginny hoped her scorn would shame Nettie. It usually worked.

"Uh-uh. Am not."

"Miguelito goes up. Says it ain't nothing but a wild canyon and a handful of Indians in mud huts."

"We're not supposed to go there," Nettie repeated. "Anyway, Pa calls it Jacalitos Canyon, and he should know. We were the first white people in this whole valley."

Ginny stuck her tongue out. "It's too bad I wasn't born back then, but neither were you. So stop boasting or they'll hear us and scalp us."

"Uh-uh. They don't scalp. They live up there so they won't be bothered by whites. That's common knowledge." Nettie sounded scared, but she didn't rein her horse around.

"Sancho says they like living out of sight of the gringos."

"Why's that?"

Ginny paused for effect. Nettie's father might be the first white man in the valley, but he didn't know everything. Besides, the Indians beat him here by a year and a mile. "Indians cut wild mustangs from the wild herds on the Tulare Plains," she said. "Sancho says they eat 'em."

"Virginia Nugent, you're making that up!"

"Ain't either."

Ahead, something snorted in the brush. "Nettie, you scared, we can turn back," Ginny croaked.

She kept her gaze in the direction where the noise came from, in case it was a bear. Before Nettie could answer, Ginny's mare caught a scent. It shot forward with an eager whinny while she held onto the saddle horn with both hands, her knees pressed into its belly.

At the mouth of the canyon, a stallion pranced back and forth, fighting the stake lines securing it around a stout oak. Ginny fought to keep her seat as the stallion reared and let out a scream that seemed to shake the tree. Her mare whinnied again in response. She dug her heels in and tried to remember what Sancho had taught her. Her back was already aching from banging against the cantle; she'd be lucky if she didn't turn black and blue.

A Yokut Indian emerged from the brush with a musket in his fist, his arms crossed, his dark eyes hard and warning. Without speaking, he pointed back in the direction they had come. Nettie spun around and rode off without a backwards glance. Ginny reined hard, but she wasn't quick enough to avoid the Indian's hand when it came down hard on her horse's rump with a loud *thwack*. The man gave a shrill "yi-yi-yi," and her horse began running. She saw Nettie far ahead, giving her horse its rein as it slid down the hillside.

Behind her, the sound of pounding horses grew louder. Over her shoulder three men raced after her, their faces hidden by bandanas, but enough contempt in their wild, unkempt hair and their swarthy skin that she felt her blood run cold. They wore bandoliers belts criss-crossed on their chests, with few bullets gleaming in the sunlight. She whispered a desperate prayer to Maria Inés's *El Señor*, Jesus.

The men were whooping and laughing, long guns raised in the air, making it obvious that they could close the gap whenever they wanted. She caught a flash of Nettie's red jacket in the trail ahead and raced to catch up. Their horses ran side-by-side down the slope until she gave heel to her mare and felt her horse leap forward. Her horse had gained by a length when it snorted and side-stepped a five-foot rattler coiled in the tinder-dry grass.

Her horse reared in terror and the two horses collided. Nettie screamed and her horse bolted down the trail. Ginny managed to keep her seat while the mare spun in a half circle, kicking and stomping at the snake. The momentum pulled her from the saddle; she found herself hanging on with only a foot in the stirrup and a fistful of mane. She dug her fingers in and hung on while the snake slithered across the trail and disappeared into a gash in the cracked adobe earth.

Nettie's horse was running flat-out toward the ranch. Ginny followed through patches of turkey melon and dried oats. She listened for the sound of hoof beats, but the bandidos had halted in a tight pack, their attention captured by Patrón's vaqueros just visible on the hillside. With another round of whoops, they turned and retreated back toward Jacalitos Canyon.

She caught up with Nettie. Their horses slowed to a walk and they rode side-by-side without speaking until the house appeared over a rise, its white walls glowing in the setting sun.

Ginny was the first to break the silence. "Probably time we get on back." Her voice felt scratchy. "No point making Sancho fret."

Nettie nodded. Her horse was caked in white patches, but its breathing had slowed. They reached the turn-off to Middle Mountain and she turned without meeting Ginny's gaze.

The sun was setting by the time Ginny reached the corral. Hurrying, she slung her saddle over a pine log that the men used as a saddle rack, hung her bridle on a stub, and when she was sure Sancho wasn't looking, she slid around the corner and made for the house.

Inside the summer house, a tortilla was burning in a haze of smoke while the cook squeezed a leaf of aloe vera onto an angry red welt on her forearm. A pot of beans bubbled on the stove alongside a smoking skillet of fried pork.

Maria Inés cast a fearful glance toward the door and spoke with an urgent whisper. "Señorita Geena. You fetch some cold water and a clean towel. Hurry, *por favor*. I no want El Patrón to see me like this." She slumped across the table with a look of agony in her face.

Ginny brought another leaf of aloe vera, water and clean rags. Outside, the scrape of benches meant the men were arriving for supper.

"Hurry. No time," Maria Inés whispered. Careful to remove any trace of pain, she pulled the remains of her singed sleeve down, cringing only once when the rough cloth caught her skin. "Hurry. You fetch the kettles out."

Ginny hurried to obey. Her face was still damp from the wash pan. She'd scrubbed her arms to the elbows, and her hair was damp and finger-combed neatly behind her ears.

The cook's eyes narrowed in suspicion. "You been with those mustang ponies again, like Patrón tell you not to? He say you do anything like that I must tell him. He weel beat you, he find out. And me, he weel let go."

Ginny's eyes widened. "Sancho lets me. I promise I won't do it again. Honest."

The cook's worried look had little to do with her pain. "You no make trouble for Señor Sancho. Already he wear El Patrón's anger on his back, worse'n any Indian. He good man. You leave him be."

Ginny froze as still as a fawn. When she spoke, her voice felt shaky. "I don't have any secrets from him."

Maria Inés's face was white with pain. "I no say nuthin' to El Patrón 'til I talk weeth Señor Sancho. We talk more while we wash dishes. You *savvy*?"

Ginny nodded. At that moment she would have agreed to fetching the gut bucket out to the hogs. Instead, she grabbed a towel and tried to carry the kettle of hot beans to the door. The cook winced and tried to help, but she nearly dropped her end before Sancho rose from his bench to grab hold and carry the pot to the table.

The salt pork was almost gone by the time Ginny managed to spear a chunk and carry it inside. On her next trip outside to refill coffee mugs, she found a piece of cornbread cooling in a kettle.

When the last man left, belching and laughing, the silence seemed better than she could recall. Patrón was gone again. She felt free. Maybe the men felt the same way. When he was gone they would show her how to saddle her pony, and sing to her with their guitars, but when their boss was around the men scraped their toes in the dust and pretended not to notice her. When Patrón was drunk, the men stood with careful faces and watched as he whipped his horse or his dog. Sometimes she would catch the look of hatred in their faces, just before they wiped clear all trace of their thoughts. She knew just how they felt. She prayed every night that her mama would help.

Tonight they stayed inside the bunkhouse to escape the mosquitoes plaguing body and soul. But she had nowhere to hide except the summer house, where the smoke from the mesquite kept them at bay. The sound of a guitar filtered through the night, Miguelito singing a grieving song for the way things used to be. The melody followed her when she carried the last of the dirty kettles inside.

"You finished, Señorita Geena? I use help now." Maria Inés's lips were pinched with pain.

Ginny began scraping leftovers into the pig bucket. Later she would tossed the scraps to them so that the hogs would return to the same place each night—easier when it was time to butcher one. When the cook had no scraps, they threw out a handful of Indian corn. Tonight they had only bones, but a pig would eat anything.

The scraps brought a memory of feeding a small dog. Her mother had brought it from Virginia. She had fed it every night, but the week her died, the dog disappeared, too. Sancho said it had been eaten by a coyote. Patrón had told her not to cry.

The skinny dog Patrón owned now was too mean for the coyotes to bother with. Maria Inés kept a goat, but she tied it inside each night. The pigs slept in the woods.

The door to the summer house was open and mosquitoes buzzed in the dusk. A tin kettle on the stove added to the heat. A deer tick crawled across her neck and she pinched it between her fingers before she laced the basin of steaming water with strong lye soap made from cattle tallow and wood ash, and waited for it to dissolve. Maria Inés began washing dishes.

Ginny took the rag from her. "I'll wash tonight. Least I can do." She traded places so the cook could rinse the clean plates in the cool water and dry them with a scrap of flour sacking.

The cook made no sign she noticed, but when she spoke, her voice was the soft tone that she saved for her goat. "Now, niña, what you and Senor Sancho up to?"

Reluctantly, Ginny told her about Caroline—leaving out the ride to the mustang hunters' canyon, and the bandidos. And the snake. She didn't intend to tell anybody about that; the whole ranch would stand in line to whip her hide with a switch if they knew. But she told about the horse and the saddle, making it sound like her idea, just in case the story got back to Patrón.

Maria Inés listened with her lips pressed together in a thin line. When she spoke, her words were surprisingly mild. "Time you learn some things. If you no going to work the women's way, then maybe you learn the men's. When everything belong to you, maybe you hire someone to cook for you. But Maria Inés, she weel be in Heaven weeth Jose Ignacio by then. Maybe Señor Sancho, too."

Chapter Nine

The winds howled all night. Rain blew in the cracks, dampening Ginny's bedding. Yesterday, she had watched the vaqueros carry the cookstove back into the main house, and this morning the kitchen was smoky with the wet wood. The sound of shouting woke her. Patrón was downstairs; she heard him raging at the cook.

"Damn it. These biscuits are half-cooked. What's the point of having an iron stove if you still cook like a squaw? You're not living on the river anymore."

Maria Inés sounded scared out of her wits. "No, Patrón. I—"

But Patrón wasn't finished. "Place stinks like the gol-dang house is on fire."

"*Sí*, Patrón."

Ginny danced across the bare wood, trying to warm up before she dressed. "This winter I'm gonna ask for a cowhide when we butcher out one of the steers. I'll tan me a rug. Maybe Sancho will show me how." The water in her washbowl was cold. She remembered her vow to be a lady, and swiped a cloth across the back of her neck.

Winter was the hard time. The worst of it was that Patrón spent long evenings staring at the flames in the cavern of a fireplace he had built for her mother. The rocks were sooty and black, and the whole room needed tending, but Maria Inés had no time for cleaning house—not for a filthy man and a girl who should be doing for herself. She didn't say so, but her eyes gave the message. Patrón didn't care one way or the other, as long as the meals kept coming regular. He knew the vaqueros wouldn't stay on without good grub, so the rooms stayed sour.

Still shivering, Ginny pulled on the britches and shirt Sancho had brought her from the bunkhouse after a small Tachi Indian boy who had ridden for Patrón for almost a full year was gored by a loco mother cow.

Sancho had hammered together a crude wooden trunk that held most of the garments she owned: a pair of worn-out britches; a stack of underwear; and a woolen shawl, a gift from Missus McConnell, one of the new squatters. She reached in and pulled the shawl against her face, inhaling the lavender she'd placed inside to protect from moth damage, before carefully folding it and returning it to the trunk.

She took her time climbing down the ladder. Ordinarily, she'd wait to see what Sancho left for her, but they ate in the room where Patrón was shouting, sick with one of his headaches. She squared her shoulders and moved down the hallway toward the sound of her father's rage. Better he take it out on her than on Maria Inés.

It made no difference that she took care to be quiet, Patrón jumped like a nervous heifer. "Don't you be skulking around here. Cat got your tongue?"

"Nothing's got my tongue. Thought the house was on fire, by the sound of it."

"Don't sass me, girl!"

She straightened to her full height. "Morning, sir."

"That's more like it. What happened to that dress you wore last week?"

"It's hanging upstairs. Worn thin and fit for a child, which I'm not anymore. You want it for polishing rags?" She felt the seat of the boy's britches and realized they were nearly worn through as well. She smelled like horses. If she had a second set of clothes, she could wash them and let them dry in the kitchen. She took a deep breath. "Winter likely to be a wet one, you think, sir?"

She could tell by the way he was twitching that he was edgy today. "Rain's good for grass," he growled. "You know that."

Maybe she could cheer him up. "You planning a trip to Hollister for supplies, you probably oughtta do it soon, right?" She hesitated. "If you don't, the creeks might be impassible, right?"

He gave a wary nod.

"Well, if you were to bring me back a fresh pair of britches, folks would think I was presentable and they wouldn't be gossiping about us."

He stared, his pupils hard-edged and strange, but she stood meeting his gaze until he looked away. His headache powder was wearing off and he his temper could go either way. Apparently this was her lucky day; the hard look softened and he nodded. "Not your fault you're growing like a colt. You remind me of . . . ."

A second later he grabbed his head, pushed back his chair and rushed out the door. The door slammed behind him, and the kitchen was silent except for the sound of Maria Inés mixing *masa* for the noon meal.

Ginny grabbed three hot tortillas and slipped out. She'd keep them in case Patrón's appetite returned. He'd be glad for something to eat.

47

***

Sancho was hanging his arms over the wall of the round corral, watching Miguelito work a crème-colored stallion with a white mane and tail. Its color was favored by the Mexicans, Miguelito most of all. He stood in the center of the pen with a *mecate* rein he'd braided from horsehair, murmuring in soft Mexican while the horse twitched its ears and pretended not to be interested. Miguelito ignored the mud and the men straddling the corral, his eyes trained on the horse as he ran his fingertips beneath the horse's neck.

Quietly, so as not to disturb Sancho on his deaf side, Ginny hopped onto the stone wall and took a seat. He was intent on the vaquero and didn't notice her until she sneezed. Then he whirled around with an oath that brought a low murmur from the other men. The horse screamed and reared.

Miguelito gave an impatient growl and jerked a thumb at her. "Get up to the casa, you two want to make noise. We working here!"

Sancho slumped in disgust, his glare shaming her worse than a tongue-lashing. She sat as still as a lizard while Miguelito picked up the end of the lead rope and began again.

Sancho watched like he was riding the horse in his mind. He murmured half to himself and half to the man sitting beside him. "Just truss it up an show it who's boss. Break its will."

"Bah! You gringos got no respect for the animal. Miguelito don't wanna make an enemy. This way make it a friend."

"Horseshit! Take a month of Sundays his way." Sancho's voice carried to the center of the pen where Miguelito was trotting the horse in half-circles.

"You say it yourself, Señor. In the round pen, I, Miguelito, am _real._"

"Psaw. A king that takes a year to train his hoss?"

"*Sí.* But when I finished, my horse will walk through fire for me."

"Arumph!"

Ginny had heard Sancho with the vaqueros more than once, arguments that went on in the corrals, in the round pen, at the table. Sometimes she heard them arguing outside the bunkhouse in the evenings.

Patrón strode up looking as angry as a bull. He shouted at the vaqueros hanging on the fence. "Get off your haunches and let's get some work done." By the time he turned and threw a saddle on his horse, the two vaqueros were mounted and waiting. Together they rode off.

Ginny slipped off the wall and left the men to their work. Sancho was in a sour mood, and she could watch the vaqueros any day. She had a couple of tortillas left in her back pocket. Maybe someone would be riding past the ranch road today—maybe even a bandido over from Jolon.

At the road she climbed into the sprawling oak and straddled one of its limbs like it was a saddle. She was still settling herself when a gust of wind whipped a strand of hair into her face, stinging her eyes shut. A moment later it happened again. With tears in her eyes, she groped for the rotten bole where she kept a bundle of waterproof gutta percha. She reached in and pulled out a collection of treasures that Sancho had acquired in a trade with an old tinker. She found a knife with a broken handle beneath a set of fishhooks, its blade rusted in two places and began sharpening the blade with a piece of flint she'd found on the trail. When it was sharp enough to cut a nick in the tree, she pulled off her hat and wedged it between her knees. The first strand of hair fell loose. She dropped it into the hat and picked up another.

Several cuts later she considered setting the blade down to feel if the sides were even, but the damage was already done. She flipped the rest over her head and sawed it off to the length of her chin, more or less.

"I'm tired of braiding. And Maria Inés won't mind if she has one less chore to do. Patrón won't even notice."

With most of her length gone, the hair coiled up like a spring. She set the blade on the limb and felt her handiwork. Some of the strands in back were a good two fingers shorter than the front. She didn't need a looking-glass to know what she'd done; there was enough hair in her hat to braid a memory wreath. She emptied the hat and plunked it back on her head. It slid down over her ears and managed to cover her eyes. A single strand slid free and she tucked it back under the hat. Patrón was going to pitch a fit; one more thing to make him ashamed of having a daughter instead of a son.

A gust of wind blew the lopped-off strands off the branch, scattering them under the tree. From the air, her golden hair looked like old sheep's wool. But there was nothing to be done. She wrapped the blade into the scrap of waterproof fabric and stowed it back in the tree.

Chapter Ten

From her perch, Ginny heard the unmistakable clip of hoof on stone; a lone rider coming along the track that led from on the Slack's Canyon road. She drew her legs up on the oak limb, careful to keep in the shadows. The morning sun was behind her. If she wasn't careful the rider would see her before she saw him.

A rider came into a clearing, his horse moving too slow for vigilantes to be chasing him. He was still some ways distant, but close enough she could make out the color of his horse, a roan. Still, he could be a bandido—Tiburcio Vasquez, just out of San Quentin prison for rustling cattle or worse, one of the three that hung out with the mustang hunters over in Jacalitos Canyon. He might be hiding from the law, burrowed up in the brush around the Dark Hole. When the sad business was done and he was ready to leave, he'd waltz up to Patrón and demand a fresh horse. And he'd get it. Theirs wouldn't be the first place to contribute a horse to a bandit's cause.

Whoever he was, he had ridden a fair piece without resting because he was sagging in his saddle. He was sure enough no vaquero; the ones she knew could ride all day and night. This one rode like a Yankee. She counted to ten, slow, the way Sancho had taught her, and by that time the rider was close enough to hear a whistle. At the pace he was coming, his roan would be abreast before she made it to ten again. She concentrated on counting while her heart raced in her chest. *Eight, nine, ten. One, two, three, four, five.* Finally, the horse rounded the bend.

She was right. He was a Yankee—taller than the vaqueros, taller than Sancho, taller even than Patrón—with a blue shirt, the kind she'd seen folded on a shelf at the mercantile in San Miguel. His kerchief hung low over his chest, limp and filthy from covering his face from dust.

The stranger wore a hat like Sancho's, only it didn't look like any horse had ever stepped on it; this one was straight and creased across the top.. He was wearing chaps so he'd ridden through the low brush where mountain lions hid, over from Hollister, across the Big Sandy and down through the west side of the San Joaquin.

Maybe he had taken the train to Hollister from San Francisco.

He was nearly abreast. Even with a grit coating he looked tawny like a mountain lion, not dark and brooding like Miguelito. And his hair was close-cropped, not braided in a long black tail the way the vaqueros wore theirs. Sancho would say he looked like he'd been raised in luxury's lap. He looked like he'd been raised in somebody's lap. The never-worn look of his clothing showed he'd probably laid out cash money for them at the mercantile in Hollister. His holster carried a long-barrel pistol that could mean business. She liked the way his mouth showed plain, not covered by a wooly beard like Patrón's, or a mustache like the vaqueros'. The easy turn of his lips gave her an urge to see him smile.

Suddenly she felt herself slipping.

"Ayeee! Confoundit!"

She hit the ground on all fours, rolled into the dust and felt a stab of pain in her shoulder as her legs flattened out under her. From the mud she caught a quick glimpse of a horse's belly blocking out the sun above her. She curled in a ball, covered her head and waited to be crushed while the stranger fought to control his horse. When he passed over her, she rolled to the side and jumped to her feet.

"What the devil?" His voice nearly pierced her tender young ears.

"Sorry, mister. Didn't mean to land so close."

"Whoa there, easy there . . .whoa!" The stranger reined in his horse, but his easy smile had disappeared into a hard, tight slash. "What the Yankee devil do you think you're doing? You got knotholes in your brain, lad?"

Ginny straightened and adjusted her hat while she considered a response. "Reckon I'd be plenty safe if you weren't dawdling on the trail."

His look of confusion was comical. "Dawdling? Are you daft?" He no longer sounded cranky, only confused, but his next words sounded mean again. "Are you in possession of your faculties, lad?" He glanced around, probably searching for other riders.

She wasn't sure what he meant by faculties. Looking over her dirty arms and legs, she couldn't see that she was missing any of her parts, but just to be sure she'd ask Sancho later, what 'faculties' meant. Meanwhile, she'd have to bluff her way through. She'd lie if she had to; that usually worked with Maria Inés, and this stranger didn't look as smart by half. He had an odd way of talking, his words lazy and slurred, like Sancho's, but more learned.

"Got my faculties," she stammered. "Just calculated you'd get here a lot sooner. Saw you up on the rise. But maybe your horse ain't so fine, you got to favor him. Yankee riders are like that, Miguelito says."

The stranger seemed more than uncommonly annoyed. He gave her a

51

sideways glance and urged his horse into a walk.

"Hey—where you going?" Maybe she'd miscalculated. If he'd come from San Francisco, he'd been on the road a couple of days, counting the stage ride. Maybe he was hungry.

"None of your concern," he growled. He straightened in the saddle and kept his head down like he was in a hurry.

Ginny tried to keep pace. "Hold up. Got something for you." Maybe the offer of a tortilla would favor the situation. She held one toward him and felt gratified when he reached for it, until he turned it over like he was looking for a mealworm.

Satisfied, he took a bite. "Say, boy. This is mouth-watering fine. Your mama make these?"

Ginny shook her head. "I helped some."

"You helped? When you aren't dropping from trees?"

Ginny nodded. She bent to remove a pebble from between her toes while he took another bite.

"Blessed Patsy, but this is tasty. I'm hungry enough I could eat a corn field," he said.

She straightened and tried to think of something to say in response. Nobody she knew could eat a whole field, no matter how hungry they were. Suddenly she wished she hadn't lobbed off most of her hair. Maybe the stranger would hang around longer if she looked like the ladies at the hotel in Hollister who called down to Sancho and Patrón whenever they let her ride to town with them. But the fancy girls had to be plumb loco because they didn't even look at Miguelito, and he was the handsomest man she'd ever seen—until today. The Mexican vaqueros didn't tip their hats to the ladies, or even look at them. They disappeared to another part of town, and she didn't see them again until it was time to leave.

She remembered her hair and pulled her hat down snug about her ears. There was nothing to be done about it; her hair was what it was and it was her own doing. She extended her hand, holding out the other tortilla. "Want another one?"

He hesitated. "Why now, I surely wouldn't mind, but what about you? What say I section it thus—and we share?"

Ginny gaped as he drew a knife from a leather sheath and cut the tortilla in even halves. He bent from the saddle and handed down her portion. *A full-grown rider worrying about a kid getting her fair share?* Nobody besides Sancho ever cared about that. For a minute she liked him better than Sancho.

"Nah, you take it," she said.

"Well, thank y'all kindly."

The rider flashed a smile that made her wish she had another tortilla to give him. She gazed up at his mouth and caught a glimpse of dazzling white teeth. He had a dimple in his right cheek that deepened with his smile, and his skin was just as clear and smooth from the front as from his side profile. Beneath the broad brim of his black Stetson he was ruddy from the sun, but not weathered like Sancho. A few strands of blonde hair escaped the brim, plastered down by the sweat of the day's ride. She had never seen a stranger's face so close before, and she was surprised by the fineness of his features.

She clapped her hand over her mouth to keep from grinning, and forced herself to drag her eyeballs away from his face before he formed the opinion that she was short some faculties. She'd know him the next time she saw him, and that was good enough for now. She was still ruminating on his smile when she stubbed her toe on a rock in the road and stumbled.

This time the stranger laughed. "Now I know what to expect, I'll be prepared."

Suddenly her tongue came unglued. "Ain't many people live up this way. Sure you ain't lost?"

He shook his head and shifted in the saddle as he studied the mix of oaks, digger pine and buckeye. "Not likely, Kaydid. I have directions to the Nugent Ranch. I reckon I'll find it before long." He added, "Nugent runs horses and cattle. He can't be far."

Ginny started to speak, and hesitated. The man hadn't asked her advice, and in cow country a person didn't offer an opinion to a stranger unless he asked. "Yep, expect you will," she agreed, more out of politeness than for any other reason. "What's a katydid?"

The man's neck got red and he didn't answer right away, "Reckon it's a scrapper wet around his ears. Like you."

"Katy's a girl's name," she said. "You got girl scrappers where you come from?"

He shook his head as he took another bite. "No. More the insult for the young lads, I suppose."

"Oh." She tried to think of something to say as she struggled to keep up. "You got a fierce set of eye lashes there, Mister. I had a calf once had some like that. Sancho said it was a double set, kind of like a freak of nature. Sort of makes you stand out with that black hat. That why you wear it?"

He laughed. "Never thought much about it, one way or another. My sister's got a set too, and yes, I expect they do stand out—on her, anyway. And, no, to answer your inquiry, I don't wear the hat for that reason." He squinted into the horizon, the beginnings of worry on his face. "Say, boy, you always so familiar?"

She felt her face heat. "Well, how's a person supposed to learn anything if'n they don't ask? Anyhow, you sort of broke the bargain."

"And which bargain might that be?" The rider gave her a closer look. "Boy, you sure you're okay?"

Ignoring the question, she tried again. "For starters, you're supposed to stop and visit with me for a spell. Like I said, we don't get much in the way of visitors around here."

"Well, I'm not from around here. Like I said, I have to get to the Nu—"

"Yeah, I know! The Nugent place. Figure you know where you're heading?"

He scowled and adjusted the brim of his hat. "I've made it across a continent. Expect I can find my way. Man I met down the trail a piece said I couldn't miss it. Should be coming up on it, any time."

Ginny swallowed. "Well then, since you're bound for riding full-chisel, mind if I swing up back?" She was itching to ride the roan. Besides, it was getting hard to talk and watch out for stones at the same time.

"Suppose that would be acceptable. Where you headed?"

"Same place as you, I reckon." Ginny was glad he couldn't see her face as she climbed up behind him.

"Fine," he answered, "then you can be so good as to show me the way."

"Sounds like you got a good fix on the direction." Now that she was astride, she was in no hurry to end the ride. She rubbed her sore toes against the horse's sides and considered.

Something about her answer seemed to set the stranger off. He half turned and his voice had an edge in it. "What is that to mean, boy? We're headed in the right direction!"

Just then, three riders appeared in the distance, driving a herd of horses. She watched as Miguelito, Jose Luis and Patrón disappeared into a draw.

"We're heading right, aren't we, boy?" he repeated, this time without his air of certainty.

"Is that a question or an answer? Kids ain't supposed to know as much as grownups. Patrón don't listen to nobody. By the way, what's your name?"

"Who's Patrón?"

"The Boss."

Something about her answer seemed to gall him. He reined in his horse, tipped his head back and demanded in the slow, careful voice he probably used on a stupid dog; "Young man, how do I get to the Nugent Ranch? I have need to talk with Charles P. Nugent. Will you simply direct me to him!"

"Depends. Is it the ranch you want to see or him?"

The rider was getting testy. Maybe his throat was dry. He didn't look to be an imbiber, but he was clearly out of patience. She stared at the horizon while he waited.

"Both," he said. "I need both. Get me to the ranch and I will find the cursed Mr. Nugent. Sweet Betsy crying in the kitchen!"

The stranger answered with considerable heat for a man with manners. Maybe he was just hot; after all, he was taking out his kerchief, swiping his forehead and tipping his hat forward again. She considered her next move. If she made him mad, she'd be walking all the way back home. "You wanna go to the ranch, oughta turn around and head the other way."

"The other way? What in blazes are you talking about?" His voice croaked like he was coming down with the fever.

"You said you knew your way. Should'a asked sooner."

"Arrrgh!" He jerked his horse around and kicked it into a trot while she grabbed around his middle to keep from falling off. She bet he was doing it on purpose.

"Sancho says if a man ain't lost, don't try to find him."

"I told you where I was headed. Sweet Patsy!" He rode a few paces in silence before inquiring, "Who's Sancho?"

His tone was peevish, like Maria Inés's when she had to milk her goat. "Can't tell you. Sancho says I'm not to talk to strangers."

"Strangers? What in Hades is that supposed to mean?"

"Well, I don't know your name, so that makes us strangers. Tight as you are with your identity, you might be a bandido. We don't abide desperados around here. The truth is, Joaquin Murrieta was one and he got himself killed up north of here before I was born. With his pal, Three Fingers Jack. Right up north at Cantua Creek. 'Cept I don't believe it, and neither does Sancho, 'cause there's more than one person claims they've seen Murrieta around, so the chopped-off head they been carrying around to show folks must be some other fellow's. Don't look out, might be yours they stuff in a saddlebag for show. Might get yerself shot, too. There's lots of guns where we're going. And there's a gunfighter named Sancho can drop you with a single shot. Comprende?"

The rider seemed amused. "Name's Jeremy Lawsen. Jeremy Beaumont Lawsen, from the Commonwealth of Virginia."

The man who had sent the letter. "Why you got two last names?" she asked. "Your ma couldn't make up her mind what to call you?"

The rider turned in his saddle to get a closer look at her. Failing, he turned back around and kicked his horse into a trot again. He slowed at a bend in the trail where a giant valley oak shadowed a rock outcropping. A few paces beyond, he halted to take a closer look at a hank of golden hair blown against the tree.

"Here," she said. His chest tightened beneath her hold and she eased her grip.

"What did you say?" His throat sounded feverish again.

She swallowed. "Turn here. This is the Nugent place."

"Well, I'll be cotton whipped! Why didn't you say so? I told you where I was going." He was mad as a hornet, but she decided to ignore his tone.

"I told you why. Sancho said—"

"Who in the devil is Sancho?"

"You sure swear a lot. Does your mother know you do that?" She couldn't concentrate if he was going to be snippy.

"Probably." He answered in a dull voice that sounded like he was dying.

"Shouldn't do that," she said. "Swearing, I mean."

"I never swear in front of females."

"Ever?"

"Never!"

"Ever tell a lie?"

"Never!"

It was getting easier to talk to him. "You're pretty sure of yourself, Mister. Never swear in front of females. Never tell a lie. Never lose your bearings. You must live a pretty mild life."

Chapter Eleven

"How much farther?" As soon as the question was out, Jeremy wished he'd held his tongue. This trip had become more than he had bargained for.

"Bet you been traveling a spell."

"Three days now. Counting the moonlight." He considered not answering, but he was beyond irritation. Besides, the kid sounded starved for conversation. He tried to keep his voice level. "Crossed a wide river with quicksand almost overtook my mount. Ran breakneck through a ravine, scarcely escaped with my life. Ate dust till I could make gravy when I spit, then got rained on to boot."

"I'm surprised folks in Hollister didn't warn you about riding out alone. Sancho says we got some of the hardest desperados in the country. Lucky they didn't catch up with you!"

The kid sounded impressed—or maybe he just wanted to take the opposite side of the argument. Either way, his clothes were covered with dust from bandana to boots. His muscles ached and he was too tired to argue. "Who says they didn't?"

"How come you took the chance, riding out here alone?" The kid was persistent.

"Made a promise to my mother," he mumbled.

The kid looked back at the trail. "I don't see no mother!"

He sighed. "That's because she's back home in Virginia."

"What's her name?"

"Missus Lawsen."

"What's she doing there?"

"She resides there."

"How come you ain't back there with her?"

"'Cause I'm out here in California. My mother had a childhood companion who died out here. She heard a rumor that her friend's kin wasn't faring very well. I made a promise I'd look in on them."

Thankfully, the kid quit asking questions. A few seconds later he realized the silence was too good to last.

"Sancho says a man ought to keep a promise. Was it a hard ride from

San Francisco?"

He heard himself sounding like a peeved nanny. "Not excessively difficult with the right company. I rode the train down to Hollister. Hotter than blazes with the cinders blowing into the passenger coach. Spent a long day picking my way from Big Sandy over the mountains on a fresh mount."

"I been that way a time or two. Gnats is the worst part. Them and the heat. Nope—dust's the worst—wind whips it up something fierce. Sancho says we got enough dirt in our lungs to grow corn. 'Spect he's right 'cept I'd rather grow strawberries. How about you?"

"How about me—what?"

"What would you grow in your lungs, corn or strawberries?"

"I confess the question has never occurred." A gnat bit his face. He swatted at it and turned back to the road, riding in silence, hoping the kid would, too. At least the worst was over. In an few minutes he could lay to rest the rumor that Charles Nugent had gone to ruin out in the far West. Surely someone was rearing Caroline Foster's daughter in the gentile manner that her mother would have wanted.

Before the kid could think up another question, he caught sight of a wreck of a ranch. He reined in before a two-story adobe style house that would look grand if it were ever finished. As it was, the wind and the rain had played havoc with the whitewash that was missing over the bricks. In the front, three columns formed arches with a gaping, unfinished lintel supporting the front door. A rickety ladder leaned against the wall like someone had walked off the job to get a drink of water and forgot to come back. The yard was a tangle of woodpiles and chicken manure. A scrawny, long-eared white goat with an over-full milk bag stood in the shade of a solitary tree.

Jeremy continued his inspection. A thin gray ribbon of smoke curled from a stovepipe on the summer house. A swallow had attached a nest to one end and he could hear chirping. A row of hollyhocks and roses was encircled by rings of white rocks. The garden had been planned by a woman, undoubtedly Caroline Foster Nugent, but she was dead. Someone else was maintaining the yard. The widower? Not the Charles Nugent he remembered; his memory was of a dark-haired man with boldness that stood out among the poor soldiers straggling back from the War with crutches and amputated limbs.

Love had clearly blossomed in the week Charles Nugent was in town. Although she had not approved, Missus Foster had allowed her daughter Caroline to marry the brash stranger from California. During the next four years, every letter her daughter sent made her fearful. She shared the letters with his mother. Together, they tried to decipher the Spanish words Caroline used, and the odd foods she described. Then the final letter arrived, written by a neighbor, Missus Imus, telling of Caroline's death. His mother had made a promise to Missus Foster that she would never neglect her friend's little daughter.

So here he was.

As he studied the ranch house, he wondered what he was going to tell his mother. Missus Foster was spending her last years as an invalid, worrying about the granddaughter she had never seen. She sent money and letters to the child, but she suspected they were set aside by a bitter father. Maybe it was more comforting to place the blame on Charles Nugent than to entertain the possibility that her granddaughter was an ungrateful brat who didn't bother to write a letter of thanks. He stood in his stirrups and tried to ease his cramped muscles until someone invited him to dismount. Whatever he chose to include in his report, the truth would need some varnishing. What he had seen so far would bring neither comfort nor peace to the ailing old lady.

A crippled cow puncher was hobbling towards them, an old-timer who seemed a fair match for his dilapidated surroundings. The kid had slipped off and stood looking around as though seeing the hacienda for the first time. He glanced at the kid's raggedy haircut and dirty face even as the kid ducked his head and drew a pattern in the dust with a grimy toe.

"This is the Nugent Ranch?" Jeremy was careful to remove all traces of judgment from his question.

"Yessir." The kid's toe continued its artwork.

"Mr. Nugent around?"

"No, sir."

"How would you be knowing that?" An ominous feeling began in the pit of his stomach and he took a closer look. "Boy, just who would you be?"

Taking off his hat, the kid slowly straightened.

Reeling with a sudden case of vertigo, Jeremy saw it all—her chopped hair, her shiny men's britches, her dirty feet with their bleeding toes.

Standing to her full forty-four inches, the girl said, "Virginia Foster Nugent, sir." Her eyes filled with tears of humiliation, but she didn't waver. "I have two last names, too."

Jeremy felt a flush climbing his neck. A thousand questions crowded his mind until he felt lightheaded. "Would . . . would . . ." There was just one last hope. "Would Caroline Foster be your mother?" He knew the answer before she nodded, but he needed to hear it from her lips.

"Yessir. But she's passed and it's my fault. Now my father rears me, but he's sick a lot."

Sick a lot! Lord a' mercy, he felt sick! What was he supposed to tell his mother? Was he supposed to turn his back and ride away? How *could* he, now that he had gotten an inkling of how things stood? Missus Foster back in Virginia could offer this child a wonderful life if the father would allow it. That was the clincher: *if he would.* Jeremy had a feeling he already knew the answer.

His horse was getting restless; he tightened his grip on his reins and used the moment to settle his thoughts. There was no need to make a decision tonight. Things might not be as bad as they appeared. In fairness to everyone, he would wait and speak to Mr. Nugent.

The old-timer arrived, panting from exertion.

"Howdy stranger. Care to sit a spell? Boss is out right now. He and a couple of hands is just west of here, rounding up horses. Surprised you didn't run into them." He spoke with the rusty accent of a Southerner who had left home many years ago.

Jeremy raised his eyebrows to Ginny, who ducked her head.

"Not my fault," she said. "I already told you. Out here we don't give advice unless we're asked."

Jeremy didn't try to contain his disgust. "In Dixie, when a man's ridden two hundred miles to see someone, we figure he means to see the fellow." He recalled a point he'd almost overlooked. "Why do you call him Patrón? He's your father, isn't he?"

The girl's eyes widened in surprise. "That's what he told me to call him."

By the time he could think of a response, the old man was speaking again.

"Name's Sancho Roos. 'Pears ya've already met Miss Virginia here. She has her ways. Can't say I've figured them all out yet, myself."

The old man stood unflinching while they sized each other up. After a bit he shifted to his good leg and waited for Jeremy to state his business.

Jeremy began. "Name's Jeremy Lawsen. Of the Commonwealth of Virginia. I've traveled west on business. My itinerary included a ride over your way to see the land prospects." He reached down and extended his hand.

"Virginia! That's where my mother was from. Did you know her?" The little girl's curiosity bordered on hunger.

He tried to answer without causing her further humiliation. None of this was her fault. "Matter of fact, I did, young lady. That's the other reason I'm here. I promised my mother I'd look in and say hello. My mother and yours were girlhood friends. She's never forgotten you or your mama." His frustration softened when he saw the effect of his words. It occurred to him that, but for her mother's misfortune, this little girl would have been friends with his little sister.

"She wants to know how you are doing. And how accomplished you are now." He bent to unlatch the strap from his satchel and drew out a soft brown bundle tied with twine. "I've been carrying this for some distance. Your Grandmother Foster sent you a packet." He glanced up in time to catch the girl and the old man exchange surprised looks.

The girl extended her grubby hands. Leaning her slight weight against the wobbly fence, she opened the bundle with awkward movements that showed little familiarity with receiving gifts. At last she had the paper loose. She dropped the string to the ground and reached inside. She held a porcelain doll. With careful movements, she shifted it so that it nestled in her arms. The doll was clad in an organdy dress with bright green ribbons, its ebony curls covered by a matching bonnet. A genuine copy of a Southern belle, it was a reminder of everything grand and gracious about the land of Caroline Foster's birth.

Jeremy grimaced when he saw what he had delivered. Compared to the girl, the doll was fussy and feminine. "Reckon your grandmother meant well . . . ," he began, taking the girl's silence for disapproval.

She stood unmoving while she took in every detail. Finally, she looked up, tears shining. "Oh, she's fine. I'll wager she looks just like Mama in her wedding dress."

A folded piece of perfumed paper fell from the folds of the dress. She glanced at the note without making a move to read it and returned her attention to the doll.

He wasn't sure how to proceed. "Your grandmother has a glorious home on the river—what is left of it after the Yankees departed it, that is. She's extended an invitation that you come to stay with her for a spell."

She held the paper toward him. "Is that what she wrote?"

She was holding the paper upside down. He took it and read slowly.

To my dear granddaughter, Virginia,

I'm entrusting this note to a family friend, as my efforts to reach you have met with poor success. My thoughts and prayers are so often with you. I would welcome you to visit, as a favor to a lonely old lady. We could share our memories of your dear mother, whom I am certain you resemble in image and thought. If this proves impractical, I would cherish a daguerreotype of your likeness and a note in your own hand, however brief.

My love to you always, my precious peach.

Your loving grandmother,
Arabella Stanhope Foster

A succession of emotions flitted over the girl's face—most surprisingly, confusion.

"You're not able to read it for yourself?" he asked.

"Some. I'm learning. What of it!" Her blush indicated she'd blurted out more than she meant to.

"Someone tutors you?" He winced at the censure in his voice. *Tarnation!* Surely her father had made some plan for her education, although, judging from the language she used, he didn't hold too much hope in that regard.

The old-timer broke in. "She got a woman across the valley helps her some. Ain't no real school short of Santa Cruz, up the coast. Hardly another young-un in these parts, neither. Boss figures she's a smart gal. Picks up what she needs from the cook and the rest of us."

Ginny seemed engrossed in the folds of her doll's dress.

"What have you learned so far?" Jeremy inquired.

Ginny faced him directly. "I can count to twelve hundred. Sancho taught me. And I listen to folks. I learn lots that way."

Lots? He had a bad feeling, given the chagrin on Sancho's face. "You don't read or stitch?" He waited for an answer while the girl fidgeted with the green ribbons of the doll bonnet.

"Not much."

"Can you recite your Bible?"

"We don't have none."

"Of course you have!" he thundered. "Everyone has a Bible!" He shook off his frustration and lowered his voice. "You're christened, are you not?"

She ventured a quick look at him before her gaze dropped to the doll in her hands. "Sancho, he teaches me what he knows. And that's a lot."

The old man eased the hitch in his hip. "We're just a bunch of vaqueros," he stammered to the dust on his boots. "We're no schoolmarms. Reckon the Boss helps with her learning when he has the time. Like she said, she gets some from the lady across the valley."

"Sweet Betsy, the girl is nearly what—ten?" It was hard to judge the age of the girl when he wasn't even sure of her gender. At her age, his sisters could write a pretty letter and read a whole slew of books from the downstairs library. Shoot, for that matter they could embroider a sampler and curtsy to their elders. He ran a hand through his hair, uncertain now just where his responsibility lay.

"Sancho says I'm twelve, give or take. I got a book. Mama used to read it to me when I went to sleep. It's full of pictures. I can read it."

Jeremy smiled at her brave effort. He turned to Sancho. "Aren't there any women on this ranch?"

"Jest Maria Inés, the Injun woman does the cooking. She gives the girl what time she has, but it ain't much. She don't speak much American. Mexican, mostly."

Jeremy turned to Ginny, feeling like someone had gut punched him. "Can you cook?" He hoped he sounded more hopeful than he felt.

"Some. I can butcher out hens."

"You butcher . . . out . . . hens."

"Sometimes. When I ain't got nothing else to do."

"What do you apply yourself to all day?" Next she was going to tell him she chased skunks to pass the time.

"Ride my horse and play with the squirrels. Once I trained me a mouse to ride on my shoulder. And I aim to tan me a cowhide this winter." She paused for breath. "Sometimes I go down to the road and wait for someone to come along so I can find out the news, same as I did with you. And I help Sancho and sometimes the cook. Sometimes Patrón lets me tag along to the Rancho Cholame, over yonder a spell."

"Your father. He's your *father*. Refer to him as such!" Jeremy tried to temper his frustration. "How often do you leave the ranch?"

"Sometimes the men, they got business to take care of, and I can't go." She kept her eyes downcast.

Jeremy had an idea just what kind of business they needed to take care of at the tavern in Soledad, and a glance at the old cowhand's red face removed all doubt. He tried to think of something to break the tension. "We'll settle things when your father returns. If you can show me where I might wash up, I'll attend to myself. Don't want to hold you up with your chores."

Ginny spoke up. "Supper ain't ready yet. Won't be 'till the sun's two fingers top of the ridge over yon. Isn't any water in the creek. Pull you up a bucket from the spring when you're ready. Tomorrow, I'll show you around the place—I'm not doing anything anyway. Me and Sancho snitched a saddle so's I can ride. What Patrón don't know won't hurt him none. That's what you said, huh, Sancho?"

She ignored the look Jeremy gave Sancho.

Chapter Twelve

Sancho followed Ginny and the stranger out the gate, but his thoughts were far from the hill country to which their horses were headed. He'd watched the way her eyes went soft yesterday, seeing the doll, and it made his heart jump at the thought that she owned something her mother would have provided if she were still alive. He'd never had anything he hadn't worked for, or swapped for or won fair and square. He'd lived a cowboy's life— nothing more to be said. What he owned at day's end were his memories.

He was thoroughly shamed at how pitiful she must appear to the Virginia fellow.

He remembered the day he stood, hat in hand, waiting to greet his boss's new bride. She'd arrived the day before, dusty and tired, so weak that the Boss had to carry her from her horse. But at eight o'clock the next morning, she was standing on the porch of the bunkhouse where she'd live until her husband built her a house. She was wearing a thin-clothed affair with a cummerbund that the morning breeze swept into the air like the sails of a ship. She looked like a queen with her white skirts billowing out, and fly-away strands of hair blowing around her pale face. The glow of her cheeks that morning reminded him of seashells he'd seen on the beach in Mexico. Her hair was the color of his stallion's mane, and as thick. She wore it wound up in a fancy hairdo like the ladies on the playbills he'd seen posted in Kansas City. Her eyes were big and scared—sea green and fringed with dark lashes.

The Boss started to introduce her to the vaqueros and she lowered her head like she was flustered. Right when Sancho thought she'd bolt and run, she looked up and smiled. She gave a little speech. He couldn't for the life of him recall what she said, except that she was glad she was there.

From that first day, he woke every morning trying to think of ways to serve her. The Boss left him to do most of the building of the new house, which was pure satisfaction. The plan was to keep a man within earshot, with an eye peeled for bandidos. Boss didn't mind losing a few head of steers, but he'd brought a lady to his ranch and he intended to keep her safe. Sancho didn't want to alarm the lady, so he made like he was her new yard man, even when the other cowboys laughed at the way he came hopping every time she needed some manure for the garden. He didn't even mind when the Boss started giving Miguelito responsibilities that he used to do.

The men had their fun. More than once he came to blows with them over their joshing. But after awhile he'd just smile when they said something to get his goat, and when they couldn't get a rise out of him, they quit.

Three years went by. He never spoke to the Boss's wife without her speaking first; didn't even let himself meet her eyes, most of the time, but that didn't keep him from thinking. For the first time he hated the fact that he was short—shorter than the Boss by a good foot or so. He hated the bowlegged shape his legs had taken on from his years in the saddle, even hated the color of his skin—the bronze, weathered layers the desert had burned into him. When he studied himself in the small shaving mirror in the bunkhouse, he saw himself the way the Boss's wife did, and the sight filled him with shame. But he had one good ear for listening. In time she began pining for her mother and the life she'd left back in Virginia. She pined for a neighbor woman to talk to, but the nearest one was some miles away, and it was hard for them to get together more than once a week. Maria Inés was in the summer house, but the Boss made it clear he didn't want his wife toiling in the heat. He wanted her in the main house, like a lady.

She seemed comfortable with Sancho, a Southern sympathizer like herself, and someone she could confide in. As loneliness began to weigh her spirit, the Boss allowed her that single kindness—along with the lemons he fetched her from San Juan Bautista. All these years later, Sancho could still taste the lemonade and the cold tea she had served under the cottonwood tree while they talked about what she might plant in this broken country. After the little gal was born, on warm days Missus Nugent spread a quilt in the shade of an apple tree and lay the baby out while she helped him prune and thin the fruit, or fill the bushel baskets when the fruit ripened. That first year, he looked down from the ladder at her playing with her baby and his heart felt nourished like the seeds she tended.

She was some kind of mother. By fall, Ginny was walking. The following year she was underfoot, trying to help. He remembered peeling a ripe peach and slicing off bits, juice dripping down her chubby cheeks. He watched as she and her mother shared excitement over the same kind of things—a striped snake in the grass or a new butterfly in the field. Sometimes the Boss came around the corner and stood quiet-like, watching. He was tall and well-built, and walked with the air of a man who was used to having things nice. Sometimes at night, the Boss's laughter rang over the yard and he would be laughing about his wife's watchdog, but to Sancho's recollection, the Missus never joined in. Missus Nugent was generous with her time, but she kept a tight hold on her feelings. She never said or did anything she would have to explain to her husband. And the Boss knew it.

***

Sancho pulled himself from his reverie while Ginny led the Virginia fellow to a couple of oak stumps near the Joaquin Creek. As good a place as any. He'd leave them to get acquainted.

"We have places on this here ranch where the hills have slid from the earth," Ginny was explaining. She might not know book reading, but she knew how to read the land. "Sometimes you can tell when the shaking is going to happen because the horses wander around like they're drunk. That's what happened last time. Right, Sancho? The earth split clean open."

Sancho nodded from where he sat in his saddle, rolling a cigarette to calm his nerves. "Ridges you see hereabouts are made from the earth pushing up. Sinks the ground in some places. Raises it in others," he said. He lit his smoke and squinted at a far-off rock formation. "This-here valley used to be an underground lake. Bits of oyster shells all over the place."

"We can ride over that way. I'll show you . . . " Ginny was chattering like a magpie, making good use of her new friend. It was just as well she was occupied. The Virginia fellow had brought up a passel of black thoughts for Sancho. He needed to let them fester up, finish the job once and for all.

Ginny led the Virginia fellow to a rock outcropping half-hidden in the wild oats. Sancho stayed behind to allow his horse to drink from the deep, sweet spring while she showed off the bedrock mortars where the Yokut women pounded their acorns. Table Mountain stood sentinel nearby, but Sancho had no eye for the mountains. Slumped in his saddle, he felt his pleurisy coming on. He slipped to the ground, squatted on his heels and tried to breathe through the tightness in his chest, a familiar pain, usually broght on when his mind returned to the past. Like today.

***

Even at three years old, the little gal had her mother's eyes. He was never sure what riled the Boss more, those soulful blue eyes or her way of speaking up when something didn't settle right with her. It seemed like the Boss blamed her both ways to Sunday—blamed her for being too much like her mother and blamed her for not being enough. He acted like his daughter wasn't there. And whiskey made it easier.

As time went on, she took to hiding in odd places—the corn crib, the hay loft with the loose-stacked meadow hay where she made pets of the mice by feeding them from the infernal tortilla she carried in her pocket. She asked Maria Inés what she should call her old man, after her father told her in no uncertain terms not to call him Papa any more. The Indian told her, "I dunno. Maybe you call him Patrón. That is what the others, they do. He like it, El Patrón."

Looking back, maybe he should have done something to try and fix the problem, but after a bit, the name didn't sound peculiar. At least not 'till the fellow from Virginia made it seem like there was something odd in it.

The Boss still smarted from his own feelings. Maybe he meant to make it up to his daughter when he got to feeling better. Hard to tell. One thing was for sure, he didn't have an inkling of what to do with her so he treated her like a ranch hand and let it go at that. It seemed like the Boss's guilt got mixed up with anger at his wife for dying, until he came to blame his daughter for her own situation. Decided that, by damn, she could just take care of herself the way he'd been forced to do.

Sancho's memories filled up his free time until he hated the idea of sleep. The night was no friend to him. He took to sleeping outside, under the cottonwood in the yard, after the vaqueros complained he woke them with his nightmares.

***

The ride was over and Sancho couldn't say for sure where they'd gone. He'd been lost in a fog since the first memory claimed him. He followed the two to the corral and watched Ginny strip off her saddle.

He pulled his own and turned his gelding to pasture. Wasn't much he could do to entertain the Virginia fellow till the Boss got back, but at least he'd worked through some of the black memories. He carried his saddle to the tack room and headed back toward the house. With some luck maybe the little gal had talked herself out.

Chapter Thirteen

Jeremy held a list of the grandmother's questions, but he already had his answers. Her list, in her neat hand, represented another world: *Who curls Virginia's hair? Who listens to her nightly prayers? Who sees to it she has new nightgowns, underthings and dresses that fit? Who makes her tea parties, and makes sure she's covered with a bonnet, and teaches her to make social chit-chat with the ladies in town?* There was no point in asking. There was no town within a day's ride, and no bonnet if there was.

Ginny babbled on. Jeremy didn't trust himself to talk; it was all he could do to listen.

"Once, Patrón came in and found me wearing Mama's straw hat. It's the prettiest thing ever. It has bits of yellow netting a person can see right through! And smooth ribbons with ties under the neck, yellow and real soft if you slide them across your lip where your mustache would be. Only you don't have one—a mustache, I mean. I've never seen a white man without a mustache. Anyway, Patrón came in and caught me wearing it, and he pitched a conniption and tossed it back in Mama's wardrobe, out of my reach."

The girl paused for breath before continuing. "Do you think it's wrong to touch someone's things after they're dead? I didn't think so, because I'm wearing these britches Nucio left behind, and Patrón ain't got a problem with them. Maria Inés says my mother's in Heaven. You got any idea where that might be? Maria Inés says she's with some fellow called Jesus. I don't know this Jesus, but I hope he don't drink whiskey around Mama in Heaven."

She chattered like a wild bird that had been plucked from a bush and stuck in a cage. It was like she'd spent too much time with a cloth draped over the wires so she couldn't see whether it was day or night. Jeremy had come along and ripped the cloth off, and she discovered she had quite a song. From what he could tell, she didn't know the melody until the notes came out, but her favorite song seemed to be about her mother.

"I think Patrón's put-out with me for letting Mama die. Me and Sancho was home alone. I was gathering eggs and I couldn't find but one. Maybe Sancho needed the eggs so Mama could get better again. Wish I could tell her how sorry I am. Maybe when I'm grown, I'll leave the ranch and I'll miss it, and it will serve me right."

At last she ran out of words.

They sat side by side in silence until a couple of vaqueros approached. The wide cut of their pantaloons gave them a swashbuckling look, especially with the lacing extended halfway up the leg. They were both wearing doeskin vests, laced in the back, and flat-topped hats with strings across their chins. Their spurs tinkled in the quiet yard, making sweet-sad music with every step. They glanced up curiously while cupping their hands to protect their rolled smokes from the wind. Waiting for the supper gong.

Ginny was apparently thinking the same thing. "Chow should be ready soon. Might as well wash up." She led the way to a bucket in the back yard. "Cold water works good. Sides, the way the men sweat, you'd think they was dunked in a batch of skunk oil. Wait till you catch a whiff. It peeves Maria Inés the way they track onto her floors!"

Obviously, no one had taught her the finer points of a lady's toilette; she rolled her sleeves to the elbows and scrubbed like one of the vaqueros. Maybe she was trying to impress him with the fact that she didn't need any mothering. If so, she was failing miserably.

Jeremy glanced at her stained britches. "Perhaps you have time to change into something fresh for supper?" He intended to meet with the father afterwards. If the girl looked tender and impressionable, it might be easier for her father to think about her future. As she looked right now, he might decide she could muck out the corrals along with the rest of the hands.

Ginny's peevish retort hinted that he wouldn't know plain truth if it punched him in the nose. "I got a dress. Reckon I could put it on for company. It's some small for me, but it's clean. And Patrón's bringing me another pair of britches when he gets back from town."

She finished drying her hands on her shirt and tucked the tails back into her britches. "Missus Imus sewed me some underthings. Sancho sneaked them home so Patrón wouldn't be beholden, but he seen the bundle and rode right over to Missus Imus and gave them back. Patrón told her he'd buy me some, but I guess he forgot. Anyway, next time I paid a visit, she insisted I bring them back home with me."

Lord a'mercy! He'd walked into a living nightmare. Legally he had rights. Tucked away in his saddlebag was the power of attorney that authorized him to act in the grandmother's stead. However, the child was not being starved or beaten. She seemed to enjoy living with a sorry excuse of a father and a broken-down ranch hand, but by all that was right and decent, he needed some answers.

She was pointing toward the table. "Best get yerself a seat."

"What about you?"

"I eat afterwards," she said.

"Afterwards? You mean with your father? That doesn't seem likely. You eat with me tonight. That's a hostess's duty. Understand?"

"Sure."

***

Maria Inés brought a pan of cornbread and plunked it down in front of Jeremy. After he speared pieces for himself and Ginny, he watched Sancho fork himself a slab and slide the pan down to Jose Luis, one of the Indian vaqueros. The others ate their beans and tortillas in silence.

Sancho waited until they were nearly finished before he asked, "Jose Luis, Antonio, either of you seen the Boss today?"

Jose motioned for them to use caution in front of the girl. "El Patrón, he need to pick up something in San Miguel. He say maybe he be home in two day."

The other men chuckled at something that went over the little girl's head. Or maybe it didn't; she picked at the ham chunks in the beans with her head lowered.

"Two days? I sent word I was coming." Jeremy glared at Sancho and then at the vaquero, but neither of them seemed anxious to take their boss's side in the matter.

The vaquero flashed a cautious glance at Ginny and frowned. "Thursday. That's what he say. He making plans to sell his beef."

Another rider smirked. "He no thinking of beef tonight."

"Enough!" Sancho motioned toward Ginny. The offender ducked his head and concentrated on his plate.

Jeremy winced at the turn of the conversation. Maybe he'd jumped his authority. Apparently around here, Indians and Mexicans didn't share food with visitors and kids, and either Nugent had more nerve than anyone gave him credit for, or he didn't care enough to set a rule. The girl was a curious little thing. He'd drawn a map to show her where her mother had come from. She had studied it intently then claimed she couldn't see the sense of his calling it "down South" when it was east. She was smart. He would give her that.

"Mr. Lawsen, you wanna ride out again tomorrow?" Ginny asked.

Jeremy caught the old man's eye and got a slow nod. Apparently he was being entrusted to keep her out of the cowhand's hair until her Pa—her

Patrón—got home. "I'd be obliged, Miss Virginia."

When they finished, the vaqueros pushed back their benches and shuffled out, still wearing the flat-brimmed hats they had arrived in. He guessed he should inquire where he was to sleep, but he wasn't overly anxious to settle into the bunkhouse. Ginny had been right about one thing; a skunk would have gone unnoticed in that place. He wondered what Caroline Nugent would have thought about the whole affair.

Someone had lit a bonfire in the yard and the men were gathering with their guitars and their whiskey. Miguelito began playing a quick rhythm with fingers that flew across the strings. The others squatted on their heels in a circle until Jose Luis pulled himself up, tossed his hat onto the dirt and began circling it with graceful steps that made his body flow like liquid. His spurs jingled to the rhythm. Silver conchos flashed firelight as he clasped his hands behind him, bowing and circling an imaginary partner.

Ginny watched from the door until Jose Luis pulled her into the dance. A moment later she was whirling and laughing while he courted her with his laughing eyes. When the dance was over, she returned to Jeremy's side, flushed and exhilarated. One of the vaqueros said something in Spanish and Jose Luis blushed.

Jeremy's baleful glance was not lost on the men. Miguelito shifted to a melancholy melody, and one of the men pulled a pair of dice from his pocket. Sancho growled and gestured toward Ginny, and the vaquero Perez palmed them with a surly glare.

Jeremy swallowed and asked a question that had been on his mind. "Any chance there's a lawman around these parts?" The silence that followed answered the issue for him. Whatever he'd done, he hadn't gained any friends.

"Tell Señor Lawsen a story," Miguelito suggested. He silenced his strings with a sly grin. "Tell him about the kind of men he might meet up with when he leaves here to go back north."

Jose Luis leered. "*Si*. Maybe he is lucky so far. But many gringos, they are not so lucky."

Jeremy shifted uncomfortably. "Came across a vigilante posse on my way in."

"Damned plague if you ask me," Sancho said.

The storyteller waited until Miguelito nodded before he began. "They say Tiburcio Vasquez was too smart for the gringos that search for him. He and his band have many amigos."

Juan Antonio interrupted. "*Si*. He one to call out anyone who would

72

betray him."

Jose Luis lit his cigarette and continued. "Once, he waits to waylay a young gringo friend."

"Like you, Señor!" The other vaquero made a dismissive gesture with his fingers. "A man who brings him food and shelter. Shares his meadow with the animals. Even gives up his own bunk for Tiburcio's woman."

Jose Luis grinned. "This friend serves him well, but his mouth has become loose. 'Drop your guns,' Tuburcio demands. 'And your gun belt and boots.' 'Why do you do this to me,' the man complains. He gives the man a hard look. 'Can you deny you speak of my comings and goings to men of the law?' 'No.' the man says. 'Then you must dismount. Take off your boots and socks. And tie this cord around your ankles.'"

"'Ah, my friend, Tiburcio, This joke goes too far,' his friend protests."

"'A slovenly knot. Retie it,'" the two vaqueros at the fireside added in unison; they have obviously heard the story before.

Jose Luis continued, unperturbed. "Tiburcio empties his friend's pockets and keeps the treasure for himself. 'To teach you a lesson,' he says, 'you will walk back to your ranch.' He ignores the man's long face, but the man does not beg. 'Struggle valiantly against the chords, and they will loosen. I will lead your horse far down the trail toward your rancho,' he says. 'You will not die.'"

"Over twenty miles," someone adds.

Jose Luis looked pleased to hold the attention of the campfire. "In time, the young gringo unties himself and begins his long walk. His boyhood calluses are long years behind him, the stones and briars, sharp. He cuts up his vest to cover his bare feet."

"Tied with strips from his shirt."

"As the strips wear, he replaces them until his shirt is no more." Jose Luis glanced at Ginny. "Then he is forced to use his undergarments, first one then the other."

Ginny glanced at Sancho, her eyes wide. "What happened when night came?"

"He survives. In the morning, chilled and stiff, he rises and walks until he finds his horse."

"From this day, he tells no one of another's business."

Jose Luis turned to Jeremy. "Señor, you are a stranger. Perhaps you come to see the little señorita, perhaps not. But the mouths of the *paisanos* are closed to you. Ride safely on your return. Have a peaceful night, Señor."

Jeremy was thankful that the firelight hid his face. The silence was a dismissal.

Beside him, Ginny was getting sleepy. It was Sancho who nudged her to her feet. "Little Missy, time to hit the hay."

She staggered to her feet in a mighty effort that broke the tension. "Mr. Lawsen, I smoothed up Pa's bedding so's it looks fresh-made. You might as well sleep there. I'll show you."

Jeremy filled in the silence as they made their way into the house. "Thanks, Squirt. That's real nice of you. Thought I'd have to share the straw with my horse tonight."

"Not hardly. We don't make company sleep with their horses. Anyway, ain't you never slept with your horse? All the hands do when they're caught out in the bush. For warmth, Sancho says—"

Jeremy held up both hands; "Whoa there, Squirt. I'm about full of 'Sancho says' for one day. How about we get some sleep. You can tell me more about Sancho tomorrow!"

"Sure thing, but Sancho says a tenderfoot can't learn too quick about the West or else he'll find himself cozying up to a rattler and killing off a king snake."

"Thanks, but I know the difference." Sancho again. Didn't the kid get any of her information from her father? She hadn't mentioned him once this whole day. In any kind of favorable light, he corrected himself.

He ducked into the dimly-lit room that Ginny indicated. The bedroom where Caroline Nugent had spent her last hours seemed out of character with the rest of the house. The furniture had apparently been carried overland on horses, from Santa Cruz, or San Francisco, shipped straight from the spoils of a war-stripped Southern mansion before the transcontinental railroad saw the light of day. The double bed was mounted on a mahogany headboard with each poster an elaborate carving of vines and spirals from the hands of German immigrant craftsman. The bed matched the wardrobe in the corner, a fair match for one his mother owned. Perhaps she and the lady who had lived here went shopping for their furnishings in an Atlanta furniture maker's. A swatch of dusty white homespun partially covered the window. Everything in the room needed a good dusting, and the sheets needed more than that.

Everywhere he looked, dirty clothing, manure encrusted boots and drinking glasses lay where they had fallen. He sniffed one of the glasses that smelled like Patrón used more than water to wet his whistle. On a dusty table, a cracked frame stood emptied of its daguerreotype. He wondered whose image had annoyed Nugent enough to remove it.

The room had the particular scent he'd come across in San Francisco's Chinatown. A smell he associated with late nights and lethargic men stumbling out of the shadows, their pockets picked clean of their gold. Underneath a piece of toweling he found a water pipe, still packed with the opium residue of its last use. He kicked it aside and uncovered a handful of white tablets in the folds of the towel. So that was the size of it; the man was a dope eater to boot. The place was a lunatic sanitarium. Blessed Patsy, what was he supposed to do?

He satisfied himself that the bedding contained nothing that might bite, sting or bore into him, and stretched out in the musty mattress in his long underwear. His mind was conjuring up solutions while he tried to settle his nerves. He didn't subscribe to the popular theory that opium was good for everything that ailed a man; he'd seen too many morphine addicts home from the war to believe in dousing a man's troubles with narcotics. Respectable trading posts were selling opium as a remedy for morphine addiction, and mothers used dope to ease their baby's teething, but that didn't make it right in his mind.

He had almost dozed off when he felt something bite his calf and hoped it was only a flea. Ginny's small voice drifted down from upstairs. "Won't do to catch a cold. Better close the windows."

He smiled. "Right. I'll take the chance."

Chapter Fourteen

Jeremy woke to the shuffling of benches. He made it to the breakfast table in time to salvage the last of the tortillas and lukewarm, bitter coffee. Sancho fished in his vest pocket for a sliver of wood and was picking his teeth as he ambled out into the yard. Jeremy wasn't sure if he was supposed to follow or not. He thought he heard the creak of a loft ladder at the other end of the hall. He was still sipping coffee when Ginny slipped through the door, clad in the same outfit she had worn the day before, but her face showed the ruddiness of a quick wash-up.

"Good morning, Virginia. Ready for another ride?"

"Sure." She circled the table searching for something. Finally she halted behind Sancho's empty spot, reached under his plate and picked up a piece of ham. To this she added a tortilla that was hidden there as well. When the last of the sandwich disappeared into her mouth, she polished off the remainder of Sancho's cold coffee.

Jeremy watched as she assembled her breakfast from the leavings of the other men. By now nothing should shock him, but she'd managed to do just that. "You do that often?" he asked.

"Often as I need to," she replied. "Sancho usually saves me a piece else I would pert-near starve to death."

"Your cook doesn't save you a plate?"

"Nah, she's pretty sore most of the time. Thinks I should be helping out, now I'm older. She's sore Patrón says I don't have to 'cause my mother was a lady."

Sweet Betsy! Gleaning leftovers from the cowhands' plates? Not his idea of ladylike behavior. Nor, he suspected, would it be her grandmother's. The more he learned, the more he was tempted to lay his fist into Papa Nugent's nose when he finally met up with the man.

Ginny wiped her hands on her worn britches and looked around unsuccessfully for more coffee. "Ready when you are," she mumbled.

I'll be singing Dixie! Jeremy grabbed his hat and followed her out of the room.

"Señorita Geena, you clean the table before you go." From the doorway, the Indian woman punctuated her words with a hard look.

He noticed the girl's attitude as she turned to the door. "Can't today. Gotta show this here fellow the lay of the land. Sancho says so."

Jeremy bobbed a meek apology and followed Ginny into the yard. "Does that happen a lot?"

"Pert' near every day." In the shed she pulled her saddle from the rack and started toward the corral.

Jeremy picked up her saddle blanket and followed. "Phew, where did this thing come from? Smells like mice slept on it."

"Yeah, well I meant to wash it, but I was some occupied yesterday."

She seemed unscathed. He wondered how she managed to shrug off criticism so easily. He had heard enough mean-spirited comments directed at her in the last two days to crush a lesser spirit. Maybe this was all she expected of life. A sobering thought.

Their path took them through land of wildlife and promise that reminded him of hill country back home. Small willows grew in places alongside spring-fed ponds surrounded by overgrown filaree—a reddish-purple plant that filled the meadows. Elsewhere, oaks offered verdant relief against the yellow grass. A blacktail doe crossed an opening in front of them, followed by a buck with a two-foot antler span.

Ginny pointed to the Winchester rifle in his leather scabbard. "Would be an easy shot, but the meat will be gamey. Sancho says rutting buck tastes worse than sour shoe leather. He says there's something in their neck, fouls the meat. Best wait till they get back to normal, he says."

Jeremy grinned. "You possess a striking array of knowledge for a young lady."

"I'd like to learn a lot more. I asked Patrón if he could write a letter to Mama's folks, so's I could tell them about me. But he said he didn't have time."

Jeremy leaned into his horse, up over an embankment. "I'll help you write one before I leave," he promised. "I'll even see it gets posted." And he'd be posting one of his own. "Where is your mail sent out from?"

"Comes by stage to Santa Margarita. Patrón rides over for it. Takes him a week, most often."

"Ah." He didn't bother to mention that Sancho had told him he made the trip in three days.

"I'd like to thank my Grandma Foster for the doll," Ginny said. "It's too fine for playing with. I pretend it's Mama when she was little. Or even me."

He glanced down at her dirty shirt and britches. "You wish it were you?"

"Mama made me a dress. Maybe someday I'll put my own daughter in it. Then I'll know how Mama felt when she had me."

Anything Jeremy could think to say might test her quavering voice. He waited until the horses had picked their way down an arroyo before he broke the silence. "Your mother played a piano. Have you given thought to learning?"

"I expect I'd like to."

"She once played 'Camptown Races,' by Stephen Foster, at a lady's social. Scandalized the countryside."

"I'd like to play camptonrazes. I'd like to paint pictures like the ones Mama has hanging in the parlor. I think I could paint. Seem to do good enough with my renderings. Sancho says so, anyway."

"Have you given thought to where you'd like to live when you're grown?"

"Anywhere but here." She glanced over to see his reaction. "I got it all figured. I'll get me a bonnet with yellow ribbons, and Sancho can tend my garden, and I'll get me a cook that don't hate me. And someone to fix my hair so I don't gotta cut it myself."

"Is that what happened?"

"Yep. Maria Inés don't got time to braid it, so I got sore and chopped on it. Patrón ain't seen it yet. He's going to pitch a conniption."

Jeremy smiled. "Your glory may be a tad short, but there's no reason it can't be straight. What say, when we get back to the house, I try to improve the 'chop' a bit?"

Ginny considered. "Expect that'll be okay."

They'd already ridden south across Middle Mountain toward a ridge on the Diablo Range where a solitary man was peering through a shiny tube mounted on a tripod that reflected the glint of the afternoon sun.

"That's Mr. Minto. Met him over at the Imus's last week. He's making a section survey so folks'll start moving into the valley. Sancho says they'll be crowding in, squatting on land that don't belong to them and ruining the range grass. Patrón says we ought to run the surveyor off afore he can finish his work, but Sancho says he gets his orders from the government so we best leave him alone."

From where they sat, Jeremy could see the Sierra Nevada mountain range. Between them and the mountains, the San Joaquin Valley stretched flat and treeless, fifty miles wide. In the vivid blue sky, scattered clouds formed a patchwork of shadows on the yellow earth. To the west, the Santa Lucia Range hid the Pacific Ocean. A trio of hawks soared in the air currents and Ginny motioned for him to stop while they watched. Ahead, two red-headed woodpeckers pecked holes into the bark of a valley oak. He sat stock-still in his saddle, breathing in the sounds and sights of the day until the brawl of a calf brought him back. A gray squirrel ran along the ground with an acorn in its pouch.

Ginny was chattering over the top of a chorus of meadowlarks. ". . . around here everything's sort of straw-colored. Bet it's green back where you're from. Bet you got a big river. That sage-green plant you smell over yonder, that's called turkey melon."

His nose caught the scent before he saw the small clumps of furry leaves growing close to the ground she was pointing to. A covey of quail called out from beneath a scrawny tree that Ginny called a digger pine. It looked like it had been stepped on as a seedling and half its needles nibbled away by a hungry steer. It was no kind of pine tree he'd ever seen.

"'Round here, if you want to know which way's north, you study the side of the tree the Spanish moss is growing. Sancho says you'll always know."

Jeremy couldn't help smiling. "We have Spanish moss back home."

Ginny's mare stumbled, both horse and rider worn out. Her mare was pulling its head to crop oats every few feet. Jeremy advised her to keep a shorter grip on the reins, and saw her face flush with embarrassment. The air had a hint of chill. To divert her, he asked about the weather.

"Gets cold enough, you need a coat, sometimes. Even in the daytime."

"Do you have a coat, Miss Virginia?"

She kept her head low, even as she nodded. "Sancho fetched me a cast-off from one of the folks in the valley. The lady said I needed the thing worse than the bed quilt she's piecing. 'Spect she's right."

Along the eastern break, rain-laden clouds were emptying their load into the mountains. He found himself wondering if the valley caught enough rain to provide good range feed for cattle. At some point on the ride, he realized he was not merely curious about another man's holdings; he was looking at it with an eye to owning some for himself.

"Ever hear Sancho talk about land around here might be for sale?"

"Might have. Talk to him. Might be he'll ride you over to some of the neighbors so's you could meet the folks."

"I'd consider myself favored."

The talk in San Francisco was all about the railroad coming to San

Miguel, only thirty miles to the west. The Southern Pacific Rail Road had laid track from Camadero, just south of Gilroy, and a man could ride it as far south as Hollister. The town used to go by the name, San Justo Homestead, until the town fathers incorporated it a couple of years earlier and named it after one of their own. Chinese coolies were breaking their backs to lay track beyond Soledad. To the east they were laying the San Joaquin line; the money-talk said it would replace the Butterfield Stage Line. The Chinese were pounding rails to Fresno and south to Los Angeles. In a few years it would be a light matter to ship goods and cattle to the city market.

Ginny continued. "Heard Sancho and Patrón talking. They say the Rancho Cholame is getting sold off piecemeal. Folks is buying up."

"Is that so?" He scanned the horizon, hoping to get a clue about where the best prospects might lie.

"He says folks is always trying to make a nickel. Says here's as good as anyplace and better than some." She pointed east, where a haze of smoke from the mining camps in the Sierra Nevada foothills partially obliterated the mountains. "You could make a good living hauling ice down from the mountains. Folks would pay handsome."

He smiled. Whatever his plan, he hadn't traveled all this way to sell ice. Part of his reason for coming west was political. The War had delivered a death blow, and his allegiance was tempered by a need for fresh air. He would never abandon his home completely, but like Caroline Foster, he had spent enough nights lying awake, thinking that his destiny lay in the open lands of the West. Out here he wouldn't stumble over the reminders of war every time he stepped out his front door. He wished he could know, upfront, what the consequences of his decision would be. Caroline Foster Nugent hadn't fared too well from the chance she took, nor from the looks of things, had Charlie Nugent. "What's the water situation around these parts?"

"There's springs all over out here. Sancho says the earthquakes brings 'em up."

Tarnation, but these Californians are proud of their earthquakes! "Year-round?"

"Enough, the cattle can drink without your having to sit watch on 'em. It's thieving you gotta watch out for." She pointed to a craggy rock formation up ahead. "We ain't on Patrón's land no more. We left it back a-ways."

In the distance, a small, low cabin made of pine with a sturdy, chinked fireplace looked to be abandoned. His palms grew clammy with the possibilities. "Where might I find the man who owns this piece?"

"Patrón would know. He's in town drinking whiskey. That's the business Jose Luis said he had to go into San Miguel for. He stays on the ranch 'til he gets lonely, then he heads into town."

Jeremy listened with dawning realization; she didn't understand that these things weren't spoken of by young ladies. At her age it might earn her a smile, but in another two years she'd have no chance for any sort of decent life. He made a quick decision. "Believe I'll ride over to San Miguel tomorrow."

"Can I go with you?" She picked at a loose piece of leather on her saddle horn, seemingly intent on her task. "I could bring Patrón home. His head will be splitting him. He might need me."

"Well . . ." He'd planned to ride out the way he came, out Slack's Canyon. He had no business traveling with a young girl. "I suggest we seek council with Sancho. If he suggests it's a good idea, I'll concur. Besides," he teased, "you could keep me from getting lost."

Ginny met his smile with one of her own. "Mr. Lawsen. . . ." she began, studying the horn on her saddle again.

"Miss Virginia?"

"We friends?"

He studied her flushed face. "A distinct possibility. However, we seem to have a problem."

"What's that?" She was leaning forward, waiting.

He noticed that she had no problem looking him straight in the eye when she thought he needed her help. "If we're to be friends, I'll need leave to call you something other than Miss Virginia. And you'll have to call me Jeremy."

He felt her gaze while he pretended to study the horizon. For some reason he remembered her comment about his eyelashes and he felt his cheeks warm.

Finally, she spoke. "Seems easier I change my ways than you."

He pretended to consider her suggestion before he nodded. "It's agreed, then, Ginny. Let's shake hands on it." Her hand felt surprisingly soft, given the range of her outdoor adventures. Her eyes were the color of the ocean back home. She smiled and her face showed curiosity and intelligence, even prettiness hidden under the scruff. He released her hand and nodded solemnly. "You'll do for a friend."

She tried to mask her nervousness with a rush of orders. "We ought to be on the watch for coyotes and skunks. Don't let your guard down out here. Let's get back so we can hear Sancho's thoughts on my riding to town." She turned her mare and galloped off.

81

"Hold up, Katydid," he called. "No point in gallivanting off to ruination. I don't intend leaving in the next ten minutes."

She reined in and waited for him to catch up. "Well, we've seen about all there is to see around here except the caves. Maybe you can come back for the roundup next spring. We'll cook up a steer to feed everybody comes over to help."

"I'd be honored, Ginny." But she was wrong about having seen everything there was to see. A man could spend his lifetime out here and not see it all. But he had a feeling after he met Patrón, he'd be about as welcome on the ranch as a rattlesnake.

Chapter Fifteen

The little gal was out riding with the Southerner. Just as well the fellow was keeping her occupied because Sancho was in no fit mood for company; black thoughts were crowding out any civil tongue might be left in his head. Time he put the memories to order. It was only a matter of time before the newcomer hit on the tough questions. A man needed to give thought to his answers.

The saddles were rough from summer dust and heat. Time he applied a coat of neatsfoot oil. Truth was, the job could hold until the rains came, but he was looking for something to keep him busy, and sitting inside the saddle room, out of sight of every living soul, was balm for the turmoil in his head. He pulled out his polishing rag, saturated it with oil and started rubbing.

***

The morning after the Missus passed to her reward brought with it decisions he knew he'd pay for. The Boss wasn't one to let another man stand in his stead; whatever Sancho did was bound to be wrong, but the coffin had to be made, and folks sent for—the Boss among them. The Boss would never accept her death without seeing it with his own eyes.

He'd put the little gal to sleep on a quilt in a corner of the shed while he sawed pine planks for a coffin. When she woke crying, he spent hours rocking her on the porch like her ma had done, crooning cattle calls he'd learned trailing a herd of nervous Mexican longhorns to Montana. In the afternoon he rode with the child over to the Rancho Cholame and asked Señor Gonzales to dispatch a rider to find Nugent. Afterwards, he dropped by the Imus place and accepted the Missus's offer to keep Ginny until the funeral.

He rode home with his face into the rising wind while storm clouds built overhead. At the house he readied the bodies for burial. Before washing them and chilling them down with stored ice from the icehouse, he massaged the hands and feet so they would remain supple. There were other things he did, things he'd seen his grandmother do to preserve the departed for burial, and he'd done so with reverence. He didn't dwell on the details; it was enough to recall that he'd dressed Missus Nugent in the white dress she'd worn on the day he met her. He'd wrapped the baby in the fine lawn shawl she'd always favored.

He chose the gravesite himself, on a ridge behind the house where he would be able to see it from the bunkhouse. All day the wind drove sheets of rain through his poncho and down his britches until he was half-frozen and glad of it. There wasn't enough misery for the guilt he carried. He pitched mud as fast as his hands could work, but the mud slipped back so he worked faster. Soon he was ankle-deep in black ooze, his legs trembling from chilblains, reminding him of his days standing knee deep in Sierra Nevada snowmelt, panning for gold that wasn't there. When the first cramp hit, he slowed his shoveling and bellowed his pain for the world to hear. After that, he kept it to himself. The rain never stopped, nor the wind, until he pitched the last shovelful and climbed out, hand-over-hand, using the reata he'd tied to his saddle horn.

The rain continued all night and into the following day. The next evening he heard the Boss coming before he saw him riding in on a horse half-dead from the run. Nugent toppled from the saddle and strode past without saying anything. He disappeared into the house and thumped down the hallway, threw open the door to the bedroom then retraced his steps. Finally, he paused at the door of the parlor where the body of his wife lay encased in a pine coffin, covered with what ice was left in the icehouse. The Boss remained for the rest of the night with his wife and his whiskey—enough that when the vaqueros finally rode in, he kept the bunkhouse awake with his keening.

Maria Inés arrived while Sancho dozed in the rocking chair. When the cook gestured toward the parlor with a question in her eyes, he shook his head. He didn't know what to tell her. In the past it had been Missus Nugent who handled the Boss.

By the time William Imus and his brothers arrived with their wives and little Ginny, Maria Inés had tortillas heating on the stove. It seemed a strange time to fill the house with commotion, but the womenfolk brought food.

Outside, a Mexican man in a black sackcoat stood watching from the edge of the crowd. Sancho recognized the slight build and the thick mass of raven hair spilling out under his narrow-rimmed, knobby hat. But it wasn't Tiburcio Vasquez he feared; the bandit had a reputation for being reasonable at times of personal hardship. It was the valley womenfolk he was afraid of. They stood outside, demanding he do something about Charlie Nugent. It was time she was placed in the ground and words read over her.

Finally, as the afternoon sun showed signs of waning, he nodded to the vaqueros who stood nervously turning their hats in their hands. In single file they passed through the hallway to the room where the Boss sat with his grief and his three-day-dead wife.

Sancho tapped on the door. When he got no response, he pounded harder. "Boss . . . we're comin' in!"

The room was silent, with only the grandfather clock ticking in the hallway. Finally, the door opened and the Boss stood, rank with the smell of whiskey and wearing the look of madness. He staggered through the hall, past the little gal who was clinging to Sancho's leg.

"Take her to rest then, by God! Take her!" The Boss sank down hard on the hallway bench and dropped his head between his hands. He remained there while the vaqueros hoisted the coffin and bore it out through the doors to the waiting wagon, melted ice running off their shoulders.

Sancho helped the Boss to his feet and supported him out the door to the farm wagon. When the little gal tried to climb into his lap, her father brushed her off. Sancho lifted her up in front of him in his saddle.

At sunset, the coffin was lowered. Sancho hardly noticed that the rain had stopped. In a way he wished it hadn't. Four vaqueros lowered the pine box into place before they crossed themselves and kissed the tips of their fingers. He barely listened as William Todd read the words. He saw Todd's wife help the little gal toss a handful of mud onto her mother's box, but Nugent sat on the wagon seat and refused to watch.

Todd read from a Bible he carried wrapped in oilcloth: "The Lord is my shepherd; I shall not want. In verdant pastures he gives me repose; Beside restful waters he leads me; he refreshes my soul." Todd finished reading and added; "Let us not forget there are two sweet souls taking the journey."

Sancho nodded. The Boss hadn't asked, and Sancho hadn't set him straight, but they were also burying a baby boy with his mama's blonde hair.

Afterwards, Miguelito drove Nugent back to the house. After the mourners left, Sancho took his Winchester and went off looking for the coyotes that had tormented the Missus's sleep. In the morning he laid three fresh pelts on top of the new grave. Then he staggered to the bunkhouse and went to bed with a fever that brought him close to meeting the Missus once again.

The next day, Nugent began to issue orders. "Keep the kid away. I don't want to see anyone," he shouted when Ginny knocked at his library door. Maria Inés clucked her tongue and led the sobbing girl off to the summer house to bake up a batch of ginger cookies. When the cookies came out of the oven, she packed two in a scrap of flour sacking and shooed Ginny off to the orchard.

Five days later, when he was strong enough to stand again, Sancho crawled into his boots and began working on a promise he'd made at Caroline Nugent's bedside. He kept close to the house, watching and waiting for what he knew was coming. Part of him welcomed the blame for letting the Missus die. The other part wanted to kill the bastard who had brought her here in the first place. A day after he was back on his feet, he found three empty whisky bottles tossed into the hollyhocks outside the parlor window. Inside, the Boss sounded half-crazy with need for a drink.

He saw Sancho outside and bellowed, "Get in here. And bring the girl!"

Sancho found Ginny hiding in the haystack. He took her hand and led her to the parlor, but he refused to enter. By the time the Boss shouted for him, he had nearly worn a track from the main house to the cottonwood tree and back again.

The truth was in the Boss's eyes as soon as Sancho walked into the room. Anger had obviously given the man plenty of time for thinking, and his intentions showed in his coolness. He had one thing left in the world: The satisfaction of cutting his hired man off from anything that remained of Caroline Nugent.

He thought the Boss meant to run him off the ranch, but Nugent was not as kind as that. Anyone who ever claimed a portion of his wife's attention had stolen something from him, and he aimed to get it back. Didn't matter that Sancho had spent time making life better for the Boss's wife and daughter; in his thinking, if Missus Nugent hadn't spent her time out in the orchard, maybe she'd have had more time for him.

"Kid, like it or not, your ma's gone. I don't want you to mention her again. Never! You understand?" Nugent waited until he saw Ginny's hesitant nod before he continued, a bit less harsh, but rock steady. "Your ma spoiled you blind. I don't want any crying around here. No carrying on. You understand?"

When the first words out of the Boss's mouth were for the daughter, Sancho felt his hair lifting. In another minute she'd be an orphan and he'd take his chances with the vigilantes. He jammed his clenched hands behind him while Nugent kept his eyes fixed just over Ginny's head. *Bastard, you can't even look your child in the eye.*

"I got a ranch to run. Your mother was the finest lady I ever met. Out of respect to her, you don't have to help in the kitchen, but you best stay out of the men's way. Now get along."

"Papa . . . Papa . . . ." Tears ran down the little gal's cheeks as she turned to leave.

"And don't call me Papa. I'm jinxed. Better off I ain't got no family."

Sancho turned to go with her, but Nugent stopped him. "You—stay!"

Damn him! Sancho was quivering so hard he couldn't speak. He stared into Nugent's hollow eyes and saw that the man was enjoying every cut of his words.

"You spent your time lollygagging around my wife. You like the yard work so much, you got a choice. Get off the ranch or take the place of the squaw's man. Don't make no difference to me. You stay, you're the new Indian. Got it? You clean the chicken coops, tend the firewood and milk the goat. Let the vaqueros run the cattle. Those are my terms."

Sancho was too stunned to see straight. Burst pride fired through his nerves, making him want to turn on his heel and ride off. It didn't even matter that he would end up doing the same chores at some other place; quitting would satisfy the hatred he felt. "Boss, you can—" As he began, he caught sight of the memorial hair wreath Missus Nugent had been working on the week she died. A swatch of her hair would need-be included. He had sheared off a lock the morning she died, had it tied tight in his spare kerchief. He could work it into the circle along with her baby boy's—the Boss need never know. And there was Ginny. There was no way he could ride off and leave the little gal alone. If he did, the Missus would haunt him to his grave. And rightly so. He heard his words, even though they nearly choked him. "I'll stay."

He started out the door in a mighty effort to reach the yard before the bile in his throat let go. It had been one thing to do favors for the lady, but both he and the boss knew why he had been given the job for permanent.

They'd loved the same woman.

In a streak of pure cussedness, he turned to challenge Nugent, and this time his glare was more than the Boss would tolerate.

"One more thing. See that my horse is saddled and brought around every morning before you eat." The Boss's voice was smug with satisfaction. Sancho felt his stomach turn over. "Ignore me and you'll be out of here as fast as your crooked legs can carry you." He stroked his week-old stubble and his smile was threatening. "Another thing. You've wasted enough time on the kid. She's got an old man. You don't need to be pretending it's you. She has any questions, she can ask me."

Sancho staggered through the door feeling like he'd been center-punched by one of those pugilist Irish fellows who came to St. Louis looking for sucker bets on Saturday nights. He had taken the bet once and still recalled having the wind knocked out of him in a whoosh. That day he felt the blow again, standing in the hallway, about to spit up breakfast or blood— it didn't matter which.

Instead, he'd choked back the need to do either, and tried to get his head around the facts. He'd wait a few weeks and see what he could do. Didn't figure on letting the little gal raise herself; Shoot, he had more memories about her mama than her old man did. Boss only saw what his Missus wanted him to see. His hired man was privy to the rest, like the fact that she was afraid of the coyotes outside her window.

He'd known. Just as he knew he wouldn't leave.

Chapter Sixteen

Sancho had spent two hours in a hell of his own making. When the little gal rode up with the Virginia fellow, he was wiping down his saddle for the fifth time with a piece of deerskin and a wad of bear grease. He shifted in time to hear her squawking about a plan to ride into town. With a god-awful effort, he bit off his retort when it appeared the Southerner seemed to think the decisions were up to a worn-out saddle tramp. Anything he did was bound to nip him in the hind-end. The Boss wouldn't take it kindly if the little gal showed up unannounced and walked in on any shenanigans. In all likelihood, right now the Boss was lying in his own filth, in one of the rooms off the mission church, being sweet-tended by one of the Indian gals made her living that way.

To his credit, the newcomer from Virginia stood quietly waiting.

Sancho hesitated. "Missy, you run on over and warn the cook there'll be an extra seat at supper. Wouldn't do you no harm to help her out, neither." He was half-surprised when the little gal nodded and started off without an argument. He took a deep breath, not sure where to begin. The young Virginia fellow was like him, poker players ready to put their cards on the table.

The newcomer began. "Sancho. . ." He cleared his throat and began again. "Ginny thinks a lot of you. I get the idea that you're pretty important to her."

Fair enough. "Well, young fellow, I'm 'bout all she's got 'cept for the cook. Maria Inés got it harder than any of us. Boss treats her like a slave. She's Injun—seems glad enough to have a roof over her head. Sometimes takes a shine to the little gal, sometimes not." He stuck a pinch of tobacco in his cheek. "Her mood depends on what partic'lar notion the Boss is in."

The newcomer seemed to relax. "Call me Jeremy," he said. When Sancho nodded, he continued. "This boss of yours, he have a particular lot of notions?"

Sancho tried to think of a reason to be loyal, but the idea faded fast. "I suspect the Boss was just riled at first. Always did have a vain streak. Reckon he woulda come outta his funk sooner or later. But that dope got ahold of him and it ain't let go. Most of his problems stem from the bottle or the pipe."

"I suspected as much."

"When the Missus died, Boss tried to put a stop to me befriending the little gal. Said he'd send me packing faster than the shine off a new pair a boots on a dusty road." The words had been grinding inside for years. It felt good to let them out.

Lawsen's eyes widened, but he kept his tone level. "What did you do?"

Sancho paused to spit his tobacco juice into the dirt. "Ashamed to say, but I went along till I was so plumb disgusted, could hardly share my boots with my own feet. Been trying to do right by the little gal without getting caught."

"You seem to help yourself to more food than a person can hold. Don't care much for ham?"

He grinned. "Not so old I can't recall hunger in a belly, myself. But she's game."

Jeremy edged closer. "How much does she hate living out here?"

Sancho shifted, trying to see behind the mask of politeness. "She don't hate it a'tall. Just hates the loneliness. And the fact the Boss ain't halfways the man he oughtta be. 'Bout time he picked himself up and stopped blaming everyone else around him." He snapped the polishing rag at the saddle leather like it was boiling.

"Does that blame include you?"

"What makes ya say thet?" He tried to determine the other man's tell while he waited for a show of cards.

"When I see a top hand spending his days wiping down saddles, I have to figure there's a story behind it."

He let his surprise show, something he'd never allow himself to do in a real poker game. "Might say I'm paying the price for killing his wife. I'm trying to make it up with the little gal." He waited for the next hand. It came suddenly, the stakes higher than he had expected.

"What would you say if I took her back with me? To her grandmother?"

He took a breath to steady his nerves. "You aiming to do that?"

To his credit, the newcomer seemed uncertain. "Not necessarily. Not right away. She'd likely balk at the idea."

Sancho considered what Caroline Nugent would have thought about the matter. That was a tough call. "Not much out here for her, but it ain't high society she's lacking."

"Her mother wanted better for Ginny."

90

Sancho shifted on his good hip and turned to study the sunset until he was afraid he would shame himself if he turned around. "Her mama was a thoroughbred. I'd sure like to see the little gal turn out like her. Been racking my brain to figure out how."

"Is there a school nearby?"

"None for three days ride. Folks too busy scraping out a living to be concerned with learning. It'll come in time, but might be too late for this young'un." An idea was forming. He could feel it in the air. "Reckon Santa Cruz is 'bout the closest place, and it's a good ways up the coast."

"Anyone she would board with?"

"Reckon there's Missus Imus, down along Little Cholame Creek. She's had Ginny to sleep over once in a while, when the Boss is caught up in his demons. Lives past the cemetery that holds her two babies." Truth was, the Imus woman was the only real lady he knew. Wasn't any use to suggest the other kind.

"Mind if I take Ginny along tomorrow when I call on them?"

Sancho bit his lip in thought. "Might come to a battle with the father. Ya up to it?" He'd hate to miss a good fight. If it happened, he'd sure curse his luck to be stuck on the ranch when the fun took place. But the newcomer seemed sure enough of himself.

"I carry a notarized document in my pocket giving me full power of authority. Missus Foster is a proud old woman. She'd have made the trip herself if she could. She wants some resolution before she passes."

Sancho digested the information. "You taking over?"

The newcomer ran his fingers through his hair like he was stalling for time. "Ginny's western bred. Her heart is here, but she can grow up a lady. And that means schooling. Maybe even a year of finishing school when the time comes." He hesitated, a question in his eyes. "Truth is, even if I wanted to take her back, she'd have a hard time fitting in. She's smarter than any kid I've ever met. She just needs some taming, and that's what I'm hoping your Missus Imus can provide."

Sancho squirmed and asked the question roiling in his head. "She coming home now and again? I could fetch her." It was not so much a question. The newcomer was asking him to agree to a whole lot here, maybe more than he could stand. But the choices weren't an old cowhand's to make.

"Anytime school's not in session. And you can visit her when you're in town. As long as you're presentable."

He felt his face flaming. "Wal now, reckon I'm a little old for some of that stuff. Burned my stomach out on rot-gut long ago. Now I tend to the tamer things. That's how come Ginny an me get along."

"That's good to know." Jeremy stood fingering his hat. "I appreciate what you've done for her, Sancho. And her mother." He considered his next words. "But there's another reason she needs to get to town. I notice the way some of the vaqueros are looking at her. It'll only get worse."

Sancho felt shame running clear to his toes. God help him if he ever failed the little gal. "Not just the vaqueros." He ventured a solid look to see if Jeremy got his drift. "Truth to tell, that's why I got myself up here to the yard. Not much escapes me."

Jeremy released the tension in his grip and put the hat back on his head. "You have the gratitude of Missus Foster. If Nugent ever decides to toss you off the ranch, there'll be a pension waiting. She wants you to have a couple of greenbacks in case things get tense and you need to get Ginny out."

He didn't want charity, but the way this fellow was putting it, it sounded like something for the little missy. He could see no harm in that. "Long as the Boss'll have me around, reckon my place is here. Got her gardens and the grave to tend." He took a closer look at the paper money Lawsen was holding out. "Doubt there's anybody in these parts'll take your paper money. Can't say I've ever seen any, myself."

With nothing else that needed saying, he turned back to his polishing.

The newcomer took the hint. "I'll go tell Ginny to spruce up for a visit."

"Ain't had much luck getting new duds out of the Boss for the kid. She ain't got 'cept the clothes on her back."

"Ginny's grandmother sent money. We'll use it to give her a better life—even if it is Yankee paper."

Sancho set aside his polish rag. "Won't serve to be too tough on the father. He was a plumb delight afore his missus died. When a woman gets under a man's skin like that, he either has to shake her off or something else takes her place." He took a breath. This was the longest speech he'd ever given. And he wasn't finished. "Reckon with the Boss, it's the drink caught a ride on his back, along with that dang dope. It's been riding him ever since."

Jeremy listened thoughtfully, and nodded. "Thanks for the caution. Nugent's suffered enough. I don't intend he should lose his daughter, too. Despite everything, if he's the kind of man Caroline Foster could choose, he's a good man underneath."

Sancho caught up a corner of the rag to clean the dust in his good eye. Time to carry his saddle into the barn before the supper call.

The next morning the newcomer had Ginny up and seated before the platter of grits and beans was set on the table. "Miss Ginny," he said, "back home, the ladies are always served first. And you're certainly the lady of the house. One slice or two?"

Ginny glanced over at Sancho and waited for his nod. "Three," she managed to stammer. "And plenty of beans." She sat back and watched as her new friend smeared hers with butter then forked himself a generous portion. She giggled as he poured her a mug of coffee and milk. She took her time nibbling on fried grits still hot when she put the fork to her lips.

The men dug into the kettle without speaking. They knew how to recognize a lady from the common kind, but this little girl had caused enough extra work with her tricks and practical jokes that they had little patience with her taking on airs. The newcomer ignored them while he kept up a steady stream of conversation about the coming railroad and the prospects for the coming year.

The little missy had gotten her hair trimmed and washed. Fluffed up, it didn't look half bad. Brought out her mother's eyes. Sancho felt his throat close up when he tried to swallow. It was a minute or two before he could manage to down the bite of cornmeal cake that was resting on his fork. When he did, he saw the little gal copying the way the newcomer cut his hotcakes with his knife. She practiced until she could make the slice, and when she looked up Sancho gave her a wink of encouragement.

Chapter Seventeen

On their way to the Imus place, Ginny showed him the spot where Sancho had been thrown by a mule. "Weren't nobody around for miles, he could see. Thought he'd bring it home for his own, leastways till its owner showed up."

"What happened?"

"There was this crazy old lady, Mariana La Loca. She claims she's Joaquin Murrieta's widow, but Sancho says that one was named Rosa. Anyway, the crazy lady was taking her convenience in the bushes. She had just hitched up her skirts when she looked up and saw her mule trotting down the trail. 'Course she thought he was a horse thief. Who wouldn't?"

"Sancho?"

Ginny nodded. "She gave a whistle liked to pierce his ears and the mule turned into pure gunpowder. Sancho said it was hell-bent-for-leather. Poor ole guy had bruises on his backside for a month."

Jeremy's enthusiasm brought to mind another story. "There's this fellow, Old Man Lynch, had to sleep in the woodshed for a good while. He was supposed to go into town for some new nails 'cause his roof was taking on water and his wife said he was a lazy, good-for-nothing fool. Well, he didn't come home right off, and she gave him a couple of extra days before she went a looking for him. Caught him in one of those rooms they keep alongside the saloon with an Injun girl named Rosa."

"You know about these things?" Jeremy sounded displeased.

"Folks talk," she explained. "Anyway, he might have gotten away with it, but a neighbor lady happened by with a burned hand, and she needed help, so Missus Lynch agreed to ride her to town for tending. Doc wasn't around, but she found her husband's horse outside the saloon. She was so all-fired mad she just opened every door till she found him, and stomped in. He was up in his cups on "Old Orchard," hardly could stand when she pulled him to his feet, he was so drunk. Well, that was that! Word is, Old Man Lynch don't go anywhere no more without Missus Lynch along."

She liked the sound of Jeremy's laughter. She remembered another story so he'd laugh some more.

"William Imus was building his stone fireplace . . . " she paused for effect, "back when he was homesteading and his little children hadn't all gotten dead from the diphtheria—"

"All his children?"

"All except Nettie and her brother. Anyway, an earthquake takes his chimney. He's plumb sore, yelling and shaking his hand to the heavens, and he done what Maria Inés calls 'taking God's name in vain.' He shouts, 'Give it another shake and put it back, God!'"

"And did the Lord comply?"

"Wait for the ending," she huffed. "Anyways, he's pretty worn out from all the work, see, and he wants to rest. So another shake comes and he gets fearful. 'Never mind, God, I'll do it myself,' he says."

Jeremy laughed so hard he nearly dropped his hat. For a minute she wondered if riding to town with Jeremy Lawsen was the same as being courted. Elizabeth Todd was sweet on a fellow who was wooing her, and her sister said she liked it, so there was probably a lot of laughing going on between them. One thing was for certain. She wouldn't consent to be courted by anyone who didn't laugh a lot.

Jeremy caught his breath. "You know, Ginny, I don't allow this is a proper conversation between a lady and a gentleman."

A lady? If he thought so, she was prepared to make adjustments in her behavior. "Jeremy, tell me about my mother. Tell me how they met."

He chewed his bottom lip, considering. "Your mother was the prettiest belle in three counties. She would have been courted by half the men alive, but they were all away defending their honor. Finally the war ended and the survivors came home. Well, she tried to choose one. She was mighty keen on keeping her father's lands the same as he had, but the world she knew was gone. Out of kilter, she called it. She'd been bred to a life that was gone, and she felt she was dying, too."

"That's sad."

"Her friends stepped in. They said her mind was suffering the war nerves. Her mother talked of taking her on a trip somewhere, but there was no money, not even a piece of jewelry left to sell. Your grandmother had given most of her silver and gold for the Cause. It was a bad time. If the War hadn't come along, your mother and mine might have had a season in Paris, but mine was already busy with a husband and a baby—my older sister."

Ginny tried to imagine a life where people got to make choices about their own lives.

"One day, a handsome western man came through town to buy up

95

some blood stock for his ranch back in California—"

"Patrón!"

"Indeed. He bought a few head of horses and arranged to have them driven west. The neighbors gave a dinner. He met your mother, and afterwards, Miss Caroline took him outside for a private tour of the garden. I remember she tucked her arm in his, and as far as I know, she never took it out again. Your father was smitten—as we like to call it where I come from."

Ginny tried to memorize every word.

Jeremy was staring somewhere distant. "You were born not long afterward." He turned so he could look her square in the eye, like he wanted her to believe him. "I see an awful lot of her in you. She caused your Yankee father to fall so completely in love that when she died she took part of him with her."

She was glad when he stopped talking. All these new ideas needed some place to hang, like Missus Imus's company teacups on their hooks.

After a few minutes he began again. "He sees your mother in you and it's put his thinking off. But like it or not, he has an obligation to you. To your mother. Your grandmother carries on about you so often. Her sons died upholding their honor and you're all she has left. I promised her I'd bring back a report about you."

Ginny felt her cheeks heat. "You gonna tell her everything?"

Jeremy acted like he hadn't heard. "I don't believe your father hates you. Sancho says he's gone sour with himself for letting your mother die. He sees her in you and he feels guilty. So he stays away. Does that make any sense?"

She turned her face toward the yellow grass at the trail's edge. "Are you going to make me leave here?" When Jeremy shook his head, she felt her legs go shaky with relief.

"Not if we can find another way. Let's see what we can figure out. Sancho says this lady we're going to see, Sarah Imus—"

"The Imuses celebrate birthdays. Nettie is her daughter. She's a year older than me. Her ma made her a raisin cake and she got a rag doll, but now I have the best doll of all." She thought of something. "See, now you're doing it!"

"What's that?"

"Saying 'Sancho says'."

She thought he'd laugh all the way to Nettie's, but he turned serious again. "How would you like to live with Missus Imus? I mean if she's agreeable?"

"Oh, no! Patrón's dead set against charity."

96

"Charity?"

"Missus Imus makes me clothes sometimes. She likes doing it, 'cause she doesn't have enough kids to sew for. Just Nettie and John."

"I was thinking, it might be possible for you to board there. Easier for her to help with your schooling."

She shook her head. "I expect she's too busy. 'Sides, Patrón needs me on the ranch."

"Says who?" Jeremy's look brought shame clear to her eyeballs.

"He don't intend I should be a burden. He said so, and I mean to keep the bargain." She watched Jeremy's face flare. When he spoke he sounded angry.

"Sweet Betsy in the morning, girl, if you were any less of a burden you'd be living in that oak tree of yours. Like it or not, you're going to be grown up one of these days. And your clothes—you're wearing rags no self-respecting vaquero would be caught dead in!" He stopped when he saw the tears she was trying to hold back.

"Anyway, Mister Imus is a Democrat." Ginny kicked her horse ahead so she could hide her face. She had been a fool to think he could like her stories. The whole time he had been laughing at her.

Behind her, it sounded like Jeremy was trying to catch up. She gave her mare another kick and felt it lunge into a trot.

"Hey, Katydid—"

"Don't call me that." She tried to blink the tears back, but she failed miserably. By the time he reined up alongside, she was awash.

"Ginny! It's not your fault—about the clothes or the reading. I didn't mean anything by it. You're smarter than most girls your age. You have a big heart, your mother's courage and the strength of one of those mountain lions you're always talking about. You're funny, and clever and brave. I just thought you might want what other girls have."

She tried to think of an argument, but the impact of his praise stole her ability to think. She had to wait for the lump in her throat to dissolve before she could speak. "Sancho says ignorant folks is called dunces. That what I am, a dunce?"

Jeremy's face turned red. "No Yankee hayseed better call you a dunce!" He sounded mad enough that she believed him. "You're not so far behind in your schooling. And when your hair grows out, maybe Missus Imus could help you some with it. Teach you manners."

"Not likely. She's pretty busy. She's been sewing up a wardrobe so Nettie can head on up to Santa Cruz to go to school when the term starts."

Jeremy looked interested. He jerked his reins and had to fight his horse for a few paces. "How about going along?"

"Santa Cruz?"

He nodded. "I expect your grandmamma would agree."

Ginny thought about traveling north with Nettie, buying a real pair of shoes and a new dress. "Would I ever see Sancho again?"

"At term ends and holidays. You could take the steamer. I could arrange it with the Imuses. You and Nettie."

She tried to picture life without the ranch. Finally she turned to him. "Jeremy, I don't have a choice, do I?"

"You want me to make up a fib, Squirt?"

She liked that he was honest with her. "What does Sancho think?"

"I talked with him about it last night. He's willing to back me up with your . . . with Patrón."

"That's why he acted so strange back there." She remembered the way he had refused to meet her eyes, had fumbled with a piece of cracked leather when it was time for her to go.

"Tell the truth, the idea's not setting easy with him."

She thought about that. "You're just making that up so I'll feel better."

"No, honest, Squirt. I promise I'll never tell you a lie."

How could she stay mad when he made her feel so important. "Jeremy Lawsen, you better not. I don't set with being lied to. Or swearing either."

He laughed. "Long as the cotton's growing, I promise."

She'd made him laugh again—and this time there was no pity. "It's okay if you call me Squirt. Or Katydid—'cept I still don't know what that means."

"A Katydid is back-home slang for a young soldier. Sort of fits you."

She wanted to smile. Instead, she pointed straight ahead. "Look, on over there. There's the Imus cemetery. That's where Nettie's brother and sister are buried."

He gave her a hard look. "You know, Ginny, not everyone dies young."

"I know." She wished she sounded more convincing.

Chapter Eighteen

Sarah Imus had a pie baking in her oven and a pot of coffee ready. Her handshake was firm and her relief obvious. At the end of an hour, Jeremy and the Imuses had come to an arrangement, while Ginny played with Nettie and John in the corner and pretended not to be listening.

Jeremy consulted his pocket watch and set his empty cup aside before he stood to make his farewells. Ginny eyed him cautiously, but he reminded himself that he was doing the right thing.

"We'll keep Ginny 'til you get back. Don't you worry none, Mr. Lawsen. And no talk of silver changing hands. We're neighbors here about." Sarah Imus smiled. "Feels good to have another girl around. She'll be welcome company for mine."

"I appreciate that, ma'am. You can expect me back inside of three days."

"Where's the father in all of this?" Missus Imus's sniff of disapproval was redundant.

"I'm not altogether certain, ma'am. San Miguel, I presume. I've been given that accounting of his whereabouts at any rate."

William Imus shot a look at his wife. "Might look for him over to the mud springs." He glanced over at the children. "Might be soaking off his drunk before he starts home." He lowered his voice even further. "Or picking up another supply of that gol-dang opium he's married to."

"William!"

***

Jeremy rode west through el Paso de Robles Rancho, glad that the Salinas River was running low enough he could get around the quicksand. A week earlier, he'd ridden the train south from San Francisco, listening while Mr. Drury James regaled the passengers with the benefits of his mud baths. James and his brother-in-law, Daniel Blackburn, had developed mineral baths from the sulfur springs on their rancho. Now they had a hotel, and the therapeutic mud was available to all takers for a modest fee.

"Nature's wonder for rheumatism," James had boomed over the clack of the rails; "soothes, cures and prevents a worsening of the course of most joint and nerve ailments." Jeremy had dismissed the prattle as that of a well-rehearsed snake oil salesman, but James didn't have the look of an opportunist. The man had continued; "The waters have wrought cures for cutaneous disorders of every ilk, spasms, even syphilis."

James invited everyone on the train to hop a stage for an easy ride down to Paso Robles so they could experience the therapeutic waters for themselves. Somewhere north of Hollister, he'd invited Jeremy to join him for a soak and a libation, and by then Jeremy figured he'd earned both. James described how fortune had favored him. On one of his cattle drives to supply the Argonauts with Los Angeles-bred longhorn beef, he discovered the vast valley of the oaks. He bought the La Panza Rancho for himself then managed to marry into local society, one of the Dunn girls from San Luis Obispo. Eventually, he purchased a half-partnership in the mud springs.

He confided that his nephews, Frank and Jesse—quiet, respectful boys who liked his wife's cooking—spent time at his La Panza Ranch. He was as shocked as everyone else when he learned that their visit was a respite between their robbing the Russellville bank in Kentucky and the Gallatin bank in Missouri.

***

At close range it seemed that James was on to something. A neat redwood building rested in a copse of huge live oaks that provided shade for an inviting sward of lawn. The noonday sun painted shadows on the grass under the sprawling oaks and the Salinas River flowed between wide banks edged with willows. The grounds were a fresh oasis in the middle of a breathtaking rancho, even though the air wafted with the unmistakable odor of eggs gone bad in a broody hen's nest.

The sign read: *Men's day—Tuesday, Thursday, and Saturday.* He was in luck. It was Tuesday.

While he paid, a carriage pulled up on a well-worn track from the south and the driver discharged a trio of older men on crutches and canes. Behind them, an attendant pushed a foreign-looking gentleman in a wheeled chair while they conversed in German.

"This is your first time?" A fellow aficionado waiting his turn engaged him in conversation.

Jeremy laughed. "Do I appear that frazzled, sir?"

"Can't speak to that, but you've come to the right place. This is indeed nature's curative for skin conditions and nerve ailments."

"I will require a room for the night."

"The hotel facilities and the clinic are two and a half miles to the south, in El Paso de Robles."

"May I anticipate finding Drury James there?"

"If you've a fondness for elegance. He and his brothers-in-law have their mansions just up the street. You can't miss them."

An attendant interrupted to guide him to a vacant bathing room. With a glass of decent Chardonnay, a good cigar and a measure of privacy, Jeremy submerged himself to his neck in a two-by-eight bathing tub filled with black mud. Thirty minutes later, the attendant reappeared to lead him to a raised platform where he rinsed off the mud. Jeremy declined the offer of a blanket. He wasn't one of the rheumatics suffering the afternoon sun in a full-body sweat. What he suffered from was a nerve ailment named Virginia Nugent—and whether the mud worked or not, he was already benefiting from the advantages of rest and inhibition. The balmy air caressed his skin. By the time he donned his fresh shirt, he was invigorated.

***

San Miguel was no sort of town, more a long row of adobe rooms standing at a right angle to a barn of a church that towered over the landscape. On his ride from the hotel, he had passed broken sheep runs and burned-out vineyards, remains of the mission. Next to them stood an empty field that probably once supported the mission garden and orchards, but now grew only dust. A bit removed from the church, a long row of adobe cells must have housed the baptized Indians, back in the day. The road leading past was devoid of life, save for an Indian boy and his rangy rooster. Farther along the wagon track, the Caledonia stage stop had a single horse tied outside twitching at flies.

Jeremy turned his horse toward the church. From close-up the adobe walls seemed solid, especially on the windowless north side of the church, but when he rode closer he could see that the whitewash had peeled away, leaving patches of straw and mud open to the elements. Still, the church was in better condition than some he'd seen in the northern towns. Lacking intervention, in another fifty years some of the mud buildings would melt back into the earth.

He rode slowly past, feeling dwarfed by the red-tiled mission. From the look of it, thieves and opportunists had hauled off everything they could, and what remained was dead from drought or bugs, including the fruit trees and the vineyards. The massive front doors were locked but still intact, although he had heard of other missions where the doors were pillaged, hinges pried off and melted down for their scrap value. Some of the roof tiles were missing. The adobe fence surrounding the grounds looked to be part of a ghost town on a slow journey back to the earth. "A damned Yankee shame," he muttered. The whole scene reminded him of the carnage that Northern armies had wreaked on towns back home.

The adobe cemetery wall was still standing and the gate open. He dismounted and approached to where a few rotting wooden markers protruded from the cracked soil. He looked around, just in case someone might take objection. The owner of a ranch wagon parked along the south wall was carrying grain sacks into the church through a side door. Jeremy followed him inside. The church had been afforded a degree of respect. The paintings on the walls were intact, even the railing at the altar. At least it hadn't been used as a horse corral like some of the other missions.

He greeted the farmer and heard his voice echo in the timbered ceiling before he slipped out and followed a covered portico along the south side of the church. Farther up he heard the pinging of a blacksmith. Apparently that part of the mission was still in use, even if the covered veranda was sagging from rot and disrepair.

He led his horse to a lone, stunted olive tree and tied up to one of the branches. A huge cow fly buzzed his ear as he stepped into the shade where noisy laughter filtered from one of the rooms into the early morning air. He wondered how the padres would like knowing that their efforts supported a tavern.

Chapter Nineteen

Jeremy found Charlie Nugent right where Sancho said he'd be, in a dingy room, its sole window shuttered to keep out the light. A weary-looking Indian woman answered his rap. From behind her, a ragged voice called from the narrow bed, "Who the hell is that? Keep the door shut!" Jeremy was not without pity for a man with dissipation. He remained outside, fingering his hat while he waited to be invited in.

"You come back when Señor Nugent feel better," the woman whispered. She was nervous, maybe owing to the fresh bruise on her cheek. Whatever her reason, she made a half-hearted attempt to close the door, but he had his boot firmly wedged and she released her hold. With a swipe of her hand she motioned for him to be silent.

"What the hell?" The man inside made a weak effort to rise from his bed before he gave up and lay back.

Jeremy filled the doorframe, blocking out the morning sun. "Morning, Mr. Nugent."

Nugent threw the damp cloth covering his forehead across the room and managed to sit up. He squinted toward the light, forcing his eyes open. In his hand, a fresh water pipe steamed its opiate toward the ceiling. "Do I know you?"

Jeremy shifted so that the light hit Nugent full in the face. "Not that I recollect, sir. No reason you should."

Nugent was inching his fingers along the bed toward a knife lying nearby on a wooden stool. "In that case, why don't you come back tomorrow and we'll meet proper-like." His question was more of a command.

"By tomorrow we'll both be gone from these premises, and you know it." Jeremy gave the door a shove and slipped in. He pushed past the woman trying to hide Nugent's pistol and holster behind her dirty skirt, and grabbed it in mid-air as she tossed it toward the bed. "This won't be necessary." He returned it to the holster, dropped both onto the brick floor and kicked the stool over on its side. In a half-dozen steps he reached the window and pushed the wooden shutter hard enough to send it cracking against the wall.

With sunrise flooding through the window, Jeremy had the advantage. He heard cursing from the direction of the bed, turned and saw Nugent cringing from the sudden intrusion of light. He ignored the man's confusion. Nothing he could do would tally the score between the father and his daughter, but Patrón's misery was sweet consolation.

Nugent was sitting up, struggling to pull on his pants. "Reckon I've lived this long without making your acquaintance, Stranger. What's the hurry?"

Jeremy smiled. "No need for ill tempers, Mr. Nugent. I'll be gone as soon as I finish what I came to do." He righted the stool and straddled it while the man groped under the bed for his boots.

Nugent straightened, holding a boot in his hand and Jeremy caught a good look at what ten years of dissipation had done. Charlie Nugent's face was blotchy and swollen with a couple of bloodshot eyes buried deep in his puffy, jaundiced skin. His untrimmed beard was tangled and filthy, and by the look of things, the man had no intention of rectifying the situation. Jeremy recalled the bed linens he'd used for the past two nights and felt his body crawling. Thank God, he'd managed to find the sulphur springs.

Nugent needed more than a bath and a change of clothes. Try as he might, Jeremy couldn't see what had attracted Caroline Foster. Nothing about him fit any standard she'd been reared to. On the other hand, even his own mother admitted the man had been handsome, She'd confessed that she could see why Caroline had left the country with her new bridegroom.

"So what's this all about?" Nugent growled. "Say your piece then get out."

"Name's Jeremy Lawsen. I hail from Virginia." He noticed that his words made the man sit up a little straighter. "Missus Foster has some concerns about her granddaughter."

"She can go straight to hell."

Jeremy shifted, hoping to gain a diversion. "Sorry you feel that way."

"Thought she'd given up her letter writing by now. Don't intend to read anything she sends. Burn the letters, unopened. You can tell her that for me."

"Expect I won't have to." Jeremy's calmness served as a warning.

The man's eyes narrowed as though he suspected he was in trouble. He parried in an effort to discover how deep. "Have you seen the girl yet?"

"I've been out there, waiting for you. Came to hash out a solution—" Jeremy tried to make it sound like he hadn't found one on his own.

"Well, now, that's a comfort!" Nugent's voice was edgy, his sarcasm thick enough to slice. He half turned toward the bed like he couldn't decide whether to stand or sit, and sank back into the straw mattress.

"—for your wife Caroline's sake."

Nugent bolted to his feet. "Don't you use her name. Ever!" His spittle sprayed the air between them. "Who are you?" he demanded.

Jeremy experienced a moment of trepidation. This wasn't going to be easy. Maybe he'd be better off conducting business outside. *Too late now.* "My mother was in your wedding. Claudia Lawsen, you might recall. She and your wife corresponded until her passing. Missus Foster is a friend. She asked me to look in on you. She's heard things regarding her granddaughter."

"So you came by to see for yourself."

"I wrote you that I was coming. Sorry to report, but in my estimation the reports aren't without merit." Jeremy brushed at a fly on his sleeve. "You may not need my help, sir, but your daughter does."

Nugent advanced to within inches of Jeremy's face. "You saw enough in two days that you're an expert?"

"I know what other girls have. Dresses, manners, friends their own age. Reading and writing. Does she have those things, Mr. Nugent?"

Nugent stalked toward the door. "She's young yet. There's time." He glanced at the sheaf of documents Jeremy was drawing from his coat.

Jeremy felt the man's confidence waver. "Well then, we're in agreement. Fortunately, I carry the means to help in that regard."

"Who the hell cares about us?" Nugent snarled.

"More people than you think. Your neighbors hold a great deal of good will toward the late Missus Nugent. They knew Ginny as a baby." Jeremy paused to give the man a chance to adjust his thinking.

"Who?" Nugent nodded toward the Indian woman who was clutching at her dirty, torn shift. "Only Concepción here. And that's because I throw her a little gratitude. Coffee and beans, right, honey?" The woman lowered her eyes and turned away. "She claims to be Mexican. They all do. I go along with it. There's some folks around here would kill her just for being Injun. But she passes just fine. They're all the same in the dark, anyhow." Nugent must have realized that it wasn't in his best interest to have her overhearing everything that was being said. "Woman—get me something to eat. Something besides those damned beans. And saddle my horse."

Jeremy waited in silence, unwilling to tip the scales of this domestic tranquility. Given reason, Nugent might well turn his venom on the woman.

When she slipped from the room, Nugent staggered unsteadily to the window and stood staring out at the empty street. In a low voice he asked, "What do those people want from me? The Fosters, I mean? I don't give a

damn about the folks around here. They've done nothing but gossip since—
"

"Is that why you kept your daughter away from them?"

"She doesn't need to hear from anyone's mouth what a rotten varmint I've become. My wife wouldn't even know me, I've sunk that low. Now you want my girl to hear it from them? Or maybe you have plans to take her back with you? Hope she forgets all about me?"

"Have you asked her what she wants?"

"She's just a little girl!"

"You even know how old she is?"

"Damn you."

Nugent's flush was a tell-tale giveaway that he did. Every year that passed separated him more from his wife. He wanted time to move backwards, not forwards. Jeremy began to understand—Ginny wasn't the only victim here. He began speaking. "Begging your pardon, but she's not a little girl anymore. She doesn't need saving from other folks. It's you giving her the pain. She was with her mama when she died. She thinks she caused it."

Silence fell in the room. Only the buzzing of a fly in the windowsill broke the stillness. Finally the father roared, "That's inaccurate, sir!"

"You ever tell her?"

Nugent's voice lost its thunder. "The cook takes charge of her."

"The cook's worn out. She's got more than enough to do without taking on a youngster."

"Look, why don't you ride on out of here. Tell the old lady the kid's doing just fine. She'll believe anything you say."

"Your daughter has no mother, and, thanks to you she doesn't have a father, either. I've seen slaves back home treated better." Jeremy tried to control his anger, to no avail. "You stand there and say you don't know? That's because you never let go of your own suffering long enough to notice hers!" He hadn't meant to raise his voice, but Nugent was standing in front of him looking like he wanted to take a swing.

"You can go to hell," Nugent repeated.

"Looks like you're already there."

Charlie Nugent didn't flinch. But neither did he have the courage to look up. When he spoke, it was in a whisper. "I come into town and have a whisky and a pipe of this damn *madak* that's got a monkey hold on me. I intend to take myself on home, but there's nothing there to hold me, so I have another. I keep trying to find some feeling for that woman, just left. But hell, I have another bottle. You think I don't know which day Ginny was born? I wish to God you were right." He slumped down on the bed, drained. But he was sober.

"That's why you're here. Today's her birthday."

Nugent cradled his head in his hands without speaking, but his silence confirmed Jeremy's suspicion.

"Your daughter thinks birthdays are something the Imuses invented."

Nugent raised his head, his bluster spent. He indicated the sheaf of legal papers with a tilt of his head. "You aim to take her away?"

Jeremy heard the desperation in his voice. "Depends. I'll tell you what I have in mind. Sancho tried to talk me out of the idea—"

"Sancho Roos?"

"He says Ginny's kin to a coyote. He's probably right. Missus Foster's old. She can't supervise the upbringing of a young girl. Believe it or not, she has some regard for the man her daughter married." Maybe that was stretching things, but a bit of flattery couldn't hurt.

Hostility shifted into trepidation; Jeremy watched the two emotions warring in Nugent's face as he stood waiting to see how much fight the man had left in him. Every creature had its breaking point. Apparently Ginny's father had reached his.

Jeremy watched the hostility drain from Nugent's face. "What's your plan?" the man asked.

"It's time she starts looking like a girl. For starters, she needs some dresses."

"You mean she's here?" Nugent looked around, frantically hoping he had not overlooked her in some dark corner.

"She's staying with friends."

"What friends?" Nugent's expression was wary. "Gossip mongers, more likely."

"She's at the Imus place. They're sending their daughter over to the coast to school next term. Missus Imus suggested it. There exists the possibility that Ginny could accompany her."

Nugent's bluster dissolved into a slight trembling of his jowls. "I won't be beholden!"

Jeremy waited. "No need, sir. Missus Foster will assume the costs to the limit of her funds. She'll have the money come directly to a bank. They'll hold it in trust to buy books, clothing and whatever else she needs."

"The old lady come out of the War with anything?"

Jeremy shook his head. "She's hanging on by a thread. Sold off to a northern banker with a guarantee of life estate. She can stay on the place till she dies. Figures she'll use her money for a good cause and Ginny's all she has left."

He waited while Charlie Nugent slumped back on the mattress and turned to face the wall. Remorseful or not, the man's pride was the wild card. Finally Nugent looked up. "What if I don't agree?"

Jeremy kept his tone cautious. "Missus Foster took your obstinacy into account. She authorized me to represent her interests. I am named as co-guardian to oversee Ginny's future."

Nugent seemed to be calculating whether the words were a bluff.

Jeremy continued. "I'm sure you grasp my meaning. We can do this one time and you share the reins, or we can have this conversation every time she needs a new hair ribbon. Understand?"

Nugent nodded, his eyes on the papers in Jeremy's hand.

"I'll give you until the sun goes down to decide."

Apparently Nugent didn't need more time. "Who controls the money?"

"As I indicated, it would be deposited to a bank in San Francisco. They would keep the funds in her account. The banker would sign the drafts." He tucked the papers back in his vest. "Keep in mind, unless I report back that you're in no condition to handle the decisions, Missus Foster will be unaware of any problem. Do we understand each other?"

Nugent met his gaze without blinking. "Yes."

"Good. Let's keep our agreement between gentlemen. I'm sure you intend to set things right with your daughter."

Nugent nodded hesitantly. "She'll come home? Summers and holidays?" Sounded as though, now that he was losing her to town, he could think of all sorts of ways to make things better at home.

"That would depend, sir. She may discover that other girls celebrate regular Christmas and birthdays. She may decide to stay in town. Wouldn't blame her."

"How she getting to Santa Cruz?"

"As her legal guardian, I intend to escort her. Along with the other young lady. I have business to attend to in San Luis Obispo. We'll ride the Coast Line Stage down to that village and provision there, board the narrow gauge railroad to Port Harford and ship out on the steamer. Once there, I'll secure her position at the school. Might take a few days, but rest assured, I won't leave until I know she's safe."

"When?"

"Best we leave this week."

"This week?"

The hard part was done. Jeremy took a final risk. "Sancho took the liberty of giving your daughter a horse and a saddle. In your name." He forestalled Nugent's objection. "You might take this opportunity to bestow the gift yourself, seeing it's her birthday." Nugent turned to study something out the window. It didn't take much imagination to understand the direction of his thoughts. "Mr. Nugent, I want this made clear. I don't give a dried apple what you do with your own life . . . " Jeremy glanced at the pipe, "however, if you ever use that stuff again while she's in your home, I'll kill you. Understand?"

"Arumph!" Nugent cleared his throat without shifting his gaze. He nodded without speaking, and pocketed the pipe.

Jeremy softened his tone. "Nugent, there's been enough hostility in our lifetimes. We don't have to be enemies over this. It would help with the gossip if Missus Imus saw us ride back together. What say, sir?"

Charlie Nugent spit at the brick floor and slowly straightened. "Give me a few minutes. Ginny's never seen me this way."

"That's where you're wrong, my friend," Jeremy muttered as he closed the door behind him.

***

Sarah Imus gave a surprised call-out when Charlie Nugent rode up a dozen paces ahead of Jeremy. "Looks like you found each other."

Ginny hid behind one of the porch posts and gawked at her father, clean-shaven and dressed in a new red plaid shirt with his bandana freshly rinsed. She looked from her father, to Jeremy, to the leather notebook in Jeremy's hand.

Finally, Nugent spoke. "Missus Imus, my daughter will be taking her schooling in Santa Cruz this term."

Ginny's anger was directed at Jeremy. "You talked him into it. It's no fair!"

Her father answered, "Ginny, it's time. Ranch will be here when you get back."

"What about Caroline? What about my horse?" she demanded. Jeremy watched as she tried to control the sheen glistening in her eyes. To her credit, she stood ramrod straight with her chin steady.

No one spoke for the space of a dozen breaths. When her father shook off his shock, his voice sounded strangled. "The horse and the saddle are yours. Just be careful."

Ginny's eyes widened. She looked behind her to where the mare was grazing on a patch of grass. Emboldened by the newfound attention, she turned back to her father. "Can I take Mama's tintype?"

Her father flushed, glanced over at Sarah Imus and nodded.

"And Mama's yellow bonnet?"

He blanched and nodded again.

Ginny looked pleased with herself. She wiped her hands on her trousers and turned to Jeremy. "Expect I'll go. Since Nettie's going, too."

Chapter Twenty

The ride down the Santa Lucia mountain range was steeper than Jeremy expected, the shriek of metal on metal from the steel brakes of the stage assaulting his ears until he thought his head would split. Judging by their giggles, the girls enjoyed being flung from side to side, partially the result of leather traces on the undercarriage, partially the fault of wheels caught in the dried grooves left over from the rainy season.

"This is better'n anything, Ginny. I'll bet my brother wishes he was here."

"Sure glad he's not!"

"Ginny Nugent, you're sweet on my brother. You want to marry him."

"Do not!"

"John and Virginia are love birds," Nettie sang.

"Stop lying. Take that back! Jeremy, make her stop telling fibs."

"Stop carrying on, ladies. These gentle passengers might take you for bandits." Jeremy hid his smile behind his palm. He'd used the excuse that he had business in the town, but the truth was he wanted to witness for himself the Central Coast that he'd heard described on the stage ride from San Francisco.

The stage descended the grade while he fought to stay upright in a rocking stage that seemed to defy gravity. He couldn't blame the driver; the man and his guard were probably keeping their eyes out for bandits in the tree cover. There were hidden arroyos and low-hanging oaks enough for a small army to hide in on this steep grade. No wonder the *cuesta* of the Santa Lucia range was famous for its holdups.

His muscles relaxed when the driver eased his grip on the reins and the stage shifted into a long, swinging rhythm that indicated a slow, easy decline. At Fremont's Camp, a fellow passenger pointed out a small structure where Captain Fremont had camped on his way south to Santa Barbara some years earlier.

The landscape gradually widened to reveal afternoon shadows and a long, curving canyon where cattle terraces ran along the golden side-hills like miniature topographical lines. Twice he noticed straight-line boundaries of piled rocks running from the base to the crown of the hills, each one edged with stunted cactus. Drury James had told him to be on the lookout for the cacti and rock fences built by Indians to keep the mission cattle safe and out of the gardens. Not too many grizzlies left now, he claimed. According to him, most ranchers planned on losing a few head to the *osos*. Gave them something to brag about.

A hostler waited at a stage stop at the base of the grade, holding a fresh team of horses that were stomping in eagerness. The changeover was made before the girls could finish their nature break and the driver shouted for them to hurry. They scarcely settled into their seats before the horses set off at a run.

El Pueblo de San Luis Obispo lived up to its name as a sleepy Mexican village. Jeremy craned his head out the small side window when the first of several shacks appeared, their white adobe walls abloom with geraniums and hollyhocks thick with dust. At the outskirts, snarling dogs gave chase to dust blowing off the wheels. Jeremy winced when one leapt too close, earning a haphazard kick from a Mexican man weaving his way across the road with an unsteady gait. The man barely missed the luggage boot. The dog yelped, and Ginny turned an agitated scowl on Jeremy. Fortunately, the dog limped off before the man could do any more damage.

At a bend in the road, gnarled pepper trees formed a boundary of sorts around a compound of shacks. A handful of horses twitched at flies from the railing where they were tied. Inside, the sound of male laughter was punctuated with the sound of a gunshot, a woman's shriek and more laughter. When a second gunshot rang out, Jeremy reacted. He had the girls pressed flat against their seats with their heads tucked into their skirts by the time a third shot rang out.

A scattering of adobe houses formed a town square that marked the heart of the village. Clearly someone had a plan for the pueblo's future. Some of the houses were one-room shacks, their dried adobe walls dwarfed by giant prickly pear cacti bursting with spiny red apples ready for picking. Beyond, wandering pigs shared stinking refuge piles with scrawny hens and scratching roosters. A brood of barefoot children joined the mongrel dogs running behind the stage.

The surrounding valley was shaped like a saucer, with a number of brush-covered peaks peppering the route toward the west. He closed his eyes and inhaled the scent of salt air. Vineyards and orchards of olives and figs seemed to be thriving in the rich dark loam spewed up by the spent volcanoes that lined the valley. According to the stage driver, the last peak fell off into the ocean.

His first stop in San Luis Obispo, as the Americans called the town, was at Young's Mercantile on Higuera Street. Clearly he was in luck. The Yankee woman behind the counter possessed a remarkable degree of sensibility when faced with a slightly disheveled bachelor and two young girls.

"Ma'am, my mother has performed this ritual a hundred times. But I've never—"

"I understand, completely, sir. I'm Missus Young, the owner's wife." With a deft flap of her wrist, she hung a handsome gray blanket across the entrance to a storage room. "We don't have much in the way of ready-made clothing for a girl her size," she explained, "although we have yard goods aplenty."

Jeremy shook his head. "No time, ma'am. We'll be grateful for such ready-made as you have. She needs outfitting from head to toe."

Missus Young appraised Ginny and prodded her into the makeshift dressing room. Out of both girls' hearing she whispered, "We keep a burn barrel outside. I'll see her clothing gets a fit burial." After she managed to extract the last piece of apparel from Ginny's grip, she swept the vaquero's clothing into a bundle and set it near the door.

Jeremy fidgeted with his timepiece and feigned interest in a row of skinning knives, but apparently he wasn't as successful as he hoped. Two Californian women entered, dressed in full skirts and white tunics, with lacy black mantillas draped over their tight chignons. Their eyes darted from the tittering of excited young girls and back to him.

Behind the blanket, Ginny was trying to figure out how to fit herself into a dress. From the sounds of giggling and whispering, Nettie must be showing her how to fit a petticoat under all those ruffles. The process was so removed from his experience that he felt his neck growing hot.

"Missus Young?" He managed to pull the proprietress aside as she was leaving the blanketed enclosure with an armload of delicates. "I have another errand, ma'am. Perhaps I could return in, say, half an hour?"

"Splendid, Mister Lawsen. Do not concern yourself with your ward. We shall get along famously. We'll expect you back in thirty minutes."

Covering his retreat with a quick, nervous cough, Jeremy headed toward the door and into the dust of Higuera Street. Outside, he checked a sheet of paper on which Drury James had penned a neat, handwritten note. Following James's instructions he headed north. His impression from the street was even less favorable than it had been on the stage, a sleepy village with cantinas and dark-looking Mexican men lounging in the shadows. From inside one shack, a woman's shriek was cut short by a man's laugh while a couple of dark-eyed, slovenly women stared dully from an upstairs window. One of them made a half-hearted attempt to rouse herself, but even from a distance he could see the fire was gone from her eyes. Several horses stood at a railing, swishing their tails while they dozed. Apparently business was brisk inside.

He filled his lungs and started up a slight incline that ran alongside the massive red-roofed church. From Monterey Street, the long building shaded an adobe hotel on the other side of the narrow track. At that moment a handful of Indian women wearing black mantillas emerged from the church, followed by a friar in a long gray robe.

Looking up the street to the corner of Palm Street, he noticed a brick building with imposing steel shutters announcing a wash house with the proprietor's name, Ah Lui, painted on a board above the door. An enterprising Chinese man was bent over, pulling steaming laundry from a boiling tub with a long-handled stick. The action brought Jeremy up short, a reminder that he'd lived in his own clothing enough days to know that he threatened to offend. The Chinese curried a reputation for being fine launderers, working round the clock if necessary. After he settled things at the Mercantile he'd circle back with a bundle of his own.

Monterey Street was more like a corral than a thoroughfare. He picked his way around piles of horse manure mixed with dust and urine, both human and animal, past a row of saloons and a barbershop. The hotel next door threatened to be a firetrap when one of the crafty-eyed loafers lounging outside emptied his smoldering cob pipe into the sawdust. He wouldn't want to be sleeping inside when a drunk stumbled to bed and tipped over a lamp. It was no sort of place for boarding two young girls. In truth, it fit the picture James had described; a hideout for highwaymen and petty thieves.

Despite the fact that the driver had managed to bring the stage in without innocent, Jeremy was in a thieves' den. He felt eyes watching him from the saloon fronts, probably waiting to pluck him after the sun went down. He started back toward the imposing mission and decided the town couldn't be all bad if it had a church. The sign in front of its sturdy doors read "San Luis Obispo de Tolosa." The Catholic missions he'd seen had all been built on rises above creeks, and this one was no exception. Shaped in the same rectangle as the one in San Miguel, this one seemed to be in better condition. At least the portico wasn't in danger of rotting through. The property to the rear showed signs of construction, no doubt owing to the fact that the parish now had a priest in residence.

He noticed tracks for a narrow gauge rail line. He'd promised Missus Imus he'd get Ginny and Nettie to Port Harford in time to catch the steamship to Santa Cruz. Problem was that Big Sol, the stage driver, had cheerfully assured him that he'd missed the last departure. Jeremy had a whole day to keep a couple of young ladies from seeing sights that would offend their sensitivities—and himself from having his pockets cleaned. Since the steamship wasn't due to leave until the following day, he had little choice but to take James up on his offer.

He crossed Monterey Street and strode past the Casa Grande, a large adobe that looked to be the courthouse. Farther up, he saw a house on a large, almost city-block parcel of land at the corner of Santa Rosa Street matching Drury James's description. James had given him a letter of introduction to his wife's parents, along with a personal assurance that Louisa James's mother could handle a couple of young females. After all, she'd raised a brood of her own.

The door inched open at the second knock and Jeremy found himself face-to-face with a pleasant looking woman in her late forties. She wore her hair in a simple upswept hairdo that lent softness to her features.

"Missus Dunn?"

"Yes." She waited as he removed his hat. He wasn't sure how one came begging a favor of this sort, so he started from the beginning; "Ma'am, I'm an acquaintance of your son-in-law."

The woman hesitated. "If you're a reporter looking for a story about those James nephews of his, I'm afraid you'll have to talk to him. I have nothing to say about those bank robbers."

He stood before the wavering door, frantically patting his pockets before she shut the door in his face. A moment later he located the letter, handed it to her and waited as she read. Mercifully, she opened the door wider and smiled. He quickly explained the circumstances of his travel.

Her eyes lit up with enthusiasm. "Oh, my, yes. I'd be delighted to board your young ladies for the night. Yourself as well. Don't give it another thought. That hotel is overrun with prevaricators, hard-drinking ruffians and ladies of the night. You're right about my daughters. Mary Louisa and Cecelia would have fits if they heard those little girls had to spend the night downtown. I'm simply delighted."

In the space of ten minutes, Missus Dunn had secured her husband's agreement and directed Jeremy to return straightaway with the girls.

Back at Young's Mercantile, he fished a leather pouch filled with silver from his pocket and began counting. On his way to the counter he stepped

115

around a young female shopper. "Excuse me, miss, I'm looking for—" He broke off as he recognized the girl standing before him in a mid-length, blue and white striped dress and new calfskin boots. "I'm looking for a tomboy about yeah tall," he teased.

"Jeremy!"

"Mr. Lawsen," Nettie protested with a giggle.

The proprietress had accomplished a miracle. Ginny wore a flat-brimmed straw bonnet that shaded her fair skin and hid her shortened locks. Her dress was neither fussy nor too plain. It also happened to be the only ready-made girls dress in the store, but Missus Young had found a skirt in her wardrobe that one of her daughters had outgrown, and a pair of neat white shirtwaist from her store inventory, both of which needed only hemming, which she promised to complete before her young customer left for the Coast. She had secured a woolen cape that would keep a young lady sheltered from the elements.

She indicated a brown paper bundle on the counter that contained a few unmentionables and a nightgown. "I took the liberty of including a carpetbag. She tells me she'll be traveling some distance."

Relief roiled over him like smoke. The total was fair, all things considered. Twelve dollars and fifty-seven cents. He didn't bother telling her that he would gladly have paid double for the opportunity to see Ginny outfitted like a young lady. He counted out Missus Foster's gift money, and on a whim, added a pair of blue ribbons and a pair of gloves from his own pocket.

As he paid the bill, he leaned close enough to whisper, "Ma'am, I'd have you to understand our situation. My young cousin here deserves to have her fresh start without undue gossip, wouldn't you agree?"

Missus Young's face reddened, and she nodded vigorously.

"Miss Virginia's going to be an upstanding member of the county some day, and we don't want her starting out on any wrong foot, do we?" He mustered the charm that he used on the ladies back home, a smile that deepened the dimple in his cheek, laying on an extra dose of Southern accent. "Ah wouldn't be wrong in thinking you'll keep this li'l transaction among ourselves, would ah, ma'am?" He waited for her fervent nod before he smiled again.

The woman pursed her lips. "You are fortunate indeed that you came to me, sir. There's no end of women who would love to have this tidbit to spread around."

Jeremy nodded. "Exactly my point, ma'am!" He smiled. "Ah can accept your personal word that no mention of this gets out to those gossips?"

The woman glowed with pleasure. "Oh, you have my word, Mr. Lawsen."

She was gathering the loose strands of her chignon when he started toward the door with his young ladies. In mute defiance, Ginny snatched up the shirt and trousers she had worn and tucked the bundle under her arm. Nettie followed a few paces behind, sniggering behind her hand.

"I look like a fool. This dress chaffs my neck. Patrón's like to turn wrathy, he finds out what we've done." Ginny looked to see if Jeremy was going to rise to her bait.

Jeremy waited until they had cleared the store before he said, "An excellent plan, Miss Virginia. You may need those duds for the spring round-up."

Ginny rewarded him with a grin. He tucked her arm securely in his, chatting until he felt her relax. If she were going to make it at school, she would need to accept the touch of another human being without wincing.

Chapter Twenty-One

While the three of them waited for the door to be answered, Ginny stuck out her right foot to study her boots. They smelled like Miguelito's new saddle. Sweet with the scent of calf hide, they were the prettiest things she'd ever seen, but they were as stiff and uncomfortable as a new-made saddle. She couldn't wait for bedtime so she could pull them off. Her new boots were sized to last for another year or two. Already a blister was forming where her heel slipped against the leather.

"How can a boot pinch my toes and slip off my heel at the same time? I'd a sight sooner gone barefoot," she griped to Nettie in a whisper she hoped would carry to Jeremy. She smoothed the wrinkles in her new dress and peered down at her hem. Something Nettie called a ruffle teased the top of her stiff boots. She swished the edges and laughed. "I doubt ruffles'll come in handy when I need to win a fair race." Her new underthings scratched. She'd never thought about folks wearing garments made special for their private parts. She wondered if Sancho had one. "Guess what, Jeremy? I have a drawstring around my bloomers like Missus Wickers at the barn dance."

"Ginny . . . ." Jeremy warned, but he was too late.

"Why this must be Virginia. And Nettie. Don't you both look lovely."

A strange lady stood smiling at them as though girls in dresses were no special thing. The lady, Missus Dunn, invited them in for tea and freshly baked ginger cookies. Ginny felt the pressure of Jeremy's hand urging her inside. She took a seat on the edge of a red velvet settee and pushed herself back until she felt her backside touching the cushion. Her feet didn't reach the floor so she concentrated on keeping them still while Missus Dunn and Jeremy chatted. The sour odor of horse sweat reminded her that she was still holding her roll of dirty clothes. She looked around for a hiding place, but the room was too tidy, too cleared of spare boots and whiskey bottles to hide anything. Seeing no alternative, she slipped the roll underneath the settee and smoothed her skirt over her feet.

"How was your trip down the cuesta?" Missus Dunn asked Ginny.

"Steep as snot. We had to get out and walk a couple of places, but we managed. We started out at a place called the Asistencia on the Rancho Santa Margarita. That's Spanish for storing place. Right, Jeremy?" She waited for his approving nod before continuing. "It's the biggest barn I ever seen. We got to look inside." She glanced over at Nettie. "Nettie picked up one of the adobe bricks. The walls is sort of falling down from the earth shaking, I expect. Anyway, the owner, General Murphy, handed up his strongbox for the driver to carry on top of the stage. Seemed like a fool thing to do, with all the bandidos supposed to be waiting in the pass. Least that's what you said, didn't you, Jeremy?" Jeremy squirmed and rubbed the backside of his collar as if his neck was getting hot. Ginny continued. "General Murphy sent two of his men along to help shoot if anybody showed their heads. Good thing they didn't, or Jeremy would have shot one himself, wouldn't you Jeremy?"

"Maybe you girls would like some tea," Missus Dunn suggested.

When Missus Dunn poured, Ginny tried to grip her fancy cup like she saw Jeremy doing. Nettie was managing just fine, but Ginny felt her fingers slipping. With horror, she felt the cup shift and slowly slide off the saucer. Hot water ran down her ruffle. It splashed over her new boots and onto the flower-pattered rug. She didn't need Nettie's gasp to tell her what she already knew; shame crawled through her until she wanted to die. For the first time since the stage had rolled out she wished she was home in the summer house with Maria Inés. "Confoundit! I done spilled my Chinee tea." She clapped her hand over her mouth.

Across the room, Jeremy was scowling.

Missus Dunn poured a fresh cup as though nothing had happened. "The ladies of our town are engaged in an effort to bring the convent school back. It would be lovely if you could attend the mission school here, closer to your home."

"I ain't Catholic," Ginny said.

"No matter. Father Sastre has vigorously inaugurated a campaign for funds. He's counting on families to come together. Education is a benefit to all."

"Where do the girls go to school now?" Nettie asked.

"One or two of the señoritas take the Coast Stage down to Santa Barbara," Missus Dunn said. "But it's dangerous. Highwaymen hide in wait at the Gaviota Pass. It's terribly risky. Bad enough that our men have to brave it."

"I think I saw where you're planning to build that school, ma'am," Jeremy said.

"We've only just begun. The Catholic ladies are planning a number of socials. It will be a year or more before we can commence construction. Their nuns will come from Soledad," Missus Dunn said. "Perhaps you girls will be our first candidates."

Ginny scowled. She wasn't sure if Patrón abided Catholics, but Maria Inés was one and he abided her.

After they finished their tea, Missus Dunn showed Ginny and Nettie their room. She opened the wardrobe and gestured to an empty shelf. "You may place your things here." She smiled encouragingly at Ginny. "If you have anything that needs washing, I'll be pleased to attend to it after supper." Ginny nodded. She wasn't sure which was worse, being found out or having to tote the bundle clear to Santa Cruz stinking like a sour mare.

She tried to imagine her mother growing up in such a room with everything so stiff and grand. The furniture, the walls, even the floors were spotless. She wondered how many hours Missus Dunn spent sweeping and scrubbing. One thing for sure, the lady was more talkative than Maria Inés. Ginny thought her head would burst from all the new ideas that had come her way in one day. Jeremy said she chattered. She wondered if Sancho ever took her for a jaybird. Another thought trumped the first. She wondered if Sancho would miss her.

Back in the parlor again, Ginny thought she'd favor slipping between the cushions and never showing her head again when she heard Missus Dunn discuss the problem of her wardrobe with Jeremy. Seemed she wasn't satisfied with the two dresses Ginny now owned.

"Good Gophers. I ain't never had so fine in my whole life." Ginny whispered to Nettie.

Missus Dunn politely pretended she hadn't overheard. "Suppose I look in my trunks? I recall that one of my girls left a riding skirt behind. And possibly a shirtwaist that would be serviceable."

Ginny shot a glance at Nettie. Her mother had stitched her wardrobe up evenings after supper. It wasn't fancy; Nettie didn't own any store-bought dresses, but she didn't seem to mind. In fact she was sitting quietly in the corner, looking out the window at a passing buggy on the street. By the look on her face, she was already missing her family.

Ginny heard Jeremy agree. It seemed strange, two near-strangers making over her. Missus Dunn liked young ladies; that was for sure. She looked like she could burst out singing she was so happy to have company.

"Mr. Lawsen, why don't you walk over and summon Mr. Dunn for supper?"

Jeremy jumped up so quickly he almost tripped in his hurry to be out of the house. Truth to tell, she didn't blame him. She'd have gone, too, but nobody asked her. "You fixing to come back?" she asked.

He smiled like he thought she might be nervous, which she was *not*. "Don't worry Katydid. I don't intend to miss supper!" He started toward the door and hesitated. "I noticed a Chinee wash house, up town. I'll drop my things by. Pick them up tomorrow." He reached under the settee and picked up Ginny's bundle. "Will feel good to be wearing clean again." He opened the door and stepped outside, whistling to himself.

The parlor slowly aired itself of the musty odor.

Ginny wanted to curl up in a quiet corner and die, but if she did that she'd miss the train ride to the Coast, and besides, Missus Dunn was beaming like she was expecting some more parlor conversation. Ginny opened her mouth and gave it her best try.

"Hope Jeremy don't get lost. Me and Nettie'll have to head on out alone."

Missus Dunn smiled. "You'll enjoy learning grammar at your new school, Ginny. For instance, you may find you prefer saying *doesn't*, rather than *don't*. And '*Nettie and I*' has such a lovely sound, don't you agree?"

Missus Dunn said it in such a nice way that Ginny didn't think to be embarrassed. "I'll try to remember, ma'am."

Missus Dunn offered her another cookie. "Perhaps you'd like to pack a few of these along in case you get hungry on the steamship?" She wrapped a dozen cookies in a swatch of white paper, chatting as she tied it with string. Ginny imagined her mother doing the same thing. "Are you girls enjoying your journey so far?"

Ginny nodded and let Nettie take the package.

Jeremy arrived back with Mr. Dunn just before suppertime.

"That's an old trick the ranch hands use, ma'am," Ginny whispered to Missus Dunn, trying to hide her relief at seeing him. "They'll show up right at mealtime so's they can get fed." Missus Dunn's smile felt like the sun shining.

Ginny had helped set the table. Now she stood in her new frock, with her hair brushed. Jeremy winked and said he had to take a second look to be sure it wasn't Nettie, and his teasing made Nettie blush. Then Missus Dunn apologized for the humble fare—vegetable soup and sweet white rolls served along with a platter of roast beef and mashed potatoes.

Jeremy said, "Ma'am, if it tastes half as good as it smells, we have much to be thankful for."

Ginny hadn't expected they would pray over their food. Her arm was halfway raised to grab a roll when Mr. Dunn began. "Heavenly Father, we bless this food and the friendships made this night. We ask your blessings for a safe journey and a beneficial year to come." She couldn't help peeking at the platter through her eyelashes. Finally, they started the food around. When the platter came to her, she was careful not to spill anything, not even her glass of milk. At the head of the table, Mr. Dunn made polite conversation, asking Jeremy how he had enjoyed the stage ride.

"Fine, comfortable ride, sir." Jeremy answered. "But your town needs a railroad to connect Soledad with the Santa Barbara stub. I'm afraid until you get one, San Luis Obispo will lose out to some of the shipping towns up north like San Miguel. I've seen the same in a hundred towns stretched across the country. It's the railroad that opens a town to progress."

Mr. Dunn agreed. "The railroad is balking at punching a line through the Cuesta Pass."

Jeremy nodded. "Indeed. I heard in San Francisco, the Southern Pacific already runs a line through the inland valley."

"That's correct," Mr. Dunn said. Ginny watched him cut his beef and talk at the same time without acting like it was anything special. The vaqueros back home never gabbed while they ate, but Mr. Dunn was continuing. "From the Mexican border over the Tehachapi Mountains, right on up to San Francisco."

She couldn't follow all the names and places. She ate quietly and listened as Jeremy talked.

"The railroad's methods have worked so far. They're getting rich, and their backers are getting richer by buying up land ahead of the tracks. Where the land's already taken, the railroads cut their expenses by demanding the townspeople donate the right-of-way."

Mr. Dunn nodded. "Folks in San Luis Obispo haven't coffered up yet. Besides, they have more important things to concern themselves with. The vigilante committee is attempting to deal with the thieves that use this town to their advantage."

"Thieves here in the township?" Jeremy sounded surprised.

"We've a godforsaken mass of filth-mongers and thieves living among us. God only knows how we will rout them. The worst of all is a local businessman, name of Jack Powers. He hides behind a cover of respectability while others do his dirty work."

"Jack Powers? Can't say I've heard of him," Jeremy said.

Mr. Dunn's face slowly turned red, like he couldn't help himself once he got started. "The devil is here in this valley. First, he's in the lowlands. They say, if you look closely you'll see him peeking out from behind those giant ragged rocks on the way up the Pass."

Ginny heard herself gasp and quickly covered her mouth. Mr. Dunn turned toward her. He'd sounded for all the world like the Methodist minister that had come riding through the valley the year before. His eyes were strange, like he thought they could all see the image he was seeing in his head. Shaking himself, he pointed to a mountain in the distance.

"There's his finger, there's his head, those are his horns. At night he comes down lower and hides in the fog that envelops this valley. Later at night he comes still lower and invades souls and has his way with them. Just to live here and try to make a living invites the devil himself. This valley makes or breaks people. Some say it's the fog. Some say it's the wind. Some, the company we keep."

He looked so fierce, Ginny couldn't contain a shiver of fright. She reached under the tablecloth and took hold of her friend's hand. Nettie was some scared, too, because she clung tight and returned the squeeze.

"Man can't blame the devil altogether. But that's its range, and its rocks. It's set a foothold here. Cleaved into the earth of this valley. Here, the Lord God has a tough fight on his hands."

Missus Dunn tilted her head toward the girls. "Mr. Dunn, that's quite enough."

Mr. Dunn came to himself with a slight tremor, and Ginny exchanged glances with Nettie.

Outside, bells began to ring. Nettie looked as excited as Ginny felt. Missus Dunn smiled and suggested they open the door to hear better. "It's the Mission bells," she explained with a warning frown for her husband. "Everything is not as dour as it would seem. Apparently they're holding a service tonight."

Mr. Dunn nodded. "Hear the pattern? They're missing a bell. It was sent to another mission in need of one. Farther north, I believe. You know what the bells are saying?" Mr. Dunn began a sing-song recitation that matched the tones of the bells. "The beans is done, the beans is done. You best get in line before the beans is gone."

"Uh-uh. That ain't what they're saying! You're spoofing us." Ginny blurted before she could stop herself. She clamped her hand over her mouth and glanced at Jeremy.

Mr. Dunn smiled like he was used to smart-mouth girls.

"That's how the bell ringers learn the rhythm," he assured her.

Finally, the bells ended and the town was quiet again. From the west where the sun was setting, the devil's fog was creeping in.

"I'll fry up a chicken for you to take with you tomorrow. But I was caught a bit short of notice tonight." Missus Dunn was apologizing for her supper again.

Jeremy cast a warning eye on Ginny and said, "Wonderful food, Missus Dunn. You give the ladies of my acquaintance a run for their reputation. Are you sure you're not a Southern cook, ma'am?"

"More cobbler, Mr. Lawsen?" Missus Dunn was obviously partial to a man who liked her cooking.

"Best I ever et," Ginny said. There, she could give a compliment, too. Jeremy couldn't fault her for manners.

Supper took long enough that Ginny's eyes grew heavy. By the time her head landed on her crisp white pillowcase, she felt like it would burst it was so filled up with new ideas. Beside her, Nettie was already asleep, like sharing a bed was no big thing. For the first time Ginny considered what it must be like, having a sister to hug. It was surprising how good it felt. The best thing she'd learned all day was to keep still and watch what was going on around her.

"Mama, you'd be proud if you saw me right now. I'm some ways to being a lady. Goodnight, Mama."

Chapter Twenty-Two

Nothing could have prepared Ginny for the Pacific Ocean—dazzling blue water spread out flat as prairie grass and bigger than forever. One moment the narrow gauge train was rounding the last curve to Port Harford, the next, she was catching her first glimpse of shimmering blue glass.

"Nettie, it's like fields of lupines laid flat by a rainstorm."

Nettie laughed and clapped her hands together. "The water takes up the whole window. Look!"

At the water's edge, the steamship Eureka waited beside a long pier that ran further out into the water than seemed possible. The October sun shimmered in a band of silver so bright that a body had to squint to see. Ginny felt the blue water feeding her, like she'd been dying and now she was alive again. From now on all of her dreams were going to be the color of the sea.

Her mama could have seen this, too, if Ginny had gotten the eggs in time. Eggs made everyone healthy. She felt her tears spilling, but she didn't try to hide her face, even when Jeremy turned. She waited until her voice lost its quiver. "Did Mama ever see this?"

Jeremy considered. "I'm not sure about this one, but she spent summers at another ocean. At a place called North Carolina. You'll learn about that in school."

"Do I have to?"

"Yep."

She considered for a moment. "Did Mama like the North Carolina ocean?"

"The Atlantic. Indeed. My mama told me so. She said that when your mama knew she had gotten herself a baby, she wrote that she hoped her baby girl had eyes the color of the sea."

Ginny felt her insides twisting. "Don't suppose she got her wish."

Jeremy pulled her close like he was a doctor examining Sancho's rheumy eyes. "Yes, Miss Virginia. Same color as that water out there. Your mother knew it, too. I recollect she wrote my mother that she'd gotten her wish."

Ginny turned back to the water. It was the only thing big enough to hold the feelings welling inside her. She wasn't about to admit it out loud, but right now her skin was barely holding it all in. "That school's going to make me learn about the Atlantic Ocean on top of everything else!"

He didn't seem a bit perturbed. In fact, he acted like it was no big thing. "'Spect so, Squirt. You can relay your experiences at branding time."

"Reckon that'll be forever," she said, unsure why she was moody all of a sudden.

Jeremy sounded disappointed in her. "Time's what you make of it, I expect." He motioned to Nettie, who was on hands and knees trying to catch a sand crab. "Let's go board our conveyance, Miss Nettie." Ginny tagged along behind, feeling like an uninvited guest.

Port Harford bustled with a half-dozen shouting men loading produce from train cars to the Eureka while passengers embarked for the trip to San Francisco. At water's edge, the Marré Hotel stood elegantly beneath the rocky hillside while the afternoon sun blazed like a fire, reflecting in the wall of glass facing the sea.

"Golly, Nettie. Look at all them windows!"

Nettie was impressed, too, but Jeremy just smiled.

The train crept to a halt at the hotel and a fancy-dressed couple boarded for the short ride to the steamship. Far from shore, sea otters swam on their backs and pried abalone shells apart with their teeth. "They pull the meat out that way," Jeremy told them. He gave them the names of everything that she and Nettie pointed out, including the seagulls waiting at the edge of the pier for scraps.

The train inched its way to the end of the pier. When it finally ran out of track and stopped, she was gripping the edge of her seat, ready to jump through the open window, smoke cinders and all. Underneath, waves washed against the pier blocks then retreated with a sucking sound. She grabbed Jeremy's coat while her head spun topsy-turvy. Still, she found herself unable to keep from staring through the pier planks. "Jeremy! We're sure-fire goners. Don't look—I'm a gonna upchuck."

"No you're not, Virginia. Look over at the horizon. You'll be fine."

When she could straighten again she tried to avoid Jeremy's look of amusement. She was grateful when he ignored her and asked Nettie, "You doing alright?"

Nettie blushed and nodded. He pulled his hat down against the setting sun and started walking, leaving them to keep up. "Best get aboard," he warned. "Time to get our sea legs before supper."

"Don't reckon I'll take supper tonight," Ginny snapped. She wasn't

126

eating with anyone who poked fun at her.

"Suit yourself." He didn't seem a bit contrite.

"I'm starved," Nettie offered, ignoring Ginny's glare.

By the time the dinner gong sounded, Ginny was tired of feeling peevish. She and Nettie tagged along behind Jeremy and stood shyly beside chairs the waiter indicated. The waiter waited until they slid into their seats before he placed placards in front of them and stood quietly as though he expected something of them. Nettie studied the menu but Ginny froze, confused and humiliated by the lines of writing she couldn't decipher.

Jeremy gently plucked the placard from her and set it down. Nettie passed hers, likewise. "What do you recommend for two lovely ladies who are traveling the *Eureka* for the first time?" he asked.

"Turf or tail?" the waiter asked.

Ginny blanched. She remembered her manners and tried to edge closer so her whisper wouldn't carry to the two strangers at the next table. "We don't eat tails back home. Mostly, we make quirts out of 'em."

She missed the waiter's valiant attempt to hide his smile.

Jeremy snapped his menu down on the table and announced, "The ladies will have mashed potatoes and green beans. And ice cream for dessert."

Chapter Twenty-Three

Jeremy couldn't help overhear a meeting at the next table between two men in the cattle business, one of them named Miller. At the one man's use of the name, Jeremy inconspicuously turned to inspect the man's looks. The gentleman of his interest had a build that lent itself to corpulence, the look of a man who liked good living. Judging from the pandering manner of the bartender, Miller, the outspoken man with a German accent, was someone with influence.

The girls settled into their dinners. Jeremy sliced into a two-inch tenderloin and offered a strip to each girl, even as he kept a careful ear on the conversation. If luck was with him, the man would be Henry Miller, whose brand claimed the hides of a million cattle from the Mexican border up into Idaho.

His eavesdropping was thwarted by a young lady.

"Jeremy, you figure to eat all that meat in one sitting?"

He nodded without trying to encourage her. Finally, Miller finished his meal, stood and stretched like his muscles were cramped from unaccustomed sitting. He viewed his surroundings with marked impatience and stepped out into the darkness, a gleam of satisfaction illuminating his face.

Calculating the opportunity, Jeremy made a swift decision. On his way across the floor he made a whispered arrangement that left his two charges to finish their meal under the watchful eye of their well-tipped waiter.

Jeremy strolled out onto the deck. "Mr. Miller?"

"*Ja*. That's what folks call me." Miller paused with a foot on the railing while Jeremy introduced himself. Apparently Miller was a family man because when Jeremy explained the nature of his trip, the watchful lines on Miller's face softened. "Expect you want something of me. You and every other man in this blamed state. Normally do my business on *da* top side of a horse. But you're here, no point wasting the breath, ja?"

Jeremy fished inside his jacket for a cigar he'd purchased in San Luis Obispo, lit it and watched the smoke obscure the fading coastline, now a speck in the distance.

Miller scowled. "You from *da* War States."

"Virginia." Jeremy hesitated. He'd heard that travelers didn't pry into stranger's affairs; he took a deep breath and a deeper risk; "Judging from your speech, sir, you're a foreigner, as well."

Miller's scowl deepened. "Ja. Guilty as charged."

"Germany?"

Miller flicked his ash with impatience. "Brackenheim. Always, my name is a matter of curiosity. I vas a young lad without funds, hoping to travel steerage to San Francisco. The boat it leaves on the tides and I meet a man who possesses a steamship ticket. A few hours before sailing, he has a turn of bad luck and takes ill. He asks I write his family. Afterwards, he dies. I search his pockets for valuables to include in his letter back home, and I find the ticket. It is non-transferable; even I can see the problem. With the purser waiting on me, I do quick some thinking. After all, the name makes no use to him anymore."

Jeremy shook his head. "You are a man of wits, sir. A fortunate one."

"Ja. Fortune follows me. I make known my adopted name on the voyage and it sticks. In later years there makes a bit of a ruckus about the deception, but after I become a man of property, the California legislature agrees to accept the legal change and grants me citizenship in the process." Miller straightened and the lines in his face relaxed.

"Wealth has its advantages."

"Being poor teaches me this. Never sell the land. *Nie!* Never!" His eyes held the look of fire as he turned to challenge Jeremy for his own story.

"Lot of good men perished back home, sir. Calculated I'd best make my own life count. A man needs to keep his face pointed in the direction he means to go."

Miller nodded, his gaze intent on Jeremy. "And where might that be?"

"My heart's set on Central California, sir. In a valley called Cholama. Over in the hill country."

Miller's eyes grew hard. *"Ja. Ein kunstwerk.* For sure, a work of art. I have just come from the Huer Huero Rancho southeast of there. A Spanish land grant I have yet to acquire, although I do not yet give up hope. Such grass as ever a man finds in this California. Wild oats grow clean to the horse's chest."

"You were just passing through?"

Miller paused to relight his cigar. "I look to my holdings in the Great Valley—the San Joaquin. Looks to be the railroad brings in farmers and cuts the state into ribbons."

"Think that'll happen?"

"Ja, sure. Happens as we speak. Farmers made to donate the land in exchange for rights to the shipping of their herds. *Vit nein* compensation."

"Yankees propose the same thing in San Luis Obispo."

Miller grunted. "That town does not see the railroad for many years. *Nein die gute ale zeit.* This you will see. The railroad, it sets one town against the others. All for the profits."

"It'll ruin the grazing in this state," Jeremy said.

Miller waved his cigar in agitation. "Ja. Zis is true!"

"Farmers are bound to come."

Miller picked a bit of tobacco from his lip. "Vit no guarantees they'll prosper. Mark my word—the farmer vill end up working for the railroad."

"Like sharecroppers."

Miller inhaled the expensive cigar with closed eyes then opened them again to study the tip of his cigar, glowing red in the darkness. "Ten years, California will be riddled with railroads. A farmer's paradise."

"But the end of the free grazer," Jeremy said.

"Range cattle will go north," Miller continued. "Already I expand into eastern Oregon. My partner and me, we buy the Whitehorse Ranch." He gave a satisfied chortle. "Let the money mongers run their cursed trains out there, ja?"

"Think I can run cattle in the Cholama?"

"For the time being. The hide business comes soon to an end. The ranchos are breaking up. This el Rancho de Paso Robles that Blackburn and his brother-in-law James hold title to, it's nice land. Ja, they do good business. Blackburn raises the cattle and ships it north to his partner in San Francisco. Godchaux butchers the meat and sells it in the city at his own price. Got the trade cornered—except for me, I suppose." He sounded pleased.

Jeremy wondered how much money a man needed before he stopped being envious of his competitor. The Miller & Lux name was familiar clear to Europe and back again. Jeremy thought about making the point, but Miller was speaking again.

"You are a clever young man. You will find your vay."

Jeremy liked the way the conversation was heading, a chance to seek advice from the most successful cattle rancher in the state. "If I might impose, sir, what's the most important thing I'll need to know?"

Miller stared into the dark waters and pondered his response. "Springs, ja, this is what matters. What use is the land without the sweet water?"

"Cholame has springs."

"There you are!" Miller glanced over and his voice quickened. "Don't be taken for the fool, like some. Out here the land can be had for spit, but don't be forgetting, for the cattle you need real acreage."

"I'm thinking three, four thousand acres."

Miller nodded. "My partner and me make our fortune on Mexican cattle until the hide market disappears. Used to be hides were the only currency. California bank notes is what the people call them." He sounded wistful. "This before the bankers come. We use leather dollars."

"And filled ships with them," Jeremy offered.

Miller's mind was elsewhere. "We try the Scottish crossbreeds, my partner Lux and me. This I learn from being a butcher *in alten,* in the old days."

"You got your start as a butcher?"

Stress lines crinkled Miller's eyes. "Ja. And proud of it." He continued, "Feed the city folks, you will own the meat trade. Your beef suits the butchers, you will retire rich!" He inspected his cigar. Satisfied that he had smoked it to its finish, he tossed the stogy into the water, glanced at his timepiece and nodded. "We talk again tomorrow. Bring your young ladies along. I am lonesome for my own daughters."

Jeremy made his way back inside to find Ginny halfway through her second bowl of ice cream and the waiter he'd handsomely bribed carrying over a third. Frowning, he shook his head and the waiter made a hasty retreat back to the kitchen. "I thought you said you weren't having any supper."

Ginny had chocolate dripping from her chin. He picked up a cloth napkin, dampened a corner in her water goblet and started to hand it to her, but she quickly swiped her fist across her mouth and hid her chocolate-covered hand in her lap.

It had been a long day. Jeremy pushed his chair from the table. "Time for bed, Katydid . . . Miss Nettie. We have a big day tomorrow." He hesitated. "You might have a belly ache tonight. Keep your convenience handy."

Ginny grinned. "My belly's been waiting for ice cream my whole life. Ain't gonna upchuck it now's I had a taste."

After a trip to the railing to watch the moonrise, the girls followed him down the hallway where the passenger berths were located. He gave them time to settle in while he kept a discreet distance down the hall. When he paused to check that the latch was locked from the inside, a sleepy voice murmured, "Jeremy?"

"Night, Katydid."

Behind the locked door he heard a small voice singing, "the beans is done . . . the beans is done . . . ."

It was too early for bed, but he felt an obligation to stay close. He crawled not too eagerly into his bed down the hall, but the stranger in the other berth was snoring and the pitch of the ship brought to mind his train passage across the plains a few weeks earlier. He waited for sleep with the memory of the train in his head. The argument for barbed wire was compelling. He tossed in his bunk and tried to wipe out the memory of seeing wooden fences in Virginia reduced to rubble by war-starved families scavenging fence boards for cooking wood.

The next morning, Miller strode into the dining room and took a seat at Jeremy's table. Ginny didn't wait for a proper introduction before she started telling him about their stage ride into San Luis Obispo. Jeremy waited until the waiter served their oatmeal and peaches before Ginny finally paused to take a bite.

"Mr. Miller, sir, I've heard it said you can ride from Idaho, clean through to Mexico and spend every night on your own holdings."

Miller had a piece of ham halfway to his mouth, but he hesitated with a frown. "Ja. There's no denying fate has favored me. But when I hear the vaqueros say I have a soft hand with a rein, this is something I value." He smiled at Ginny. "Zat and my fine family."

Ginny interrupted her repast to give him a devilish-sweet smile. "What's your real name? Jeremy's burning to know." She continued smiling despite Jeremy's warning boot to her shin.

Miller noticed. "Let her be. She asks an honest question." He leaned close and whispered, "It's Kreiser." Smiling, he added, "But tell no one."

"She's good for your secret," Jeremy promised with a glance at Ginny.

Miller smiled. "No secret, not really. I tease with the young lady."

Jeremy let out a slow stream of air he hadn't realized he was holding

"It is good to meet new friends, but you don't be asking I sell you any land." Miller sounded adamant. "Once I buy, I never sell. But I know a man with land to sell. I write the particulars. If you get to him before me, well, I wish you luck."

"That's mighty kind of y—"

Miller's eyes grew hard. As abruptly as his smile had changed his continence, his scowl was back, reflecting his reputation as a ruthless trader. "*Nien.* Kindness has nothing to do with it. I buy up all the Spanish land grants I find in this state. Now my sights are trained on Nevada." He stood and bowed to the girls. "I bid you *guten tag,* ladies."

Chapter Twenty-Four

The ship's docking added confusion to an already bustling waterfront. Jeremy hired a transom to carry the girls and their luggage through the street from the Santa Cruz pier to the two-story school on the hill, careful to steer them aside when a black buggy with brass railings and a matched pair of tawny horses might have run them over.

The transom carried them along Pacific Street and they watched the fog lying offshore like it was waiting to pounce. They passed a burned-out hotel and what looked to be the charred remains of a livery and Chinese wash house, judging from the partial remains of a sign on the ground. A hand-drawn ladder truck stood nearby with a cadre of volunteers cranking water on the still-smoking remains. Farther up Mission Street, an Italian-style mansion was being constructed along a tree-lined row of wealthy homes that looked to be vacant. "Summer homes for the wealthy, most likely," Jeremy explained to the girls.

On Center Street, Ginny pointed out a gothic church with wooden steeples and curved arches. "What's that?"

"It's a place where people worship God. I'm sure your teachers will make provision for you to attend service on Sundays."

Ginny craned her neck until the church disappeared before she caught sight of a young boy riding his pony across a grassy knoll. Her eyes turned wistful. "I hope Sancho takes good care of Caroline. She favors oats with a touch of molasses. Maybe he won't remember that."

"Sancho won't forget," Jeremy said.

The school was at the top of a hill, a grand two-story white building with a profusion of windows. Jeremy studied Ginny's reaction. Nettie had already attended the previous year and was taking everything in stride, but Ginny gawked like she was entering some royal palace. He noticed the way her hands clutched at her skirts.

"You're going to like it here, Ginny. It may not seem so now, but you're going to thank your grandmother one day." He was gratified to see her hands relax.

A tall woman in a starched black dress greeted Nettie. At the sight of her returning student, the headmistress, Miss Standish, relaxed her stiff demeanor and reached to smooth a loose strand of hair into her crisp gray-streaked bun.

Jeremy watched as the woman inspected his other charge, her eyes running the length of Ginny's outfit from her cropped hair to her stiff new boots. When her eyes flickered to him, he was satisfied with her understanding nod, an affirmation that she was not unfamiliar with young girls who possessed roughness at the edges. She summoned a teacher waiting nearby. The young woman advanced and took Ginny's arm. They disappeared through the doors, heads together as the teacher directed a question at her. Jeremy followed the headmaster into her office.

The next morning, Jeremy tried to ignore the spark of panic in Ginny's face. When it was time to say goodbye, he handed over a packet of writing paper with the address of her grandmother neatly printed on the inside cover next to his own. He explained that her letters would reach the ranch if she addressed them in care of General Patrick Murphy at Rancho Santa Margarita, California. Sancho had promised to ride over to pick them up. The only post office closer was at the Rios Caledonia adobe in San Miguel, but it was likely that her father would forget to pick them up if she sent them there.

Jeremy was careful to ignore her tears as he patted her awkwardly on her shoulder. "You have a home in Virginia anytime you need it. And kin there who love you." To his ears he sounded like her big brother. "Any messages I can deliver your grandmother?"

Ginny's voice sounded shaky. "Reckon I'll be working on a letter, myself. Missus Imus says it's important to keep a sense of kinship among your own." She sat stiffly on a velvet chair in the school's parlor. To her credit, she kept her chin jutted up level with his, even though her lip trembled.

He fought the urge to check his pocket watch. "A satisfactory plan if you ask me, young lady." She was too smart to miss the way his eyes darted to the window.

Realizing their time was at an end, she panicked. "Don't expect me to be perfect all at once," she snapped. "It ain't in me. Sancho says I'm half jackrabbit and half cottontail."

Jeremy smiled. "Sancho says' again, huh, Squirt?"

She was using every trick she could think of to keep from crying. "No telling when I might say something to give offense!" She folded her arms tightly against her chest and rocked forward like she was comforting herself.

"When I come back to the ranch, you better not be tugging at my hair no more."

Jeremy bit back his smile. "Fair enough, but I won't be calling you Miss Nugent, either, Katydid."

Suddenly, she seemed struck by a number of questions that needed immediate answers. By the time he managed to break away, the stage was loading at the bottom of the hill. He rushed out the door then turned to see her and Nettie watching from the window. From the middle of the street he gave them a last wave and started running. Two blocks later he managed to throw his valise onto the top and climb aboard just before the stage lunged to a start.

"Sweet Lord a' mercy!" He pulled out a kerchief and swabbed his face with hands that shook like a soldier with a case of the war fits. If he'd known what escorting a young lady entailed, he might have begged off.

***

The stage ride north provided ample opportunity for reflection, and by the time he arrived in San Francisco, he had a name for his spread: Cottonwood Ranch. In his pocket he carried a letter of introduction from Henry Miller for a meeting with a mercantile and real estate entrepreneur by the name of John Parrott, a man who in years past, had conducted a private banking business that some claimed had loaned money to Mariano Vallejo at five per cent per month. Now retired, the man had sold his banking interests to the San Francisco Bank, but word was that he still made their financial decisions.

After depositing his luggage at a boardinghouse run by a married couple from New England, the Stewarts, Jeremy sat at his desk and added his note to Miller's letter of introduction.

The next day, in a meeting at the Palace Hotel, Parrott responded after hearing his plan. "I'll arrange a meeting with a man I think can help. He heads up a bank in one of my buildings."

The hotel dining room was a dazzling reminder of what the South had lost. Jeremy tried to keep his attention on the importance of this meeting, without being distracted by the gilded banisters, the crystal chandeliers, and the air of prosperity and entitlement that saturated the room. He shrugged off his irritation and addressed Parrott over the top of his menu. "If I might be so bold as to inquire, it's rumored that a block of commercial buildings over on California Street belongs to you, sir."

Parrott smiled at the waiter who was attempting to appear inconspicuous. "Let's order."

He explained, when Jeremy asked, that he'd built the entire block with the labor of indentured artisans from Hong Kong, hired for a dollar a day plus a ration of fish and rice. He explained that the exterior walls were faced with granite imported from China, laid over interior walls of Chinese brick. The Granite Block took his crews only four months to complete. Now he was leasing out offices to government and private corporations for thousands of dollars every month.

Over Porterhouse steaks and champagne, Parrott advised him of the political climate. "Not much different from the carpetbag politics where you came from, down South," he warned.

Jeremy winced. "Then, sir, I'm afraid I'll be trading flame for fire."

Parrott smiled. "I'm an honest man, Mr. Lawsen, and would bestow on you a bit of old-fashioned advice, if I might. It's the best I can do for a newcomer such as yourself."

"I'd be much in your debt."

"Then watch your step, young man. There are thieves and villains in this city disguised as financiers who will rob you or have you assassinated for what you own." He turned to see who might be listening. "If I could sell out my holdings for fifty cents on the dollar, I would abandon this country forever."

Jeremy waited as the waiter refilled his champagne. "That surprises me, Mr. Parrott."

Parrott continued. "I am at times disgusted at the corruption that happens in this city—in this state. Keep above the temptation to get rich at any cost."

"You have my pledge on that, sir." Jeremy raised his glass in a toast.

***

The bank was located in one of Parrott's granite buildings. The upstairs office had been appointed with every conceivable luxury that an army of skilled craftsman could provide. Again, Jeremy blocked the comparison to the shattered bank where his mother still traded. Prosperity in San Francisco had not come on the back of the South. The prosperity he saw all around him only kindled inside him a stronger promise to build a fortune of his own.

He felt an immediate liking for Milton Latham. It seemed that the two had lined up on the same side of the fence because Latham gave him essentially the same advice. "Stay clear of the Comstock crowd that operates in this town. They're looking to increase their investment stocks with the blood of honest ranchers and businessmen. As things look, they're a fair way to succeeding."

"How they doing that?"

"One way is to grab legal title. There are men in the Cholama—you've probably met a few—who arrived early, picked the best land and never bothered to file on it. To do so would mean they'd have to travel up here to the government building, and it's a long trip. Those men are only squatting. They probably won't think twice about it until they start getting pressure from incoming settlers. They're probably only thinking about the taxes they're saving."

"You saying the crooks have that angle figured?"

"Looks that way. They're filing claims right out from under some of these fellows. Next thing they know, some of the ranchers won't own their own land. You take care if you see strangers nosing around your area."

"I'll do just that." Jeremy pulled out a small tablet and reached for a sharpened quill on the desk. "What can you tell me about establishing a crossbred cattle operation in California?"

Latham's smile brought a flood of heat to Jeremy's face. "Put away your notepad, son. By the time we're done, you'll have your facts in your head where they'll do you some good."

Jeremy accepted the banker's outstretched hand. "You know your business, that's obvious."

Lathrop smiled. "Seems logical that a banker would be an expert rancher. A matter of weighing the risks and the strengths of his collateral, wouldn't you agree?"

Mr. Latham had already opened a bank account for Jeremy. In the banker's presence he notarized the document he wrote up. Jeremy signed over his bank draft, and with a flourish to his signature, he became a westerner.

Outside the bank again, Jeremy recognized Henry Miller's portly form astride a buckskin gelding. He was staying at the California Hotel, but he'd dropped by to see his friend, Latham.

Miller extended his hat, but his expression was devoid of the warmth of their previous meeting. "Lawsen, you beat me to the bank dis time. Don't be expecting it next time. I have da reputation as a hard man and I see I earn it."

Chapter Twenty-Five

Living alongside an ocean felt purely wonderful except for the fog and the chill night air. Most nights the dampness kept Ginny awake shivering until she learned to ask for a second blanket. She lay in bed listening for the fog horns. On clear days she watched the ships and steamers on their way between San Francisco and San Diego. Lessons were harder. She spent long hours trying to catch up with Nettie, who already knew how to read and write.

School was exciting and taxing, both at the same time, and some days the routine rubbed like her new shoes. Rising at dawn was the easy part. She was usually dressed before any of the others, just for the novelty of washing her face with freshly-poured water she didn't have to haul from the spring. The hard part was having the doors locked. She hated living with the feeling that the walls were closing in and there was no apple tree to escape to.

Some of the girls griped about the cold oats and thin milk, the hard brown bread without butter, but Ginny missed the fresh meat, even the scrawny chickens that she and Sancho butchered. Everyone expected her to take to reading, writing and 'rithmetic like she'd been doing them her whole life. The teachers acted sympathetic, but they refused to accept excuses.

One day, loneliness seemed to stall her every effort. She barely passed her cursive test because she confused her "*q's*" with her "*g's*" and wrote a line of "*the gueen quarded the qate with a guill.*" The other girls snickered at her baby mistake. During arithmetic, the teacher assigned the class to add columns and she forgot how to carry hundreds. She heard the words Sancho had taught her criticized and her pronunciation corrected a dozen times a day, until she felt like she was turning into someone she didn't know.

That evening she refused to take her turn in the kitchen. "I'm not doing dishes," she muttered to the other girls who were donning their aprons. "I'm full-up tired of doing house work. My grandmother pays for my schooling and I shouldn't have to."

The senior girl in charge summoned Miss Standish and she arrived panting, her thin chest heaving with indignation. "You will comply or suffer the consequences," she calmly stated.

Ginny tilted her chin in defiance and repeated the words slowly, "I . . . ain't . . . cleaning . . . the . . . kitchen."

She watched Miss Standish's lips flatten into a thin line. "You will comply. Or I shall send you home before you cast a contagion on my other scholars."

Missus Whitman arrived, her mouth pursed in an "o" of astonishment. Ginny felt a momentary stab of guilt. She turned to Miss Standish. "I reckon Patrón will hear about how you're working us like servants. My grandmother, too."

"Silence!"

Ginny tilted her chin and fired her last dart. "Patrón won't be able to come fetch me home until after round-up."

Miss Standish stood to her full five-feet-ten and pointed a thin finger toward the hallway. "You will spend the night in the storeroom with no supper. You will reflect on your behavior while you write your apology."

The basement room was a small, dank room with an oil lamp that Miss Standish removed on her way out. Through the closed door, her housekeeping belt rattled until the proper key was inserted it into the lock; afterwards the only sound Ginny heard was the click of heels. Panic beaded on her forehead until she thought she would faint, but she made no sound. A thin light pierced the darkness and she traced its origins to a spot that was eye-level with the street, covered by a bundle of rags. She brushed them aside and saw the dirty window.

A wooden box rested on the floor beneath a counter; she used it to boost herself onto the ledge. The lock was stuck, but she tried again, her head pounding. On the third try she felt the brittle pot-metal latch break off in her hand. She gave a quick glance at the door before easing the window open and filling her lungs with salt air.

She was awakened in the middle of the night by a bright orange orb of the full moon shining into her window. Common sense warred with her claustrophobia until freedom's song won over restraint. She was in enough trouble that a little more wouldn't matter, she decided, as she eased herself out of the ledge. Outside the dusty, enclosed space, she started toward the Ohlone settlement located toward the bay, down in the Potrero. The dirt path was rough and patchy. She wrapped a raggedy blanket around her shoulders and watched the full moon slide behind a cloud.

Darkness made everything eerie and distant, but she recalled the direction. The settlement was on the left, near the Evergreen Cemetery. On a walk with her class, two mornings earlier, she'd gawked at the half-naked

Indian children until Missus Whitman had threatened her with a demerit if she didn't keep her head straight ahead like the other girls.

A narrow bridge at the edge of the settlement straddled a ditch dug by Costanoan natives to keep their horses from straying. A horse whinnied and she stood still, wishing she'd brought a carrot. It turned away while a mongrel dog circled her warily as if deciding whether to growl.

Most of the shacks were closed up against the damp ocean air. She stole close to the dying embers of an abandoned fire, careful to stay in the shadows. From the corner of her eye she saw someone—or something—moving in the shadows. A furtive movement at the edge of a far building caused her heart to dance nearly out of her chest until a skinny dog slipped out from behind a wash tub. She'd given no thought to what might happen if she got caught, but the skinny dog brought a number of possibilities to mind. Maybe the sheriff would haul her back to Miss Standish, who would banish her from the school with a disgraceful letter to Jeremy and her grandmother. Maybe she would get caught and never be heard of again. She wasn't sure what Indians did to nosy town girls, but she offered the dog a pat. It edged closer and began to sniff her, its tail wagging furiously.

Men's voices rose and fell from somewhere on the commons, laughing and whooping like the vaqueros at Patrón's bunkhouse. A crack of light escaped through an opening, widening as a door opened. The room glowed with a pit of light in the background. It was a sweathouse like she'd seen in a drawing of an Indian village in her classroom. The walls were plastered with mud like the summer house that Maria Inés's husband had built. A fire burned in the center, feeding a thin stream of smoke through a hole in the roof.

Suddenly, a naked Indian man slipped out and closed the door behind him while she gaped. The moon rose over the hills and started toward the ocean while she crouched, too scared to move. Suddenly the door opened again and a handful of naked, glistening men burst out. They began running straight toward her for a few paces, until they turned and plunged, whooping, into the frigid creek flowing between her and safety.

She turned and fled across the bridge without looking back, racing as fast as her feet could carry her to the dirt road leading to the school. Her blanket slipped. In the moonlight the pumpkins growing alongside the track looked like crouching Indian men. The neat rows of corn looked like Indian women waiting to thrash her with their wooden spoons for disturbing their sleep. Ignoring the stitch in her side, she struggled back along Coral Street and up the incline where the two-story school building pushed gloriously against the moonscape. She was winded, doubled over with a stitch in her side by the time she arrived.

When she could breathe again, she pulled off her shoes and carefully slid the basement window open. The climb back through the splintered window was harder than the escape had been. When she was safe inside again, she turned to inspect the damage that she'd have to explain to Miss Standish. Her hands were dirty, her shoes were muddy, and her shirtwaist was covered with dust from the sill. She waited until her heart had settled before she swigged down the drinking water Miss Standish had left for her, She remembered, just in time, to save some to pour onto a rag and began to scrub the dirt. She shook out her skirts and picked burrs from the hem with the aid of the moonlight. Finally, when she had swabbed away the signs of her adventure and wiped her shoes clean, she lay down again on the ledge and tried to quell her trembling.

In the minutes before sleep arrived, she felt her loneliness easing. Her last thought was a promise to herself that she would tell no one, not even Nettie, of her adventure. Safe now, she felt the old Ginny blending with the new Virginia. The two, mixed together, seemed to fit better than either one by itself.

***

Eventually the weather turned dreary and the rains came. The Santa Cruz River emptied into the Pacific, fed in part by the rivers in flood stage that separated her from her Cholama Valley. The mid-term break was nearing and the other girls were making plans to spend Christmas with their families. She sent a letter home, but she received no answer, so that December brought a dull ache of homesickness while she practiced for her first Christmas play. Jeremy sent a letter, carefully printed in block letters. She asked Missus Whitman to help her read the hard words.

Dear Katydid,

It's fair quiet without you around. Even the horses think so. Hope you're not kicking up a ruckus for your teachers. I expect by now you have more stories to tell. I'll have to satisfy myself with Sancho's stories until next we meet. He's a fine teacher and I am working hard at learning to ranch in this Cholama. Things you take for granted are hard lessons for me, I must declare

When you come home for a visit you'll have to ride over to see my barbed wire. Sancho calls it my high-falutin bob-war. I've caused quite a stir, as my cook would say. Your father wants to run me out of the valley and Sancho has

offered to help him.
Take care and send a note when you can. Your mare's just fine.
Your friend,
Jeremy

The night of the Christmas program arrived. Ginny peeked from the cloakroom where the students were donning their costumes. The room was crowded with mothers and fathers standing together, the women dressed in fine dresses with lace trim, and bonnets with curls framing their faces. Her gaze lingered hungrily on the ladies and their finery. Some of the farmers stood with their arms crossed self-consciously like they were out of place in the commotion. Sancho would be among them if he were here. She abandoned her search when Missus Whitman warned her to get in her place.

Miss Standish began her welcome address.

Ginny had never performed in front of anyone, so she focused her attention on two smiling men in the back row. One was a head taller than the other, looking for all the world like Patrón standing next to Sancho. The room might be filled with strangers, but she could still pretend that they were in attendance. Her mother, too, all three of them smiling while she sang the carols she had worked so hard to learn.

At the close of the program, Ginny watched her friends rush to greet their parents. Nettie dragged her along to meet her aunt and uncle, and after the introductions were made, Ginny stood not knowing what to say when the aunt asked if she had family in attendance. Nettie's uncle was a minister. He held Methodist revival meetings over on the peninsula near Monterey. He inquired politely after her kin and she felt her face heating. Obviously, he and his wife knew nothing about ranching or they would know that winter was no time for traveling. Patrón had stock to tend. Some of the vaqueros had been released for the winter and the ranch was as short-handed as could be.

She looked around at the excited faces and fought back tears while she carried a plate of fig bars and Swedish lace crisps to the corner. "Why do folks think Patrón would come?" she muttered to herself. "He didn't answer my letter, asking. At least he could have done that."

He could have ridden over to Hollister and taken the train. He could have ridden in early and collected the supplies for the rest of the winter, taken the stage and stayed warm and dry for most of the trip. Nettie's aunt and uncle had come all the way from Monterey, but Patrón wasn't one for wasting precious hours while city folk sang and made merry around a piano. It didn't matter to him if he looked bad in front of these town folks. It didn't matter to her, either. They just didn't realize what it took, ranching in the Cholama.

***

Sancho watched Ginny singing from a spot at the back of the room with one shoulder braced against the wall. His belly burned with the shot of whiskey he'd taken for his rheumatism as much as for courage. His grimy denim trousers were dry from sitting close to the wood stove inside the saloon, as was his heavy ranch coat and his battered hat. He faced the crowds without his usual trepidation. Dry and warm were things to be thankful for, even among the suits and frippery.

The little gal stood in the front row, dressed in a white robe that made her look so sweet he had to look twice. With his dim eyesight, it appeared that she had gold wings attached to her back and a narrow halo that twinkled every time her head bobbed. He imagined he heard her clear voice rising above the others, taking the notes high like a sweet mountain songbird. Her voice made the assembly sound like angels had filled the room.

He recalled only one Christmas in his whole life. It was the year when his ma waited for everyone to gather before she lit the single candle she had perched on a fresh spruce tree she'd cut and dragged in after the younger ones had gone to bed. There weren't any gifts, but he hadn't known to expect any. The surprise was the tree with its bits of colored quilt scraps tied up into the branches. For those hours the house smelled like a forest after the rain, and afterwards the shack held the tang of gingerbread.

Like a proud papa, he wiped the moisture traveling down his cheek. "Caroline Nugent," he whispered, "hope you're watching this little gal. She's sure somethin'."

Chapter Twenty-Six

Ginny raced though a breakfast of oatmeal and bread without butter that the school provided for any girls who hadn't returned home with their family. She finished her kitchen chores and changed into her britches, piling on layers of cotton and woolen shirts under the oversized ranch coat that Sancho had brought her. Over all of this she added the woolen scarf Missus Whitman had knitted her as a gift, along with a Bible with her name written inside. Her shoes were already oversized, so an extra pair of woolen socks made the fit snug. With a quick hug for Missus Whitman and a whispered farewell to Nettie, who was sick in bed with a fever, she followed Sancho to the stage.

With a last look at the dingy gray Pacific, Ginny turned her attention outside of the swaying stage as it rolled along El Camino Real and headed east. The stage rolled through pine forests with wet, drooping branches and the fetid stench of decaying leaves. In several places the women passengers had to disembark and trudge through the mud while the men pushed and prodded the stagecoach with broken tree limbs. She was glad she was wearing her old boots, but even so, she would have walked barefoot to save her good ones.

The stage had gotten mired in the mud at a couple of creeks that fed the Salinas, so they were two hours late rolling into the Caledonia stop in San Miguel. Now the sun was too far set for starting out, but the Boss hadn't handed over money for rooms, and Sancho couldn't abide sleeping in the long, low room the stage stop set aside for the single men. It had no windows—made that way so the men wouldn't get themselves shot at night while they were sleeping—and he didn't cotton to sleeping in an airtight room like a rat.

At San Miguel, they wasted little time. Sancho collected their horses from the livery. He'd brought Caroline. The mare whinnied in recognition even before Ginny caught sight of her.

"We got to get to shelter before nightfall," he warned Ginny. "Even so, we'll be in for a soaking."

"That's okay, Sancho. Nothing will dampen my day."

"There'll be a drop in temperature." He squinted at the sky. "We're riding overland, across the mountain."

"Long as my Bible don't . . . doesn't get wet. Glad you wrapped it in oilskin."

He walked the horses at a pace that gave lie to his need to hurry. The animals were cold and stiff from standing and needed to warm their muscles. Gradually, they picked up their pace until the miles and the hours passed with an increasing sense of urgency. She was not scared—not with Sancho—just in awe of the storm mounting around her.

The rain began in slow drops. Within minutes it was falling in a steady torrent that obliterated all traces of the trail. They pulled on slickers tied behind the saddles and rode with heads hunkered against the rising wind. Sancho halted once to retie the scarf that kept his hat anchored to his head, and to squint ahead at the darkened, obscured track. Finally, he shouted to Ginny to pull into the tree covering to the right of the trail.

"There's a grove of willows over there, Get under them and let's see what happens with the storm. When it lets up, we'll ride again."

He glanced around, trying to get his bearings. Already his legs were aching. He knew the little gal had to be scared; she would be chattering like a bluejay in a nest of squirrels, otherwise. If he had his facts straight, there was a nesters' cabin ahead, set on flat land near the Estrella River. If they could find it they would have shelter, and with a little luck maybe even some dry wood to burn while they waited for a break in the storm. Shouting to her to follow, he gave his gelding free rein. The horse's night vision had brought him back to the ranch more than once.

The horse picked its way toward the flood stage of the crashing Estrella River. Suddenly it halted dead in its tracks and refused to move, even with his urging. In the pitch darkness he knew better than to force the issue. He slid from the saddle to see what the trouble was and struck his elbow against the side of a wall. "Dang me, but you found the cabin, horse." He turned and shouted against the wind; "Get down here, Missy!"

Over his shoulder he saw her huddled in drenched misery, her lips, her entire body, chattering as he lifted her to the ground. he pushed the door open and a rat skittered into the corner. In the inky blackness he bumped his leg against something hard and swore under his breath. The little gal stuck to his right side while he fumbled with his waterproof container of matches. Striking one, he managed to locate a pile of broken, rat-chewed debris alongside the chimney. He flung a handful into the broken fireplace and used a second match to light it off. When it caught, he slowly added more until the tiny flame flickered and spread.

"Missy, I'm going out to unsaddle the horses. You keep the fire going. I'll be right back."

***

Ginny nodded and faced the fire. She could remove her outer garments as soon as the wood blazed, but for now, until Sancho returned, she remained huddled in her wet coat. From what she could see, they had struck a vein of pure luck. A broken, abandoned chair would provide dry tinder.

Sancho returned to dump the saddles and blankets on the floor. "I tied the horses right outside," he said as he turned to the fire.

"Sancho, there's something over there in the corner," she whispered, grateful that he stood between her and the noise.

"It's a rat, likely," he cautioned, lifting his rifle to use as a weapon or a club, whichever the situation called for. Another rustle under the pile of chewed pilings and a critter darted toward the door. "It's a possum," he whispered, lifting his Hawken rifle to his shoulder. He halted just in time. A shot at this range would frighten the horses into breaking their reins and stampeding. Instead he could only shake his head in disgust as the ugly critter slunk out the door. "Dangnation! Would have made some good eating." He limped across the room and slammed the warped door as hard as he could.

"I'd sooner go hungry than eat that thing. It had a tail!"

"Reckon you'll get your wish then, Missy." He rummaged in his saddlebags, found a sack of beef jerky and tossed it to her with a scowl.

Ginny spread her slicker on the rough floor. Using her saddle as a pillow, she flopped down and faced away, pretending to sleep. She knew Sancho was listening to the storm because she heard him feeding the fire, trying to make the wood last. Judging from his listlessness, his damp legs were stiff and cold. He shifted under the weight of the poncho, struggled to his feet and paced until she fell asleep. Sometime in the night she sat up, startled by the sound of grating wood. It sounded like a rat chewing, yet not quite the same. Sancho was hunched over, kneeling on the floor. She squinted in the gloom, but it was impossible to see what he was doing. She'd have to break her silence.

"What's the matter?"

"Go back to sleep, Missy." His voice was hoarse.

"Tell me!" He didn't need to treat her like she was a baby.

His growl sounded resigned, like he knew she wasn't going to give up. "Missy I'm worried about the sound of that river. Figure to bore out a hole in the cabin floor. I'll stick my finger through it from time to time. If I can feel the water then we got to go. With luck we'll last till the sun comes up. Then we'll ride hard for the ranch."

Ginny followed the core of wood he pulled from the hole. She watched while he dipped his finger in as far as it would go. When he lifted it, his finger came up dry. She let out a sigh of relief. The flames were lapping the last scrap of wood, but the room felt almost cozy.

"Go to sleep, Missy. You'll need your strength for tomorrow." He sounded tired.

The silence called for an apology. "Sancho, I'm sorry about the Christmas program. I was just lonesome when I wrote home about it. If it wasn't . . . weren't for that old program, you'd be home safe and dry by now. And I'd be with Nettie."

"Shucks, Missy, I wouldn't have missed that singing for nothing. I swear I seen your Mama listening over in the corner." She felt him squeeze her shoulder. The wood snapped against the rain. In the darkness, Ginny summoned her courage. "Sancho, why did Mama die?"

She could tell by the way his body stiffened, that he didn't want to talk about it. When he spoke, she heard his reluctance.

"Can't rightly say. People say it was her fate."

"Were they happy?"

He hesitated. "For awhile. Happier than any two folks I ever seen. Can't always judge a thing by how long it lasts. It's kind'a like this here storm. By tomorrow it'll be over and we'll wonder what all the fuss was about. Maybe they had more in a little while then some folks have in a lifetime."

"Oh." He hadn't mentioned the eggs. Maybe Jeremy was right. Maybe eggs had nothing to do with it. The certainty that she had killed her mother was the one thing she could be sure of. The idea had filled her thoughts for as long as she could remember, and now Sancho's words seemed to dim that thought right inside her head. What if they were right and she hadn't killed her mother? Her brother? What if dying just was? She'd need to fill the space with something else. But what? She'd have to ponder on that.

Sancho continued. "She died doing what she loved, caring for you and trying to have another young 'un. She was sure proud of you."

She lay awake, thinking, until she must have dozed off. When she woke the rain had slowed and Sancho stood at the door, squinting at the coming dawn.

"Come on, little gal. Time to get a move on. We'll be back at the ranch afore anyone knows we been gone."

The horses covered the last miserable miles like they knew they were heading to the barn. Ginny's heart was thudding with excitement by the time the ranch came into view, the hacienda lit up like the Piedras Blanca lighthouse she'd seen from the steamship on her way north—carving light out of the fog. She gave the house a wistful look, but she rode toward the tack room. She wasn't about to ask for special favors.

Sancho was right behind. "Go on up to the house, Missy. I'll take care of the mare."

She was drenched and dog-tired, but she'd bite off her tongue before she'd pass on her obligations. "I've made it this far. May as well finish. Caroline needs a rubdown and some grain."

She unsaddled and started rubbing her horse with straw. Even in the half-light, she saw a glimmer of respect in Sancho's surprised glance. Around their ranch, horses settled for a quick roll in the mud and a shake after the saddle was off. Grooming was something she had learned in town, watching the livery stable hands. Caroline nickered gratefully. Ginny made sure the tack room was shut tight before she followed Sancho to the house.

Their reception in the kitchen surprised her. The fact that everyone stopped talking when she and Sancho walked in made her think that maybe they were worried. Maria Inés gave her a grin, and Jose Luis and Juan sat quietly, watching. Although neither said so, she got the impression that maybe they had been discussing the idea of riding out to search. Miguelito pointed to her layers of shirts and coats. "Señorita, you have got *muy grande* in town!"

She looked down and laughed. She waited until the vaqueros wandered out to their horses before she started unpeeling. Starting with the huge coat, she removed layers of sodden wool until she could feel the warmth returning. Hunkered up against the stove, wrapped in a woolen blanket, she thought she recalled her mother doing the same thing on a rainy day like today.

The room smelled of tamales and coffee—both hot enough that the window was steamed—the stove hissing and snapping, and a pot of coffee simmering on top.

She filled her stomach and, after a trip to the privy, she readied herself for sleep. Later, she'd ride out and find a holly bush. She'd pick a branch red with berries and make a wreath with some of the evergreen boughs that grew on the hillside, and carry it to her mother's grave. When the sun cleared she'd sit with her Bible and show her mother how she had learned to read.

Chapter Twenty-Seven

Ginny spotted Jeremy riding point on a small herd of Durham cattle heading toward his ranch. The heifers were swollen with pregnancy and Jeremy was taking his time easing the herd. At the end of his gloved hand, a rope was attached to the nose ring of a young roan bull that looked so splendid, she stopped her horse to watch.

"Look what the sun brought out," he called over with laughter in his voice. "If it isn't Katydid." He peered close, in feigned surprise. "What happened to your freckles? All that school work wearing them off?"

A bubble of joy escaped at the sight of him. Maybe it was irritation because he still thought of her as a little girl.

"Don't call me that! Anyways, you got your work cut out for you, Jeremy. I ain't never . . . I haven't ever seen such a bare-bones operation." He was still laughing when she nudged Caroline alongside. "How's that barbed fencing you're so worked up about?"

Jeremy smiled good-naturedly. "You'll just have to wait till term's end to find out."

"Why? Is it stuck on a train somewhere between here and Illinois?" He was ignoring her. She tried again. "You need it now if it's going to do you any good!"

"Yep."

His grin infuriated her. He was even starting to talk like a cowman. "What good is wire fence without anything to hang it on?" she asked. He was studying the far mountains like she wasn't even around and that made her even more irritated. "Gonna rain again tomorrow, Sancho says. Don't watch out, you'll get flooded and have to go back where you came from!"

"Yep."

She raised her voice when he turned toward his ranch, leading his bull. "You think just because you got some cattle and some land you got a ranch? Where's your house?" Her voice sounded shrill and childish.

"Don't need a house. Frees up my mind for the cattle!"

"You'll be lucky it don't snow but a couple times this winter. Else you'll be freezing in that tent of yours."

149

"Yep."

"Jeremy Lawsen, you're impossible!" She laughed at her inability to get a rise out of him and saw him twinkling with good humor. Coming home felt good clean to her toes. Surely none of the girls at school had such a place. "I promised Maria Inés I'd be home to help. Gotta go keep my promise. Bye, now."

A few miles later she had to move to the side of the road while a muddy wagon rolled past. It was loaded with manufactured wire studded with steel barbs twisted right onto the wire. The freight hauler looked chilled, likely from fighting the heavy load over the hundred-mile road from Hollister. Ginny thought about the tortillas she used to carry in her pocket.

***

Every night of her holiday, Ginny said a prayer for letting Sancho fetch her home. She tried not to think about having to return in two weeks. Too much was happening. The valley was bursting with new settlers. William Imus ran a post office from his house on the Slack's Canyon stage road where the McIntosh mail stage made its stop. It was called Imusdale. The stage ran twice a week from Hollister, clear across the hills.

One afternoon she and Sancho rode over to pick up the mail and she shared some of the current events the older girls had been talking about at school. According to them the battle lines between barbed wire and free range were dividing the country, same as the War had. She was proud to be able to talk to him about it.

"Jeremy's leading the countryside with that rolled wire he's bragging about."

"That he is." Sancho said. "The livery and the mercantile fellows in Hollister saw his wire, they cabled East. Each is hoping to be the first to offer it for sale."

"Maybe he ain't as dumb as he looks," she mumbled.

Sancho gave her an intense look. "That what you're learning in school—to see the sour in people? If it is, best come on home. Save your efforts."

She ducked her head and mumbled an apology.

He wasn't ready to let it go. "What you got against Jeremy? Seems to me you owe him a fair bit."

Her face heated. "Yeah, I know. He just bothers me sometimes. He treats me like I'm a kid."

He snorted. "'Spect that's because you *are* one. Give yourself a few years and he won't seem so irritating."

An image of Jeremy the day he arrived, thick dark lashes feathering his cheeks while she gawked. She thought of the times when his image was stuck inside her head while she waited for sleep. Each time it happened, she smiled at the comfort it brought, but Sancho was a friend and she didn't recall *his* grizzled old face filling her head while the sandman dallied.

Before she could think of a response, they arrived at the post office where a group of men stood outside, arguing the merits of the wire. Some of them were polite. Some looked worried. One of them sounded hopping mad. The arguments flowed freely, with everyone talking at once and no one listening.

"Never thought to see the day anybody ruined the West with such a perversion."

"Manifest Destiny. It's the God-given right of white men to control the earth. Says so in the Bible."

"You're dead on there. God favors the white man. God favors the Union. No two ways about it."

"You Southerners took pains to see that blacks weren't included in your definition of a man. Called them bucks, a breeding term—same as deer or elk. No reason to treat a buck like a man, isn't that what you say?"

"Bucks? Ain't that what you call Indians? Bucks and squaws? Who are you to claim the Bible? Hypocrite is what I call you."

Sancho broke in. "Reckon we're all neighbors hereabouts. No reason this thing needs to get ugly." He crouched, glaring while the two most rabid-sounding arguers backed down, their eyes trained on the ground while their faces flamed with anger. Ginny backed off a few paces, unsure what she should do. She wished Jeremy was here.

Mr. Imus produced a newspaper that told of the range wars being fought in Texas and Wyoming. He agreed with Sancho. A new homesteader, George Gould, was arguing with Charles Harlan that the range wars were a struggle between the big ranchers and the small.

Sancho tried to reconcile the argument. "Reckon the big ranches'll make a fortune running livestock on public lands. They won't give up a single acre they don't have to—even if it ain't theirs. Wait and see."

Mr. Gould's face got red and he sputtered, "They don't have to. All they have to do is fence in the springs."

Gibson McConnell waited until the group was quiet. "I'm considering wiring my spread."

Harlan continued arguing with Mr. Gould like he hadn't heard. "Serves the big boys right. In Texas, ranches count their land by the number of days it takes to ride across on horseback!"

Ginny tried to imagine a ranch bigger than the Rancho Cholame. But judging from the talk, it had been broken into homestead sites. Some of the new neighbors had already chosen up land for farms, and those who could afford it were filing claims. Jeremy was right; the time for pre-empters and squatters was coming to a close.

"I aim to claim up legally. I intend for my great-grandchildren to be buried in this valley someday," Harlan said.

On the ride over to Jeremy's, Ginny listened as Sancho told her about the newcomers having trouble farming on a hundred and sixty acres. Cattle prices were down and recession was making money scarce. Some of the area was in another county, and those folks had to file at the new county seat in San Luis Obispo. To save themselves a trip, some saw an unclaimed parcel on the map and signed for it, sight unseen. They hadn't counted on the rocks and the topography.

Some folks did the same thing at the Monterey county seat in Salinas. Afterwards they rode out to Cholame, saw their holdings and realized they were trying to farm on grazing land. Mr. Harlan claimed most of them wouldn't stay but a year.

Ahead, a few head of cattle were milling around while Patrón sat astride his big stallion, arguing with Jeremy. Ginny and Sancho were too far away to hear anything but occasional fragments.

". . . take care your cattle don't get out of that damned pasture and . . . at my springs. . ."

Jeremy was there, too, standing loose-limbed, trying to stay calm. "I'll do my best, neighbor."

It seemed like the whole world was going crazy with anger and dispute—all except Jeremy, who seemed like he was tired of strife. Ginny tried—and failed—to recall even one time when he'd raised his voice in an argument. Maybe the War had taken the ire from his heart and changed it to acceptance so he could go on living. But his calm manner was lost on Patrón, who turned his horse and trotted off. On his way past, he pulled his horse up to get a better look at Jeremy's new Durham bull.

Sancho grinned and leaned in toward Ginny. "Nothing like a purebred bull to improve a man's fortunes. Your old man's mad there's a fence between his cows." He winked and waited as the Boss rode past with a tightening of his jaw.

Sancho rode over to where Jeremy was piling posts. "Send her home with plenty of daylight," he called over his shoulder as he headed to catch up with his boss.

Jeremy waved and nodded.

Ginny waited for Jeremy to tell her his plans for the fencing. She hadn't thought about the need for posts. He was using juniper trees the size of a man's arm, skimmed bare. Where a tree stood in line with the fence, he had his men tack wire to it. Where they had no other option, they dug a posthole in the ground. On hard rock, they left the post floating and sank the next one a little deeper.

Two of Jeremy's cowboys were griping about their calluses and blisters. She heard the tail-end of the conversation. ". . . got us working like dang farmers out here."

Jeremy came walking up just in time to hear the last. His face turned red, but he ignored them.

"I'll bet they save their choice words for when you ain't . . . aren't around," Ginny whispered. Her cheeks felt warm when Jeremy nodded and winked.

The cowboys were starved for female company; either that or they were clumsy. One of them dropped his pliers three times in less than a minute. The other seemed unable to find the right fencepost in the wagonload of tree trunks he was pawing through.

Jeremy shook his head in disgust. "I think you better ride on home, Squirt."

"Me, what have I done?"

"They work slow enough without an audience. Best let them be."

"I'm not bothering them. They can pound posts all day for all I care."

"That's the problem. They see a pretty girl, they're not pounding anything but their chests."

"Jeremy!" Ginny protested, "I brought you dinner."

Jeremy rubbed his thick cowhide work gloves together to warm his hands. His face glowed with honest appreciation. "Well now, you're an angel in a new hat. I'm in a race against time. We're trying to set the posts while the ground is soft from this last rain."

Ginny laughed. "Hope you like beef stew and tortillas. Wanted to make some dried pear cake and hot Chinee tea like we have at school, but I ain't . . . haven't learned how yet."

"This'll do just fine." He pulled his canteen off a post of new-strung wire and took a swig while Ginny occupied herself with the food basket.

"You're chopping down all the juniper trees."

"Ground sprouters. They'll grow back. We have no other choice."

"How much longer will your fence take?"

"Hard to tell." He pulled off his gloves and glanced down the fence line. "Most of my time is spent riding the line, helping to settle disputes in the surveying. Sometimes all I do of a morning is to soothe feelings among my hired hands who think they're fencing themselves out of a cowboy way of life."

"Are they?"

Jeremy capped his canteen. "Probably. But it can't be helped. Another five years, everybody will be fenced in."

"Or out. Least that's what Patrón says." She turned to study the triple row of wire on the new fence. "What's going to keep the cattle from running through that skinny little wire?"

"They'll learn. But until they do, I aim to help them remember." He stuck a tortilla in his teeth and jumped up, mumbling, "Here's my plan." He grabbed a handful of thin cloth strips and waved them in the air. "The men'll hang these from the wires like a bird deflector in the garden." He tossed her one. "I've been spending my nights tearing short strips. Animals can see color. They notice movement. Hopefully they'll catch on."

"What if they don't?"

"We'll be riding fence day and night for awhile. Fixing breaks."

She sat watching him work until the sun started to set and the evening turned cool. "Time to head on home."

"Thanks for bringing dinner, Ginny. You're getting to be a good cook."

For once Jeremy wasn't teasing. The warmth of his compliment warmed her as she packed her basket into the saddlebag and mounted her mare. She glanced at him from under her lashes, confused at her feelings. "I got a pair of bloomers, one of the church ladies give me. I'll tear some rags for you. It'll tickle me to think of them blowing on your fence."

Jeremy looked up and shook his head. His face turned red and he glanced over to see if the men had heard. They hadn't. She laughed as she rode away.

Chapter Twenty-Eight

Ginny and Sancho made the ride back to Soledad on a sunny day, the first of January. She recited the multiplication table for his benefit. She had taught him the letters of his name and he'd carved them into the backside of the *bosal* he twisted for her mare. She found it wrapped in a bit of gunnysack beneath the digger pine tree he'd cut for her to decorate on Christmas Eve.

In his lilting, hesitant English, Miguelito told the story of Jesus and how El Señor was born in a small cave in a valley like Cholama, and how sheepherders brought gifts of lamb and pelts for Jesus and his beautiful madre. Missus Whitman had already read them the story, but Ginny liked the way Miguelito told it.

No one met the stage when she arrived in Santa Cruz so she made her way up the street alone, hefting her carpetbag. Other girls were arriving in buggies and wagons driven by their fathers, who handed down their valises then toted them inside. Miss Standish stood at the gate, talking earnestly to each parent. Something she said was causing a considerable amount of agitation on the part of the listeners.

Missus Whitman approached her and gratefully accepted the persimmons Ginny brought her. "Dear, let me help you with your bag. We can speak in your room."

Ginny followed her teacher through the hall and into the room she shared with the other first-year students. She waited as Missus Whitman set her valise on the bed.

"Sit down, dear." She sat on the edge of her mattress and waited to hear the reason for her teacher's grave demeanor. "Dear, your friend Nettie is . . . has passed to her reward. She died a few days ago."

The room seemed to be spinning, so Ginny tried to focus on something. She chose the coat hook while her mind tumbled with confusion. Clearly she had killed Nettie by being her friend. She saw her mama's daguerreotype hanging above the wash basin, a reminder that she was to blame. Guilt reared its ugly head and she kept hers lowered, hoping to be invisible as she cringed, trying to concentrate on Missus Whitman's voice.

". . . her aunt and uncle saw to the burial. We had to inter her right away. I've sent word to her family."

"Can . . . may I see her?"

"You may visit her gravesite on our next outing, weather permitting. We will hope for a temperate day." Missus Whitman prepared to take her leave. "I'm so sorry, dear, I know you loved her. No one is allowed near her bed. We've had it swabbed down."

"Will I die?" The selfish thought was out before she had time to think about it. She deserved to, she knew, but . . . .

Missus Whitman seemed to understand. "God willing, no. It's fortunate that she fell ill as most students were leaving."

"Can . . . may I miss supper? I'm not hungry."

Missus Whitman smoothed her hand over the top of Ginny's braids, her touch warm and soft. Her eyes were sad, but her voice took on the sternness she used when she taught arithmetic. "Food is necessary to maintain one's strength. You may return to your room after dinner tonight. But tomorrow, you need to resume your kitchen duties."

That night, supper caught in her throat. Everyone talked in subdued voices, but Nettie's name wasn't mentioned; it was like she'd disappeared the way her own mother had. After Ginny finished eating, she crawled into her straw mattress and bit down hard on the corner of her sheet to muffle the sound while she sobbed for all the dead people in Heaven.

The Lord is my Shepherd. I shall not want . . . Missus Whitman had made her class memorize a psalm about shepherds and green pastures. It was her favorite prayer. Ginny liked to think of Jesus as a shepherd like in Miguelito's story. In her bed, sniffling tears, she felt closer to her mother than she could ever remember. Close to Nettie and Jose Ignacio. Close, even to the dead vaqueros who hadn't known Jesus before they were tossed off their horses on the Bar N.

Sleep came when she was too exhausted to fight it any longer.

***

When spring arrived, Ginny wrote two letters.

> *Granmother,*
>
> *I have to rite a letter for class. Jeremy told me about you paying for school. I like school and misses whitman says I'm smart. Sancho made me a bosal for my horse. My friend died and I visit her grave on walks. The rain falls hard here and it gets some fogged. My best learnin is ciphering. Now I know how, I like adding numbers and carrying them over.*

156

Thanks for sending Jeremy. I'm sorry mama got sick. My next letter will be better.
   Your grandater,
   Virginia Nugent

The following week Missus Whitman assigned a second letter.

Jeremy,
   Expect you will read a letter if I rite one. So this is it. I rote my granmother. She mite rite back. I expect your working hard. Hope your bull don't die. Raining plenty here. Bet you could use some for your grass. I'm sorry to tell you Nettie passed on. She was my best friend forever. Expect you might want a lock of her hair. Here it is.
   Your friend that ain't a katydid.
   Virginia Nugent

April 3, 1879
Katydid,
   I enjoyed your letter. You'll be glad to know the bull is hale and hearty. The fences are still standing and nobody has taken a potshot at me over them. I'm sorry to hear of Nettie. Her parents have taken it hard. A letter from you might ease their burden. You've had two hard passings, but true friends do not all die. Some will remain with you through your life, I promise. I'm happy to hear the apple blossoms are out. I'll tell Missus Imus of your gesture. Take care.
   Your friend,
   Jeremy

She'd been watching for the apple blossoms so she could put a bouquet on Nettie's grave. She'd found the headstone in the Evergreen Cemetery, a marble block that came almost to her waist, carved with a little girl's hand reaching up to the heavens with a rosebud. The headstone had crisp lettering with the date Nettie died—December 6. She tried to imagine her mother's name carved into marble and lasting forever, alongside one for her brother that read, *Baby Nugent.*

April 5, 1879
Patrón,
   Missus Whitman says I should stay with her in Oregon for the

summer. Expect I might if this stands with you. Expect I can learn more from watching her than at the ranch. Keep feeding my horse. Give her oats. Don't swear at her either.

Virginia Nugent

Her father didn't reply. Sancho tried writing in a tight, cramped hand, with a stub of pencil he'd sharpened with his skinning knife. Missus Imus finished the note off for him.

Missy,

Grass is gone up and real dry. Cook is ornreyer than ever. Times is real bad at your place. Do what you need to do for yourself. Oregon sounds like what your mama would want.

Your friend, Sancho

November, 1879
Dear Katydid,

We lost some fine neighbors. Last month William and Sarah Imus took their son John and moved on. They followed William's brothers over to Arizona. Probably wanted to keep together with the horses they're supplying the army over there. They said the opportunities for selling beef to the miners was just too good to pass up. Missus Imus said she'd be obliged if you would keep a thought in your heart for her and her lost ones. She will think of you often and will visit if she is able.

The other two brothers, Charles and Edwin and his Rose, left here last year—restless, I suppose. I suspect they couldn't abide the changes that were taking place in the valley—including my fence. But change is part of life. You're not too young to understand that. The barbed wire issue has pretty much settled down. I made a friend in Gibson McConnell, who shares my interest in the wire. My cattle are increasing. Take care. We miss you. Seems I have only the meadowlarks now to chirp at me. Write when you can.

Your friend and almost uncle,
Jeremy

February 15, 1880
Jeremy,

Wrote Patrón two letters and never got an answer. I decided not to visit the ranch until he writes, since Sancho aint sent word things are better.

If it is fine by you I will visit Oregon again this summer with my teacher. Don't make much sense coming home to what I left without something changing.

Sorry this letter aint as fine as some the other girls write. Expect I have to work harder. Give Sancho my love. And Karoline, my horse.

Your friend,
Virginia Foster Nugent

Feb, 1881
Dear Katydid,

On the 1st of this month we had 7 earthquake shocks. The first 2 were very hard ones. They knocked down several chimneys, the adobe storeroom Edwin Imus built on his place and the end of William Imus's adobe barn, although the Imuses weren't there at the time. Mr. Parkinson got the worst of it. He had his chimney knocked down and the quake opened up several springs on his property. You can see them clearly from the road, boiling up with the smell of rotten eggs. If you were here you could take a bath in a four-foot sinkhole of hot water and never mind the winter cold!

I counted 30 quite large cracks in the ground running across the road. The jarring set me off my feet and took a couple of my rock fences with it. Hope you're learning to read well enough you can decipher this note. Sorry I don't have more news to tell. Your father is poorly. Sancho is well. Maria Inés is limping with a sore foot she tries to heal with plants she finds on the ranch.

Fondly,
Uncle Jeremy

September 1882
Dear Jeremy,

You ask what I've been doing. I'm keeping real busy. I'm growing ten ways to Sunday, that's for sure. Grew 3 inches since school let out. Missus Whitman made me lower my own hems. I don't tell her how much I hate sewing. My fingers are worn to stumps. We stitched up a taffeta skirt to wear with a hand-me-down shirtwaist a lady gave me. Missus W. had me to soak the collar in starch and press it with a hot iron till it was crisp as meringue.

This summer we made jelly and crocheted dollies. Some church ladies come by every Wednesday and read the Bible, and take tea and bitty slices of lemon bread and I get to serve.

You still promise to come to commencement (I copied the word off a book) if I finish my schooling? Expect you will be surprised when you see me. You and Sancho are my best friends and the only ones who write. Except Grandma. She's faithful to a fault, as she calls it.

I attended an event this summer and saw men play a game called polo. It's played on horses trained special. You asked about my plans when I'm grown, and I decided I'll train thoroughbreds for polo. Sancho and Miguelito could help. You could be my partner. We could go a fair ways to getting rich. I figure to get me a maid to serve strawberries and cream for breakfast. What do you think?

Your faithful friend for life,
Virginia

October 16, 1882
Ginny,

Polo horses sound like a fine idea. Your spelling has improved to the point that I would accuse you of having someone else write your news. But I know you are proud, and smart, and your words are your own. Your grandmother is proud of you, too.

The ranch has changed since you left home. Sancho says it's pining for you and I tend to agree. You may be surprised when you come for a visit, which I would recommend you do, soon. Your father isn't well. He has seen fit to offer some of the stock for sale and the ranch is quieter than you remember. I do not wish to alarm you, but it has been four years and you may be taken back at what you may find after all this time.

You never ask about the ranch. I hope that doesn't mean you've forgotten your friends. You're a young girl and you need to return to your roots soon. We can talk about the polo idea.

Your favorite friend and almost uncle,
Jeremy

April 2, 1883
Dear "Uncle" Jeremy,"

I am amused that you feel required to lecture me like I was a child. If you could see me you would not think to call me Katydid. I am tall as a willow except not so thin and shapeless. Missus Whitman says she is hard pressed to keep the boys away, but that is not true, exactly, although there was one this summer in Oregon who asked permission to write. Missus Whitman let me use my grandmother's funds for a flat-brimmed black hat, and I coil my hair in a roll that makes me appear older. I purchased my first grown-up dress for a cotillion in Portland and that's where I met the young man. I shall wear it to my graduation ball next year. You must plan to attend. Perhaps I will save a dance if you stop calling yourself my uncle.

Fondly,
Virginia

May 9, 1883
Ginny,

I've been hoping your father would write, but since he hasn't, I'm taking it on myself. It's time to come home. Your grandmother's money has run out with her passing. Maria Inés needs some help. Your father isn't up to doing much, and I know he misses you even if he doesn't say so. Sancho has been trying to keep things nice for you, but nothing is the same.

You've had nearly four years of school, and from your letters it would seem you've learned as much as many girls do in twice that. From the substance of your stories about traveling with your teacher, Mrs. Whitman, you have become quite the young lady. Your mama would be proud. Your grandma, bless her departed soul, was proud of you and grateful for your letters.

Jeremy

Four years. Had it been that long? Ginny set the letter aside and turned to study the ocean in the distance where the familiar bark of a seagull stirred her back to the present. Her clothing lay in neat piles on her bed waiting to be placed inside her carpetbag. She unwrapped a white handkerchief to expose the treasures that she'd determined to carry with her: small gull feathers she'd collected on walks, the pressed dogbane gathered from the Indian settlement, small pebbles she'd found near Nettie's grave. She ran her hands over the small volume of Shakespeare that Missus Whitman had presented to her along with a certificate of completion for the year's coursework—given to her with no fuss or finery, but what did it matter, she was going home.

She'd been longing for this letter in spite of the fact that she was frightened at the prospect of returning. Curiously, her heart skipped in anticipation of meeting Jeremy again. She'd carried the image during a thousand lonely nights when she longed for the ranch, the moment when he saw her again and realized how much she had changed. She closed her eyes and saw his flare with approval at the beautiful woman she'd become. Perhaps it was childish of her, but she was determined that she would have her moment of triumph when she stood before him.

Smiling, she lifted a stack of shirtwaists and stuffed them into the tight spaces of the carpetbag that remained. The Coast Line Stage would be arriving soon. Just enough time left to say her final goodbyes, and to collect addresses of the girls who would remain her friends forever.

Chapter Twenty-Nine

The Rios Caledonia Adobe was playing host to a number of loafers and loungers with nothing better to do than to place wagers on the exact minute the stage would arrive. A hostler was bringing up a matched pair of horses to replace the weary teams that pulled the red and yellow Coast Line Stage from Pleyto, forty miles back.

"El Camino Real, the King's Highway. If this is the way kings traveled, I'm happy to be common," the woman next to Ginny grouched. Ginny forced a smile for the sake of civility. The woman had dozed off between Natividad and Lowe's Station using Ginny's shoulder as a convenient pillow.

The man in the middle jump-seat was given to winks and grins of a disconcerting sort; either that or he suffered from a tick of his eye. Fortunately, he had the presence of mind to spit on the leeward side so his chewing tobacco didn't jump back in on Ginny again.

"Look over yonder. That's where this very stage was held up a week past. All the women relieved of their valuables," he announced with apparent glee.

Ginny was tempted to trade her window seat, just to give him something to look at besides her, but fortune smiled. At Jolon Station, he grumbled one too many times about the beans and bread the station master's wife served. "Judas Priest! We get fed another pot of beans, gonna have to take a physic just to get my bowls untangled."

When they started out again, the driver condemned him to a topside seat with the luggage. The loss of one occupant eased the cramped quarters inside, but it had no affect on the dust and grit. Ginny was sore from the hard seat, cramped from squeezing into a fifteen-inch-wide space alongside two bulky women, and seasick from riding backwards accompanied by the see-sawing movement of the leather-sprung wagon.

Some hours later the stage jerked to a halt at the Caledonia stop.

As soon as she disembarked, Ginny planned to pull off her linen travel duster and shake the dust out. The amenity provided by the Coast Line Stage covered her from head to foot, for the good it did. She would need to follow the other passengers over to the Salinas River to bathe the grit out of her skin, her hair, even her teeth. But dust was only one of the discomforts; the route festered with gamblers.

Sure enough, at a bench outside the tavern, two men were paying off their wagers. It seemed that at every stop someone was busy procuring their drinking money in that fashion. She squinted to see if one of them was Sancho, but undoubtedly he knew better. He was standing in the roadway, squinting with his good eye as if he were expecting to meet a child. Her expectations were no more accurate. It wasn't until she shaded her eyes that she was certain it was him. The past four years had been hard; that was evident. He seemed gaunter than she remembered. She could tell by the stern set of his muscles that frowning had become more natural than smiling.

She called his name and watched his face transform, first to disbelief and then to joy. Too soon he turned away, mumbling an excuse about having to retrieve a serape from his saddle to replace the linen duster.

Ginny tried to ignore the leering glances of the men milling about the station, speculating on whether she had someone to pick her up since there was no buggy waiting, only a pair of ranch horses, one so familiar that it brought tears to her eyes. She lifted her head and glided past the men with all the confidence she could muster. She wanted to hug Sancho, but the stranger who stood before her didn't raise his eyes and she lost her nerve.

"Sancho, before we set off, I need to find my way to the river. I better wash off one layer of dust before I pick up another."

He nodded, but he seemed incapable of speech.

When she returned, scrubbed and combed, her mare stood nearby. Ginny stroked her shaggy head. "You hardly know me, do you girl? It's been far too long. But I'm home now."

The ride was strained and silent; Sancho seemed too preoccupied to say more than a few words. "Got a new road over the hill, along Vineyard Mountain." A few minutes later he added, "Cuts some distance off the trek." Three miles later he offered, "Reckon most of the new folks is pleasant hereabouts."

Finally, Ginny protested. "Sancho, it's me. You act like I'm a stranger. Maybe I stayed away too long and you've forgotten all about me!"

When he met her gaze directly for the first time, his eyes glistened. "Missy, it's just that for certain-sure I'm riding alongside your mama right now. You're a dead-ringer for her."

For the next mile it was Ginny who rode in silence as emotions washed through her. She felt homesick, even as she traveled closer to the ranch. She would die before she'd admit it to Sancho, but part of her felt fearful about what awaited. How could she be afraid of her own home? Four years ago she had cried at having to leave, but that was before Jeremy's letter arrived. In the slit of a letter opener, everything familiar had ended. She reminded herself that she had been planning her graduation since she arrived at the school. What had changed with the note was a reminder that she had no choice in the matter of her life. In the aftermath, she had spent time reflecting on her attitude, as Miss Standish advised. After the initial feeling of pettiness passed, she was left with gratitude for the sacrifices her grandmother had made and for Jeremy, who convinced her she was good enough and smart enough.

At the far side of the Vineyard Grade, Sancho suggested they rest their horses. She dismounted and saw the small tombstones at the Imusdale Cemetery. She walked over to read the names of the graves of Willis Imus and his sister, Vina.

"Mister and Missus Imus didn't have much to show for their years here, did they?" She gazed across the valley to Castle Mountain. "Wish I'd known my brother."

Sancho straightened from checking her mare's hoof and his gaze met hers in silent understanding.

When they reached the ranch, Patrón was nowhere to be seen, but Maria Inés came hobbling from the summer house, wiping her hands on her apron, her face wreathed in a huge smile. "Señorita Geena! Es time you come home!" Her embrace was warm and filled with the essence of chilies and tomatillos.

A few minutes later Ginny made a tour of the house. The outside ladders had been pulled away, but the decay remained. Worse than the dirt and the squalor, her mother's presence seemed to be gone. She studied her surroundings, surprised at the anger welling up inside her. "I'm not calling him Patrón anymore."

Maria Inés was close enough to hear. "What you call heem, Señorita Geena?"

"I'm not calling him anything."

"Gonna need some name, Señorita. My people call father, *Tili*."

"I'll call him Charlie."

Sancho unstrapped her carpetbag from the back of her saddle and quietly carried it inside. The men sounded busy down at the corral. She heard the cries of the calves and smelled the dust of the cattle while memories brought up tears she thought she'd outgrown. She arrived just in time for spring roundup.

165

Dust nearly choked her when she climbed the loft ladder to her old bedroom. She wanted to head down to see what was going on at the corral, but first she needed to haul out her bedding and replace the straw to rid it of the stench of the rodents that had apparently taken up residence while she was gone. If she didn't take advantage of the waning sunshine she'd be up all night sneezing. But a loft was no place for a lady.

She descended the ladder, picked up her carpetbag and moved it into the empty bedroom down the hall, an unused room that her mother had intended for a nursery. Charlie had burned the crib and the rocker one night, and the room had gone unused all these years. A cot stood in the corner, made of rawhide strips that would hold her bedding after she scrubbed the cover and filled it with clean straw. Cobwebs claimed the corner. She swiped at a dirty window panel and realized she would need a basin of hot water and a cloth to do the job properly.

Her old vaquero britches slid over her hips, just barely, but the fit was too snug for decency and showed more calf than ankle, even with her high-top shoes. The riding skirt Missus Dunn had hemmed four years earlier made her seem more woman than girl. It was obvious what she'd be doing this evening after supper—pulling stitches. She'd grown to the height of the Dunn girls. In her domestic arts class she had learned the need to bundle rags to have on hand for her woman's time of the month. Missus Whitman had been strict about tempering practicality with her lectures on maidenly virtue.

She reached into her trunk and found her mother's camisole. When she laced it up, her breasts spilled over the top. A perfect fit. She unloosened her hair and let it fall to her waist in soft curls that no longer hinted of oak trees and broken knife blades. Down the hall, her mother's oval mirror stood where she had last seen it. Ginny pushed open *his* door and halted. Taking a quick, nervous breath, she picked up the wooden frame in both hands and carried it back into her room. With the mirror polished, she studied her reflection and was pleased with what she saw, but the soft-eyed beauty clad in her mother's camisole seemed a stranger. Sancho thought she was a dead ringer for her mama, and as she traced the curve of her breast, she hoped he was right.

On one of his trips down the hall, Sancho carried in a cardboard hat box that contained a Stetson the color of new calf and with the feel of velvet, a homecoming present from Jeremy. She plaited her hair into a loose braid down the center of her back and tied it off with the ribbon he had bought her four years earlier. When she finished, she donned a dress and made her way to the kitchen.

She kept busy helping Maria Inés with supper. When it was over and the dishes finished, Ginny knew she had to face her father.

Charlie was already ensconced in his chair when she entered the library. He hesitated before offering her a glass of whiskey, the gesture both pathetic and touching. She started to shake her head. Instead, she held out her hand and waited as he poured a portion into a glass. The taste burned her lips. She wanted to cough, but she forced herself to sip as though drinking hellfire was something she did every day.

He watched her with a sad, sweet longing, like he was seeing her for the first time. The comment Sancho had made, *the spitting image of her mother*, stuck in her head and she shivered. Taking another sip, she glanced around the room.

"Everything looks so familiar."

Charlie gave a casual glance at the ceiling and nodded. "No point changing anything. Nobody comes in here."

She studied the whitewashed walls, dirty with soot, and saw the room as her mother must have seen it, lovely and filled with possibility. With a bit of cleaning, and the furniture restored and repositioned; with the addition of some drapes like the ones Missus Whitman had made for her summer cottage, the room could be lovely. "Perhaps I could make some changes. Maybe if I—"

"Leave it! I don't want it touched."

Ginny took a deep breath. Her voice wavered, but it held. "I will require the key to the parlor. From now on it will be mine to use as I see fit." She hesitated. "There's no point in discussing it. Mama never intended for us to keep it as a shrine. If you don't wish to go in, I will understand. But I will use it as *she* intended. Please give me the key."

For a moment he looked shocked. Slowly, his look of anger dissolved and he walked over to the gun rack where his weapon rested in a green felt rack. He picked up a small rifle, carried it back across the floor and handed it to her. "This was your mother's Winchester 66. She didn't shoot it much, but it's yours if you want it. From both of us."

Ginny held the straight-grain walnut stock in her hands and rubbed the cool gunmetal barrel against her cheek. It was her mother's repeating rifle, a wedding gift from her father, manufactured the year they were married.

A faint memory caught her off-guard—a day spent in the pasture watching them shoot at tin cans set on a stump. She was eating a slice of bread and she looked around to share it with the tree squirrels, but they were hiding. Her mother had been happy that day. Her father, too. He had helped hold this rifle against her mother's cheek and they had laughed when she hit the target.

Now it belonged to her.

"Th . . . thank you, Charlie."

He nodded and returned to his whiskey. For a moment she wanted to throw her arms around his neck like she had that day, but the notion passed.

"Charlie, I need the key."

Chapter Thirty

Eight o'clock came and went. She grew tired of making conversation with Charlie fidgeting with the need of whiskey, but trying to ignore the bottle standing on the dusty sideboard. Finally, she escaped to the stuffiness of her new bedroom and its dubious mattress. The brass on her rifle gleamed in the lamplight; she couldn't resist an impulse to work the lever action before she turned out her lantern. It chambered easily. He had kept it oiled all these years.

The coo of night-birds and the chirp of crickets kept her keyed up long after her body willed her to sleep. Finally, exhaustion settled her nerves and she slept. The sound of rattling pans woke her before sunrise. She arrived at the cook house just as Jose Luis and Antonio trudged past, carrying a barrel of water until they saw her. The exertion lining their faces was interrupted by the shy glances they gave her.

Suddenly bashful in their presence, she kept her head down and concentrated on the platters of newly butchered beef liver and potatoes that Maria Inés was frying. When the food was ready she lugged the skillets to the long, makeshift tables that had been set up in the yard for neighbors arriving for the round-up. Everyone joined the vaqueros in a hurried meal, but this time there was no laughter, no bantering, no bragging about who would rope the most; it was as though each man and woman was there out of obligation. When she returned with the coffee pot, someone recognized her and the table erupted in a frenzy of welcome. The food was forgotten while men and women showered her with hugs and pats. Some of the cowboys had been boys the last time she saw them; now they had families of their own.

By the time everyone returned to their plates, Ginny was flustered and disheveled, grateful for the bottomless coffeepot she found herself occupied with. Her wrists were unused to the weight of the cast-iron skillets, felt like they would break by the time the last man left. A few laughing and chattering neighbor women began transferring pies and pots of beans from their wagons to the tables while they peppered her with questions about Santa Cruz.

The braying of calves from the corrals created an irresistible temptation. In the cook house, Maria Inés kept her eyes averted as if she had no thought except the tortillas she was preparing. Ginny hesitated, torn between duty and the familiar desire to join the men. Finally, she picked up a load of dirty tin plates and started scrubbing. The sounds outside seemed so familiar, she could track the activity without seeing it. Vaqueros from the neighboring ranches were trying to separate their cows from the common herd. Miguelito was on horseback with a coiled lariat, working the cattle. The men had undoubtedly ridden hard, scouring the land for every last stray. Some of the more experienced cows hid their calves—sometimes in the same arroyo each year or under the same bush, while others moved easily into the milling circle. The stragglers were the challenge.

She washed another dish while she imagined the scene at the corral.

Charlie stood heating the iron that held his brand, the Bar N. Sancho handled the *senal*, the ear mark while the vaqueros roped the calves with their reatas. The first roper, the header, aimed his loop for the horns while the second, the healer, tossed a well-placed loop around the hind legs. They stretched the ropes taut and laid the animal out flat while a third man straddled the calf, keeping his knee on the neck until Charlie could brand it. The men were quick. In less than a minute, Charlie was finished, the young bull calves castrated and the calves, more angry than hurt, released to run bawling back to their mothers.

All morning the squalling of the calves and the braying of mother cows filled the canyon until Ginny was almost crazy with longing. By the time the sun was high overhead, the branding had winded to a halt and the vaqueros who had finished stood waiting to close the gate, collect their gear and douse the fires. In the silence she realized that everyone was heading for the yard. Charlie would be in the lead, eager to slip into his room and emerge with a bottle of whiskey.

She saw them coming, tired, dusty men with ravenous hunger and a powerful thirst for whiskey and coffee. Ginny smoothed her hair away from her damp face and straightened, trying to repair herself while she scanned the crowd for a glimpse of Jeremy. Her quick count tallied thirty-five men and women. Jeremy was not among them.

She and the other women spread the food on the long table beneath the cottonwood: Platters of cornbread and tortillas, pans of beans and fried potatoes, baked pumpkin, greens of monkey weed, miner's lettuce and lambs quarter, boiled corn and dried apple pies. A young steer was roasting on the spit. Ginny sipped a cup of panoli she had made with Maria Inés's help from roasted corn, pulverized and mixed with sugar.

When their work was finished the vaqueros would drink whiskey. They would fill their bellies and play their music long into the night for whoever chose to stay and listen. A few unfamiliar cowhands bolted to the front of the line. They had arrived on fresh horses and dismounted behind the barn, trying to blend in with the dusty, exhausted crew. When they finished eating they would plead the need to do chores back at the home ranch. Sancho had pointed it out to her once, and she made a point to watch for them. Sure enough, she saw them lingering near the tables. 'Grubbers' he called them. Others were waiting at the fringe, most likely outlaws waiting to eat before they returned to give their bosses a report.

She turned to retrieve a stack of clean plates from a pregnant Missus Harlan who was washing them. Suddenly she felt a stranger leering at her from a few feet away. Her eyes drifted down to a pair of expensive Anaconda snakeskin boots that no self-respecting cowboy would wear, even if he could afford them. The man wore calfskin gloves that didn't look as if they'd ever held a tool. She removed her apron and rolled it in a ball while she waited for him to speak.

He continued to stare, apparently in no hurry to break the unholy silence. For want of any better idea, she made the first move, a hostess's inquiry into his supper needs. When he gave her a condescending half-smile and a wink, she turned to stand next to Sancho and one of their neighbors.

Sancho hadn't missed the exchange. "You keep your distance from that one," he growled. "He's nothing but a wolf looking fer his next meal." She nodded, unsure how Sancho knew the man. "You leave that one to your father. Hear me?" Sancho glanced across the yard with a worried look. "Not sure why Jeremy ain't here. Something must have come up."

Her welcome home party was going horribly wrong. Jeremy hadn't even bothered to show up. She moved away before she shamed herself with tears, a reminder to herself that she was a grown woman, no longer a little girl. The lesson held when she saw the reaction of the stranger. He smiled and she glanced around to see if anyone was watching, but Sancho had disappeared.

The stranger caught her alone while she was carrying a load of dishes to the washpan. "Miss Nugent, I apologize if I startled you."

"You didn't."

The stranger stood before her, his smile widening. "Permit me to introduce myself. George Hayes of San Francisco."

"My father's over at the corral, showing off his horses. I suggest you catch up with him there." She coiled a strand of hair in a nervous gesture that highlighted her self-consciousness.

His eyes darkened with amusement. "Oh, I'll do just that. Trust me. But for the moment, I wish to make your acquaintance. You see, I fully expect us to be friends some day."

She thought she'd misheard. "You must be mistaking me for someone else."

He smiled tolerantly. "Quite sure I'm not. I represent the Comstock group, associates of your father. But let's not speak of business. I had no idea Charles Nugent had a grown-up daughter."

"I . . ." She started to protest, but stopped herself. He seemed friendly enough; maybe she had overreacted. She reminded herself that she was old enough to make her own judgments.

He scanned the crowd, apparently seeing no one more interesting, because he turned back, smiling agreeably. "Have you taken time to eat, yet, Miss Nugent?" She shook her head. "Well, let me rectify that. There's no reason why a beautiful woman should be toiling like a peasant." He led the way to the table and casually laid a slice of raisin pie on her plate. She was flattered by his concern. He speared a chunk of beef and laid it alongside a scoop of baked squash. "We'll leave off those infernal beans. You deserve better, Miss Nugent."

She felt her neck heating. "Call me Virginia."

***

Ginny was in the orchard when George Bender Hayes swung from his horse and started toward her. She was dismayed to see that his valise was tied to the back of his horse.

"You're leaving us so soon, Mr. Hayes?"

"My ill fortune, to be sure. A week in this god-forsaken country and you arrive on my last day here," he groused. "What abominable luck."

"You would stay longer if you could?" Ginny bit her tongue at the unladylike prodding. But she was touched by his sincerity. Perhaps she had been mistaken in her earlier opinion of him.

"I would extend my stay, but business calls me back to San Francisco. You and your father must visit. I have an acquaintance about your age. She would be delighted to have a new friend."

Ginny kept her eyes to the ground and strove to contain her disappointment. "Charlie doesn't travel much."

"Then you must come alone. I'll arrange it with your father."

"I've only just arrived. I doubt he will agree."

He smiled again. "There is a new play opening soon. You might enjoy it. Are you fond of theatrical productions?"

Ginny colored. "Oh, yes. I've seen several in Ashland."

"Then I shall make the arrangements. Now I must bid you adieu." He grasped her hand and brought it to his lips as though she were a high-born lady. Plucking a card from his vest, he handed it to her before managing a graceful leap into his saddle. At the road he turned back and tipped his hat.

Ginny remained in the orchard, hugging her arms against her sides. She glanced at the business card in her hand. *George Hayes.* Taking a twig from the apple tree, she traced his name in clear block letters in the dirt. After wiping the name clear with the back of her hand, she wrote it again, this time in cursive, adding his middle name, *George Bender Hayes.* She coiled a strand of hair around her finger—a habit she despaired of breaking—and traced the words into the air, *San Francisco.* Sighing, she turned to where the dust from his horse had already settled. "I wish I would hurry and turn seventeen."

Sancho was sitting in the shaded canopy at the bunkhouse. She found a seat and watched him working a strand of horse tail that he'd secured to an oak tree. A hank of tail hair was piled nearby, trimmings from the wild Spanish Bard horses captured from the Tulare Plains, their tails chopped short to show from a distance that the horses were claimed. He reached for a piece and began hitching a new set of reins.

Ginny watched his fingers ply the coarse hair. "Who's it for?"

"Depends. You need one?"

She shrugged. He finished one or two every winter, working on them in the rainy evenings while the vaqueros gambled. He liked to keep his hands busy, as a remedy to his rheumatism. When he wasn't playing cards or mending his gear, he was making horsehide reatas or bosals to trade or sell.

He steamed the hair in a large vat simmering on an outside fire, a tub filled with dye. He'd already spent days cooking, straining and laying the hair over strung ropes to dry. Now he was ready to begin.

"Where did you learn this, Sancho? All the other fellows make salt and pepper reins, but yours have every color in the rainbow."

He reached for another handful. "Never told no one this before, but in my younger days I was a hell-raiser. Spent time in the Arizona territorial prison. That's where I learned the trade, so to speak." He gave a sheepish grin. "Might say I had time on my hands."

Ginny considered. "What did you do that was so bad?"

He cast a sheepish look around. "Judge said it was a question of whose brand was on some calves we was trailing."

"You rustled cattle?"

His ears reddened. "Different world back then. Spent a couple of years seeing the error of my ways." He added another strand of color and glanced over to see how she was taking the news.

"My mother know about you?"

His grip eased slightly. "Yep."

"And my father?"

"Whatta *you* think?"

She didn't bother answering.

He jabbed his thumb toward a hank of dyed horsehair. "Remember anything I taught you?"

She pulled up a strand. "Reds from the madder root and the cactus apples. Yellow from sunflowers. Orange from ground lichen. Juniper berries, the green." She held one up to the sunlight. "You said the plants around here are washed out."

"True enough. Injun paint brush gives a real pretty brick color, though. Use that a lot. Brown, I get from the sumac." He grabbed another handful. "Ain't the dyes I have trouble getting nowadays, it's the horsehair. Wild horses are all gone."

"Looks like you have enough to make a rope all the way to China."

He had piles of hair collected under tarps and stuffed in wooden boxes stacked against the wall of the bunkhouse.

"Don't know about stretching clean to Chinee, but takes pert near four miles of horsehair just to make up one little halter. More than that for the reata. They call the reins a mecate, down Mexico way. Up here, Yankee cowhands call them a McCarty. Reckon some folks don't take to Mexican talk." He paused to spit his chew into the dirt. "No matter. Them ropes'll last a lifetime."

She picked up the end. "You never said who it was for."

"Jeremy asked to buy one." His voice hardened. "You two in a pucker? The other day you spent all your time with that bank feller."

Ginny lifted her head and felt heat flooding her face. "Mister Hayes knows a lot of people in San Francisco. He goes to theatrical performances and musicales nearly every night."

"That what you want?" Sancho tugged at a knot.

She gave him a look. "I think he's interesting, that's all."

"Kind of slobbery around the chops, you ask me."

"Well I didn't. Sancho, he invited me to visit him in San Francisco."

His face wrinkled into a scowl. "Wonder how many little gals he pays

174

notice to? Maybe only the ones that'll own a ranch, someday?" He snorted. "Fellow strikes me as a coyote."

She'd never heard him speak rudely about anyone; it wasn't fair he would dislike the only person who had ever treated her like a grown-up. He was jealous because she had made a friend. At any rate, she'd heard enough. She stalked off toward the house, leaving him sitting with his horse hair. She planned to spend the afternoon with her rifle and an empty tin can.

Chapter Thirty-One

Jeremy watched his men riding off to the roundup at the Nugent Ranch with longing in his gut. Ginny was back. It took everything he had not to leap into his saddle and race the other men over to the ranch. He imagined her with her neat pigtails, a sprinkling of freckles and that irascible expression that never failed to bring a smile to his face—or his heart. *First thing tomorrow*, he promised himself. *I'll see how she likes my gift.*

He gave a last look at his disappearing men before he bent to pour his foreman a cup of coffee. Pouring one for himself, he squatted near the fire. "Troy, we have a problem."

"Looks that way."

"Here's what I've considered." He drew out a rough map on the ground. "But I'm going to need your help."

"Shucks, Boss, you know you don't have to ask."

Troy Hart was a good man, a displaced Southerner who had left enough of himself back home on the battlefield that he decided to try his luck in a new climate. He had hopes of setting up a spread like Jeremy's. They'd become friends in the laying of fence line and at mealtimes, suffering each other's cooking.

***

In the weeks that followed, each time a fence was cut the site was entered on the map while he and his foreman kept watch without appearing to do so. Soon enough it became obvious that a pattern was developing, and they set the trap. The culprit was a drifter who wanted a few more weeks work before he got turned out. Jeremy was hiding in a draw at midnight, near where they anticipated the next cut would occur, when he heard Troy's whistle. He rode up in time to catch the drifter cutting the second strand. They confiscated his wire cutters and threatened to turn him over to the law.

The culprit whined, appealing for mercy in a voice that lifted an octave. "Sheet! You ain't goin' to string me up over this!" You son of a seadog. It ain't even again' the law."

Jeremy considered. The drifter was right; cutting fences wasn't against

California law, not yet, at least, but give the legislators another week. He smiled. "We're not going to hang you."

The man's confidence rebounded; he edged toward his horse while Jeremy conferred with his foreman.

When the man was almost to his stirrup, Jeremy yanked the reins from his hand. "We've decided to turn you over to the cowhands." He turned to his foreman. "Troy, bring those wire nippers along. The boys may find something on him to trim."

The drifter's voice rasped with panic. "What I got to do to make this right? I was only trying to make some steady work for myself." He spit and rubbed his worn boot on the inside of his other leg, a nervous gesture that belied his cocky tone. "Sides, I was sore. It ain't right, fencing in the range. Land belongs to everyone."

"Be that as it may, your stay is these parts is finished," Jeremy told him as he fished eleven dollars from his money clip. "Here's two weeks pay. You pack up your gear and quit this country for good. Understand?"

The next morning, Jeremy made it a point to be standing alongside the cook stove when the crew arrived for breakfast. He waited until the last man sat before he helped himself to a plate of salt pork, potatoes and beans.

"You men know what I expect. You'll mend fences, dig a post as well as brand and rope. Is anyone unclear about any of this?"

The men glanced at each other uncertainly.

"I'm glad we're in agreement," Jeremy said. "Clearly you've thought through your stand on the fencing question?"

The men nodded.

He glanced from one man to the other and made a decision. "Today we start on the new bunkhouse. It's time you have a real house."

***

Sancho happened by while Jeremy's men were hammering stud walls into place. Jeremy met him with a mug of coffee.

"Riding fence are you? Hop down and I'll show you a fine cup of coffee."

"Arumph."

Jeremy poured a cup for himself. "Notice the new grass? Makes a cattleman proud to be alive." He took a sip and added, "When nature cooperates, it's an easy living."

Sancho kept his gaze on the ground, but his hand on the mug trembled with palsy. "One of these years the drought's going to kill our way of life."

"I surely hope you're wrong, neighbor."

"'Spose that's one thing we can agree on," Sancho muttered.

Jeremy started toward a pile of lumber waiting to be unloaded. "How are things over your way?"

"Surprised you'd ask. There's a gal over there thinks you're mad at her."

Jeremy winced. "I had a problem come up at my ranch. Had to miss the round-up. Felt like hell. Didn't even see her."

"Well, someone did. Looks like we got trouble." Sancho relayed his version of the events.

"Sweet Betsy!" Jeremy punched the air with his fist "A banker friend in 'Frisco warned me about that coyote." He dropped the board he was trying to pick up and glared at his crew. "You men got work to do?" When they picked up their hammers again, he was careful to keep his voice low. "You think she's getting man-crazy? She's just a kid."

Sancho seemed to be holding back a smile. Even his tone had a bite of humor. "Ya had a look at Ginny, lately? Could be some fellow can see what you're missing."

"Ah, she's just a kid," Jeremy repeated, his voice less sure than before. He remembered his failed promise to call on her.

"She's rounded out. Getting all soft like her ma. 'Spect it won't be long till she'll be wanting to be taken to the dance in a real buggy." Sancho toed the dirt like he was studying it for snakes.

Jeremy grinned at the idea of Ginny dancing. "Well, for crying out loud. You let her know, come this Saturday night I'll take her to the roundup dance at the new hall. That way she won't feel shy."

Sancho nodded and ducked his head like he was hiding something.

The sun was high overhead. Jeremy glanced up and asked, "You want to take the noon meal with us?"

Sancho nodded toward the pot simmering over the fire. "Nah. Know only too well what you bachelor ranchers is having—beans and more beans." He started for his horse and hesitated. "Come to think of it, Ginny sent this along. It's her hellfire stew."

"Stew again?"

"Must think you're partial to it. But there's enough for yer men."

"How long has it been since I tasted her stew? Four years?"

"Her chow goes down pretty good these days."

"Ginny in the cook house?" Jeremy tried and failed to fit the image in his head.

"Best not laugh. Missy hear you, she'll pepper it up. Things could get a little comp-li-cated when it hits the gut." Sancho was still laughing as he turned toward home.

***

Jeremy's first glimpse of Ginny, she was standing inside her father's adobe in a thin, flowing dress of gauzy lilac like the one on the porcelain doll he'd brought her years ago. It was the sort of dress that Southern belles wore back home. He squinted in the dim lamplight to be sure it was her, standing there with her long blonde hair caught up in some sort of fat curls that made green pools of her eyes. His heart raced in a strange conflict of emotions that would bear meditating on if he made it through the next few minutes. He opened his mouth to announce himself, but his words caught in his throat. He coughed. Confused as he'd ever been in his life, he lifted his hand to knock on the door. Behind him, a lad in another wagon pulled into the yard, jumped to the ground and brushed past.

"Ready, Miss Nugent? I brought Pa's wagon. And a quilt for the dust."

Jeremy watched as she smiled beguilingly. She started forward and paused when she noticed Jeremy standing there, hat in hand. Her smile hit him with the force of an anvil.

"Oh, Jeremy. Are you going to the dance, too? I suppose we will see you there. Joseph was so kind to stop by and invite me. *Personally.*"

He gulped and noticed Sancho watching from his seat on the porch. The situation was utterly beyond comprehension; he felt his face heating as Ginny maneuvered the lad into the wagon.

She turned and smiled. "Jeremy, would you mind following behind us so you don't kick up dust? We'd so appreciate the courtesy." She turned back to the lad and Jeremy heard her explaining, "Mr. Lawsen is a close friend of the family. Practically an uncle."

He waited until the wagon circled back toward the oak tree at the end of the lane before he turned to acknowledge Sancho's canary grin. "What just happened here?" His voice seemed rusty.

"What'd I tell you?"

They trailed the couple at a safe distance until they reached a park-like glen along the Big Cholame Creek where a brand new, two-story hall had been erected the week before. Without a church or a school, the park and its new town hall were the closest thing to a community they had, not counting the Imusdale post office. He found a place to park his buggy and leaped down, feeling foolish in a conveyance suited for women. People were arriving with pies and covered dishes, children and babies bundled in blankets. The sounds of fiddle and banjo came from downstairs while women carried their food up the stairs to the second floor.

A mosquito buzzed Jeremy's ear and he cuffed it with a vengeance while Ginny's lad helped her from the buggy. When the wind chose that moment to flare up, he watched two shapely legs flash from under her thin dress.

"Judas Priest, can't she keep herself decent?" he groused as he twisted his horse's reins around the railing. His instinct was to slug the fellow who had benefitted from the view at close-hand.

The new building smelled like raw pine. The musicians stood in a corner, warming up on their instruments. A fiddle, banjo, guitar and harmonica blended with a washboard and spoons played by a couple of younger boys.

The first round of dancing began and Jeremy watched from the sidelines as Ginny and her lad took the floor. He stood trying not to be obvious as they twirled, cut under and promenaded without a misstep, chatting and laughing instead of concentrating on the steps. Ginny threw her head back and laughed at something the boy said. Jeremy couldn't help but wonder where she had learned to dance.

After the second round, he realized he was acting like a concerned father instead of a young man with a rare evening off. He made his way outside to smoke a cigar with Enoch Lee and his brother Eli, and to make acquaintance of some homesteaders and quicksilver miners who had recently moved into the valley.

After a few minutes of small talk, George Gould asked the question everyone seemed to be waiting to hear; "Those fences holding up okay?"

Jeremy paused to light his cigar. "So far." His interest wasn't in fences tonight. He felt strangely in the mood for a fight.

A little man was scowling from the shadows. Eli Lee introduced him as his friend, Frank Bass. Jeremy glanced up over his flaring match, giving himself time to form an impression before he spoke. The two made a strange pair; Bass, scarcely chest high to his friend Lee, but they apparently shared a fondness for varmint hunting with their long guns. Bass bragged he had a recipe for squirrel pie that lit up the cabin when the wild onions were ripe and ready for stewing. But he wasn't here to exchange recipes. Tonight he seemed to have something more on his mind.

Bass stroked his bushy beard and glanced over at Eli before he turned to Jeremy. "Don't seem right, you start something will affect the whole valley. A man's right to hunt ought'a be considered."

Jeremy kept his eye on the two Lee brothers. "This valley's a big place. I don't mean to take anything from you. Just want to protect what belongs to me."

"Wildlife belongs to everyone," Bass muttered.

"Heard tell out on the prairie, whole herds are stampeding. Getting tangled in broken strands. Some of them running for miles. Choking to death on the barbs stuck in their lungs," Enoch Lee said.

Jeremy frowned. "Folks on the flatlands have different problems. Prairie fire and lightning. Thunderstorms that make the wildlife panic."

William Todd tapped his pipe against a nearby tree and casually refilled the bowl. "Been doing some reading. Seems our hills help a lot. Keeps the critters from stampeding. I'd say let's wait and see."

"I'm doing more than wait and see. I'm building my future, one post at a time," Jeremy said, favoring his critics with a glare.

"More like one blockhead at a time," Bass muttered.

Jeremy made a movement toward him, but the new postmaster broke in.

"Seems a shame to waste the evening arguing over something we can't solve. Let's celebrate the fact that the Red Rock School District has been officially formed. We have more in common than what divides us." He turned to the man on his right. "You're to be congratulated on spearheading such a fine idea. Isn't a man here who won't benefit from having his children educated. So let's enjoy the music." He directed Jeremy toward the music. "Time for you to take one of the ladies around the floor, my friend."

Jeremy nodded and stubbed out his cigar. When the others drifted off, he turned to Todd. "Appreciate what you just did, sir."

Todd nodded. "'Spect I'm as close to the law as we have around here. Now you leave it be and enjoy yourself."

Jeremy caught a glance of Ginny dancing with a second young man— and a different one after that. At least she had the good sense to spread her attentions around, he thought, as he guided a homesteader's plump wife through the Virginia Reel.

H managed to maneuver himself so that he was standing next to Ginny at the refreshment table when the music ended. "Enjoying yourself?" he asked, aware that his hands were sweating. She nodded, too winded to speak. A waltz began just as she finished her glass of cider. Before Jeremy could claim her, a young man led her out onto the floor.

Jeremy turned and headed for his wagon.

Chapter Thirty-Two

The silence of the cook house woke Ginny before the first beams of morning light filtered through her window. Outside, the vaqueros were milling beneath the cottonwood tree, muttering. She rose from her bed and bolted to her feet, grabbing her black skirt with her teeth while she thrust her arms into the white shirtwaist she had worn the day before. She ignored the oval mirror, slipped on her shoes and ran to the door without waiting to pull the buttonhook through the fastenings.

The men were standing in the orchard, their feet pitching clouds of dust in the orchard rows while they watched an Indian woman walking down the track to the entrance of the Bar N. From where Ginny stood, the woman made a graceful silhouette against the rising sun, her tule reed mat slung over her back as she limped down the road. A wide basket—probably filled with the acorn meal she had been up late grinding—rode on her low, broad forehead, with only a loose hand to balance it. Her free hand held a rope connected to a goat, its trim hooves giving off puffs of dust as it followed.

Maria Inés!

Ginny gripped the door frame until she feared she would pass out. From the corner of her eye she saw Sancho holding back a faint smile. Charlie forced his way past, swinging the door hard against the wall as he strode into the yard. For once speechless, he stood staring in the direction that his vaqueros were facing. It was Sancho who made the first sound. Ginny heard him laugh. He pivoted and the two men faced each other, sparks flying between them until Sancho turned and limped toward the corral.

In a few minutes he was back, leading an old mare harnessed with the new mecate he had just finished. He strode past the yard without glancing over, but his challenge was clear to everyone watching—Charlie most of all, who refused to shift his gaze from the back of the departing Maria Inés. When Sancho reached her, he took the basket from her head and tied it across the horse's wither before handing her the reins. He stood aside while she mounted.

When the horse was lost to sight, Ginny felt a headache beginning. She knew before Charlie spoke what his next words to her would be.

"Meals better be on time from now on, girl."

***

Ginny kept the bean pot simmering. After every meal she added to it as the men ate their way through the contents of the big cast iron pot and looked around, scowling, for something else to curb their insatiable appetites. Maria Inés had left enough tortillas for the first meal, but the pile was depleted and dinner only hours away.

On his way to the corral, Charlie stuck his head into the summer house and bellowed, "I want fresh-baked bread from now on. No more of them damned tortillas." She jumped at his next words. "Time to put your fancy education to work."

She kneaded enough bread dough for six loaves and set them to rise in a crockery bowl covered with a bit of cotton flour sacking. Between shaping loaves, adding sticks to the slow fire, frying potatoes and all the rest of it, she made a dozen trips to the root cellar.

By the time she found her way to bed, her feet were blistered from wearing her shoes without stockings. She pulled them off and rubbed her toes. With a start, she realized she hadn't gotten around to hooking the buttons.

She woke an hour early the next morning in order to have the oven hot for coffee and baking. Sancho cut the stove wood smaller so she could regulate the oven temperature more easily, but the sun was barely over the hills before he apologetically hung two tree squirrels outside the door. She cleaned the animals and plunked them in cold water before returning to her other chores. Flies were already gathering on the gut bucket by the time she carried it to the hogs. Afterwards, she made her way back to the table, lowered her head and wept.

"This is . . . .isn't . . . wh . . . wh . . . at I went to school for. I don't want to cook. I don't wan . . . want my hands to get rough and dry like hers. I want to live."

After a few minutes she dried her eyes with the apron that had become part of her. The loaves of bread would last a few days and then it would be time to do it all over again. What did Charlie expect from her, a miracle? Ire built inside her until she felt herself growing hot, like the embers in the stove waiting to be fed. "He's not going to win. He's not!"

Saying the words aloud helped. So did action. She stalked across the yard to the summer house and began throwing flour into a huge crockery bowl. She added lard, salt and the soured goat's milk Maria Inés had left behind, and began working the dough between her fingers until the pieces crumbled into small bits. As she rolled the pie crust into shape, she vented her anger on the dough. By the time she finished she had made two observations. This would be the best pie the men had ever eaten, and she was going to get herself to San Francisco.

A noise in the yard caught her attention. *Jeremy!* She made fists and gathered her forces to let him know how he had hurt her. She'd been home a whole week. A whole week! How dare he!

The pie was cooling when Jeremy ducked and entered. Despite her anger, Ginny's hands went to collect her stray strands, but she realized that no amount of finger combing could make up for the fact that she'd forgotten to even comb her hair. There was no hope for it. This wasn't what she'd imagined—to be humiliated like this. She turned away so he wouldn't see her tears.

Apparently he didn't notice because he made a lame joke. "Whooee!" It's hot in here. How do you manage it?"

The fire was stoked for the midday meal. So was her anger. "Don't notice it being any hotter than usual."

His response was dangerously casual. "That so?" He grinned. "I'm sorry I haven't been over. It's been a hard week—"

"You've had a hard week?"

He nodded. "I wanted to come, meet you proper. But I had to. You need to . . . you look tired."

Tired? She had dreamed of how she would look. And he'd ruined everything.

She decided to give him an earful. "I'm so sorry to hear that. Tell you what, Jeremy, you just mosey out and tell the men I won't be serving any meals today. Invite them over to your place. I'll shut down the stove and take a nap."

"Hey now!"

She plunked the Dutch oven onto the table and began filling it with the two squirrels and a handful of carrots and potatoes she had just picked. "Here you are, riding all the way over from your place. I'll bet you're purely tuckered out.

"Not too bad—"

She shoved the pan into the oven and turned. "Checking up on those cows and calves can really soak the starch out of a man. I know because it sure works up the appetites around here!" Choosing that moment to take a long look at the garden, she waited until her voice calmed and her eyes dried before she turned back.

Jeremy sat watching as she mixed icing for a raisin cake that waited near a crock of fresh-churned butter from the Guernsey cow her father had purchased for her to milk. He was probably accessing the stoop to her shoulders and the exhausted look of her eyes, where darkened circles gave evidence to the long hours she was putting in, but she couldn't care. She glanced up at the sun and mentally gauged the time she had left before the men returned for their meal. Even this gesture was wasted when the clock in the main house began chiming.

They sat in silence while the clock finished. Jeremy spoke first. "Your father's wrong to use you like this. You're too smart and fine for this. Let me help you."

He sounded regretful, but she was too angry to care what he thought. She broke off a brittle laugh. "Yeah. Look at me! Tied to the stove with my apron strings."

Jeremy watched her, his eyes dark and intense, like he actually cared. But if he did, he'd have come by before now. In the next moment she lost her generosity of spirit when he took a sip of the coffee she had ground before the sun was up. She wanted him to offer sympathy, but instead he sat watching her with eyes that hid his emotion.

She felt her humiliation heating to anger. "You men! When you work up a sweat, you can take a rest. Or climb into a waterhole. Even manage a siesta."

He raised his hand as if to ward off an attack. "Whoa, I'm not your foe here."

"Maybe not." She rubbed her hands on her apron as though she could wipe this nightmare from her skin. "But I'm too tired to tell the difference."

Jeremy's eyes widened into softness that unnerved her. "Your father getting you any help?"

She snorted. "Charlie's idea of helping is to ride on into Hollister for provisions so I don't have to take time away from the stove. I haven't been off the ranch in six weeks. Not since the night of the dance."

He absorbed this information with a long sip from his mug. Was it her imagination or were his hands shaking? "Why do you stay?"

She considered his question, not for the first time. Not even the first time that day. "He wants me to fail. I came back looking like my mother and he can't stand it. He's trying to get me to leave him like she did." His eyes narrowed and she realized the idea wasn't so far-fetched. "I won't go."

"What can I do?"

"Jeremy, do you have any idea what I do around here all day?" A basket of beans sat waiting for her to snap and blanch, but she ignored them.

His tone was annoyingly calm. "A fair idea, I suppose."

"You suppose?" She was spoiling for a fight and he was as handy a target as she was likely to find. "I'm up first every morning. I fix breakfast for everyone, all by myself. Then I pack up whatever they need, if they're riding out for a few days. Then I clean the dishes and start dinner. After Maria Inés took her goat, Charlie brought home a cow. I strain the milk and set it to cooling. Some days I make butter. I beat that cussed churn until my back could break." She held out her hands. "Look at my blisters." She held them in front of her until he turned. "Then there's cake and bread to make, twice every week. And when I'm not cooking, I have to set up whatever's ripe in the garden so we'll have something to eat this winter. If the men don't do it, I gotta crush the grapes for Charlie's homemade wine."

Her voice grew louder until it echoed in her ears. "Then there's the days I wash clothes and hang them to dry. Takes the whole day. Then I iron everything with those heavy sad irons I heat up on the stove. Charlie likes his shirts done just so, and he tosses them back at me if they have a wrinkle."

By now she was pacing. "I don't allow us to live like animals anymore. So the beds get changed, the floors swept. I carry all my own water. It's either that or watch Sancho struggle with it."

She was gratified to see Jeremy squirming. From the oven, the scent of stewing squirrel filled the room. The clock in the hall chimed the half-hour, reminding her that she was getting further behind by the minute. She didn't care. The vaqueros could dig clay for dinner for all she cared.

"When I have time, I clean out the stove and the milk buckets and tend the pickles and the chilies over there soaking in brine. Sometimes Sancho picks a bushel or two of peaches that can't hold any longer, and I stop everything and split them and put them on trays so they can dry. Then, after a few days, when I have a minute, I turn them, and when they're dry I collect them in gunny sacks."

Jeremy's face was getting red—served him right.

"I make ten, maybe more, trips down to the cellar every day. When I'm done I grind meat scraps for sausage. Oh, then there's the jerked meat. I slice pieces of beef and pepper them, and hang them overhead to dry. Kitchen's so hot they cure themselves." She glanced over to see if he was still listening. "And when I have nothing else going on, if we butcher I put up mincemeat, head cheese and blood sausage."

She paced from one end of the room to the other, avoiding Jeremy's long legs by sheer determination. Each time she came to Maria Inés's corn meal basket, she cursed the woman anew. "Last time I spoke to anybody wasn't hungry was at the dance."

She picked up the basket of beans. "Most nights I get myself to bed by ten so I can start all over again." She broke off a bean and tossed it into a bowl. "Come winter, I'll have to get up and stoke the stove and unfreeze the water before I can start cooking." She snapped another bean in two while Jeremy watched.

She brushed back a strand of sweat-dampened hair. With it went her anger, leaving her with only the satisfaction of Jeremy's concern. "I'm sorry you wasted your money on my schooling. Maybe next time you can send word you're coming and I'll have a chance to wash up." Her dress was damp and sour, sparsely covered by her apron. Grease stained her front where the apron did not cover it. She laughed ruefully. "I probably remind you of the first time you saw me."

Jeremy sat with an inscrutable expression in his dark eyes. Suddenly he stood and gathered her into his arms. His kiss melded warmth and concern, and something more. By the time it ended, Ginny wasn't sure whether she had imagined it. She stood with her cheek against his, her eyes closed, and waited for him to speak. Instead, he released her and started toward the door.

She found her voice as he ducked under the lintel. "Jeremy?"

His own voice was muffled, as confused as her own. "We'll find a way out of this, Ginny. Trust me."

His words had a soothing effect, but his kiss had uprooted her life. She stood in the kitchen and listened to the sound of him riding off and everything in her wanted to run after him. But there was nothing he could do. Charlie had no money to hire another Maria Inés, even if he could find one. The mines had siphoned off all the cooks for hire; probably even Jeremy was feeling the pinch. His cowhands had to fend for themselves, but they knew better than to complain.

If she had to guess, she'd say it was pity that prompted his kiss. He'd said nothing about tender feelings. His emotions had nothing to do with thinking of her as a woman or he'd have said something. She dismissed the idea. He was probably already suffering the pangs of regret.

With nowhere to turn that didn't remind her of Jeremy, she made a decision. On the way to the corral she met Charlie and the vaqueros coming for their meal. She brushed past them without slowing, amused at the look of confusion on Jose Luis' face. Trust him to worry about missing a meal.

"Dinner's ready. Serve yourselves. I'm going riding." She caught the shock on Charlie's face and met his gaze. "You get me some help or I'll go back to frying tortillas."

Chapter Thirty-Three

Ginny was helping Sancho butcher out a steer for the fall roundup when Charlie rode in from San Miguel with an Indian girl behind him. Holding a skinning knife in her right hand, she watched as he dumped the girl off into the dust then turned and rode on to the corrals.

"What's he done now?" she asked.

Sancho stood squinting, his hand over his eyes. "'Spect he's brought you some help."

"Her?"

"'Spect so."

"How old you think she is?" From across the yard, the girl rose to her feet, but she remained stooped like she was searching for something in the dirt. Her stiff, uncertain movements made her appear more like an old woman than a child.

"Pert near your age, first time we butchered out them hens, I'd say."

Ginny swallowed and approached the girl. "*Tienes hambre?*" You . . . you hungry?

The girl nodded.

"What's your name? *Cómo se llama?*"

"Arciela."

"Come, Arciela."

The girl remained unmoving, her face hidden beneath a filthy thatch of untrimmed hair.

"*Viene!*"

When the child made no move, Ginny took her hand. The child looked up and she saw the sightless eyes, fixed and unmoving. The child was shaking. Carefully, Ginny led her into the summer house. She fixed a bowl of beans and watched the child feed herself with her fingers. When the girl finished eating, she poured her a cup of milk and watched the child spill it in her haste. After what seemed like forever, the child stopped for breath.

Ginny wrinkled her nose at the unwashed odors coming from such a small body. "Come. We'll fix a bath. I'll find you something to wear. Maybe Sancho has some trousers in the bunkhouse." The girl clearly didn't understand, but she permitted herself to be led to the spring. When they finished scrubbing the layers of dirt off and returned to the cookhouse, the girl clean and dressed in oversized cast-offs, Ginny was an hour late with her chores.

"You're no bigger than a minute. You can't even lift that water bucket." She heard Maria Inés's voice in herself and she softened her tone as she led her to a basket sitting outside the door. "Here. You can clean the beans. It'll be fun."

She led the girl over to the table, easing the crook in her neck as she settled the girl to her task. The girl didn't understand English, and Ginny felt a reluctance to speak Mexican—that had been Maria Inés's language. Swallowing her impatience, she took Arcelia's hand and showed her how to pick stones from the beans they would cook for supper. The girl spilled her scant pile and began again.

Ginny returned to the summer house and watched from the doorway as the girl's fingers gained speed. An errant breeze caught a hen's feather from the ground and deposited it onto the table. The girl must have sensed it because she patted her surroundings until she found it. With her eyes closed, she caressed the soft feather across her lip. Ginny's legs went limp with the memory of comforting herself in the same way, imagining her mother's touch.

Sancho arrived a few minutes later, carrying the bowl of beans cleaned of stones. The girl followed at his heels.

Ginny barely spared them a glance. "Sancho, will you show Arciela where the walnuts are? She can gather them if you show her. It will keep her occupied until I can finish up here."

Afterwards, she filled the dish pan with warm water. Arciela could help with the dishes.

***

Two months passed into another season. Fall was here and the nights were getting shorter. The child slept upstairs in the loft now, so quiet and invisible that it sometimes seemed like a ghost inhabited her old room. Today Charlie had ridden in, haggard and eye-glazed, hounded by the demons that seemed to close in each year when the weather turned cold. Instead of retreating to his library, he disappeared into his room and closed the door.

Ginny finished her chores and started to her room, carrying a candle against the darkness. She made her way down the corridor while the clock in the hall was striking ten, her mind occupied with a never-ending list of chores. The last of the food was put away, out of reach of the rats that plied the summer house after she left it. With luck the coyotes would occupy themselves with the scattered calf parts the vaqueros had left behind and they wouldn't venture close enough to the house to wake her. Tomorrow the vaqueros would carry the stove back into the house, but tonight she was so exhausted that every step was an effort. In less than a minute she anticipated being dead to the world.

She passed her father's door and hesitated when she heard a soft mewling coming from his room, the sound that a kitten would make. Arciela sometimes played with the kittens, but she understood that they were not to come into the house. Ginny pressed her ear against the door, afraid to open it in case Charlie was not yet passed out. She'd never been inside his room with him still in it. The idea caused a shiver of fear.

There it was again, louder, and definitely not a kitten.

The door opened easily. In the candle glow she saw her father's form, heard his snoring, and smelled his presence in the sickly sweet scent that she associated with his headaches. Another sound came from the floor where a small figure huddled in a fetal position, sobs racking her body. *Arciela.*

"What happened, Arciela? What is it?" She turned the girl and noticed the blood stains on the shift that she had wrapped around herself. A sleeve was missing. "Oh, Charlie. How could you?" Her questions trailed off as she stared in horror at the bruises and welts. One eye was puffy and swelling.

She pulled open the drapes to capture the moonlight so she could make sense of what she was seeing. A loud snore interrupted her and she froze as the smell of whiskey drifted from the bed. She managed to bite back the scream that would bring Sancho running from the bunkhouse, but as she covered her mouth with a shaking hand, she heard her own mewling. Nausea washed over her, churning her stomach until she thought she would need the bedpan that sat half-exposed under the bed.

Her father thrashed in a drunken stupor, partially buried in the crumpled quilt her mother had brought west as a wedding present, but she spared him no further glance. He moaned and turned onto his side, and a water pipe filled with residue rolled to the floor. A shiver of shame and revulsion ran down her, but she choked back her sob. Trembling, she reached over and picked up the torn sleeve from the bed.

Without making a sound, she lifted the child and carried her from the room.

Fury drove her movements as she tossed things into her carpetbag. When she finished, she left Arciela on the porch and went in search of her mare and the saddle, grateful that for once Caroline responded without

191

whinnying when she led the horse out of the corral to the front of the house. Fortunately, the men had passed out from their celebrating. Under normal circumstances she wouldn't get past any of the vaqueros—probably not Sancho, either, but he was exhausted, and his hearing bad.

With the child settled in the saddle, Ginny made one last trip into the parlor and helped herself to the pile of silver coins in the strongbox. She pulled her Winchester from the gun rack. Hanging nearby was the six-shooter that Sancho had taught her to use. She put the rifle back and took the revolver, instead.

In a final act of defiance, she pushed Charlie's leather chair away from the fireplace and traded it for the crude table he used for trimming his leather. Surreptitiously, she carried lamps and chairs, piling everything in the center until the room looked like a warehouse. When she finished, her mother's influence was gone.

The horse stood quietly while she wrapped a poncho around the girl and climbed into the saddle behind her. Turning, she followed Maria Inés's path down the dusty trail, trying not to make a sound. Charlie would not wake until the men came in for breakfast, and they were welcome to draw any conclusion they wanted.

Her horse started in the direction of Jeremy's ranch, but she yanked the reins when the memory of his kiss imprinted itself. "I'm not worth your effort, Jeremy. And now I'm a thief, as well." She tucked her pistol in her waistband and turned the mare toward San Miguel.

The sun was overhead when she reined in at the mission cemetery. Inside the fenced enclosure a woman's low, keening voice came from the area where the Indians were buried. Ginny woke Arciela and helped her down. Together they walked through the cemetery gate.

Maria Inés was kneeling over her husband's grave, clad in the shift and the sandals she had worn the day she left the ranch. Wordlessly, she took the child's hand and the anger in her eyes told Ginny that she understood. The girl would be cared for.

Ginny returned to her horse and found the money hidden inside her saddlebag. She removed the pitiful pile of coins and divided them in half. Maria Inés shook her head angrily. Not Charlie Nugent's money. Ginny tried again without success, but she realized that Maria Inés was right; if the two Indians tried to spend it, Charlie might accuse them of theft.

Ginny stroked her mare's damp neck while she crooned in its ear, her thoughts turning to dread. "Maybe Sancho was right. Maybe this would have been easier if I'd never given you a name." She led the horse over to where the little girl was waiting. "The horse is for you, Arciela."

Surprisingly, Maria Inés's expression was soft and understanding. On a whim, Ginny enveloped her in a hug, clasping her so tightly that she felt Maria Inés's breasts against her shirt. As she breathed in the woman's familiar scent, she felt the woman's arms tighten around her own.

By the time the northbound stage pulled out of the Caledonia Station, Ginny had made arrangements with the stage manager to write a letter documenting her gift to Arciela. She left a dozen silver dollars in his care with the understanding that the child be returned to her mother, Concepción.

Inside the stage, she slept as the horses galloped north.

Chapter Thirty-Four

San Francisco

"Virginia, what is this?" I won't allow this riff-raff in my house. You'll learn to adjust to my ways or suffer the consequences." George Hayes strode into the bedroom, holding a kitten by the scuff of its neck.

"I found it yesterday in the park. It was lost and alone." Ginny sat at the dressing table, her hands folded into tight fists as she strove to keep her voice calm and dignified. Her husband detested bursts of emotion.

"Get rid of it!" He tossed the kitten at her and stormed out.

The kitten hid under the bed until Ginny coaxed it out with a scrap of pink ribbon. She clutched the mewling kitten with one hand while she used her other to massage the throbbing pain behind her temples. The nausea was there again. She closed her eyes and waited for it to subside. When she was able to stand upright, she moved listlessly about her room, idly fingering the tassels on the servant pull-chord alongside the brocade and velvet window coverings. She glanced at the gilded, over-sized painting of a fleshy nude reclining on a sofa—a wedding gift from her husband. She wondered if one of his actress friends had posed.

Sighing, she realized that she didn't really care. What she wanted was for someone to burn it, along with the other fussy, overstated furnishings. Everything had been done to make the house seem well-appointed and luxurious—on a bank manager's salary, no small feat; even his friends wondered how he managed. The truth was, her husband filled the house with items from the auctions of the dispossessed and the bankrupt. Victims of ill-fortune. As the man who foreclosed on them, he was in a position to know all the best bargains. Undoubtedly he had learned his decorating sense from the brothels. He seemed to love everything else about the fancy houses— why not the furniture?

Actually, she was relieved that he enjoyed his whores and actresses—it saved her from having to indulge in what he considered his husbandly rights. Sometimes she feigned a headache to spare herself even those token visits.

She was convinced that he only came to her room to instill in her a proper fear. He considered her sexually inexperienced, too thin and outspoken to a fault; she spent long hours trying to decide why he even bothered with her at all. It had been only days after their hasty wedding ceremony that he engaged in a massive campaign to change every fiber of her being. He'd made it clear in the months she'd lived under his roof that she was everything he despised in a woman.

George's friends were social strivers like himself, mostly at the fringe of polite society, name-droppers all. The feigning of a headache, the taking of lovers, the managing of servants were topics that the wives of her husband's associates discussed for hours on end, practically their only area of interest. In public, George fawned over her like an adoring bridegroom.

According to one of the wives, who offered her opinion under the influence of too much champagne, his envious friends thought he must have hidden talents to attract a clear-eyed beauty like Ginny, who would have been accepted in far higher circles had she not been married to the infamous Mr. Hayes.

Ginny didn't have the heart to share the story of her whirlwind romance. It was too embarrassing to explain that their relationship was founded on a bottle of champagne, the night she arrived.

"Try more, my dear. It's straight from Paris. Sparkling, like you."

"I don't . . . think I . . . should."

"Nonsense. You should enjoy yourself. We'll have something to eat. Later."

She recalled the salon and the well-coiffed matron who squeezed her into a corset and slid a velvet dress over her curves. In her alcoholic buzz, she watched a stage actress arrive for a fitting and exchange a familiar kiss with Mr. Hayes. When he proposed over dinner, she was tipsy enough that she laughed and said the idea was ridiculous.

The next morning she woke feeling ill. He came in her room with a vial of medicine for her tomato juice, and it seemed as though she slept all day. And the one following. By the third day she refused the tomato juice and he returned with a syringe. After that, the days faded into each other while a matronly woman kept watch. Finally, Mr. Hayes appeared again with another proposal.

"Get up and get dressed. We have a wedding to attend."

She dimly recalled the witnesses in the judge's elegant chamber. Mr. Hayes thought the joke was on her, but the joke was really on him because he'd gotten a fool for a wife. The witnesses swore they heard her agree to the judge's questions. Mr. Hayes cautioned that her forced, scribbled signature would hold up in a court of law, given the judge's aspirations as a solid Republican, and his own contributions to the party.

He'd found her revolver the night she arrived and locked it in his desk. She intended to find it before she left. He wasn't getting anything that belonged to her—not willingly, at least.

Her introduction to the ways of society started the week she arrived, when her new husband insisted she use her remaining money to outfit herself appropriately. She tolerated the fittings of the gaudy, low-cut gowns in a stupor, feeling ill at having sacrificed her mare for such a paltry cause. The wardrobe accomplished another task, which she had disregarded at the time; it eliminated all her spending money and any way for her to return home. Penniless, she was stuck in the city of her dreams.

***

Ginny shook herself from her reverie; revisiting the past did little to settle her nerves. In an effort to escape the suffocation of the stifling house, she picked her way down the wooden steps, around to the narrow side-yard where the air was perfumed with a wrenchingly familiar scent of bay leaf. She lifted her arms and gathered the laurel branches against her, crushing the pungent scent into her clothing. *When I am grown I shall live in a garden.* Her words came back with haunting clarity.

Returning upstairs, she found the packet of Jeremy's letters and spent the afternoon reading them. One elicited tears.

March 15, 1883

Dear Ginny,

Your last correspondence seems so changed in tone, I have been hard-pressed to set it aside and go about my ranching as I ought. Your letters are a welcome part of my life and I would be lost without them. Maybe having you gone these past years made it easier to think of you as a child, but in truth, your letter made that impossible any longer.

Your concern for others and your view of the world are those of a compassionate woman. I'm proud to have served a small part in that, but remember the honor belongs to you. Your efforts to improve yourself through conviction and deed make me realize that Cholama will be welcoming home a lovely and polished young woman when at last you deign to honor us with your presence.

Please take pity on us here in the Cholama. Trust me when I say that many hearts and souls in the valley are pining for your return. We would, if we could, meet your stage with brass band and bugle. Come home to us, Ginny.

Jeremy

Every word spelled out feelings she had been hiding even from herself. How young she had been, how naïve; he was better off without her. Bundling the letters, she walked to the fireplace and dropped them in, one by one, watching as they signified the death of her dreams.

It was time to get on with her mess of a life and make a plan. There was no point in delaying the news, even if it meant sacrificing her only pleasure. When her husband realized she was with child, he would ban her from the sorry nag he permitted her to ride side-saddle in the park, on mornings when it wasn't raining. In the stifling custom favored by the men of his set, wives were to remain sequestered in their houses until their waists were svelte again and the baby deposited with a nanny. At least she would be spared the humiliation of having to appear in public. Even though she had seen her eighteenth birthday, she knew she looked tawdry in the dresses he made her wear. How she longed for the britches of her youth.

Her husband stuck his head in her room and frowned. "I have investors in town. If you were anywhere near capable of overseeing the staff, I would invite them to dine in. It would save me a fortune." At her dressing table he fingered a bit of French lace purchased from a bankrupt merchant. "No matter. Poor deluded chaps, they'll think I have the loveliest woman in San Francisco on my arm. You're good for that, at least. As long as you manage to keep your mouth shut."

He leaned over and took her chin between his thumb and index finger, like Miguelito would take a mare. She stared into his smirking face without betraying her thoughts, until he seemed to lose heart in the game. He straightened and his tone took on the icy directness she had come to expect when the two of them were alone.

"Fix yourself up. Apply the rouge pot to that pallor. You look sickly. We are dining at the Palace Hotel. Have the maid cinch you well. You're getting fat."

She sat unmoving, willing herself not to vomit.

From the hallway he called back, "Wear the red velvet. Low-cut. That's why I take you along."

His door slammed and Ginny winced. She had to tell him. Soon. The red velvet gown could barely fit her thickening waist. It would take her most of the day to modify it if she wanted to eat, and she must—for the baby's sake. She didn't dare defy him; he had given her the back of his hand once when she said something he considered inappropriate at a dinner party. He had smiled and acted the smitten husband until they arrived home, then he hit her, splitting open her lip. She would make a good impression. It was easier. She would look stunning, talk in soft, correct tones so the gentlemen would toast her, their eyes bright with whiskey lust. Afterwards she would return home and grow a baby.

***

As they entered the carriage entrance of the Palace Hotel, Ginny was momentarily stunned at the opulence. She ogled the high ceilings and glass walls bathed in light from a hundred crystal chandeliers. She followed her husband along a hallway gilded with gold trim and deep red wallpaper, stepping carefully on marble floors that radiated the crisp click-click of stylish women's shoes. Ahead, a couple entered a hydraulic elevator and disappeared.

The maître d' escorted them to a huge, rounded table covered with fine Irish linen, with a half-dozen different wine glasses at each setting. Within minutes, three other couples arrived. That left one chair.

Ginny was about to inquire who the other guest would be when he came strolling across the floor in the person of Jeremy Lawsen. As luck would have it, he was seated next to her. She could do nothing but avert her flushed face and pray that she could get through the evening without shaming herself. Her corset thrust her breasts nearly out of her dress. She glanced down at her exposed bosom and used the moment of introductions to pull her lacy shawl up about her shoulders.

"Mrs. Hayes, how nice to meet you again." Jeremy took her hand and held it firmly in his own as she tried to control her trembling. He released his hold, but she suffered from the devastating effect on her senses when his gaze lingered a moment longer.

Her husband obviously didn't recall meeting Jeremy at the ranch. In a chillingly mild tone, he responded. "I didn't realize you have already made acquaintance of my wife. How fortunate." Taking a sip of wine, he smiled at the two of them and Ginny felt her insides tighten.

"Our families are old friends. The Fosters of Virginia." Jeremy's smile was deceptively benign. Ginny could have kissed him. "Perhaps you've heard of them. Old plantation family."

The others at the table purred appropriately. The women, especially, looked at Ginny with renewed interest. One smiled approvingly.

"Can't say I have. Imagine they've been left destitute with the rest of the rebels." George Hayes' smile was self-satisfied. "She's fortunate to have a protector."

Ginny saw Jeremy's jaw clench while he fought to let the comment pass.

The rest of the evening was a disaster. Ginny giggled at an inappropriate comment and spilled a drop of wine on her dress when she reacted to her husband's pointed, warning look. She tried not to drink more than a half glass of wine, but he continued to top off her goblet until she hardly knew what she drank.

Jeremy chatted amiably, trying to ease the situation by introducing topics that would make her look witty, but each time her husband managed to turn the compliment around. Her head was splitting by the time he ended his game of cat-and-mouse.

Her final act of the evening was one of defiance. With nothing to lose, she dipped her damask napkin into her water goblet and deliberately wiped her make-up from the bruise on her cheek. She faced her husband without blinking and watched the veins in his cheeks engorge with rage while the women across the table gasped.

"We have high doorknobs in our home," she said. "I'm so careless."

Chapter Thirty-Five

Jeremy straightened and wiped George Hayes' blood from his hand as the man lay sprawled on the dining room floor with a broken nose. Jeremy's decision to smash his fist into the pompous, controlling bastard followed an evening spent with his stomach knotted at the fragile shell of a girl Ginny had become. She had picked at her food like a bird and jumped every time the man turned his dissipated face in her direction. Even her laugh had been false and self-conscious, and the dress she was wearing would have done a Charleston hooker proud.

Her last act of defiance was pure Ginny. He could have kissed her. Instead, he had decked her tormentor. "You ever touch her again, I'll kill you. That's a promise, Mister Hayes. And I keep my promises."

It was all he could do to leave her in the company of her husband and take himself off in the opposite direction. He walked for hours through the fog, past drunken couples and wharf-side vagrants while he fretted on what could be done. What a guardian he'd turned out to be. The only time she ever really needed him, he had let her down. He held no illusions that, had he not forced himself on her in the cook house, she would never have fled to the only other person she knew enough to trust when her world collapsed around her.

The fog closed out the lights, leaving him alone with his thoughts, and he returned to the day she disappeared.

Sancho had ridden onto his ranch and together they pieced the story together. He left word with his foreman to hide her, should Ginny come to him for help, and he and Sancho rode into San Miguel. Maria Inés gave them another piece of the story when she took them to the bruised, sleeping little girl. Someone claimed to have seen Ginny riding in the direction of the Coast, and Jeremy followed her trail while Sancho rode on back to the Cholama to see what he could do about keeping the ranch together.

After losing two days on a false trail, Jeremy returned to San Miguel. He was in the process of boarding his own horse, determined to take the next train to San Francisco, when a familiar whinny caught his ear. He found Ginny's mare being led off to a local ranch by her new owner. It took all of his available silver to add a bit of profit for the man's trouble, but he managed to buy the mare back.

He decided to ride to the ranch and deliver the mare into Sancho's keeping, pick up some spare clothing and money, and make the trip to San Francisco. He rode all day and night, but it was of no consequence. By the time he arrived in the city, three days later, she was married.

He asked around and it appeared that she had done so willingly. No one had any tale of her having seemed reluctant—only slightly dispirited. The judge claimed he was told she was in a family way and claimed that he didn't question the haste, given the reputation of her husband. It had taken longer to find a way to ingratiate himself into a dinner invitation that included the illusive Missus Hayes.

The lights of the Palace Hotel lit the entire block. Jeremy stepped out into the night with champagne and beefsteak churning in his belly. He headed into the wind, in the direction of the Bay, muttering to himself. "I don't blame her for hating me. I'm the one who talked Charlie into bringing the little Indian girl in the first place."

At the waterfront a drunken sailor bumped against him and swore. "Watch yerself, Gov'nor. You ain't so fine."

The fog soaked through his dinner jacket, but Jeremy ignored the chill. He deserved to suffer. *I forced my feelings on her. No better than her old man. She was too young to know her mind. It was clear she was heading for a showdown with her husband. That last trick with the napkin was a red flag waved in front of a bull—a signal that she wasn't afraid of anything.*

It was partly strategy and partly blind luck that had him dining with Hayes that night. He had hired a private detective to keep an eye on Ginny. When the detective's sightings grew scarce, Jeremy sent a letter of introduction to Hayes, figuring to wheedle an invitation to dinner. After that, the rest had gone as planned.

On the morning following the dinner at the Palace, Jeremy stood in the fog-enshrouded street and watched as Hayes emerged from the three-story wooden house and boarded a hired buggy that headed off in the direction of the financial district. Jeremy waited another half-hour and knocked on the door.

***

When the maid announced Jeremy, Ginny's hands went to her belly in an involuntary gesture that brought a knowing smile from the Irish girl. Ginny tried to meet her eyes, but the girl kept her expression vague, her eyes lowered. They would speak of this later. One problem at a time.

Outside, the fog had swallowed all trace of her husband. Willing away her nausea, she paced the room trying to decide what to do. Finally, she reached for a loose-fitting morning gown, gathered her hair into soft curls that flowed down her back and secured them with a ribbon at the nape of her neck. Her husband's anger would be worth the comfort of seeing Jeremy again. Taking a steadying breath, she started for the stairs. She opened the parlor door before Jeremy looked up from his coffee. He stood smiling, but his expression froze when he saw the swollen lip and the ruddy mark on her cheek.

"Damn him to hell!" He didn't ask what had happened. He didn't need to.

She forced herself to meet his gaze after first assuring herself that her old look of defiance was firmly in place. "Hello, Jeremy. You shouldn't have come."

"Well, it looks like you might be wrong there, ma'am." His eyes slammed shut, leaving his ridiculous lashes fanned across his cheek until she had to make fists to keep from kissing them. His voice husky, he continued in a rush. "Blessed Patsy, how could I stay away?"

She stood silently, allowing herself the welcome sight of him. Warning herself not to touch him, not to tempt fate. Just seeing him was more than she deserved. Taking a step, she swayed and almost fell as a bout of dizziness claimed her.

"Ginny, are you sick? What's wrong? How badly did he hurt you?" He rushed to her side and caught her in a warm embrace that eased her fears as her world went black.

When the world came back into focus, she was lying on the velvet settee near the window. He'd opened the drapes, undoubtedly to judge for himself the damage her husband had done. As he knelt at her side, she shut her eyes to hide her pleasure. Without thinking, she lifted her hand to the smooth contour of his tense cheek, feathering his skin while her heart pounded with satisfaction. She felt him controlling the tic in his jaw and she gave him a feeble smile.

"Ginny," he repeated, "what's wrong?" Beneath her fingers his Adams apple bobbed. Turning, he touched his lips to her fingertips and this time it was his eyes that shuttered. The two of them sat in silence while the clock ticked in the corner.

Finally she admitted, "It would appear that I am in the family way."

Jeremy's smile wavered, but it held. "Congratulations."

"I've been thinking I want a girl." In response to his unspoken question, she added, "The world doesn't need another George Hayes."

His blush indicated his agreement. "You'll love it, filly or colt."

It should be yours. If only I had trusted you. Shifting, she resorted to a more businesslike tone, even while her fingers itched to return to his face. "I can't wait to show her the Cholama." The name reminded her that they were on borrowed time. "Tell me about home." Judging from the cloud gathering behind Jeremy's eyes, the news wasn't good. But true to form, he tried to soften it for her sake.

"Sancho's about the same. Kind of lost without you. Your Pa lost some of his best men with his use of that little Indian girl." He couldn't meet her eyes. "Sancho stayed, but not because he wants to."

"For my mother?"

"And for you. He wants to keep things up for your return."

Panic roiled inside her and she had to glance away. "Not while my father is alive. I just couldn't."

"You need to prepare yourself. The way he's going . . . . "

"I don't think I'm ready." She glanced outside, but the storm felt like it was coming from inside her. "I watch my husband succumbing to his demons and I hate them both for being so weak."

"Your father's not perfect. Nobody is."

Hearing the words, she felt herself relax for the first time in months. She wanted more for her baby than a legacy of hate. Maybe it was time.

Jeremy was still talking. "You've known this was coming. You've spent your life trying to save him from it, but it's time."

She nodded, even as her eyes slammed shut in shame. "Jeremy, if he goes before I can get home, would you—"

"Name it."

"Will you see to him for me?" When he nodded, she continued, "And make it our secret? From my husband, I mean?" She wondered what he must be thinking, but his slow, intense nod indicated that he understood what she was asking. Thwarting George Hayes's plans for the ranch would appeal to him.

"Say the word and I'll take you home right now. You can have your baby on the ranch." His eyes seemed to burn with a desire to rescue her. But she had no intention of bleeding her shame onto him.

"Not yet. I have to finish here."

The maid gave a hesitant knock before carrying in a teapot and two cups. Jeremy watched her suspiciously. His skepticism followed her as she poured the tea and tidied up the sideboard, apparently in no hurry to leave.

Ginny followed his glance. "Jeremy, this is Rose. She's a good friend. She won't tell Hayes you were here."

He glanced at Rose, embarrassed. "I appreciate your loyalty. I was just trying to convince her to leave—"

Ginny shook her head emphatically. "I'm no hothouse flower, despite my husband's best efforts. I'll see my baby born and the father's name on the birth certificate. When I return to the valley, it'll be with my head held high."

"You don't owe him anything. He beats you."

The word was an accusation; she felt her cheeks heating. "He's touched me for the last time, I swear it."

His eyes studied her so gravely that she fought off tears. "Your father's missing a gun. Know anything about it?"

"Meaning—what? I'll be careful for the baby's sake."

"Meaning he may push you too far."

"I wouldn't waste a bet on him—let alone a bullet."

He smiled. "I'd put my money on you, comes to that." Despite his attempt to appear lighthearted, he looked worried and it was her fault. All of it. But she would not allow her poor judgment to sully his name, or his future. She gave a bright, false laugh and waved her hand to dismiss his concerns. "Jeremy, tell me about your cattle."

He took the hint and spent the rest of the visit describing the Cholama. It seemed he had just arrived when it was time to go. Rose brought his coat and he pulled an envelope of paper money from inside a pocket. "Ginny, I want you to keep this. Just in case."

Ginny felt her nerves go cold. "George will find it. I know he will. He has a sixth sense for such things."

Jeremy handed the money to Rose. "Hold on to this for her. She's going to need it, and I may not be here. Don't let Hayes find it."

Rose nodded and tucked it into her pocket.

Ginny offered her hand for a formal farewell while possibilities crackled between them. She longed to walk him to the sidewalk, but she restrained herself. The fog had lifted. No telling who might be watching, even a private detective hired by her husband.

She started toward the stairway. "I'm already homesick. I won't watch you leave." In truth, her head was beginning to ache. When the door closed behind him, she raced up the stairs to her bedroom and opened the curtain hoping to catch a last glance as he walked away. Instead, he stood across the street, under a lamppost, cupping his hands to keep the flame of his cigar from the breeze. As he straightened, his eyes searched the windows and he saw her. With a tip of his hat he turned and started walking.

She watched until he reached the end of the street. No one followed him.

Chapter Thirty-Six

Jeremy's note was delivered by a stranger who waited at the corner for her to leave her house. It instructed her to meet him on Market Street.

Ginny smiled at her reflection in the shop window. She looked a proper nanny in the worn black skirt and shirtwaist she had borrowed from Rose. When the stiff autumn breeze cut into her, she pulled her shawl tighter and pushed the perambulator into the press of shoppers. At the Geary Street Bakery, she picked out a crusty loaf of sourdough bread for the pot of soup she planned for supper. Her husband had given her no household allowance in the past three weeks, but she had formed an arrangement; she was teaching Rose to read, and in exchange, Rose agreed to look the other way while she prepared supper on the cook's day off.

As the cable car rumbled up Market Street, she caught a glimpse of a familiar man leaping off into the street. She called his name as loudly as she dared, but he continued through the crowd, apparently searching for an address on one of the buildings. "Jeremy?" she called again, glad that she wore the maid's disguise as an excuse for her bold manner.

He turned at the sound of his name and scanned the crowd. When he failed to notice her, he turned and continued on. She called again, this time close enough that he recognized her voice. They nearly collided as she pulled off the spectacles she wore as part of her disguise.

"Thank God I found you." His eyes scanned her face, searching.

"There you are!" They burst out in unison. Ginny recovered first. "I'm taking my daughter on a walk. For all intents, I'm the nanny."

His eyes widened at the baby in the buggy. "I'm glad you could get away. I came to talk sense into you. And to see a man about a loan."

"A loan? Oh, Jeremy! Are things so bad for you?"

He seemed puzzled by the question. "The loan isn't for me. It's for your father."

"Oh." Glancing skyward, she expected to see fog encompassing the city. It would suit her mood. Instead it had rolled out to sea, leaving the sky streaked with feathery clouds and sunshine. "We're a troublesome family.

You'd do better to leave us to our own follies."

An acquaintance of her husband gave her a quizzical look as he passed. A few steps further he turned for another look before continuing on his way. Thankfully, Jeremy realized the impropriety of standing on a public street; he took her arm and guided her in the opposite direction. "Let's find someplace where we can talk."

Ginny relished the opportunity to spend a few minutes alone with him. "Can we eat?"

"If you want. I have no appetite except for you." He searched the sidewalk for a restaurant with no apparent urgency, as if he was accustoming himself to the novelty of seeing her again. When he turned back, his eyes sought the perambulator.

Ginny anticipated his question. "Her name's Caroline Rachel. Carrie. She's almost two months." He was watching the baby with an expression that warmed her insides. Maybe she had managed to do something right.

Inside the restaurant, he helped her to a corner table. "We have a lot to talk about."

"I'm so glad I received your message."

His face reddened. "I've been watching your house. My man has," he corrected. "I receive his reports." He waited until the waiter ladled chowder into her bowl before he pressed his hand on hers. "My man hasn't seen you leave the house in weeks."

She wasn't sure how to respond. "I'm . . . it's been difficult."

"High doorknobs again?" he asked, his eyes blackening with rage. She lowered her head and fussed with Carrie's outer wrap, but he persisted. "Tell me he hasn't hurt you."

She looked up and saw him studying her with such intensity that she had to look away. "Jeremy, don't make such dire assumptions. I'm fine."

He frowned. "You look anything but fine."

She didn't intend to put him in harm's way over her troubles, not if she could help it. Her face heated and she found herself chattering. "My goodness, I haven't had such delicious chowder in forever. I prefer plain fare. I can't abide some of the dishes they serve in the city."

He studied her closely for several seconds before mercifully changing the subject. "So this is Carrie. She's a pretty little thing. Like her mama."

Ginny glanced up to see if he was serious. "You said I looked like a boy."

"That was a long time ago. You've changed considerably." His laughter seemed strained. Hers as well. She thought he was trying to hide his anger at her until she saw his pupils constrict and realized he was scared. "Are you ready to go back with me?" he asked.

"I can't. Not yet. Something's wrong. He spends hours alone in his office. I think we're in trouble."

"He's a prevaricator, Ginny. It's just catching up with him."

"I know." She studied her fork, shamed at the situation she'd involved him in. He allowed her to eat while he teased the baby with a corner of his napkin. Something in his smile unleashed the old, familiar Jeremy. Suddenly it seemed important that he meet the baby. "Carrie needs holding. Would you mind?"

His eyes showed a brief second of panic. "It's been years since I held anything but a colt or a calf."

"Same principle."

He took a cautious hold, cradling the baby in one arm while he surrendered a finger. "Quite a grip you got there, Little Missy."

Ginny felt her eyes filling. "How's . . . how's Sancho?"

"He misses you terribly."

"And Charlie?"

Jeremy looked up. "I'm sorry I don't have better news. Most of the livestock's gone. Sold to pay the bank."

"My husband's bank owns the note."

"It was a bad loan from the start."

"I didn't know. I met my husband . . . Mr. Hayes . . . at the ranch."

"It never occurred to me that you'd go to *him*."

She dipped her head, shamed. "Did you know he was the one who introduced my father to the dope? He told me the night you joined us for dinner." Her voice broke. "I haven't spoken to him since. He also showed me a document. In the eyes of the law, we're legally married."

"You're sure about that?" Jeremy asked.

"He boasted that he has friends in high places."

"Don't be too sure about that. I have a man working on it." Jeremy glanced around and leaned forward. "You don't have to go back."

Ginny hesitated. "He'll find me."

"You promised—after the baby came." Jeremy pressed her harder. "I'm not leaving you here. What will it take to make you see sense? If you won't come home for me, then think. Your father's dying. He wants to see you . . . and the baby."

Her heart raced as Carrie played with his finger. "It's too late for my father and me. Too much water under the bridge."

Jeremy's eyes narrowed in frustration. "You're a mother now. Maybe it's time you considered why he's the way he is."

She met his eyes across the table. "I've had time to think. And I had some things figured wrong, didn't I?"

He nodded and it was as though the sun came out across the table. "People aren't all bad—or all good. We make mistakes."

She understood. He was talking about the kiss; he didn't need to said so, it was there between them. She'd ruined whatever might have been between them. She dropped her gaze to her plate and tried to force a few bites, but her food had no flavor. She was happy when the waiter arrived to take their plates away.

With a wink for the baby the waiter said, "You make a handsome family."

Pain crossed Jeremy's forced smile. "We should be going, Ginny." He reached underneath his chair for his Stetson, suddenly all business. "I'll be back as soon as I get your father's signature. Four days at the most. Meet me at my banker's. Will you promise to do that?" He pulled a card from his pocket. "His name is Parrott. Can you find a safe place to hide this? Don't underestimate your so-called husband. He means to have you at all costs."

Ginny swallowed. "He means to have the ranch. I'm just an obstacle."

"Obstacles have a way of disappearing, Ginny. Four days. I'll be back. Promise you'll meet me Friday at Parrott's?" He handed her the card.

She reached up to tuck a strand of his hair back under his band. "I'll be there."

Chapter Thirty-Seven

Ginny sat soundlessly in the darkened parlor and fidgeted with the lace hankie in her hand. Rain crashed against the window sills, but she'd drawn the drapes to give the dunners and bill collectors an impression that no one was home. The muted ticking of the big grandfather clock in the entry was the only sound in the house. The cook and Rose were gone. Had it been only a day since she'd laughed with Jeremy over lunch? Her fogged brain tried to remember all the events of the last twenty-four hours.

She had scarcely returned home when Rose greeted her at the servant's door with a warning that someone was waiting in the parlor. Ginny slipped into the kitchen, changed into her afternoon gown and managed to greet the visitor with a cup of tea. Her own cup was trembling as he explained that he held a demand that they vacate the house within twenty-four hours, taking only their personal effects. A policeman was stationed outside to be sure they complied.

The magistrate was rocking nervously on his toes while he studied the newels on the stairway landing. She drained her tea and attempted a modicum of small talk. His response was cordial, but vague, as though his mind was on more important matters.

She gave up her attempt when he set his cup down and met her gaze with an apologetic half-smile. "I'm here to see your husband, Mrs. Hayes."

She gulped and fabricated a quick falsehood. "I'm sorry. He's not home. I've only just arrived, myself."

She opened the letter he held out for her. The court order was filled with confusing terms. Words like "embezzlement, "opium use" "mismanagement" leaped out on the sheet like fire-hot branding irons.

"The contents are for Mr. Hayes only," the magistrate protested.

She met the apologetic eyes of the policeman and understood that her so-called society life was over.

"I'll see he gets this," she promised, hoping her voice didn't quiver.

When the door closed behind her, she raced upstairs and found her husband sitting in his office, staring blankly at the drawn window. When she attempted to open the blinds, he roared and lunged at her, overturning his desk in a shattering of glass and wood. His eyes looked bloodshot and filled with madness. Suddenly she feared for her baby, sleeping downstairs. She turned and fled the room. The policeman outside would know what she should do, even if it meant public humiliation. She had nothing left to lose.

Her foot was on the stairwell when she heard the click of the lock behind her.

Back downstairs she found Rose preparing fresh tea with a wary look for her mistress's breathless state. Ginny knew she looked frazzled and half-mad, but it was too late to worry about appearances. She closed the door into the kitchen and slumped against the table before her legs failed her. "You must leave. Now. There's no point in jeopardizing your reputation at our expense. That's exactly what will happen when this gets out."

"I won't go, Miss."

"You will." Ginny found a sheaf of paper and used her schoolgirl cursive to pen hasty letters of reference. She finished with her married name and thrust them at Rose. "Find Cook and see she gets her letter of referral. Take the money Mr. Lawsen left. I'll get more from Mr. Parrett. I have his address."

Rose nodded, her eyes wide and frightened. "Miss, you can't do this."

"I must. I'm so sorry, Rose. Good luck with everything."

She managed to nudge Rose through the servant's door, the girl still listing reasons why she should stay.

***

The front door was locked to prevent entry from the magistrate or one of his minions. The baby was safely asleep in a corner of the parlor, near the valises and cases that contained their meager possessions. If the policeman was still stationed at the front entry, they would escape through the same door that Rose had exited a day earlier.

Upstairs, her husband was dry-firing her empty revolver, clicking it again and again in a maudlin exhibition of madness. If not his, then hers. He clicked again, and she realized the frequency was increasing. She was poised at the bottom of the stairs, cowering in indecision when something made her understand that his thin hold on sanity was evaporating. She needed to act, now. She peeked out the window and saw the policeman. She wouldn't involve a kindly family man in her family drama. She would get the baby and herself to safety.

Quickly, she rummaged through the downstairs rooms looking for anything she could pawn or sell.

Anne Schroeder

"It's too bad your father didn't buy me the diamond necklace he promised. I could hock it for sixty dollars," she whispered to the sleeping baby. In his study she found seven dollars. It belonged to Carrie, even if Mr. Hayes had suggested the baby wasn't his. In his top drawer she found his set of diamond-studded cufflinks, along with his gold pocket watch. She slipped them into her pocket, trying not to remember the night she had fled her father's house. Technically, a wife couldn't steal from a husband. If he pressed the issue, she would repay him, but for now it would buy her and her baby a train ticket home.

Back upstairs, she forced the office door open and found Mr. Hayes sitting on the floor near his overturned desk, having just fed bullets into her father's pistol. The hammer was cocked, the barrel shaking so badly that she braced herself for an explosion.

She blurted out the first thing that came to mind. "George, you must be thirsty. Please. Let me get you something. Bourbon?" He glanced up eagerly, but she could find nothing except a pitcher of water. She poured him a glass, but he knocked it away. His hand jumped at the sound of glass breaking on the floor and she frantically tried to divert his attention.

"George, dear, we must put the gun away."

She edged closer and tried to reach across him, hoping he was too drugged to react. Instead, he pushed her away, the movement so angry that she was afraid he would shoot them both. She began inching toward the door, careful to keep her fear from showing.

"It's not fair," he whimpered. "Don't they know how important it is to keep up appearances?" I only married you because of the ranch." His voice hardened when he realized she was still in the room. "I'll demand your share. Sell it and use the money for my defense. That's what I'll do."

"My father's alive. You have no right." She cringed at her blunder. She must remain calm.

"I can hear it now—the boys on the streets selling newspapers for a penny each, shouting 'George Hayes arrested for embezzlement! Read all about it.' People will crowd into the galleys to watch my shame. They'll cheer when the verdict is read." His nose was running, but he made no attempt to wipe it. "No doubt they'll find me guilty—the small-minded idiots who run the legal system. Damn them anyway."

Downstairs, someone shouted, "Police. Open up."

His eyes were glassy and his pupils huge. He fixed a stony stare on her and snarled, "You bitch! I'll kill you for ruining me."

She heard the desperation in his voice and her heart sank. "You'll kill

212

me? And your baby?" She glanced from him to the door, afraid he would shoot if she tried to flee. His eyes shifted to madness and he started to raise his shooting arm.

When her legs wouldn't move quickly enough, she pitched herself on top of him and tried to wrestle the gun away. Their fingers fought for control of the trigger and the gun fired, hitting the ceiling. The impact threw her against the desk as the chandelier exploded in a blast of glass that caught him across the face. Blood ran from a scalp wound, but it was the deranged intensity in his eyes that unnerved her.

Downstairs, the door broke open with a splintering of wood and boots started up the stairs.

She grappled to get control of the pistol and remembered the months she spent kneading dough, the muscles she had developed from hard work while he spent his time in dissipation. The revolver made an unsteady arc upwards. She tried to force his hand off the grip, but his thumb was on the hammer. It clicked and she saw the smooth bore of the barrel pointing at her forehead. She closed her eyes, already hearing the explosion. Sweat made the handle slippery and she tried to keep her hold, but it was useless. Her hand slipped off and the muzzle exploded with a flash.

The circling smoke looked so serene that she was transfixed. Her head was ringing and the room had gone deathly silent. The sharp smell of gunpowder tickled her nose. Then a policeman lifted her to her feet. Another policeman pressed past, mercifully blocking her view. Other hands helped her through the crushed glass to the landing. From downstairs, Carrie's cry drew her back to the present. She took a step toward the stairs and started down, clutching the railing with both hands.

***

Rose was waiting at the door of the courthouse, dressed in the black skirt and white shirtwaist. She slipped through the excited crowd waiting in the rain, grabbed hold of Ginny's hand and placed the money in her palm. Together they pressed past the reporters and the photographers with their bulky cameras set up in the hallway.

Rose sounded like she'd been practicing her argument. "Miss, surely you'll be wanting someone to help out, now that you're alone."

Ginny hesitated. "Rose, how old are you?"

"Sixteen, miss."

Sixteen seemed like another lifetime. Was it only two years ago? "Soon as this is over, I'm going home."

213

Rose hesitated, sucked in a breath and said in a rush, "I could go with you, miss."

The baby reached for Rose's cuff and pulled it into her mouth.

"Don't you have any sisters or brothers who'll worry about you?" Ginny asked.

Yes, miss. Eighteen of them. Some back in the homeland, some spread to the winds. I'm saving my pennies so my sister can join me. She turns fifteen next year, miss."

Ginny remembered the penny jar in the tiny servant's room where Rose slept. "The work's harder in the country."

"I'm from the country, miss. I don't know no other way."

The baby weighed her down. At the far end of the courtroom the bailiff was calling her to the stand. She needed to make a decision. Rose made her laugh and she hadn't had a real friend since Nettie. "Here, take Carrie. We'll catch the train as soon as this inquest is over."

From the witness stand she watched Rose jiggle Carrie in the hallway. A neatly-dressed, bespectacled man in a dark suit entered and whispered something to the clerk. They both turned and looked directly at her, and the man smiled encouragingly. *Jeremy's private detective.* Ginny recognized him from the time she saw him reading a newspaper on a park bench while she played with Carrie on the grass.

The judge's questions were direct, but kindly phrased. "There will be a reckoning of your husband's finances, Mrs. Hayes. You are to sell or dispose of nothing." He leaned in and his eyes seemed apologetic. "Is that understood?"

"Yes." She hadn't planned to ask, but Carrie deserved something. "Does that include my personal clothing?"

Several men in the courtroom guffawed, and the judge's face grew red.

"Silence!" The judge leaned closer. "Of course not. You're free to take your personal effects. The court is concerned with your husband, not yourself."

Ginny waited while the courtroom quieted. She glanced at the shrewd, tight faces of some of the moneylenders and shivered. Clearly there were men in the city who wanted the value of her red velvet gown to salve their losses. When the judge finished questioning her, Jeremy's detective escorted her and Rose from the courthouse. The jeering crowd of merchants who were owed money pressed close, waving their claims in the air. The detective, Mr. Prester, forced a path through them.

Ginny kept her face down and her eyes focused on the marble floor, allowing herself to be led into the sunshine. Mr. Prester had a buggy waiting. Once inside, he took a seat beside her and pulled the flaps down to block the jeering crowd. Rose and Carrie sat across. Trembling, Ginny pressed her head back, closed her eyes and waited for her heart to slow. When Carrie began fussing, Rose passed the baby to her. Ginny buried her face in the baby's hair to hide her trembling while the buggy lunged and swayed through the city. When she opened her eyes, the buggy was pulling up to her steps.

Already it was a stranger's palace. The policeman standing guard blocked their way until Mr. Prester produced a copy of the judge's document authorizing Ginny to remove her effects. Satisfied, the officer stood aside and allowed the three of them to enter. Ginny used the opportunity to feed her baby while Rose and Mr. Prester found carpetbags and packed their clothing. The two of them carried the bags to the buggy. Rose returned to the house and carried out a bag of baby things. Ginny followed with Carrie.

Her last glance of the house from the moving buggy made her feel like she had remembered what is was to breathe again.

She retrieved a crumpled and rain-smeared card from her case containing the address of the shop where she had purchased the dresses. The proprietress would recall her, she had no doubt. It was she who had whispered a quiet offer to repurchase, should the young madam require cash for any reason.

Chapter Thirty-Eight

Ginny braced herself with one arm on the seatback and another around her baby while the jolting farm wagon rolled toward the ranch. Fortunately for them, Troy Hart, Jeremy's foreman, was collecting his mail at the new stage stop and had offered her and Rose a ride. She hadn't had the presence of mind to think that far ahead. No one knew they were coming and she wanted it to be a surprise.

The sky was flawless blue, the air dry and fresh with the scents of sage and juniper—with a hint of turkey grass added to the mix as though God had stirred up a pot of fall color just for her. Rose gawked at the wide, sandy streambeds and the dotting of oaks still green with summer color, and she felt herself filling with pride. Above them, a falcon hunted the yellow grass, its wings spread in the wind current. A meadowlark sang from a sagging willow near a stagnant pool of water.

Ginny held Carrie up so the baby could see and hear, while the wagon picked up speed on a downhill stretch and the valley spread out before her. Clearly the Cholama had suffered a hard year; the autumn hills were brown from lack of rain. Clouds of dust hid her view as she huddled on the spring seat, trying to shelter her daughter from the worst of the grime. The wagon lumbered down the lane until the driver pulled to a halt beneath the cottonwood tree in the yard. Ginny waited, unable to move, her eyes hungry to see everything in one glance.

In the orchard, someone lifted his hand to shade his eyes and slowly started toward them. She could feel Sancho's excitement the moment he recognized her.

"Missy. . . that you?"

She handed off the baby to Rose and jumped to the ground. With her long skirts bunched in her fists, she began running. "Sancho, I'm home!"

By the time she reached him she was winded. She stretched to give him a hug and saw that his face was wreathed in a toothless grin. "Well, tan me to leather, If it ain't Miss Virginia."

"Sancho. I'm so glad you're still here." She wasn't sure what to say first. Or where to look. The peach trees were losing their color, the leaves just

216

beginning to turn. In the orchard the pomegranate tree was bursting with color. A bee brushed her cheek and she laughed. "Oh, Sancho! Everything's just the same." As soon as she said it she realized she was wrong. The baby fussing back at the wagon reminded her that everything had changed. Troy Hart had unloaded her bags and was helping Rose down.

Sancho caught the movement in the wagon. "I reckon not everything."

She glanced toward the house. "Charlie?"

He gave her a sympathetic look. "He's in bed. Seems to be hanging on for someone."

She felt her heart soar with gladness. "I need to see him."

Sancho nodded. "Thought you might. You're sure your mother's daughter. A thoroughbred clean through."

She took his arm and pulled him forward. "I have a couple of girls I want you to meet."

The expression in Sancho's face when he met Carrie was worth coming home for. His weather-roughened fingers held the baby's tiny finger and he leaned in close, making her gurgle with pleasure at the tickle of his beard.

Then it was time for the next homecoming.

Ginny paused at the door. Her heart, beating like a hummingbird's only moments earlier, settled while she waited in the doorway and tried to reconcile the man lying in her father's bed with the man she used to know. The fierceness was gone from his frame; what remained had withered. A stranger would have argued that such a small man could not instill fear, but the surprise for her was that she could look at him and feel peace.

Charlie was clean-shaven and trimmed, and his eyelashes fanned the hollows where cheekbones used to be. He lay in a bed with sheets and a feather tick pillow that looked fresh-washed. His face was thin, with skin the color of Miguelito's yellow stallion. Even the whites of his eyes held a sickly yellow hue. His hair had turned whiter than Sancho's.

He must have felt her presence because he turned slightly so his face caught the afternoon rays coming through the window. She wanted to speak, but she wasn't sure how to address him. He was no longer Patrón, nor even Charlie.

"Papa?"

His eyes opened and he squinted to see. A slow smile framed his missing teeth as he wheezed a greeting. "Ginny?" She knelt beside the bed, afraid to disturb him. Silence clung to the walls and she waited for him to break it. "Ginny . . . I'm so sorry."

Her eyes filled, but she managed to whisper, "Sancho says you waited."

She wasn't sure if he heard her. At any rate, it didn't matter. He swallowed and continued. "So sorry. I had such plans. And then—all gone."

It was in her mind to tell him that it didn't matter, but the words choked her. She found a tin cup and fed him a few sips of water, but most of it ran down his chin. He licked the remaining drops with a grateful sigh, his mouth and his words parched like August grass.

He glanced up and she saw the weight of his own demons waiting to claim him. Time to lay them to rest. "Papa, I thought I killed her and that's why you were so angry with me. It took me a long time to understand that I had no part. But you blamed me."

His eyes slammed shut and for an instant the old Patrón was back. "It wasn't you. I killed her. Me." he panted. "I brought her out here and I couldn't protect her. I promised her I would."

She reached out and took his thin, trebling fingers, and she could feel the veins beneath his paper-thin skin. "No, Papa, she just died."

"Why . . . she . . . leave?"

"Because she knew we had each other." Hearing them for the first time, she believed her own words.

"Can you forgive her? Me?" His eyes glowed with such intensity that she choked. It was time to set the past aside.

She turned and accepted the baby from Rose, who was waiting in the hallway. At the cooing sound, her father struggled to raise his head. "Papa, meet your granddaughter. Her name is Caroline Rachel. We call her Carrie." She held the baby low and watched his face fill with wonder. When his strength failed, he dropped back on the pillow and his smile was almost as she remembered. His fingers twitched like he wanted to touch the baby, but his strength was gone. Time to let him rest. "I'll be back to sit the night with you, Papa."

He was asleep before she closed the door.

She escaped into the orchard to sort her thoughts, the collision of memories, real and imagined, harder that she had expected. Later, she left Sancho to entertain Carrie while she helped Rose put together a meal of stewed tomatoes and tortillas along with a pot of beans he had simmering on the woodstove. They took their meal to the table in the yard, just the three of them.

"What did you think of San Miguel?" Sancho had reluctantly turned the baby back to her while he ate. Now he was trying to ease her nerves with small talk. And it was working.

"Oh, I was ever so surprised. The train tracks run right through town.

And with a way to get crops to market, the town has grown. There's a new feed mill. Stores and houses—even streets! The mission church is holding services again." She thought about the last time she was there. "The railroad people punched a hole right through the Indian housing to put in the tracks."

"Heard that was done with the new priest's blessing. Had to happen."

"Well, it was a blessing. And when we rode to the end of the line we took the mail stage right into the new Parkfield station. There'll be a town here soon. It's purely a wonder."

"Makes things easier, that's for sure." Sancho's attention rested on the baby. "Wait 'till you see the new school they built over Red Rock way."

"Over by Jeremy's ranch? That will be good for his neighbors." She hesitated. "And this ranch? What's left of it?"

"Not much. Sheriff held a public auction for most of it. You got only the hundred and sixty acres fronts the road here. But it's enough to raise horses."

"My father's gift to me and my children." She was glad she had to attend to her baby's feeding so she didn't have to look up. Sancho wandered off to allow her privacy. When he returned, the conversation continued. "Think he knows I'm home?" she finally asked. "I mean, he seemed to. But he's so tired."

"He knows. Been fighting to stay alive. Sent word with Jeremy." He fidgeted with his coffee cup. "Didn't want to send a letter. Figured your husband might forget to give it to you."

"Yes," Rose said. "Surely that would have happened."

Ginny looked from one of them to the other and felt her eyes fill. "It's good to be home."

Rose took the baby from her and disappeared into the house while Ginny gathered herself for her midnight vigil.

She woke the next morning, her muscles cramped from sitting in the small chair. Carrie had awakened twice during the night and she'd tended the baby's needs while her father slept. After the final feeding, she left the lamp lit and read aloud from the Bible she'd left behind on the night she fled. She must have dozed because she was awakened by a faint sound, then silence. She moved to open the door and stood aside as Sancho entered, but the truth was in his face when he turned.

He returned shortly with a pallet made of barn wood. Numbness crept through her limbs. Not guilt or sadness, not even regret; those would come later, when she had time to consider her part in this ending, but she thanked God for bringing her to her senses in time. She had brought her father the promise of a hopeful future and had seen his mind settled. She had brought him the peace that had escaped him these long years. That was enough for today.

She eased into the hallway and closed the door. "We'll wash him after breakfast. I don't intend to bury him without a proper funeral."

Someone was riding up the drive toward the house. "Fitting time for Jeremy to ride in," Sancho murmured.

She wasn't prepared for the yearning that filled her. "He's come to see Charlie."

Sancho squinted at the cloud of dust coming up the road at a gallop. "It's his hoss. Danged if it ain't!"

Jeremy reined to a halt at the base of the cottonwood tree, gray tufts of dirt still flying around his horse's feet as he jumped to the ground.

Ginny walked toward him, shaking the wrinkles from her skirt to keep her hands occupied. She noticed that he was similarly occupied with shaking his duster, aware of everyone in the yard watching.

Jeremy stood awkwardly twisting his Stetson like he wanted to take her in his arms, but he said, simply, "I was on my way to San Miguel to catch the train. Ran into the stage driver and spared myself the trip."

"My father's gone."

He studied her face and seemed relieved by what he saw. "You're okay? I mean, you had time with him?"

She nodded through her tears. "There's the burial yet. I don't know who to ask."

They studied each other while their eyes spoke for them. It seemed as though this meeting was stolen from both the living and the dead, as if they were standing on a bridge between what had been lost and what might be, given grace and luck. She was afraid to step forward, and too eager to step back. Maybe he was, too because they both waited, searching each other for a sign. Finally, the lines of tension on his face smoothed.

"There's a whole settlement of people here now. I'll put out a call, if that's all right with you," he said.

She nodded. "Most of the people who helped bury my mama have left, but maybe there's a few who remember her. It will be good to see them again."

"They'll be honored to help." He tore his gaze away and leaned to chuck the baby under its chin, an awkward bachelor's gesture that belied his shaking hands. She smiled, wanting an excuse to touch him. Apparently he understood, because he jerked as though he remembered something.

"It's not the right time, but I have something for her." He slid his hat back on, freeing his hands to unfasten his saddlebag. When he found the package he was searching for, he pulled it out and handed it to Ginny, carefully so that their hands met beneath the package. Slowly, she slipped her fingers into his while the baby's body hid them.

"Look, Carrie, Mr. Lawsen brought you a present."

She waited to see what was inside, but she had a feeling she already knew. The feeling grew with every twist of string and paper until she thought her heart would burst. Sure enough, a porcelain doll lay in the wrapping, dressed in a frilly frock like the one he'd given her so many years ago. She breathed in the new-doll smell and watched as Carrie batted at the doll's curls with her tiny fist.

"I think we'll put it up until you're older." She smiled. "Mr. Lawsen's a bit rusty when it comes to judging what little girls like." She set the package on the table and handed the baby to Sancho.

Jeremy glanced up and tipped his hat to the girl watching shyly from the kitchen. "Hello again, Rose. I hope you've come to share your tales of the famous Wednesday escape with some of our bachelors. I know one foreman in particular who will be happy for your company. "

Rose dropped a curtsy. "Yes, sir." Coloring, she glanced at Ginny and giggled. "Ginny says there'll be no more of that—miss and sir, I mean."

Ginny nodded, glad that her face no longer heated with the shame of her circumstances. "I'm as poor as a church mouse. There's no need putting on airs for the neighbors. Rose and I are sisters now." She glanced down, suddenly shy. He was smiling at her in a way that made her heart stop.

"Ginny," he took a breath, "let's take a walk."

Under a laden apple tree he released his breath and turned toward her, pressing her against the bark of the full-leafed tree that sheltered them. "I'm sorry about your father. He had his struggles, but he cared about you."

She felt her tears falling in spite of her resolve. "I know he did. It's been a long night." She shook her head and burrowed her cheek against his chest, feeling his heart thumping. "I'm glad you're here."

He lowered his mouth and whispered, "I rushed this kiss the last time. I don't intend to do that again."

Their first kiss had been filled with mystery and confusion. But this time a woman stood where a girl had once been, sure now of what she wanted. It was Jeremy who had been reduced to uncertainly by a girl he had never thought to love, their places reversed in a kiss that offered reassurance to him and confidence to her. It was a strange time to realize that nothing was as it had been only minutes earlier. When they broke apart, reluctant and breathless, the orchard seemed different to them both. Jeremy straightened and his eyes held a certainty that made her feel cherished and safe.

"That little girl will need a father." He kissed her again. "Your father asked me to take care of you both."

She smiled through her tears. "My father hated your barb wire. And I think he hated you. So don't go acting all noble."

"Maybe. Maybe not." His chest was warm and his words rumbled deep against her cheek. "Marry me and find out, Katydid."

"I told you not to call me that."

"I recall you gave me a lot of orders. You were a bossy little thing."

Her smile was back, despite her next words. "I'll be wearing black for a year. I owe them both that much."

He hesitated. "People will understand if you only do six months. But I won't press."

"We'll take it one day at a time."

Chapter Thirty-Nine

By Spring the hillsides were bursting with early color. A month later, the creeks were still running clean and shallow, enough to wash out a portion of the stage road to San Miguel. The previous night had brought a deluge, but Ginny was restless from too many days cooped up inside. She wanted to see for herself the overflowing springs and the new quicksilver mine that was bringing in homesteaders, in a slew of new wagon traffic along her road. Sancho rode with her while Rose stayed behind with Carrie.

She insisted on saddling her own horse with tack she lugged from the rack. "My mare looks a little thin," she teased. "You sure you and Jeremy brought the right horse back?"

Sancho's nostrils flared with indignation. "Guess I'd know. Been taking care of that hoss since before you was born."

"Is that so?" It felt good to joke again.

They started toward the distant range where the hills were exactly as she remembered, craggy rock outcroppings towering over the same blooming chamise, blue curl and bunch grass. The pastures were abloom with a blue tinge of lupine and the air was perfumed with scent. Thanks goodness it was too early for rattlesnakes. "Felt the earth jar lately?"

"Nah. Been quiet since the big one in '81. Broke off a few rocks on the round corral. Cracked the adobe some, but we managed. 'Spect Jeremy wrote you about that one."

"His letters made me feel like I was still here. I owe him so much."

"'Spect the feeling's mutual."

She rode a few minutes before she broke her silence. "You think Rose is going to marry that fellow who's been calling on her?"

"Don't know why not. Troy's a hard worker. Jeremy thinks a lot of him."

"He's helping her learn to write."

"That what the two of them do at the table every night?"

Ginny heard herself laughing. "She says they're watching the moon. She's never seen a finer one. Calls it *la Cho-luna*. She wants to board the new school teacher here when the school opens. She's going to do the cooking

223

and send half her earnings home to her sister Maureen so she can come to America. It's all planned."

"How 'bout you? Your widow year will be up before long. You two make weddin' plans yet?"

"He says I'm nineteen, getting on to being a spinster."

Sancho shook his head. "Nah, that don't happen 'til you're twenty."

She smiled. Sancho looked happier than she'd ever seen him. Younger, too. "Jeremy wants to take me home to Virginia to meet his mother for our honeymoon. Carrie and me. Rose will stay and cook."

"Rose is good company."

"I'm glad she took Charlie's old bedroom. Even though it's bigger, I couldn't make myself move in there."

Sancho nodded, his mind somewhere else. "Room's got a passel of memories, that's for sure."

She recognized the joy behind his worn skin, as rough and patchy as worn leather, with eyes that reflected quiet satisfaction. She felt the same. "It's been nice living here, just the baby and us. Gave me a chance to find out about myself before I become someone else's wife."

"Reckon your ma felt the same. She had a friend in me."

"Thank you for what you did with the memory wreath. I saw her hair. And my brother's. I hung it in the parlor."

"She'd like what you done there. Room's got heart now." Sancho looked up and felt a familiar stab of pleasure at the landscape. They had ridden a far piece across the canyon, up the arroyo toward the tree line. He shifted, favoring his aching hip. Time to ride back. His mind wandered to the first time he saw the valley. With nothing but time, he let his memories surface. Miss Virginia wouldn't mind. Maybe on the ride home he'd share the story with her.

The next morning a buttermilk sky delivered another fine day. Changes were in the air. Ginny bubbled with happiness as she sat playing with Carrie beneath the cottonwood tree after the lunch dishes had been cleared from the table. "Spring is here. I can feel it clear to my toes."

Rose was more pragmatic. "I'd say you're enjoying a bout of love, Ginny."

Ginny felt her face heat. "Jeremy and I are riding down to San Luis Obispo after we see a minister. He's promised." She turned to Sancho. "To visit our friend, Mrs. Dunn. And see the opening of the convent school. It'll be part of our honeymoon. She'll be surprised to know we're married."

Sancho shook his head. "'Spect not. Women got a feeling for those things."

"Arciela's coming back. I spoke to her mother. She's thirteen now, old enough to help out with the baby." Ginny laughed. "They'll be good for each other. Carrie can be her eyes. She'll be chasing Gila monsters around the yard by the time she's a year. She sees enough for two people."

Sancho checked the sun's afternoon position with a satisfied nod. "If Jeremy's coming over, you better skedaddle."

Ginny handed him the toddler and raced into the house.

After she finished bathing, she slipped into one of her mother's dresses, the green-sprigged calico that made her eyes look like the ocean in fog. She dallied, weaving a wreath of roses into her hair that matched the scented soap she'd used in her new hip bath. She'd picked the bathtub out of a picture in the Montgomery Ward catalogue and had it shipped down from San Francisco on the train. The stage driver hauled it over from San Miguel on a mud wagon, and the money from her velvet dresses paid for it all. Cool and refreshed, she strolled outside just as Sancho was boosting Carrie so she could pick a peach blossom in the warm spring evening.

Back inside, she poured herself a cup of coffee and called to Rose, "I'll start supper. You'll want to clean up before that cowboy comes by tonight." She laughed at Rose's blush.

The almond trees were blossoming. They'd be thick with nuts this year, but they could spare a couple of blossoms for the table. Sancho cut a sprig with Carrie perched on his good hip. At eleven months she could walk enough that she was into everything. Before supper she'd pestered him into finding her a dried apple left on a tree.

"Got me a hankering for cobbler," Sancho called across the yard.

Ginny paused in her stirring. "Got dried peaches already soaking. Rose'll make the crust. There's enough to do around here for two. No sense in working ourselves into a lather, like you say."

She saw Sancho wipe his knife blade on his pants and return it to its pouch before he followed Carrie into the cook house and perched her on the tule basket, out of harm's way. He sounded winded. "That mare of yours is due to foal any day. That's a fine stallion you bred her to."

Ginny hesitated. "Sancho, when I was away at school, I saw men play something called polo on specially trained horses. I wrote Jeremy about them. It's a field game that rich folks play." She hesitated. "A good polo horse will bring top dollar."

"Don't say!"

"I'm thinking Cholame would be a fine place for a polo ranch.

Miguelito could come back."

"You might be on to something. He's married now, to a fiery little California gal who keeps him on his toes. He had a bad bout of it, but he's worked out his anger. Maria Inés was his mother, you know. She kept the secret all those years. His wife would be good company."

A butterfly flew into the room and lit on Carrie's hand. Sunshine peaked through a patch of white cloud and Ginny sighed with contentment. "I never want to leave here again."

Sancho sighed and his breath seemed tortured. Ginny watched as he caught himself and frowned. "Don't wish that on yourself. Places are for seeing. Go and enjoy. This all will be here when you get home again."

Ginny sighed. "I suppose. Look at us. This place is getting to be quite a town. We have a school. And a meeting hall. A livery and a mercantile—the miners saw to that."

"Imus wouldn't recognize the place, he seen it now. You gals hear anything from 'em?" It seemed that he struggled to speak, but maybe she was imaging it.

She nodded. "Rose heard some of the brothers are coming back for a visit this summer. They have family living all over the valley now."

"Heard one of 'em use the name Parkfield the other day. Has a good ring to it."

Ginny laughed. "Why it sure does! Why didn't we think of that?"

Sancho pulled a piece of string from his pocket and made a lizard loop for Carrie, who giggled and reached for it. By the time he finished, he was winded. "Your ma wanted the world for you. And Jeremy's just the one to give it."

"He's taking me to Paso Robles next week to see a play at the Hot Springs Hotel."

"Well, that's just fine."

"And he's teaching me to shoot his shotgun." Carrie was getting fussy. Ginny stopped to lift her up and hand her a molasses cookie. "Sancho . . ."

"Huh?"

"Do you think Mama was happy here?"

He hesitated and it seemed as though his eyes changed color, but he smiled and the light was back again. "Happy is where your heart is, Missy. Ain't no other place it can be."

"I suppose you're right." She thought a moment about how happy her mother must have been with a husband she adored and a baby like Carrie. Other memories surfaced. Gratified, she set her toddler down and

226

straightened.

At the road, Jeremy's buggy was turning in. She watched him pull to a halt, her heart hammering the way it had the very first time she laid eyes on him. His eyes widened when he saw that she wore the flowered dress instead of her black widow's garb; she could tell by his smile that he'd gotten her message.

"Keep an eye on Carrie. I'll be back." She scooped up her skirts and started running toward the wagon.

Jeremy caught her and swung her into the air, her petticoats splaying beneath her gingham dress. His hands spanned her waist, over the whalebone stays of the corset she'd struggled to have Rose cinch for her. His skin, fresh-shaven and glowing with new spring sunshine, made him seem young and determined. She ran her fingers across his cheek, stopping when her thumb caught at the corner of his mouth, her breath captured when his smile froze in intensity. She was weak by the time her feet met the ground again.

His lips found hers, and afterwards her neck and the fine strands of hair that escaped her ribbons. When their lips and eyes were satiated, they fell in beside each other, matching slow steps as they strolled hand-in-hand along the Cholame Creek and watched its flowing ribbon cut through the sand.

"It's the same way with life," Jeremy said, nodding at the water. "We're all rushing to get somewhere."

"Maybe." Ginny was content where she stood.

He reached in his pocket and brought out a packet. "I have reservations for the musicale at the Hot Springs Hotel. It's official. We'll be gone two nights."

"Two nights? We can't travel together."

He grinned. "I've made arrangements for that, too. We'll attend a wedding at the Estrella Adobe Church on our trip to Paso Robles—our own. We'll honeymoon at the Hot Springs Hotel. Rose can tend Carrie for three days."

Ginny considered. "I thought we'd wait for the Methodist preacher."

"The riding circuit? It takes him a month to do his route. It's 300 miles. His horse could break a leg. I'm not waiting for him."

Ginny felt herself heating. Her last wedding had been forced on her in a drunk judge's chamber with an angry man's grip on her wrist, threatening her when she faltered in her response. She shook her head to clear her thoughts. *No purpose in revisiting that nightmare.* Still, a shudder of fear crawled down her spine. "What if I say it's too soon?"

Jeremy frowned in feigned dismay, thinking that she jested. "Too late. I already paid the minister his fee."

Ginny saw the good man standing in front of her who offered only safety and solace. Shrugging off her trepidation, she tugged his hand to start him back toward the house where dinner waited. "Let's go share the news. I think Sancho will be relieved to get his girls married."

***

On the morning of their wedding, Rose insisted on staying home with Carrie. Sancho seemed worse and she wanted to keep an eye on him. Ginny handed Jeremy her carpetbag and watched as he lifted it into the buggy. From the shade of the cottonwood, Sancho coughed with enough force that he struggled to remain standing. "I'm afraid that my happiness may come on the wings of sorrow," Ginny said.

"Sorrow?" Jeremy straightened and offered his help in mounting the running board.

She turned to tuck her hand beneath Jeremy's elbow. Her tears formed a clot in her throat and she struggled to speak. "Jeremy, I think Sancho's ill."

Rose insisted that Sancho should move into the main house, but he shooed them away with a wave of his hand.

"You gals leave me to the bunkhouse and get about your lives, you hear?"

She turned after kissing Carrie, and allowed Jeremy to help her into the buggy. "As a safeguard, keep Carrie away from Sancho until we know what ails him," she whispered to Rose.

The miles to the small church in Estrella were achieved with a minimum of dust, owing to the recent rains. Jeremy reminded her that April was the best month of the year for travel. She laughed and replied that he was preaching to the choir, a phrase that Missus Whitman had often used.

Reverend Knightson looked up when their horses pulled alongside the parsonage. "I thought you might be the folks for the funeral."

"Someone die?" Jeremy asked.

"We got us a diphtheria outbreak. Any of yours taken sick lately?"

Ginny felt her stomach clench. She glanced from Jeremy to the Reverend, unsure what to do. It was too late to turn around and go home. Best they place their trust in God and Rose. Jeremy nodded and indicated that the service should commence.

The Reverend suggested that Dwight Reynolds, an Estrella farmer, and his wife serve as witnesses when they happened to be at the parsonage unloading two sacks of barley and a weaner hog to fulfill his tithe.

Cholama Moon

As soon as the words were said, Ginny felt herself relax. The ceremony was hurried and lacking in social fineries, but she had a new dress and a bouquet of lupine blossoms that she picked from a field. She'd seen the corrupting influence that velvet dresses and faux jewels could create; she didn't need anything more than she had to be happy. Jeremy would see her through whatever life offered. She felt blessed. *Missus Jeremy Lawsen.* She wanted to write it in the sand.

Her honeymoon trip to Paso Robles included a theatrical performance, fine Chardonnay wine, time well spent in a mud spa, and afterwards, hours alone with Jeremy—each kiss stirring in her an awakening after the memories of force and drug-induced attacks that had disturbed her sleep for two years. After her first hour alone with Jeremy, she wondered how she could have been so foolish as to feel she knew anything about the marriage act. She took a deep breath and managed to confess her foolishness to him, and later, to laugh at her fears.

Chapter Forty

After three days, for all her happiness Ginny Lawsen leaped from the buggy and raced into her house before Jeremy had time to rein in the horses. At the corner of the summer house she found Carrie secured to a tree with a piece of Sancho's reata, pursuing a butterfly. To a mother's eyes she appeared the picture of health.

Sancho was a different story. With an apologetic glance at Jeremy, Ginny quietly changed into her work dress and traded places with Rose, who was dead on her feet from fatigue. Jeremy took his daughter on a walk through the orchard.

Ginny rinsed a cloth in fresh water and wiped Sancho's fevered brow. His neck was swollen, with a bluish hue to his skin and a rough, barking cough that Rose had been careful to contain with a pile of red bandanas that she had provided for his use. The windows were open for ventilation, but even in the fresh air he labored to breath. She watched him lying with his eyes closed, so still that he looked dead except for the hoarse inhale-exhale of his labored breathing. She waited for him to open his eyes before she spoke.

"You know something, Sancho? You never told me your real name."

Sancho looked up with a haunting, worn expression. As quickly as it appeared, it was replaced by a faint smile. "Getting ready to make my tombstone, are you?"

"You know better than that. I just want to know, that's all. Mama knew, didn't she?"

He nodded. "'Spect that's a fair request." He hesitated while a cough consumed him. When it ended, his voice lowered to a whisper. "I'm trusting you to keep this between the two of us."

"Promise."

His voice was barely audible. "Missy, say hello to Ecclesiastes Malachi Roos."

Ginny thought she'd strangle from her effort to keep a straight face. "Ecclesiastes. That's from the Bible."

His face looked puffy and unnatural, but his words sounded disgusted. "Ma had a passel of young'uns. Reckon she just run out a names. Took to opening her Bible to whatever name was on top. Got two brothers, both named Proverbs. Different first names."

Ginny choked through her tears. "See, it could be worse," she whispered. He snorted and she continued in a stage whisper. "Your secret is safe with me, Ecclesiastes. It's a lovely name. Really! A gift from your mother."

Sancho nodded and closed his eyes.

For the next two days she spent her waking hours tending Sancho and trying to keep Carrie from harm while Jeremy returned to his ranch. At night, unexpected wind gusts tore crumbling chinks from the adobe brick of the bunkhouse. Chills knotted Sancho's muscles, but not for lack of blankets. Ginny and Rose kept the woodstove stoked and a kettle of chicken broth handy, but despite their ministrations, Sancho's coughing worsened. He tossed as if old memories plagued his sleep until Ginny thought her father was the lucky one, already out of his misery. As intolerable as the nights were, they brought with them moments of clarity.

Tonight he fought the pain gripping his chest. His breath came hard, squeezing his lungs and numbing all feeling in his arms. The next jolt was worse than any earthquake; this one took his body and he seemed to be watching himself from a distance. A bright light lit his eyes and he smiled as though he had forgotten the pain.

Ginny sat beside him, imagining that he was meeting her mother again. He would be watching with wonderment as the lady in white gestured to him from the other side, the way he had always described her. She was wearing a thin white dress, her skirts flowing in the breeze as she beckoned for him to join her.

Ginny could almost hear his thoughts: Sweet Jesus, the joy in her eyes was a memory he hadn't let go of and there it was, waiting. There were others beside the white lady, watching and waiting, some holding out hands to guide him forward. He saw it all, but it was the vision of the lady that grew more radiant with the light from her eyes.

He struggled to breathe and suddenly it didn't matter. Life was sweet and easy, and peace was there, waiting. One last breath and he was over the divide.

Ginny sat with her Bible until she was sure that his spirit had left him. Only then did she place the coins on his eyelids and pull a length of sheeting over his body. Her whispered farewell was strained by unshed tears.

"Adios, my dear friend. You're with *her* now."

The words signified an ending. Sancho, Charlie, both gone, along with everything they had worked for. Sancho had made good and lasting friends in the valley who would need to be notified. She would send word to the postmaster. He would know what to do. Tomorrow they would have a burial and tears would flow in earnest, but tonight Sancho was right.

Jeremy and Carrie were waiting. *Her* life was waiting to begin.

Author's Notes

At the edge of Ginny Nugent's valley the Temblor Range was born, in technical terms, the southwest slippage of the North American plate against the Pacific plate at a rate of six centimeters a year. To a girl of the nineteenth century like Ginny, tectonic science was unknown—its results, mere curiosity. Her world was bounded by her Devil Mountains and *La Luna Cholama*, the moon that illuminates her fractured valley.

This remote section of Southeastern Monterey County, California's Cholame Valley –pronounced Show-lam Valley —is only five miles wide. In 1878, from there to San Francisco or Los Angeles took three days by horse, mail stage or train. Rugged and filled with natural beauty, the valley has played host to Indian tribes, Spanish land grants, Mexican bandits, wild mustangs and earthquakes. Today it is known as Parkfield, the epicenter of the San Andreas Fault.

In this era of California history the great Mexican land grants are being broken off. Public land is being offered to homesteaders and preemptors (squatters.) People are pouring into California from many areas of America and overseas. The Salinans—the white people derisively call them "Diggers"—have been disenfranchised from their land. A fast-growing population brings a railroad, which means towns, trade and transportation. Within seven years, the Cholama changes from being a handful of isolated ranches to a growing community with active social life.

Although the Nugent family is fictional, most of the historical figures, homesteaders, politicians and events in the book are real.

Nettie Imus entered the story when I saw an online photo of her grave market at the Evergreen Cemetery in Santa Cruz, California. Nettie was the 10-year-old daughter of William Imus, the first white settler in Cholama Valley. Her brother and sister are buried in the Imusdale Cemetery there. According to Donalee Thomason in her historical reference book, *Cholama*, Don Imus, the radio talk show host, is a descendent of the original Imuses.

About the Author

Anne Schroeder's love of the American West was fueled by her Norwegian grandfather's stories of hardscrabble farming and neighbors sharing. She shares her own stories in Ordinary Aphrodite, a light-hearted journey of small steps from the boomer generation.

She earned a B.S. in Social Science at Cal Poly, San Luis Obispo. Now she writes from Oregon and California's Central Coast, and shares her love of the West with her husband of many years, her children, grandchildren and two dogs.

Many of her short stories and novels have earned awards including the Will Rogers Medallion and LAURA Short Fiction Award. Most of her books are set in California and Oregon, including her Central Coast Series of early California history. Anne served as President of Women Writing the West and WILLA Literary Award Chair. She is a member of Native Daughters of the Golden West and Western Writers of America. She blogs at
http://anneschroederauthor.com
http://facebook.com/anneschroederauthor

Historical Novels by Anne Schroeder

Central Coast Series
Maria Inés
The Caballero's Son
Cholama Moon
Palomita, Dove of the Gabilans (coming 2022)

Boy in the Darkness
Walk the Promise Road
Norske Fields

Branches on the Conejo Revisited
Ordinary Aphrodite
Gifts of Red Pottery

Excerpt of Maria Inés
(Book #1 in the Central Coast Series)

Chapter One

Alta California
September, 1818

The fury of the storm seemed to be a warning. The few who still called themselves the People of the Oaks whispered that the flooding was the gods' anger because they had left their villages and their traditional ways to dwell among the padres at Mission San Miguel Arcángel. But others argued not. For them the rain was a blessing from the true God.

"Let the rains come," a young woman prayed as she lay waiting for her next birthing pain. "Let us be safe this night." She was a *neophyte*, a baptized Indian with a name given to her by the padres and she felt afraid in this new place. But no travelers would arrive seeking hospitality in this weather. Tonight *El Camino Real* was flooded, the thin wagon track that followed the rivers and valleys from the border of New Spain, north to the Missions of Alta California. "Let the rains come," she repeated. "Let our fields and our hearts be renewed."

Her heart was one with the forces raging outside her walls, ancient winds whipping through the olive grove, ripping off branches and pitching them into the north wall of the dormitory. The sound of singers and cantors in the nearby church were muted as whorls of rain lashed the clay-tiled roofs, windows and rough-hewn doors.

Alfonsa lay inside the adobe room assigned to her husband, Domingo. Restlessly, she stirred in her birthing bed, feeling its sturdy willow frame flex beneath her. A fragrant layer of pine needles sent out a sweet fragrance, sap freed by a layer of heated rocks in the trench beneath her. She breathed deeply and her mind saw the forest where, a few days earlier, she had walked from sunrise to sunset to gather pine boughs. Domingo had built the bed in the way of her ancestors to please her, a deep rectangular trench dug into in the hard-packed adobe floor holding five rocks still hot from the fire. His mother bound the frame with woven *tule* grass to protect the skin from the heat. Now Alfonsa now rested safely above the half-buried stones and waited.

"It is good, 'mingo," she whispered, and her heart swelled with gratitude. She longed to tell him this, but he was not present. His mother had chased him from the room because the old taboos did not allow him to take part in the birth. The two were both at evening service, along with every other neophyte, and she was alone.

A basket of pine nuts lay nearby, a gift he had brought so she would have strength for her ordeal. She glanced at the basket, but her body was filled with anticipation, not hunger—a thing her husband would not understand because his belly was never full, even after he had taken his meal. Alone but unafraid, she bit down on an olive twig to blunt her moan from the world outside. "The rain is God's gift," she whispered through cracked lips. "Our prayers are heard."

Another pain engulfed her. She shut her eyes, bit into the twig and tried to hold onto yesterday's memory when Padre Juan Martin had stood in the courtyard, his hands raised to the sky as a warm breeze wafted his robe like the wings of a dove. Strong and fervent, his voice swelled to the cloudless sky as he led his people in prayer for rain. Rain so that there would be more wheat in the fields and vegetables in the gardens. Food for the *escolte*, the Spanish soldiers protecting the Mission. Food for the padres and their guests. Grain to trade to the other Missions and to send to the governor for taxes. And if there was any left, food for the neophytes, for her and her baby soon to be born.

The summer heat had been intense, the rain sparse, but the Spanish Governor de Solá had levied extra taxes in the form of wine and cattle hides. Many workers died in the latest round of hunger and typhoid, leaving fewer to gather the crops. She did not complain like some of the others who groused under their breath about the six hours of labor required of them—

even though the padres worked as hard as any of them—but drought made things harder. Her belly, big with baby, made drawing water difficult; carrying the burden basket pulled down her shoulders and strained her back with the pressure of the strap. This is why she knew God had sent the rain for her, and just in time.

"Aiiiyaah." Another pain, this one harder.

Her lips moved in the prayer of the Holy Mother who had given birth in a room no bigger than her own. Alfonsa swallowed her sob. "Hail Mary, mother of God . . ." She repeated the prayer that brought her strength in trial. Surely the Holy Virgin had shown courage at the birth of her son. *New life comes—blessing and pain.*

Across the room, the shadowy figure of an old woman swayed in prayer. Not the Latin chant of the padres and the choir, but in rhythm with the ancient people: prayers to the sun, moon, rain, golden eagle as they had been prayed in the village of the spirit woman's childhood.

Tonight, fire shadows danced on the wall. From a standing position, her old body swayed back and forth, translucent in the light of the flickering firelight, her ancient bones limber from a lifetime of sitting upon the earth. With almost every sway her forehead brushed the wall in front of her, allowing crushed limestone from the wall to mottle in the deep furrows of her forehead. Streaks of white caught in the strands of her hair, making her seem even grayer than the day she arrived. Her hair was long then, but she had singed it short with firebrands to show she mourned the loss of the old ways.

"Grandmother," Alfonsa whispered, "you've come." *NenE'*—the name the people called the mother of her mother. *NenE',* the storyteller. In her dream, Grandmother told about *T'e Lxo,* the thunder. *T'e Lxo* roared from the sky in a dance with the lightning, and afterwards it was here, over this chosen valley and over her people, the stars would spread their blanket when the world was washed clean and the streams refilled.

Back and forth the old woman rocked. *Brish Brish.* Alfonsa knew she imagined it, so soft a sound, so soft a color, yet both stirred something deep inside her, a feeling that the old ways would never totally disappear. Grandmother was only here in spirit. She would be no help with the coming baby, but someone would arrive—maybe sooner, maybe later—when the common prayers in the church ended and the final meal of the day had been distributed.

A knotted rosary lay limp in Alfonsa's hand. Domingo had left her to her labor, but she listened for his footstep. Did not Saint Joseph wipe Mary's brow at the birthing of their son? *Ride the contraction as a wave,* the older mothers told her. But what did that mean?

Outside, the huge bells tolled against the crashing of the storm. Lightning flashed nearby, filling her room while thunder soon followed. A strong gust of wind blew through the cracks around the door, cooling her skin. Smoke stung her eyes as the intrusive wind fingered the fire in the corner.

She returned her gaze to Grandmother, who stood motionless, listening to the song of the wind.

Did the wind tell the old one that her granddaughter would have a blessed and strong grandchild? In the woman's wrinkled face and sad eyes, strange secrets remained hidden from human understanding. Grandmother would know the meaning of the images that came during Alfonsa's own sleep, strange words that woke her when she cried out, sometimes with a few human words, but sometimes with the words of other-world spirits. She wondered about the spirit world the elders no longer talked of, but it would do no good to ask. When she was a child she had questioned Padre Juan Cabot about them and he said the dead do not come back to the living. She left it at that. Padre should know these things, yet the belief did not leave her.

She felt the power of the river carrying her and her unborn child. In a moment of release from fierce pain, Alfonsa raised her arms.

"My people," she sighed.

Another vision, one in which she gazed down from the starry blanket into the valley. She saw her people by the river, milling among their huts of *tule* grass bundled together with bark strips. So small, so simple. She found herself wailing in her dreaming. "Why can't I bring my baby into this world in a hut like my grandmother's? In my people's village? With the smell of grass and bark. With the songs of my people. Under the stars as *T'e Lxo* shouts from the sky.”

Grandmother continued to rock on her toes and Alfonsa understood what was deep inside the old one's heart—fear. Fear for the baby about to be born.

“God help us,” she whispered, her throat dry.

She managed a swallow of water from her drinking vessel, an abalone shell carried from the sandy beaches to the west. Suddenly the pungent scent of burning sage chased the sour smell of sweat and rancid grease from the tight, closed room. For this she was grateful, but not for the pagan smoke that would bring the wrath of Padre Martin upon them. She rose on her elbow and tried to fan the air away before the scent embedded itself in her hair and her skin.

“No, Grandmother, you must not. Padre says these things are of the devil. Superstition. You mustn't.” Before she could prevent it, the old shadow woman managed to smudge her belly and her breasts, up to her chin with the black soot, her chants summoning the ancient spirits to provide for a strong baby, a safe birth. Spirits the old woman summoned were powerful. Alfonsa felt her body relaxing under the sweet cleansing. A moment later Grandmother's spirit faded and the room was empty.

A small sound issued from the doorway. It was *Oxwe't*, the mother of her husband, returning from the church. The shadowy image of Grandmother faded into darkness and the room was empty again except for the two of them. The new arrival wrinkled her nose and glanced around. A faint smile flickered over her customary frown.

Alfonsa felt the need to talk.

“*Oxwe't*, this room is built with skill and hard work. Your son honors us with his devotion.” As she expected, the woman slipped to the floor without speaking. Domingo had explained to the padres that no Yokut woman would speak to her son's wife, not even if they passed in the field, but his pleading was dismissed like a mosquito's buzz. Padre claimed the old taboos were pagan. God required a man's wife to care for his aging mother.

His mother made a bed in the corner of the small room and said nothing unless her son asked a question of her.

The scent of sage filled the small room with promise. One after another, several families had lived in this room and baptized it with their odors, their greases, sicknesses and deaths. The odors lingered after the families departed. She was happy with the sage that now cleansed her nostrils, willing to risk discovery of the pagan ritual.

Soon her trial would be over and Domingo would be at her side. He worked full days in the burning sun, forming adobe tiles and bricks. On each, he marked a small "x," his own mark before the clay dried. Many others worked with him so that in the summer season several thousand "x" tiles piled up in the courtyard. He used some of his handiwork to build tight adobe rooms like the one Padre had given them to use.

Once the baby comes, I will scrub this room, she vowed. *With wild soap and lime it will be made new again, just as the ones Domingo builds now.*

A new cramp gripped her and she allowed her thoughts to flow into her calm place. Mercifully, she drifted into darkness.

When she awoke, the weight of the storm had broken. Outside, a clay tile torn loose in the wind dropped onto the ground—most likely a weak tile made by one of the others; her husband's tiles were strong as the oak limbs they were formed on. As strong as God, whose will must be obeyed.

Moments later she felt pressure building between her legs and raised her head, her body rigid. The pain was increasing, and with it the pressure to push. At her keening sob, one of the neophyte women rushed in. She bent and saw the dark place where the baby pressed. She turned toward the door and called, "Ayeeee. It is time."

Señora Marcia, the wife of one of the soldiers, slipped into the room, her crisp black skirt crackling against the quick tap-taps of her leather shoes. A neophyte woman followed carrying a cooking basket of steaming water with a hot rock inside, which her practiced hands swirled to keep the red-hot rock from burning through the basket.

Yes, it was time. She felt the child slipping from inside her. In her dream, white mist covered the canyon, a bright and swirling whirlpool. Her spirit wanted to enter, but the mewling made her hesitate, a sound so faint that she wasn't sure her ears could be trusted. She opened her eyes and saw hands cradling a tiny bundle. Boy or girl it didn't matter, only that she hold it before the angels came to take it to Heaven, for surely it was too tiny to live.

The baby's cry was pitiful, the bleating of a goat. She felt an ache of another kind when she heard Señora whisper, "Bring the Padre."

Made in the USA
Monee, IL
06 March 2022

92301727R00134